**One less snake**

Beyond the yellow tape, police officers worked as an efficient team around the base of the park's centerpiece bronze statue. An older man sat slumped on a marble step at the statue's base. He seemed oblivious to the activity buzzing all around him. His head was bowed as if he'd fallen asleep.

"Even *Media Today* can't get away with printing out-and-out lies," Annie reminded me. "Before going into politics Bruce used to work as a trial lawyer. He gave my late husband his first job at his law firm. At the first whiff of libel, Bruce will sue, and the newspaper editors know it."

"I hope so. Even though Griffon Parker is a snake, his stories seem to sell papers," I said, feeling my face heat. "He's won plenty of awards for his investigative reports. I hate what he does and who he hurts. He's a weasel. A weed. A sorry excuse for a human being. And—"

"*Dead*," Annie finished for me.

# The Scarlet Pepper

## DOROTHY ST. JAMES

BERKLEY PRIME CRIME, NEW YORK

**THE BERKLEY PUBLISHING GROUP**
**Published by the Penguin Group**
**Penguin Group (USA) Inc.**
**375 Hudson Street, New York, New York 10014, USA**

Penguin Group (Canada), 90 Eglinton Avenue East, Suite 700, Toronto, Ontario M4P 2Y3, Canada
(a division of Pearson Penguin Canada Inc.) • Penguin Books Ltd., 80 Strand, London WC2R 0RL,
England • Penguin Group Ireland, 25 St. Stephen's Green, Dublin 2, Ireland (a division of Penguin
Books Ltd.) • Penguin Group (Australia), 250 Camberwell Road, Camberwell, Victoria 3124, Australia
(a division of Pearson Australia Group Pty. Ltd.) • Penguin Books India Pvt. Ltd., 11 Community
Centre, Panchsheel Park, New Delhi—110 017, India • Penguin Group (NZ), 67 Apollo Drive,
Rosedale, Auckland 0632, New Zealand (a division of Pearson New Zealand Ltd.) • Penguin Books
(South Africa) (Pty.) Ltd., 24 Sturdee Avenue, Rosebank, Johannesburg 2196, South Africa

Penguin Books Ltd., Registered Offices: 80 Strand, London WC2R 0RL, England

This is a work of fiction. Names, characters, places, and incidents either are the product of the author's
imagination or are used fictitiously, and any resemblance to actual persons, living or dead, business
establishments, events, or locales is entirely coincidental. The publisher does not have any control
over and does not assume any responsibility for author or third-party websites or their content.

THE SCARLET PEPPER

A Berkley Prime Crime Book / published by arrangement with Tekno Books

PUBLISHING HISTORY
Berkley Prime Crime mass-market edition / April 2012

Copyright © 2012 by Tekno Books.
Cover illustration by Mary Ann Lasher.
Cover design by Olivia Andreas.
Interior text design by Kristin del Rosario.

ISBN: 978-0-425-24704-4

BERKLEY® PRIME CRIME
Berkley Prime Crime Books are published by The Berkley Publishing Group,
a division of Penguin Group (USA) Inc.,
375 Hudson Street, New York, New York 10014.
BERKLEY® PRIME CRIME and the PRIME CRIME logo are trademarks of
Penguin Group (USA) Inc.

PRINTED IN THE UNITED STATES OF AMERICA

10  9  8  7  6  5  4  3  2  1

ALWAYS LEARNING                                                     PEARSON

*For Jim . . .*
*the love of my life and my partner in crime.*

*For Martin H. Greenberg.*

*Marty Greenberg, the creative force behind Tekno*
*Books, passed away during the writing of this novel.*
*Without his insight and dedication to the book*
*world, this series would never have happened.*
*May he always be remembered for helping*
*the underdog and giving new voices a chance.*

# Acknowledgments

Once again as I immersed myself in the fictional world of Casey Calhoun and her White House adventures, I had the pleasure to meet, interview, and learn from so many wonderful gardeners, journalists, and dedicated bureaucrats.

My dear friend Judy Watts shared her experiences as a newspaper editor. Former *Washington Post* editor and fellow novelist Patricia McLinn patiently talked through Casey's life and her neighborhood and helped me to mold my Washington gardener into a three-dimensional character. And the incredible Eddie Gehman Kohan, who reports all things food- and garden-related from the White House in her Obama Foodorama blog, offered her insights on what it's like to report from inside the White House. I can't tell you how much I appreciate these three talented ladies.

On the gardening front, my gratitude goes out to Amy Dabbs, the Tri-County Master Gardener Coordinator, for sharing her passion for organic gardening, and to Master Gardener and fellow writer Shannon Cavanaugh, for her enthusiasm for her garden and her writing. Keep those newsletter articles coming! And thank you, Kathy Jentz, editor of *Washington Gardener*, for answering my D.C. gardening questions on the fly through Twitter. What a wonderful invention. I don't know what I would have done without it.

A special thank-you goes to Miranda Kenneally, YA novelist, for showing me the ropes at the State Department. You turned my latest D.C. research trip into an unforgettable adventure.

Of course, enormous thanks go to Brittiany Koren for offering me the chance to bring Casey Calhoun to the pages of this book. Brittiany, you're a great friend, a hard-nosed editor, and one of the best cheerleaders in the business. A big thank-you goes to Michael Koren for his understanding and patience during all those times Brittiany locked herself away in her office in order to help me hash out all the details.

Thank you, also, to Rosalind Greenberg, Larry Segriff, John Helfers, and Chuck Wiseman at Tekno Books for your support and to the awesome staff at Berkley Prime Crime, especially Natalee Rosenstein for giving me the chance to continue Casey Calhoun's story, and Robin Barletta for making the process of publishing a book fun.

Last but not least, I must thank the incredible authors in the Lowcountry chapter of Romance Writers of America, Sisters in Crime, and Mystery Writers of America, whose unflagging support has kept me pounding away at my keyboard, especially Nina Bruhns, Julie Hyzy, Margie Lawson, C. J. Lyons, Tracy Anne Warren, and Joanna Wayne for patiently listening and giving advice as I worked out plot problems, figured out promotional efforts, and whined like an annoying little girl while writing this book. Once again, I couldn't have done it without you!

# Prologue

*If I am shot at, I want no man to be
in the way of the bullet.*
—ANDREW JOHNSON, THE 17TH PRESIDENT OF
THE UNITED STATES

**M**Y wary gaze scanned the West Wing corridor. The creamy walls were lined with framed photos of White House events, both past and present. A smiling Richard Nixon shook hands with the Chinese premier on one side of me and John F. Kennedy stood grim faced in the Oval Office during the height of the Bay of Pigs missile crisis on the other side.

No world-changing decisions were scheduled to be made today. I kept my pace steady as I made my way past the steps that led down to the Secret Service's offices in the West Wing's basement and toward the Press Briefing Room. It was quiet—too quiet. My shoulders tensed.

The large potted begonia in my arms was missing about a third of its variegated leaves. Several of its canes were broken, and a large crack ran the length of its bright yellow ceramic pot.

Both the pot and the plant desperately needed atten-tion, but I'd been instructed to take the begonia from the vice president's office, through the twisting, surprisingly narrow hallway, and deliver it to the Press Briefing Room regardless of how awful it looked.

"Who am I but the assistant gardener?" I grumbled under my breath. The plants in the West Wing, or anywhere else in the White House, for that matter, were kept in peak condition. First Lady Margaret Bradley loved plants almost as much as I did.

At her direction every office in the West Wing had at least one potted plant. A grand idea, in my opinion, even if it did increase the gardening staff's responsibilities.

Twice a week, a gardener traveled from office to office watering, feeding, pinching off old flowers, and replacing any plant that lacked the green perfection expected at the White House. We carried out our work with pride. This was the People's House, a beacon of hope, a symbol of freedom.

No one on the gardening staff would willingly deliver a begonia with missing leaves and broken stems, but today wasn't a normal day at the White House. As I rounded a corner, I passed the President's Chief of Staff, Bruce Dearing. He leaned his rotund body toward Frank Lispon, the White House press secretary. The tall African American man looked as if he was trying to become one with the wall's Sheetrock to avoid Bruce's protruding belly.

"I wouldn't be surprised if someone slipped poison into the nasty gingerroot tea he's always drinking. The man writes wild rumors. Speculations," Bruce said in his low, growly voice. He poked Frank in the chest with his pudgy finger. "And he calls them *investigative reports*?" His finger poked Frank again. "Can't you ban him from the White House?"

"I'll see what I can do," Frank murmured with an embarrassed glance in my direction.

A sudden commotion rose in the hallway near the Press Briefing Room. Startled, I almost dropped the poor begonia.

President Bradley, surrounded by a bevy of staffers and a detail of Secret Service agents, passed through the double glass doors from the West Colonnade and breezed into the West Wing. Surrounded by his entourage, he hurried down the narrow hallway—which suddenly seemed to shrink—apparently on his way to the Oval Office.

Remembering the Secret Service's admonishments to keep out of the way, I flattened myself against the cream-colored wall as he passed without even a nod in my direction.

Once he was out of sight, I balanced the large pot between my hip and the entranceway to the Press Briefing Room and reached out to grab the handle.

I'd just started to pull the door open when someone in the direction of the Oval Office shouted, "Bomb!"

*Bomb?*

Before I could move, breathe, or even think, the Secret Service, with the President at the center of their detail, backtracked through the hallway toward me. They moved as a single unit like an angry bull.

With the President's safety foremost in my mind, I knew I needed to stay out of their way. If I blocked them, or even slowed them down, the bomb might go off and the President could end up injured or even killed. I couldn't outrun them to escape out the double glass door, but I needed to get out of the hallway and to safety.

My heart started to pound. Despite the Secret Service's explicit instructions to hurry toward the nearest exit at the first sign of trouble, I tossed open the Press Briefing Room's door instead.

And thudded against the muscular chest of a large man clad all in black.

A black knit balaclava covered his face, leaving only his cold eyes exposed. He clutched a rifle in his hands, which he used to shove me back into the West Wing corridor.

"Gun! Gun!" I shouted. My legs got tangled with the legs of one of the Secret Service agents desperately trying to rush the President to safety. We crashed to the ground.

The President!

I'd given the gunman an opening.

Using all my strength, I tossed the potted plant at the shooter as he took aim. The large ceramic pot slammed into his chest with enough force that he fell on his backside.

A Secret Service agent leapt over me to get to the gunman. The sharp pop, pop, pop of gunfire had me instinctively covering my head. But the gunfire hadn't been aimed at me.

The agent who'd charged fell.

Three more masked gunmen, dressed exactly like the first, stepped over the fallen agent and their masked buddy as they poured into the corridor.

One gunman grabbed the President. Another grabbed my arm and pressed the barrel of his rifle against my temple with enough force that it pinned me to the floor.

"Bang!" he shouted. He ripped off his balaclava. "You're dead. The President's dead."

I glared up at the man snarling down at me and pushed the barrel of his rifle away from my face. The man had distinctive streaks of silver running through his brown hair and an unfriendly gleam in his eyes.

Mike Thatch, special agent in charge of the Secret Service's elite military Counter Assault Team, or CAT, as its members liked to call themselves, had designed and directed these training sessions. Apparently he also took an active role in carrying them out.

Thatch reached out a hand to help me up. I refused it and sat in the corridor, cradling my head in my hands.

"You have to take this seriously, Casey. You have to follow our directions. Think about it. The bomb was obviously a diversion. The gunmen were the real threat in this one. What should you have done?"

"I don't know," I said.

We weren't at the White House, but at the Secret Service's James J. Rowley Training Center in Laurel, Maryland. Although the West Wing corridors looked like the real thing, there weren't actually any offices behind the doors. And an agent had played the part of the President.

Training sessions such as these were commonplace for Secret Service agents and members of the President's staff who worked within what they'd termed the "kill zone," a small but potentially deadly area that surrounded the President at all times. If bullets were to fly, these were the people who would be in the direct line of fire. They needed to know how to react.

As White House assistant gardener, I rarely worked anywhere near the kill zone. But in response to growing political unrest throughout the world and an increase in credible threats to the President—not to mention the unpleasantness we'd encountered this past spring—the Secret Service had decided to expand its training sessions to include all members of the White House staff, no matter how lowly or removed from the seat of power.

The nine other members of the White House and West Wing staff attending today's training session, including the press secretary and the Chief of Staff, had reacted with swift resolve to the threats thrown at them. With the aid of the Secret Service agents, all had saved the President.

I'd been the only one who'd failed the test. And not just once, but three times now. What was wrong with me?

"Get up and do it again," Thatch barked.

When I raised my head, I caught sight of CAT special agent Jack Turner watching me. Like the other CAT agents, he projected the hard-nosed image that he was a warrior from hell. Stoic, humorless, and all about the mission. With a vicious tug he tore the already pushed-up balaclava from his head and plucked a begonia leaf from his short black hair.

He'd been the unlucky rifleman to get knocked down by my flowerpot?

"Sorry," I mouthed as he brushed off the potting soil covering his chest.

This past spring Jack had played Watson to my Sherlock. There was something about him that had gotten under my skin, something that made me feel safe. It might have been his expressive green eyes or his steady calm voice.

Whatever it was, I'd shared with him intimate secrets from my past that I hadn't even told the grandmother or two aunts who'd loved and raised me. He'd stuck by me even when doing so became hazardous to his health. I considered him a close friend.

The grim set of his mouth didn't look too friendly now. He exchanged a look with his SAIC, Mike Thatch, which only seemed to deepen his frown.

"I'm sure I'll get it next time," I said to Jack, braving a smile.

"I doubt it," he grumbled and exchanged another heated look with Thatch. He then offered me a hand up.

My muscles, tired and bruised from having been tackled from every angle imaginable, screamed as he hauled me to my feet. A sharp pain stabbed me in the ribs when I bent down to scoop up the potted begonia. I bit back a yelp.

"Okay"—I hugged the cracked ceramic pot to my sore chest. Several more leaves dropped from the hopelessly battered begonia onto the tan carpet—"I'm ready."

But no matter what I tried that day, I couldn't puzzle out how to save myself or the President.

# Chapter One

*People say I am ruthless. I am not ruthless. And if I find the man who is calling me ruthless, I shall destroy him.*
—JOHN F. KENNEDY, THE 35TH PRESIDENT OF
THE UNITED STATES

## One month later

"I can't imagine a more painful way to die," the elderly Pearle Stone, lioness of the District of Columbia's influential social circle, commented as she ambled her way across the White House's lush green South Lawn.

"The poor dear," her silver-haired friend, Mable Bowls, whispered back while dabbing at the sweat on her forehead with a lacy handkerchief. She sounded a trifle more excited than upset. "Do you know the cause?"

"One can only speculate," Pearle replied gravely.

"A mystery to be solved then?"

"I believe so, my dear."

Their conversation was none of my business. And yet I found myself matching their stride as I walked behind the two older ladies dressed in matching light blue stretch polyester pants and flowered tops. My ears were so alert the backs of them prickled.

Who were they talking about?

*Mercy goodness, Casey, the church made a grave mistake*

*when it overlooked curiosity as a deadly sin.* Aunt Willow's oft-spouted warning slapped me back to my senses. *I vow your curiosity has caused more trouble in your life than all the sloth, gluttony, greed, and envy heaped together.*

On the dawning of my fortieth birthday, I believe I had to finally agree with my pearl-wearing, mint julep–sipping Southern belle relative who'd helped raise me. Considering the danger I'd stumbled into this past spring, it was becoming too dangerous *not* to agree.

Curiosity could prove deadly.

I'd promised to change my ways. No more sticking my nose into other people's business.

These past several months I'd been excruciatingly careful. Not that it'd been easy. Temptation seemed to lurk around every corner. It came with the job.

Since the beginning of the year, I'd tended lush lawns, nurtured luxurious flowerbeds, and cultivated the newly planted vegetable garden at the President's Park, which included the White House and its gardens. Although I held quite an impressive security clearance as assistant gardener, I swear the only murder I wished to become involved with these days was the kind found within the pages of a book.

Truly, I'm simply a gardener, which by definition means I should lead a quiet, unassuming life. I had no intention of squandering this great opportunity to serve my country and teach others about my passion for organic gardening.

That morning I'd followed my normal routine. Well, as normal as could be expected when tasked with herding a group of volunteers more interested in gossiping than gardening through the Secret Service security clearance checkpoint at the southeast gate and toward the First Lady's vegetable garden.

That was when I'd happened to overhear the ladies' rather interesting conversation.

"Do you think we should warn her or just go ahead and start planning her funeral?" the elderly Mable Bowls continued with a titter.

"It's not our place to gossip. She'll learn about it soon enough." Pearle Stone had the grace not to sound too happy about the budding scandal.

I had no business listening to them. But, let's be honest, unless I planned on sticking my fingers in my ears and singing "la, la, la," it really was impossible to ignore the society matrons' conversation. The pair suffered from hearing loss so acute that stage whispers carried shorter distances.

I tried to focus on the fragrant sweetgrass basket I was lugging down to the fifteen-hundred-square-foot vegetable garden at the base of the hill, nearly as far away from the White House as it could get without leaving the South Lawn. I'd wanted the garden right beside the back door—that's where gardens belong—but the Secret Service had vetoed that idea, citing security concerns.

So every morning I loaded my basket to the rim with an assortment of tools and gardening gloves and made the trek across the lawn. It was so large and heavy that it took two hands to manage. Even without distractions, I struggled to make my way down the hill without leaving a trail of white gardening gloves like a modern-day version of Hansel and Gretel.

"I imagine Griffon Parker will publish the story soon," Mable said, her voice growing even louder. "And it had better be spectacular. I've heard he's about to lose his seat in the press pool."

Dread tiptoed down my back at the mention of Parker's name. I picked up my pace, listening intently again.

This past spring I'd run afoul of *Media Today*'s star White House correspondent when he'd attacked my organic gardening proposals. I doubted the weasel could get a grocery list right even if it were written out and handed to him.

"Do you think *Media Today* would truly replace him with a television reporter?" Pearle asked.

"D.C. would certainly change without him around to stir the pot. At least he's still here now and kicking. I heard the story he plans to write will kill any and all political

aspirations the poor dear's husband has cultivated." Mable
tsked.

"Bruce's sights were on the presidency. And now . . ."
Pearle said sadly. "Poor, poor Francesca."

*Francesca*? I whirled around, searching the group of
volunteers behind me.

Francesca Dearing, my most dedicated gardening volunteer, was also married to the President's hard-nosed—
and plump as a ripe eggplant—Chief of Staff, Bruce
Dearing.

Let me tell you, President Bradley didn't need this kind
of trouble. His approval rating had recently plummeted
thanks to this spring's banking scandal. He couldn't afford
to have another erupt so soon.

Although I didn't spot Francesca among the dozen or so
volunteers trailing me across the South Lawn, the petite
Annie Campbell was only a few paces behind me. Francesca and Annie grew up in the same small town in West
Virginia and were as close as any two women I'd ever met.

I held my breath, hoping Annie hadn't overheard the
snide remarks. But how could she not have heard?

Annie's gaze met mine. Her shoulders noticeably tightened.

"Mrs. Bowls, Mrs. Stone," I called, desperate to get
Mable and Pearle's attention.

"Is it Bruce or Francesca that Griffon Parker is after?"
Pearle Stone wondered quite loudly.

I picked up my pace to catch up with them. "Mrs. Stone!"

"Does it matter?" Mable crowed. "Soon the two of them
will be forced to pack up their things and disappear back
up into the mountains."

With a strangled cry, Annie rushed past me. Her hair,
cut in a pageboy style and dyed a red that was much brighter
than a woman her age could honestly claim, bounced with
each agitated step. Her gardening outfit, which looked as if
it had fallen out of a high-priced designer's closet, swished
as she went.

Pearle shook her head as she watched Annie jog the rest

of the way to the vegetable garden at the bottom of the hill. "That one would be nothing without Francesca."

Mable tsked again. "Didn't Francesca swear she'd rather die than return to that Hicksville of a hometown?"

"That she did," Pearle replied. "Many, many times." She stopped and turned toward me. Though her stiff movements betrayed her advanced age, her indulgent smile made Pearle look positively angelic. "Did you want something, dear?"

She looked me up and down with her keen, assessing gaze. Not a single strand of her curly, blue-tinged hair moved.

"You don't have your hat," I said, deciding not to mention Francesca. The damage had already been done. Admonishing the pair would only give them cause to keep their focus on the gossip surrounding Francesca.

"Speak up, dear," Pearle said.

"Your hat," I repeated, louder this time. "Where is it?"

D.C. had been in the grip of an intense heat wave for the past week. The humid June air already felt warm enough to make a beetle sweat, and the sun had only barely peeked over the horizon. In a few hours this area of Washington, which had once been swampland, was going to feel like the interior of a seafood steamer. I didn't wish to lose any of my volunteers to heat exhaustion.

"My word, she's quite right. Where is your hat? You know how badly you freckle in the sun," Mable Bowls scolded. She grabbed Pearle's arm to help support her as several volunteers breezed past us. Mable enjoyed reminding everyone how she was only seventy-nine, a full six months younger than her "ancient" friend, and still as spry as a spring chick.

"I believe I must have left it back at your house, Mable." Pearle tapped a slender, neatly manicured finger to her chin. "Yes, I believe I did." She turned her angelic gaze toward me again. And smiled. "Would you be a dear and—"

"I beg your pardon," I said as my cell phone belted out the first few lines to Katy Perry's bubblegum pop song

"Firework." It was a playful tune that reminded me of the biblical parable that no one should hide their light under a bushel. "I'd better take this."

I usually sent my calls to voice mail when I was working. However, if Pearle, who reminded me too much of my grandmother Faye with her genteel smiles and refined manner, finished her request, I knew I'd soon find myself on a wild-goose chase in search of the lady's garden hat.

Praying the caller didn't hang up before I could answer, I dug into my pocket for my cell phone. This wasn't as easy as it sounded considering how I had to juggle the large sweetgrass basket in order to manage it. Several garden gloves slipped to the grass.

"The harvest celebration is next Wednesday, and there's still quite a bit that needs to be done. This phone call might be a question regarding one of the details," I explained. We'd been coordinating the garden details with the White House chefs, which was the easy part, and with the First Lady's high-strung social secretary, Seth Donahue, who tended to give me a searing headache.

As more gloves tumbled from my sweetgrass basket like leaves in the fall, I flashed a self-deprecating grin and turned away from the two sweet, although half-deaf, ladies. "Hello?" I said as I pressed the phone to my ear. "This is Casey."

"*Casey*," the woman on the other end implored in a raspy whisper. I lowered the phone and glanced at the caller ID display. It gave no number. No name.

The readout simply read, "Unavailable."

"Hello?" Did I know anyone with a blocked phone number? Not even Secret Service Agent Jack Turner blocked his number.

I don't know why I picked that moment to think of *him*. Or why my heart suddenly sped up. He'd not called in weeks, not since my disastrous training session with the Secret Service. And to think I'd started to convince myself that Jack had developed feelings for—

"*Casey.*" The raspy whisper turned more urgent. "*You have to help me.*"

"Francesca? Is that you?" It sort of sounded like her. "Where are you calling from? Is this about Griffon—?"

"Don't say his name! Not even over the phone."

"Okay," I said. "Aren't you signed up to work today? I could use your help in the garden."

"I don't have time for that right now. You know the charity murder mystery dinner you've been helping me plan? I've had an idea about it. We need to talk. Can you meet me at the Freedom of Espresso Café in a half hour?"

"I'm sorry. I can't. We could talk while we work here, though."

"Oh, no, I can't do that. I'm very busy. I have to deal with"—she sighed loudly—"*that reporter.* But I need to run an idea by you while it's still fresh in my mind."

"Francesca, I'm at work. I have responsibilities and gardens to tend."

"Casey, you don't understand. I need your expertise with *plants.*" She whispered the last word into the phone. It came out muffled, as if she'd cupped her hand over the receiver, as if she didn't want anyone around her to hear. How she spoke that one word, as if she were talking about something dark and sinister, sent a shiver down my spine.

"*Plants?*" I asked. But she'd hung up.

# Chapter Two

*If it were not for the reporters, I would tell you the truth.*
—CHESTER ALAN ARTHUR, THE 21ST PRESIDENT OF
THE UNITED STATES

"IS something wrong, dear?" Pearle asked as I frowned at
my phone.

"I don't think so." I jammed the phone back into my
pocket, which caused more gardening gloves to tumble out
of the basket and onto the lush fescue. "It's just that I'm—"

"Yes?" Pearle leaned forward. Excitement danced in her
ice blue eyes as she waited for me to hand her a piece of
juicy gossip for her and Mable to chew on.

"It's nothing," I said and forced a broad smile to my lips.
"Here." I handed her my floppy straw hat to wear. "I don't
want you to get overexposed to the sun."

I continued down the hill toward the vegetable garden,
scooping up gardening gloves as I went.

"There *is* something wrong," Mable pronounced as she
and Pearle followed me across the lawn.

"She does look troubled," Pearle agreed. She adjusted the
straw hat so it sat at a jaunty angle atop her blue-tinged hair.

"Who was on the other end of the call?" Mable wondered aloud.

"Someone who clearly doesn't know our Casey well," Pearle said. "She's dedicated to the White House and her plants."

I smiled at that. The volunteers, most of whom were old enough to be my mother, if not my grandmother, had adopted me as their own. Even Francesca, in her own self-absorbed way.

What many people don't realize is how much the White House depends on its volunteers. With all the regular day-to-day demands pulling its paid employees in several directions at once, the White House's relatively small staff couldn't possibly handle running the household plus the numerous special projects—such as decorating the White House for Christmas, organizing daily public tours, opening the garden to the public twice a year, or developing and maintaining a world-class vegetable garden for the First Lady. Volunteers regularly offered a helping hand in the First Lady's office *and* in the gardens.

Although volunteer positions were highly coveted and generally had many more people vying for any given position than was needed, in Francesca Dearing's case, it had taken a bit of bribery to convince her to come to help out in the vegetable garden.

But I'd wanted Francesca. Her experience in growing prize-winning vegetables in the D.C. area was well known in the plant community.

Up until about six months ago, I'd spent most of my career working under the canopy of live oaks thickly draped with Spanish moss in Charleston, South Carolina. While D.C. and Charleston shared deep roots regarding our nation's history, they existed in very different microclimates with unique problems. I needed to recruit a knowledgeable volunteer with on-the-ground experience, someone like Francesca Dearing.

Unfortunately Francesca had existing obligations to charitable and political organizations. When I'd asked for her help, she'd politely refused. It wasn't until she'd learned about how I'd solved a murder this past spring that *she'd* contacted *me*.

In addition to her passion for plants, Francesca devoured murder mysteries. She never missed an episode of *Castle* or *The Mentalist* and had read nearly every cozy mystery series in print.

Although I'd tried to explain otherwise, she fancied that she'd found herself a real-life amateur sleuth. In exchange for her help, I agreed to play along with her fantasy.

Since there were no crimes for us to investigate, thank goodness, she invented a game of her own. We would combine our knowledge of mystery plots and . . .

Oh, I hesitate to admit this. I promise you my stern but loving grandmother Faye raised me to have better judgment. It was simply that I needed to make the First Lady's vegetable garden an unquestionable success. To do that, I needed Francesca's local expertise.

So, yes, I did agree to play her silly little game. In exchange for Francesca's assistance in the garden, I agreed to help her plan the perfect murder.

For charity.

At a dinner.

No one was supposed to die.

No one *had* died, I reminded myself.

*Not yet*, my pesky inner voice chided.

Just because Francesca had called out of the blue with an urgent need to talk about the charity murder mystery dinner on the same day rumors were swirling about her impending social death didn't necessarily mean she was planning to host a *real* murder dinner. That was just my fanciful imagination working overtime . . . I hoped.

My cell phone sang its cheery pop song again. I set down my basket at the edge of the First Lady's vegetable garden and reached into my pocket. Again, the caller ID readout proclaimed, "Unavailable."

"You should answer it, dear," Pearle said as she came to stand next to me.

"It's probably important," Mable agreed as she stood on the other side of me.

"I doubt it." If Francesca wanted to talk to me about murder, she knew how to find me. I needed her help in the garden.

**AN HOUR LATER MY CELL PHONE STARTED TO** sing again. I paused in tying a young pepper plant to its bamboo stake and checked the caller ID.

"Unavailable."

She'd called at least four other times in the past hour. Not that I'd talked with her. I'd hit the "ignore" button, only to have her call back fifteen minutes later, which only fed my concern that this Griffon Parker business was straining her nerves. It would be wrong of me to turn a deaf ear to her cry for help.

My finger skipped over the cell phone's "ignore" button, and I answered the call.

"Cherry leaves," Francesca said.

"Cherry . . . *What*?" I must have misheard her.

"Cherry leaves," she replied as if I should know exactly what she meant. "They could be ground up and put into a tea."

Francesca couldn't be serious. I handed the soft cotton strips I'd been using to tie up the pepper plants to Mable and stepped away from the gardening bed. Gordon Sims, the chief gardener at the White House and one of my closest friends in Washington, was helping out in the garden this morning and could answer any questions the volunteers might have in my absence.

I spotted his full head of silver hair gleaming in the morning sunlight over near the tomatoes. An easy smile lifted the corners of his mouth as he waved in my direction. His smile grew a bit wider as several of the older volunteers mobbed him, swallowing him up as if he were a rock star, with Pearle and Mable leading the charge.

"What's going on?" I asked Francesca. "What are you talking about?"

"I was on the Internet last night," Francesca explained. "That's where I read about the cherry tree. Did you know its twigs and leaves contain cyanide?"

"I did know that." With the cell phone pressed tightly to my ear, I walked away from the volunteers. I didn't want anyone listening in on my end of what I suspected would turn into an odd conversation. "But, no. No, cherry leaves."

I stopped near the South Fountain. That was when I spotted Jack Turner dressed in the Secret Service's Counter Assault Team's black battle uniform, striding down the hill like a man on a mission.

What was he doing here? And alone?

I hadn't seen or heard from Jack since the disastrous training session with the Secret Service. I figured he was embarrassed to be seen around me.

"But if the cherry leaves are poisonous," Francesca argued, "then if we added a handful to someone's herbal tea it would be the perfect murder weapon, right?"

"The tea would likely make someone sick," I warned. "I'm sure if anyone were to *accidentally* ingest it, he'd likely notice the symptoms and get himself to the hospital in plenty of time to be treated."

Jack walked past the garden and straight toward me.

God, he looked dangerous in his uniform, and not in a bad way. My heart started to beat a little faster.

"That wouldn't do," Francesca murmured.

"What did you say?" I asked, completely distracted by Jack. He stopped several feet from me and mouthed, "I need to talk with you."

I held up one finger and smiled.

He didn't smile back.

"It has to be the yew leaves then," Francesca whispered. "Just as you had suggested last week. You frighten me how you come up with these scenarios. It's the perfect murder plot, you know, even in real life."

Real life?

"No, it's not," I blurted out. "It'll work for the mystery

dinner. But in real life, the police would run toxicology tests. They would still figure out who had a motive."

I'd said that last part too loud. Jack's head snapped in my direction. His frown deepened.

"It's not what you think," I mouthed. I'd promised Jack and my family that I wouldn't get involved with even the whisper of another murder investigation.

I knew I wasn't a younger, hipper version of Miss Marple. Even though Miss Marple and I both loved our gardens and our mysteries, *I* wasn't a fictional character. I was flesh and blood and bones and this past spring had learned first-hand just how badly I could get hurt. Murderers tended to go after obstacles with, well, *murderous* intent.

Imagine that.

"We'd have to leave a suicide note on the body. And perhaps some pills," Francesca continued, despite my pro-testations that she needed to stop. Apparently she'd stopped listening to me . . . again. "No, not pills. An empty pill bottle. That would slow the police down in their investiga-tions. Of course, we also have to make sure to muddy up the motive."

Francesca and I had discussed this part of the murder plot—the motive—many times. In novels, the obvious sus-pect never turns out to be the murderer. There's always a twist.

"This is still for the mystery dinner, right?" I asked.

Jack checked his watch. His frown turned into a scowl as he started to pace.

"Of course it is," Francesca said, gentling her voice as if she were talking to a child. "But what you've suggested is so perfect. It could be real. That's what I like about it. If someone followed your suggestions, she *could* get away with murder."

"This is still just a game?" I asked again.

She laughed, a high-pitched birdlike titter. "You wouldn't think that I—?" She laughed again. This time it sounded forced, nervous. "*I wouldn't*—"

"There are rumors that your husband's career could be ruined because of an article Griffon Parker plans to write, and all of a sudden you're obsessed with wanting to talk about how to commit the perfect murder for real. What would *you* think if you were in my shoes?"

"You—you know about Griffon Parker's story?" she sputtered and then quickly drew a deep breath. "What exactly have you heard?" she demanded.

"I haven't heard anything. But I'm worried about you, Francesca. I don't want you to do something—something . . ." I stumbled for the right word. "Irreversible."

Jack's head snapped in my direction again. He dredged a hand through his short-cropped black hair, turned, and started to walk back up the hill. If I was going to find out what he wanted to talk to me about, I needed to get Francesca off the phone.

"I don't think we should talk about this anymore," I said. "I have to go."

"Perhaps you're right." She was silent for a moment. "Sometimes I wish I could get away with murder. It would solve so many troubles in my life right now."

"And create about a thousand more," I warned as I jogged after Jack.

"Of course you're right. It's just a game we've been playing. And a way to help raise money for the garden club. I'll think of a way to handle Parker."

"Legally?" I pressed.

"Naturally," she drawled a moment before she disconnected the call.

"Jack!" I called as I ran after him.

He stopped and slowly turned toward me.

"You—you needed to talk to me?" My heart started pounding again. I swallowed quickly.

He scowled at his watch. "I'm sorry, Casey, but I've got to go."

"What did you need to tell me?" I asked while following along with him as his long stride carried him back toward the White House. "Or did you want to ask me something?" Like out to coffee or dinner? Like a date?

"I wanted to—" he started to say, but shook his head. "It wasn't important. I've got to get back on duty."

"Maybe later, then?" I said and then mentally kicked myself for sounding so blooming needy.

I didn't need Jack. Or anyone.

"I didn't want to know anyhow," I grumbled. But he'd already disappeared inside the West Wing.


**"THAT'S THE LAST TIME I HELP OUT WITH THE** volunteers, Casey," Gordon Sims warned later that afternoon.

I glanced up from the pile of paperwork on my desk, which I'd been hopelessly trying to organize, and found him leaning against the open door frame that connected the grounds office with his own office situated directly underneath the White House's North Portico.

With thirty-five years' experience tending the President's gardens, Gordon's incredible knowledge of plants, along with his relaxed demeanor, made him an invaluable asset to the numerous administrations he'd worked under. Over the years, he'd weathered nearly every kind of disaster imaginable. Very few things in his life upset him.

"Why's that?" I asked, surprised that he was complaining about this morning. Apart from Francesca's absence, everything had gone smoothly.

"While you were chatting on your cell phone, those ladies treated me like I was a juicy tomato they wanted to squeeze. I think a couple of them came close to actually squeezing." He shivered dramatically.

He watched while I struggled to decide what I needed to do with an invoice from one of our approved vendors. I dropped it back into my in-box and spotted a handwritten to-do list for the upcoming harvest day festivities.

"You loved every moment of it. Admit it, I did you a

favor," I said somewhat absently as I ran my finger down the list. It'd been a good day. Nearly every task had been checked off.

Gordon's smile faded. "Did you see the newspaper the East Wing dropped off when we were outside?"

"No, why?"

"Your kitchen garden was featured in an article," Lorenzo Parisi, Gordon's other assistant gardener, chimed in from where he sat at his drafting desk on the other side of the room. Above his head on the whitewashed cinder-block wall hung a colorful schematic for the First Lady's vegetable garden next to a design for the White House grounds, made by Fredrick Law Olmsted, Jr., that dated back to 1935.

He tossed the newspaper across the room for me to catch.

The newspaper wasn't *Media Today*, I was glad to see. So there was no danger the odious Griffon Parker had penned a scathing attack on the First Lady's garden or her organic gardening program. The newspaper was one of those free political rags that employed homeless men to hand out copies at all the Metro stations.

The headline on the second page read, WATERCRESS-GATE: SCANDAL IN THE WHITE HOUSE VEGETABLE GARDEN.

My shoulders sank in concert with my heart. I swallowed before reading the first paragraph. Then the second.

"'The First Lady's garden is an elaborate hoax designed to dupe the American people into eating their vegetables,'" I read aloud. "Why in blazes would anyone even think that?"

Paragraph after paragraph, facts were jumbled together with conjecture. The article then concluded with, "It's impossible to believe the plants in the White House's garden could have grown so quickly in the chilly D.C. spring climate or produced so much. We are forced to conclude the garden has been staged."

"Oh, for heaven's sake!" I tossed the newspaper at my desk.

It landed with a satisfying slap. "The plants in the garden are on display for any tourist to see. We'd have had to sneak in at night week after week, replacing baby plants with slightly bigger ones. Even then, someone would have seen us!"

"It's just a throwaway newspaper, Casey," Gordon soothed. "No one takes those articles seriously."

"I suppose not." The article just below it on that page touted, PRESIDENT'S LOVE CHILD.

"Bogus or not, I wouldn't let Seth see that article," Lorenzo said with a smirk.

"He does seem to be gunning for you lately," Gordon agreed.

I wondered if the First Lady's social secretary was one of the unnamed sources. Would he stir up trouble for the First Lady just to hurt me? Probably not.

"Now that you know the story is out there, you won't be blindsided by it if a reporter asks a question about it," Gordon said as I rubbed my temples to ward off a Seth-sized headache. "That's how these things work."

"I doubt anyone in the press is that interested in the vegetable garden." Lorenzo slid his dark Mediterranean gaze in my direction. "The rumors swirling around Bruce Dearing are distraction enough for everyone."

Gordon nodded his agreement. "I heard the press secretary complaining in the hallway this morning that none of the journalists listen at the daily press briefing. They're all too busy Googling on their BlackBerries, trying to scoop each other, and *Media Today*, on their witch hunt for a scandal. I can't remember ever seeing a darker cloud hanging over any member of the West Wing, especially not over the President's Chief of Staff." Gordon had to raise his voice to be heard over a sudden series of loud bangs. The grounds offices were adjacent to the carpenters' shop, where they'd been frantically working all week on a special project for Seth Donahue.

"Don't forget about those nasty rumors that circulated about a year ago about the press secretary and the Chief of Staff," Lorenzo said.

Lorenzo grinned in my direction when I took the bait and asked, "Rumors about Frank Lispon and Bruce Dearing? What were they about?"

"Nothing," Gordon said. "Just some nasty backstairs gossip that doesn't deserve repeating." Gordon wiped his hands together as if brushing off a day of hard labor in the garden.

*Repeat it, repeat it!* I wanted to scream.

But I didn't. I was no longer a slave to my curiosity. I didn't need to know everything about everybody. And I was mighty proud of myself for my extraordinary display of self-control.

"Does the scandal have to do with—?" The words popped out of my mouth.

"Lorenzo"—Gordon turned away from me—"are you still planning to attend the First Lady's volunteer appreciation tea? I need to send word to the East Wing who I'm sending in my place by the end of the day."

Lorenzo rubbed the back of his neck. "Actually, I can't do it this year."

I didn't blame Lorenzo for wanting to wiggle out of going. From what I'd heard, I'd rather catch a bad case of the mumps than attend this year's volunteer event. But I was surprised by Lorenzo's sudden change of heart.

Lorenzo was the kind of guy who lived for the chance to rub elbows with powerful people like President John Bradley and First Lady Margaret Bradley. Appearances mattered to him. He wore suits to work even though we all worked in the gardens. When he worked outside, he wore a dark green garden apron over his dress shirt to ward off stains. He looked as if he should be puttering around an English estate. Even now at the end of the day the creases in his pants were sharp enough to scythe grass.

I, on the other hand, wore sensible loafers, khaki pants, and knit tops. Although I started each day looking fresh and professional, I rarely ended that way. Even when I managed to avoid getting splattered with mud during one of our many gardening projects, Milo, the overgrown presidential puppy, would happen.

The fluffy fifty-pound, six-month-old goldendoodle had developed a bad habit of digging in the lawns and gardens. Lately the task of cleaning up both the garden and Milo's muddy paws fell into my lap.

Lorenzo conveniently kept his distance whenever Milo was in need of a bath, claiming to be allergic. I suspected he wasn't allergic to dogs, but to dirt.

"I thought you were looking forward to the volunteer appreciation tea. What's happened?" Gordon asked Lorenzo.

Lorenzo's tanned cheeks turned a strange shade of puce. "I . . . um . . . will be busy that afternoon. I . . . I have a date."

"You do?" I shouted, overjoyed to hear it. His former girlfriend had been tragically murdered this past spring, which had crushed him. Both Gordon and I had been worried about his dark mood for months. "That's wonderful news! Who is she? Do we know her?"

"Um . . ." Lorenzo rubbed the back of his neck. "Let's stick to talking about gardening." He swiveled his chair back around to face his desk.

Although I was the new girl in the group—Gordon and Lorenzo had worked together for the past seven years—I had hoped Lorenzo would have accepted my laurel leaf of friendship by now. We worked long hours together, sacrificing nearly all of our social lives to make sure the grounds always had a showroom shine. Apparently, because the First Lady had personally hired me to develop and implement an organic gardening program at the White House, Lorenzo would always view me as an outsider and a threat.

"Ohh-kaay," I said as I frowned at the back of Lorenzo's head. "Perhaps we could—" I stopped when my desk phone rang.

The brisk, no-nonsense Secret Service agent on the

other end of the line skipped the greeting and said, "Ms. Calhoun, we have a situation at the northwest gate."

"A situation?" I sat up straighter, causing my desk chair to let out a loud squeak.

There was no reason for anyone in the Secret Service to contact me, an assistant gardener, about any kind of situation that would concern the security of the White House, unless I was somehow responsible for causing it.

After that disastrous training session at the Secret Service training center, I'd been trying to keep a low profile and avoid any and all "situations."

Oh, hell, whatever it was, I'd simply have to fix it.

Lorenzo had turned around and was watching me with an expression of concern until he realized I'd noticed. He quickly spun back to his desk.

"What's going on?" I asked.

The Secret Service agent didn't answer right away, which wasn't a good sign. "Mrs. Dearing is at the northwest gate."

"Francesca?"

"Yes, ma'am. She's brought a guest that she insists you need to meet. She said you asked her to bring him here."

"She did?" I hadn't asked Francesca to bring anyone to the White House. And I still had no idea why the Secret Service would consider anyone at the gate a situation. "So what's the problem?"

"Mrs. Dearing's guest hasn't been properly vetted. We can't admit him. You should have known that," he scolded. "You'll have to come out here."

"That's not a problem. I'll be right out."

I started to hang up, but stopped myself. There had to be something else going on.

Secret Service agents didn't rattle easily. On a day-to-day basis they calmly dealt with dozens of suspected threats against the President in addition to managing overzealous protesters and the occasional mentally ill patient looking to make the six o'clock news. The men and women who protected the White House and its important residents were too well trained to be bothered by something as simple as an unexpected visitor. "Are you sure there's nothing wrong?"

"Ma'am . . ." A low chuckle garbled his words. "Mrs. Dearing's guest, well, he seems to be wearing a skirt."

# Chapter Three

*Sometimes I wake at night in the White House and rub my
eyes and wonder if it is not all a dream.*
—GROVER CLEVELAND, THE 22ND PRESIDENT OF
THE UNITED STATES

**N**OT knowing who or *what* to expect to find at the
gate or what Francesca was thinking, I emerged
from the White House basement and onto a paved sunken
courtyard adjacent to the North Portico. Although it was
close to six o'clock that June evening, the oppressive heat
wave made the warm summer air feel like an old damp
dishrag. Even the breeze felt hot and wet.

I crossed the courtyard and climbed a concrete stairway
to the curving driveway that bisected the North Lawn.

Not for the first time, I felt a surge of pride as I turned a
full circle and took in the sight of the White House's soar-
ing columns. Every inch of the People's House held a piece
of every important man and woman who'd walked these
grounds. Stone garlands of oak leaves, acorns, roses, and
acanthus leaves had been expertly carved into the White
House's entranceway by stonemasons under the direction
of President Thomas Jefferson. President Harry Truman
had planted the boxwoods that lined the driveway.

These were the types of things I hoped to not only protect but highlight as assistant gardener.

Even though I served at the pleasure of the First Lady and President, I considered the entire nation my client. Not everyone who visited Washington, D.C., would have the opportunity to tour the inside of the White House. Those who did would only see a small portion of the rooms. But the grounds were on display for everyone to enjoy.

As I took the same path many presidents had walked, I couldn't help but think that I must have been born under a lucky star.

I'd come from chaotic beginnings, traveling like a gypsy with my parents from city to city, country to country, often changing our names as we'd flee in the night. Whether my parents were criminals or con men, to this day I still don't know. My father had abandoned my mother and me shortly after my sixth birthday. The next day, a man with a stubbly beard had murdered my mother while I'd watched. When she died, she took her secrets with her.

It wasn't something I liked to think about, but the memories refused to leave me alone lately. They buzzed my consciousness like a swarm of annoying gnats.

Because I'd lived with a string of false identities for as long as I could remember, it took some time for my grandmother Faye to rescue me from a foster system that didn't understand how to heal a child as broken and angry as I'd become.

Treating me as cautiously as one would a wounded animal, Grandmother Faye spoke very little and demanded even less as she carried her tense, bitter grandchild back to Rosebrook, the centuries-old Calhoun family home located in the heart of historic Charleston, South Carolina.

The four-story mansion was filled with long shadows perfect for hiding. The house became my sanctuary, my place to curl up and lick my wounds. I often hid up in the attic, where the past could be stored and forgotten. I lived in my own world, cut off from my grandmother and two aunts who desperately wanted to love me.

Then one day as I gazed out an attic window, I fell under the spell of the enchanted walled garden that enveloped Rosebrook.

Hugging my legs to my chest, I'd watch from that high window with fascination as my grandmother and my spinster aunts, Alba and Willow, worked, often on their hands and knees, tending the flowers, planting vegetable gardens, pruning back ancient hedges with fat, tree-sized trunks. The skirts of their knee-length flowered dresses swished like waves on a beach as the women moved from plant to plant. Their hands were always moving in a smooth rhythm that seemed to calm the fury and fear raging inside me.

No matter the season or the weather, the three women worked in their garden with a consistency that had been foreign to me, a faithfulness I'd never realized existed and yet had yearned to find.

One dreary winter morning I crawled down from my perch in the attic and joined the older women as they tended the flowerbeds. Grandmother Faye had smiled, bringing a new brightness to her cornflower blue eyes, and handed me a trowel. Together we planted a rosebush. With its bare roots and thorny, leafless branches, I despaired that the dead stick would ever grow.

But my grandmother gently encouraged me, guiding my hands while teaching me how to care for the hopeless twig. Come spring, a miracle occurred. First the bright green leaves broke through, softening the bush's sharp edges.

Then the flowers arrived.

Pink. Passionate. Beautiful.

Seeing those flowers, my heart had started to beat again.

The gardening lessons that my grandmother and aunts had lovingly taught me—lessons that had been handed down through generations of Calhouns—were what I carried with me all the way to the White House.

To honor my family and show them in deeds what words could not, I needed to prove myself worthy to tend the President's gardens. The next test of my mettle was coming up in less than a week with the First Lady's first vegetable harvest. In this, I would not fail.

Not even Seth Donahue or Griffon Parker could trip me up.

With pride and passion for my work fueling my step, I headed down the semicircular North Drive toward the northwest visitors' gate.

"This way, Ms. Calhoun." A well-built member of the Secret Service's Emergency Response Team, dressed in black military fatigues and lugging a futuristic-looking P90 submachine gun, came up from behind me.

"Is something wrong?" I had to jog to keep up with his long stride.

The number of uniformed division Secret Service agents manning the gate had nearly doubled.

"Potentially, ma'am," he said. "You need to provide us with advance notice before bringing high-profile guests to the gate."

"High profile? I didn't—" I started to explain, but stopped myself. Shifting the blame wouldn't change anything. I dug my teeth into my lower lip and pressed on, determined to deal with whoever Francesca had brought and quickly move them to another location.

"Good evening, Fredrick," I said as I spotted my favorite guard at the whitewashed clapboard gatehouse. His bright red hair and flushed, round cheeks gave the bulky Secret Service agent a boyish look.

He smiled as he greeted me. "Your guests are over there," he said with a tilt of his head toward the front of the gatehouse.

I saw Francesca Dearing first. I envied her effortless sense of grace. About twenty years older than my almost forty, she reminded me of a glamorous movie starlet from the golden age of Hollywood. She had a timeless taste in clothes, stylishly coiffed brown hair with just a touch of gray, and an apparent knack for always knowing the right thing to say. As a result people wanted to know her and be around her. Including me.

Dressed in a fashionable pink pantsuit, she hugged the arm of the man standing beside her. His square jaw complemented the muscles bulging in his bare arms. Wavy black hair hung wild about his face. His brown eyes shimmered with laughter. His expression held an arrogant smugness that suggested he thought he was God's gift to women.

And, as I'd been told, he was wearing a brightly colored flowered skirt . . . er . . . kilt with a black T-shirt. Below his knobby knees he wore a pair of black combat boots very similar to the standard-issue boots used by the military branches of the Secret Service.

The uniformed division agents manning the gate kept their professional demeanor firmly in place. They were highly trained and prepared for anything. But mischief danced in their eyes as I passed.

I suspected I'd hear about this again.

"Casey," Francesca said, "you don't have to worry about anything. You said you needed my help with the harvest preparations and here I am. I'm going to make the First Lady's harvest an unqualified success. Starting with him."

A uniformed division agent behind me snickered.

I turned around to glare and noticed that even the sharpshooters on the White House roof had their binoculars trained in my direction. Unwilling to be intimidated, I gave a wave.

I whirled back around as Francesca began the introductions. Not that they were needed.

"You're Gillis, Gillis Farquhar," I said, interrupting Francesca, and thrust out my hand. I doubt I would have recognized Gillis if he hadn't been wearing that outrageous outfit, the same outfit he wore on his weekly gardening show. Take away his colorful kilt, muscular arms, and strong, naked calves, and he'd look rather ordinary.

"Crikey! Aren't you a bonny lass to know me?" His Scottish brogue rolled across his tongue. "You've seen my show?"

"Who hasn't?" I said.

Gillis Farquhar was the Gordon Ramsay of the gardening world. He hosted two weekly gardening television
shows and a daily radio call-in show, and he'd published
nearly a dozen how-to books. His latest, *Gardening the
Farquhar Way: Organic!*, was working its way up the bestseller lists.

Clearly I wasn't the only one to recognize him. A small
crowd of tourists, mainly women, gathered outside the iron
fence, cameras snapping away.

"Gillis! Gillis!" several of the women called in near
hysterics.

He tossed his long hair while waving at the crowd and
blowing kisses, which only encouraged his fans to yell
louder. More tourists came over to the gate, craning their
necks to see what was happening.

"I was going to suggest we sit in Lafayette Square and
talk, but we'd be mobbed."

"Oy, canna we go inside, lass, so I can shake hands with
your Mr. President man?" He blinked his brown eyes and
smiled.

I so wanted to accommodate Gillis. Gardening celebrities turn up at the White House about once a . . . never. But
without prior clearance, there was nothing I could do.

"I'm sorry, but we'll have to—"

"Ms. Calhoun, you can't hold a meeting here. Didn't the
training session teach you to stay out of trouble?" Mike
Thatch, the special agent in charge of the CAT, trotted
toward us. He snarled as his gaze took in the growing
crowd pressing against the fencing. "You need to get your
guest away from the gate. Now." The White House Police
had already started to herd the crowd of women away. But
Gillis kept waving at them, attracting them back.

"What should I do?" I whispered to Thatch.

"Plan ahead next time. Give us some advance notice,"
he snapped and returned to directing his agents on crowd
control.

Fredrick, bless his kind heart, directed us to step inside
the whitewashed guardhouse. He spoke quietly on the

phone for a few minutes before producing two visitor's badges, which he handed to Gillis and Francesca. "You have permission to use a conference room in the EEOB. I'll serve as your escort."

"Dog's baws!" Gillis exclaimed.

"I beg your pardon?" I asked.

"Just my way of saying it's excellent, lass. We get to go inside after all. Lead on."

"It's not inside the White House," I cautioned.

"Then where are we going, lass?"

I pointed to the Eisenhower Executive Office Building.

"Cor blimey, that rickety old place?"

Fredrick rolled his eyes. I rather liked the French Second Empire design of the building. With its steeply sloped mansard roof, the five-story, block-long structure looked as if it belonged in a quaint Paris neighborhood or a doily-draped living room crowded with figurines and knick-knacks.

"Does your girlfriend have a favorite flower?" I asked Fredrick as he hurried us through the metal detector inside the guardhouse and away from Gillis's screaming fans. Several news reporters came over from the West Wing press room to see what the fuss was about.

As we crossed the lawn toward the Eisenhower building, every few steps Gillis would stop to wave. I glanced back at the crowd and saw that the journalists had converged on SAIC Mike Thatch. His expression grew all the more grim as he answered each of their questions.

Tomorrow his name would likely appear in several newspapers. Thatch would not thank me for thrusting him into the spotlight. Nor would he let me forget it.

"Violets," Fredrick replied, barely moving his lips. "My Lily likes violets."

"Really? Not lilies?" I asked.

"Go figure." He shrugged.

"Monday morning I'll bring a potted arrangement filled with violets for you to give her." I touched his sleeve. "Thank you."

We entered the Eisenhower Executive Office Building located beside the West Wing. The EEOB, built in the 1880s, like the Treasury building on the other side of the White House, was connected to the White House through a tunnel. The large building housed medical offices, a bank, and offices for most of the White House staff. We followed Fredrick up a flight of bronze baluster stairs to a small conference room on the second floor.

Once we'd settled in around the oak conference table, I tried to reach Seth Donahue, the First Lady's social secretary, to include him in the meeting, but he'd already left for the day. I made a mental note to call him over the weekend to brief him on whatever plans we made.

Over the next hour, Gillis provided several ideas of how he could assist with the harvest. He volunteered to teach gardening lessons to the schoolchildren scheduled to attend. Francesca focused on how his presence would attract additional media attention.

I frantically jotted down notes while wondering how I could make all these changes before Wednesday. However, while it would mean more work, his suggestions had merit. It'd be a mistake to dismiss them.

The day had faded into twilight by the time the meeting ended and Fredrick escorted us back to Pennsylvania Avenue. Deep shades of orange and red streaked across the evening sky.

"We can continue our planning session tomorrow morning at the public garden. You are still coming?" Francesca asked.

"Of course I am. I'm bringing the petunias," I said, relieved that Francesca had found something other than murder plots to occupy her mind.

"Wonderful. And if you have any upcoming meetings with the First Lady, please include me. I want to make sure she knows—"

"Mrs. Bradley's schedule is always full," I interrupted, wondering why I hadn't realized it sooner. Francesca hadn't been interested in helping me. It wasn't friendship that had inspired her to invite Gillis to the White House. She was using the vegetable harvest as a way to bolster her husband's faltering career. She wasn't the first wife anxious to forge a close relationship with the First Lady. "I'm sorry, Francesca. Mrs. Bradley doesn't have time to sit in on meetings such as these, especially not with twins on the way. She receives briefings on our progress, of course."

"You'll make sure she knows I'm working on the plans, though, and that I was the one who brought in Gillis, won't you?"

"I'll send an update to her office first thing in the morning," I promised and then thanked Gillis for volunteering to help out with the local schoolchildren.

"She'd said I'd like it here." His gaze darkened as he stared intently at the White House behind me. The gleam in his eyes was one I'd seen in many of the politicians around here. Ambitious. And power hungry. "She was right. I do like it here. I can't wait to use my organic gardening method in these gardens."


**I HAD TO MANUALLY CLOSE MY GAPING MOUTH** as I watched Gillis swagger through a throng of adoring fans before ducking into a sleek black town car waiting at the curb.

"Bruce won't be done for at least another hour. Annie gave us tickets to a late-night jazz concert at Ford's Theater. It doesn't start for hours," Francesca said. She stood next to me as she hugged herself and gazed out over the tall iron fence that encircled the White House northwest gate. Now that Gillis was gone, she looked as lost and uncertain as an abandoned puppy. The corners of her eyes crinkled as she implored me to take her back to my office.

"I don't want to go home alone and face the answering machine. Please, Casey, I could help you hammer out the details for the harvest."

"I don't know." Until an hour ago, all the details had already been hammered out. Francesca and Gillis had changed several activities. If I spent more time with her, what other changes would she make?

"Please, Casey." She gripped my wrist with crushing strength. Unnerved, I tried to pull away, but she held on with brute force.

"You're hurting me," I said, wincing.

"Sorry." She released my wrist. I doubted she realized she'd grabbed me in the first place. "Let me help you so I can feel as if I'm doing something productive instead of sitting around and worrying about what that journalist might do."

"Sure, come on," I said with a sigh.

Back at the grounds office Francesca chatted happily about nothing really. I only half listened. I was too busy worrying about what Gillis had meant when he'd said he couldn't wait to get his hands on the White House gardens.

The First Lady didn't need anyone to develop an organic gardening plan. One was already being implemented. Mine.

I glanced over at Francesca as she happily carried on a conversation without any help on my part. Gillis had taken time out of his busy schedule to come down from New York to Washington. What would he want with my job? By the time Francesca and I had tamed the towering piles of official forms on my desk, I'd concluded that I'd misunderstood what Gillis had been talking about. He didn't want or need my job. And it was late.

The windows across the hallway from the basement office were draped in darkness. The arched concrete hallway, which tended to carry the slightest sound along its length, had fallen silent. Not a clank or a whirl of whisks could be heard from the busy chocolate shop down the hall. Only a hint of rich, dark chocolate aroma lingered in the air.

I closed my eyes and breathed in the sweet scent. Attached to that scent was a faint memory that fluttered in the deep shadows of my mind. Something had happened in a quiet, chocolate-scented room once a long, long time ago. I couldn't quite remember what.

I didn't want to remember. Memories were dangerous.

I jumped to my feet, stuffed my belongings into my backpack, and slung it over my shoulder. "I'm calling it a night," I announced.

A few minutes later Francesca and I crossed the North Lawn. While Francesca gossiped about West Wing staffers, my thoughts strayed. I wanted to get home and into a cool shower.

We were halfway to the gate when the door from the West Wing press room swung open to release a steady stream of reporters. There must have been an evening briefing.

"Do you know what's going on?" Francesca asked.

"It's probably just a late briefing on the budget negotiations." Even so, I wondered if a crisis had erupted somewhere in the world and if it would affect the upcoming harvest events. It amazed me how a skirmish half a world away could upend even the White House grounds office's schedule.

"I haven't heard about any breaking news events." Francesca scowled at the approaching reporters. "I do hope you're right that it's about the budget debate and that it doesn't have anything to do with Bruce." She drew a deep breath. "*Or me.*"

"Those rumors are about you, aren't they?" I asked. Francesca represented the epitome of grace and good manners. My grandmother would love her. "What did you do?"

Under the glow of the White House lighting, Francesca's healthy pink glow drained from her face as she watched the number of reporters swell. "I can't be here."

"Facing them would suck the power right out of the rumors. I know. Remember when Griffon Parker targeted me this spring?" I tried to catch her arm, but she pushed my hand away and hurried toward the security gate.

"Ms. Calhoun!" a reporter called.

Great, Francesca wouldn't stop and talk with me now. Not with a reporter dogging my heels.

"Ms. Calhoun!" the reporter called again.

Although the grounds crew would sometimes chat with the press, official contact had to be approved through either the communications office or the East Wing.

Quite frankly, with all the talk of scandals lately and the "Watercressgate" article, I had no desire to talk with anyone in the press corps. For all I knew I was about to stumble into a political briar patch.

So even though my grandmother had taught me better manners, I pretended I didn't hear my name being called as I rushed through the northwest gate's security barriers and jogged to catch up with Francesca.

Lafayette Square (which throughout its history has been used as a graveyard, an army encampment, and a zoo) was relatively quiet tonight. The long-term protesters were there. Connie, a nuclear arms protester, had lived in front of the White House among her large, handmade poster board signs for the past three decades. Beside her was the new unfriendly guy, who wore a camouflage hat pulled low on his head. He sat in a battered lawn chair and held a handwritten sign propped up in his lap that read, "Every American Deserves a Safe Workplace." A small handful of tourists milled about. The stifling humidity must have chased everyone else indoors.

"I'm sure it's not as bad as you think," I said as I caught up to and matched Francesca's long stride.

"It is," she cried. "I can't face it. I can't face them."

Her whole body began to tremble. "They know, don't they? That's what the press conference was about. Bruce will be devastated. I—I can't face him. I can't face either of them."

"Why? What did you do?"

"Please, Casey." She picked up her pace. "I can't talk about it."

I hated to let her run away in such distress. "We don't know what Frank Lispon said at the press conference."

"*Frank*!" She used his name like a curse. Tears coursed

down her perfect cheeks. She pushed me away and turned her head the other direction so I couldn't see her. "*Frank,*" she moaned.

"Ms. Calhoun!" That darn reporter had followed me into the park and was fast closing the distance between us.

Francesca darted behind a statue of Andrew Jackson sitting astride a horse.

"Miss Calhoun! I've a source who insists the First Lady's organic garden is a farce. Would you like to comment on that?" The reporter's voice boomed across the park.

Grimacing, I whirled around to face my accuser. "That news article was nothing but a pack of lies."

An older man in a tweed suit with hunched shoulders and a stooping back rushed toward me. His determined stride was quick and jerky. He had a pinched expression around his eyes as if he was too proud to admit he needed glasses.

I don't know if it was his personality or his looks, but whenever I saw him, he reminded me of a pesky weasel that tore plants out of garden beds just for the fun of it.

"Griffon Parker." I wrinkled my nose with distaste. "You'll have to request an interview with the East Wing. It's unfair of you to ask me questions. You know I'm not in a position to comment."

"But you're in charge of the First Lady's gardens," he pressed.

"You'll have to submit your questions to the East Wing," I repeated. Chief Usher Ambrose Jones, who'd spent nearly all of his adult life working in some capacity at the White House, had taught me the technique. Calmly and professionally repeat your point until the other side gives up.

Unfortunately, when I turned to look for Francesca, Parker stuck to my side like a prickly sandspur.

"Come now. You wouldn't want tomorrow's story to be one-sided," he threatened. "Let's be honest here. Claiming the First Lady created an *organic* vegetable garden is good PR, but it's not real. My source tells me—"

"Before you write this glorious exposé of yours, do

some research," I said, feeling the blood rise to my cheeks. I didn't care what his source was telling him. His source was wrong. "The First Lady's vegetable garden is *not* an organic garden. No one at the White House *ever* said it was an organic garden. We're utilizing organic practices. There's a difference. Google it!"

I jogged away from him before something unladylike slipped out of my mouth. My face burned with frustration and embarrassment.

Good gracious, I shouldn't be allowed within a mile of the press, especially not Parker. Why couldn't I learn to keep my mouth shut? Why did I let him get under my skin?

Now when he's writing up his story tonight, all he'll remember is how the assistant gardener snapped at him.

Instead of biting his head off, I should have *calmly and professionally* asked for more information. Who was his source? What exactly had his source told him? If Parker had a source who was criticizing the First Lady's garden, that was something I needed to know.

Was his source the same person who had fed that other newspaper its information for "Watercressgate"?

Now I would have to swallow my pride, go back, and find Griffon Parker to do just that.

I spotted the weasel leaving Lafayette Square. With his head turned down and his gait more jerky than usual, he looked as agitated as I felt.

A beautiful dark-skinned woman dressed in a crisp navy blue suit appeared out of nowhere. She flicked her black hair, tinged with deep auburn highlights, out of her face as she followed Parker. She remained at his side dogging his every step as he'd done to me.

Good. I was glad he was getting a taste of his own medicine.

She was slightly taller than my five feet seven and yards more glamorous. Her shoulder-length hair hung perfectly straight like pressed silk. It was clear by her tight expression that Parker had done something to make her unhappy. Either that or she'd been sucking on lemons. She stopped and raised both her hands in the air with a wide, but graceful, gesture as she spoke.

I wondered what he'd done to upset her.

"It's none of my business," I reminded myself.

"*Look at her.*" Francesca suddenly appeared at my side. She grabbed my hand and dragged me closer.

"Who is she?" I asked.

"What does she know?" Francesca whispered.

"You can't do this, Parker," we heard the woman say as her voice rose.

Parker ignored her as he stepped onto the section of Pennsylvania Avenue that ran between the White House and Lafayette Square. This part of the road was permanently closed to all but foot traffic. He scurried down the pedestrian street toward the much busier Seventeenth Street.

"You stole my research!" she shouted after him.

"You can't prove it," he hollered back.

"You're the only one who could have taken those papers from my desk. You had no right." She followed him, her heels clacking against the pavement.

Parker drew a breath, straightening his hunched shoulders. When he turned to her, the cold look in his beady black eyes made me draw back. "I don't know who you slept with to get here, little girl, or if you're here to meet the company's racial quota, but I do know you don't have the balls to take my place. You can't even hold on to your precious research," Parker growled.

The woman raised her slender hand to slap him, but hesitated. She looked at her hand held at the ready and smiled.

Francesca moved us even closer as the woman spoke, her voice low and hard. "I'm not so sure the CEO of *Media Today* would be happy with your performance right now, especially after he hears about how you—"

"Don't threaten me," Parker snapped.

"I'm not. I'm—" She spotted Francesca and me and closed her mouth.

Parker took the opening and scampered down the street like an oversized rat. I wanted to follow.

*Stay out of it*, my pesky inner voice warned. Their argument was none of my business. I needed to go home. I wanted to go home.

"Wait up," Francesca called. She grabbed my arm and held on tight as she chased after the female reporter.

# Chapter Four

*Things don't turn up in this world until somebody turns them up.*
—JAMES A. GARFIELD, THE 20TH PRESIDENT OF THE UNITED STATES

**F**RANCESCA gave me a hard shove just as we caught up with the dark-haired, picture-perfect reporter in front of the white-bricked Blair House.

Windmilling like a madwoman didn't save me. I tripped over both my feet and plunged into the reporter. She gave a cry of alarm and wrapped her arms around my shoulders to save us both from landing in a heap on the ground in front of the White House's official guesthouse.

With a frustrated shake of her head, the reporter demanded—in colorful words I won't repeat—to know what the devil I wanted.

I glanced around. This was Francesca's game, not mine. Where had she gone?

"I'm sorry I fell on you like that," I said, still looking around for Francesca. I'd never known my fellow gardener to be so slippery.

The press credentials hanging from a lanyard around the reporter's neck read, "Kelly Montague, *Media Today*."

So this was the television reporter rumored to take Griffon Parker's place? I silently wished her success.

"Yes? Can I help you?" Kelly tapped her high-heeled shoe. "I'm in a hurry."

"It's Griffon Parker," I blurted out.

She folded her arms across her chest and waited for me to continue.

"He's causing a problem for a friend of mine." I looked around for Francesca again. *Why did she run off like that?* "Come to think about it, he's causing trouble for me, too."

"It seems no one in D.C. is safe from him," Kelly quipped.

"No kidding. He's a menace, and he's writing an article attacking a friend of mine. If she could find out what the story was going to be about, I'm sure she could use that information to do some advance damage control."

"Yes?" Kelly raised her perfectly arching brows. "What do you expect me to do?" She started to walk away.

"Well, I . . ." This wasn't going as smoothly as I'd hoped. "I . . . um . . . the argument you were having with Parker just now, I was wondering if it had something to do with the Dearings. I overheard you say that Parker took some papers of yours. It wouldn't happen to have anything to do with Bruce or Francesca Dearing, would it?"

"I don't know what you're talking about." Kelly picked up her pace. Her quick, no-nonsense stride made it clear that she didn't want me to follow.

I narrowed my gaze and watched her hurry away in the same direction Griffon Parker had gone. There was no reason for me not to believe her. And yet I was certain Kelly Montague had just lied to me. Why else would she have jerked as if I'd sucker-punched her at the mention of the President's Chief of Staff and his wife?


**THAT NIGHT I DREAMED OF RICH CHOCOLATE** scents and Paris. Warm and comforting, the dream had been going along quite well until I tumbled headfirst into a deep pit in the middle of the South Lawn, a pit where the First Lady's vegetable garden should have been.

An angry wind slapped me over and over as I clawed at the pit's walls, reaching for the edge that moved farther and farther away from me. Or was I falling deeper into the hole?

Tired and humiliated, I tossed my head back and cried out for help.

That was when I noticed a man cloaked in dark shadows that wrapped around him like a trench coat. He stood at the edge of the pit, his shoulders straight, and watched my struggles. Why didn't he reach down and pull me to freedom? All he had to do was stoop a little.

"Who are you?" I cried.

The man didn't speak or move. He remained at the edge of the pit until several streaks of lightning blazed across the sky.

The stricken face staring down at me was one I'd long ago blotted from my memories. I hadn't seen him for nearly thirty-five years, and yet I saw him now as clearly as the day he'd tweaked my nose and walked out that apartment door and never returned.

Suddenly I was no longer the successful organic gardener on the brink of her fortieth birthday, but a frightened six-year-old living in Phoenix, Arizona, and James Calhoun was my world.

"Daddy?" My voice belonged to a fragile six-year-old girl who no longer existed. "Daddy? Why won't you help me?"

Why did he abandon me? I needed him. Why did he walk out on Mom and me?

"I neeeed you!"

He could have saved my mother. He could have saved me from—

Another flash of lightning lit up his face again. This time it wasn't my father staring down at me. It was Jack's.

I woke with a start.

The bed, the dresser, the cracked plaster on the ceiling of the brownstone's bedroom gradually became real again. I didn't dare move for fear of falling back into that nightmare and becoming trapped in the pit again. I stared at the plaster ceiling, finding solace in the silence of the night.

Unlike in my dream, no storm raged outside my window, and I had no father.

Not anymore.

He'd left ages ago.

I inhaled the thought with my breath, practicing the relaxation techniques a childhood therapist had once shown me.

He'd left his only child unprotected.

I breathed out.

He'd left me to die.

Don't think about the rest. Push the door closed. Push the door closed. Don't remember.

It was dangerous to remember.

I pressed my fists to my eyes.

Ever since the murder of that poor Treasury official this past spring, the ironfisted control holding back my past had started to weaken. It was worse at night when I dreamed.

I sucked in another deep breath.

Don't sleep. Don't dream.

Breathe out.

Learn from the past. Guard your heart. Don't ever let it get hurt like that again.

I choked a bit on that last breath, but I shook my head and snapped out of my funk.

Focus on the present. Griffon Parker was making everyone's life miserable. That was a real problem that I could grab on to. I needed to do something to stop Parker from destroying Francesca and the First Lady's garden.

But what?

*But what*?

After a night of tossing and turning and worrying, the next morning I was no closer to coming up with a scheme to thwart Griffon Parker than I had been the night before. As soon as I woke up, I scoured the newspaper, finding no mention of scandal on the front page or the whole front section. I flipped through the entire newspaper, scanning every article.

Not one article mentioned Francesca, her husband, Bruce, or the First Lady's kitchen garden. Surprisingly, none of the articles in Saturday's paper had been penned by the perpetually unfriendly Griffon Parker. We'd been given a day of reprieve, a day to figure out how to best Parker at his own game. Instead of relief, I felt all the more anxious to meet with Francesca and brainstorm.

"We're late," I called to my roommate, Alyssa Dunn, while pacing the front entranceway.

"Five more minutes," Alyssa called back.

"We don't have five minutes." I trotted up the narrow Victorian staircase. "We're already five minutes *late*. The ladies can't get started without me, since I'm bringing the plants."

Alyssa and I rented the upper two floors of a three-story brownstone in the Columbia Heights neighborhood. The building, built in the 1890s, was an architectural treasure with its ornate scrolling oak woodwork. Located just two miles from the White House, I often commuted to and from work on bike or on foot.

Pretty much everything within the capital city was within walking distance or a short Metro ride away from my front door.

"You're going to have to drive us. It'll take too long to walk. Alyssa! I mean it." I banged on her bedroom door. "We need to leave now."

"I'm coming." The bedroom door swung open just as I raised my fist to bang on it again. Alyssa breezed into the upstairs hallway as if we had all the time in the world.

She'd pulled her shiny black hair into a simple ponytail. But that was just about the only thing simple about her polished look. Although she often complained about the fifteen pounds she'd gained since she'd moved to D.C. to work as a congressional aide for Senator Alfred Finnegan, I couldn't see where she was hiding it. The white sundress with bright yellow sunflowers accentuated her curves, curves in all the right places that I wished I possessed.

Flawless makeup, tanned legs, and hemp sandals from a designer I knew she'd mentioned, but for the world of me I couldn't recall (nor cared to recall)—Alyssa looked stunning.

"*What are you wearing?*" Alyssa and I each pointed at the other's outfit.

"We're going to be planting a flower garden in Burberry Park, not attending a garden party," I reminded her in case she'd forgotten. I had dressed in an old T-shirt and denim shorts that had faded over time. Old. Comfortable. And completely appropriate for renovating a public garden.

Alyssa frowned as she touched the hem of the flowered sundress she wore. I eyed her strappy sandals. They'd be ruined before the end of the day, not to mention how muddy her feet were going to get.

"These are the oldest clothes I own." She sounded truly bewildered that I'd think there was anything wrong with what she was wearing. With a carefree shrug, she hooked her arm with mine and directed me down the stairs. "I don't think we have time to stand around and debate fashion. I thought you said we were running late."

"You're right. Besides, fashion is a debate I'll never win with you." Designer labels were like a second language to her, one that I didn't speak a word of.

"Do tell me that your Secret Service man is planning to help out today."

"No, he's not. And he's not my—I mean he's not—oh, forget it. Jack's not going to be there." My cheeks burned as I remembered how he'd come down to the garden to talk with me. And only me. What had he wanted to say?

"Interesting," Alyssa murmured as she watched me too closely.

"It's not interesting, because there's nothing between Jack and me to be of any interest." I disentangled my arm from hers and gathered the tray of patriotic red, white, and blue wave petunias that were waiting for us on the front stoop. "And you're driving."

As Alyssa drove up to the nearby park, one of the many leafy green oases dotting the city, I spotted a small crowd milling around the park's periphery.

Francesca and her close friend Annie Campbell were coordinating the beautification project. Many of the same volunteers working in the First Lady's garden had signed up to help, including Senator Alfred Finnegan's wife, Imogene.

I suspected Alyssa had insisted on tagging along with me this morning because of Imogene's involvement in the project.

"You'd better let me out here," I said. The few parking spots along the park had already been taken. Doing a delicate balancing act with the large tray, I slid out of Alyssa's little red convertible.

While Alyssa parked the car, I crossed the road to the park and searched the crowd for Francesca.

She should have been easy to spot since she nearly always wore pink. This morning, the only person dressed in pink was me in a faded pink T-shirt that had been a freebie at a breast cancer awareness walk.

Perhaps Francesca had decided to stay home to avoid facing the rumors that had been swirling around her. But if Francesca wasn't around, that meant Annie Campbell would have to handle all the details on her own.

Poor Annie. Unlike Francesca, Annie was rather hopeless when it came to plants or thinking for herself. In the First Lady's garden, Annie served as gofer for the other volunteers. I couldn't remember ever seeing her put her hands in the soil even once.

Prepared to take a leadership role in assigning tasks, I joined the small crowd milling about. Oddly, none of them greeted me or appeared at all interested in my flat of wave petunias. Instead, their attention was focused on the yellow police tape that encircled the small park.

A cold shiver tiptoed down my spine.

"What's going on here?" I called out to a police officer who had just finished tying off the last of his yellow tape to a saucer magnolia tree. With a clipboard tucked under his arm, he headed toward an opening in the tape border where another officer stood watch.

I trotted to catch up to him. "Excuse me," I called.

"What?" he snapped, obviously tired of fielding questions from the public.

"What's happening here?" I asked.

"I'm sure it'll be in all the papers, ma'am," he said, indicating that I should move away from the police tape. "Please step back. We've got work to do."

Not one to be easily discouraged, I stood my ground. "I'm supposed to meet with a group of volunteers. We're planting a community flower garden."

He nodded when he spotted the tray of red, white, and blue petunias I was lugging. "You'll have to do that another day. As you can see, the park is an active crime scene."

"Actually, I can't see anything." I rose to my tiptoes, but all the action seemed to be happening on the other side of the large bronze statue in the middle of the park. "What happened?" I asked.

The officer glanced around the cordoned-off area and then back at me. He shrugged. "Apparently some guy offed himself."

"In the park?"

He nodded.

I was about to ask for more information when Annie Campbell hurried toward me. Her shiny red hair bounced with every agitated step. Her dark purple silk sundress was as stylishly inappropriate as Alyssa's cute outfit. "Casey! There you are. And you brought the flowers. Aren't they pretty? I already called the ladies and told them that we needed to reschedule. I didn't have your number, or else I would have called to tell you not to come."

"Really? I thought I gave all the volunteers my cell phone number."

"Did you? Oh, well, I just got a new cell phone and lost most of my contact numbers. If you give it to me again, I'll be sure to take better care of it. You can trust me on that."

"Oh, I trust you," I said to boost her confidence. She always seemed so unsure of herself and apologetic of her shortcomings. "As soon as I find a place to put this tray, I'll give you my cell phone number. Do you know what happened?"

"Not really." She grabbed my arm. "I think we'll be able to see better around the corner."

I let her lead the way around the periphery of the park even though I should have gone back out to the street to look for Alyssa. She must have parked the car by now.

"Have you spoken with Francesca?" I asked as we followed the yellow police tape.

"Several times. She even called early this morning to say that she was feeling under the weather. I have to be honest with you; I think she backed out because of what Pearle and Mable were saying yesterday. I'm supposed to have dinner with her tonight. I hope to find out what's going on then and help her make a plan for damage control."

"You're a good friend, Annie. I'm glad she has you."

Annie lowered her head. "I hope I can do enough."

"I hope so, too. When I saw Francesca last night, she sounded distraught about the article Griffon Parker is going to write. But she wouldn't tell me anything about it. The longer I spent with her, the more it seemed as if she was coming . . . unhinged," I said, remembering the strange way she'd kept running and hiding.

"Francesca? Unhinged?" Annie adamantly shook her head. "She's the most levelheaded person I know. She knows how to handle the press. I'm sure it's the whispering behind her back about what may or may not be 'the scandal of the decade' that's getting under her skin. Francesca and Bruce are as honest as you can get in a political couple. There's no way that Parker fellow could have anything of substance on either of them."

"I don't know about that. Even if it wasn't 'the scandal of the decade' Parker knows how to make it sound as if it is that terrible." That was what he did when he went after me this past spring.

"Oh, here we are." Annie pointed across the yellow tape. She'd been right; we could see what was going on much better from this street.

Beyond the yellow tape, police officers worked as an efficient team around the base of the park's centerpiece bronze statue. An older man sat slumped on a marble step at the statue's base. He seemed oblivious to the activity buzzing all around him. His head was bowed as if he'd fallen asleep.

"Even *Media Today* can't get away with printing out-and-out lies," Annie reminded me. "Before going into politics Bruce used to work as a trial lawyer. He gave my late husband his first job at his law firm. At the first whiff of libel, Bruce will sue, and the newspaper editors know it."

"I hope so. Even though Griffon Parker is a snake, his stories seem to sell papers," I said, feeling my face heat. "He's won plenty of awards for his investigative reports. I hate what he does and who he hurts. He's a weasel. A weed. A sorry excuse for a human being. And—"

"*Dead*," Annie finished for me.

# Chapter Five

*Facts are stubborn things; and whatever may be our wishes,
our inclinations, or the dictates of our passion, they cannot
alter the state of facts and evidence.*
—JOHN ADAMS, THE 2ND PRESIDENT OF
THE UNITED STATES

"*D*EAD?*" I squinted at the policemen working diligently
within the taped-off area of the small park. "What do
you mean Parker's *dead*?"

Annie gestured toward the statue of some long-forgotten
hero and the man slumped at its marble base. The man—
not the statue—was dressed in the same tweed suit Griffon
Parker liked to wear. His stark black hair was slicked back
in a style that had long lost favor. His long narrow nose and
leathery skin reminded me of Parker.

All of his features matched, and yet . . .

"That's not him," I said, shaking my head. "It can't be.
He's like kudzu. No matter how hard you work at pulling it
out, the darn thing just keeps popping back up somewhere
else."

"People aren't plants, Casey. And there's no sprouting
from the roots for him." Detective Hernandez from the D.C.
Police approached from the other side of the yellow tape
with his hands pushed deep into his pockets. "Your friend
is correct. You're looking at the infamous Griffon Parker.

But don't go blabbing anything I've said just now to the press, okay?"

A pair of stony-faced medical examiners lifted the body, carefully lowered it into a black body bag that had been arranged on a gurney, and zipped the bag closed.

Although I didn't feel any fondness toward the crusty reporter, and I mean none at all, I found his death troubling.

"What are you doing here anyhow?" Hernandez asked. "Don't tell me you listen to a police scanner in your free time and run to every reported location hoping to find a crime scene."

"I would never do that! I didn't want to see this." I rattled the large tray of patriotic petunias to make sure he noticed them. Not that I doubted the detective had missed them. "We're planting flowers. Or we were."

"Bad luck, then," he said and scratched his mustache thoughtfully.

"I can't believe it," I repeated needlessly.

The detective shrugged as if he didn't care what I did or didn't believe, which only drove home the fact that Griffon Parker had wilted to the point of no return. Never coming back.

"*Francesca*?" Why had she been so adamant about talking about the perfect murder plot yesterday?

"I beg your pardon?" Detective Hernandez leaned across the yellow tape and asked.

"Did I say something?"

"You said someone's name."

"Did I? I was just—just muttering to myself." My head felt icy cold despite the summer heat. Even as I shivered, a bead of sweat formed on my brow.

Francesca wouldn't have gone and done something . . . irreversible. Would she?

As I stared in horror at the crime scene behind Detective Hernandez, I had to admit that I honestly didn't know the answer to that question.

"You may not believe this, but I—I'm not used to stumbling across dead people," I told the detective.

"You do seem to have a knack for finding trouble," he grumbled.

I'd met the hard-boiled detective three months ago after discovering a dead body in Lafayette Square. I think Hernandez was wearing the same off-the-rack gray suit and ice blue tie he'd worn the first time we met.

Although he was well into his fifties, he had the trim physique of a much younger cop, if perhaps a bit more worn around the edges. His brown hair, the same rich color as his eyes, was streaked with gray and thinning on the top. To compensate, he sported a thick salt-and-pepper mustache that made him look as if he'd stepped out of the pages of a pulp fiction novel.

Hernandez, with his keen eye for details and diplomatic style, often found himself in charge of the politically prickly, high-profile cases.

He was good at his job. *Very* good.

I had no doubt that in time he'd use those sharp senses of his to tease out the facts. When he did, would he end up following a trail of evidence back to Francesca?

*And me?*

"You don't look so good, Casey. You're not going to be sick, are you?" he asked and backed away several steps.

"You do look awfully pale," Annie said. "It's the heat. You need to sit down."

I swallowed hard and shook my head. It wasn't the heat. I'd spent nearly my entire life tending to gardens in sweltering temperatures. "It's walking into the scene of a murder that has me feeling . . ."

*Worried.*

I glanced around, wondering why Alyssa hadn't returned from parking the car. She would know what to say to Hernandez. Or what not to say.

"I have no idea why anyone would want to kill Parker," popped out of my mouth.

"Off the top of my head, I can name at least two dozen reasons, but I don't think that's relevant here. So far there's no sign of foul play. None at all. I don't think Griffon Parker was murdered," the detective said.

"But he wouldn't have—" I started to say, but stopped myself before spouting off anything that might trigger Hernandez's sharp instincts. He'd learn soon enough that Parker wouldn't have killed himself before publishing the damaging article that promised to destroy Francesca and Bruce Dearing.

Hernandez stroked his thick mustache thoughtfully. "Now, Casey. Don't go putting any crazy ideas into your head. That reporter's death has the makings of a walk-in-the-park open-and-shut case. You know how rare those are? Very."

"The nice young officer on the other side of the park"— Annie gestured to the police tape that ran behind the park's statue—"said Griffon Parker killed himself. Is that what you think happened?"

"My officers shouldn't be making conclusions like that. This is an ongoing investigation," he said, giving the petite Annie a thorough inspection.

I quickly introduced the two of them. Annie fluffed her bright red hair as she smiled at the detective. "Annie does volunteer work in the First Lady's vegetable garden," I added. "She also organized the group of ladies who were supposed to be planting these wave petunias around the statue today."

"Nice to meet you, Annie." Detective Hernandez reached across the tape. His expression softened as he clasped her hand a moment longer than necessary. I also didn't miss that he glanced down at her naked ring finger. "I'm Manny. Manny Hernandez."

Spots of color rose in Annie's tanned cheeks. "It's good to meet you, Manny."

I wondered if I should have felt slighted. He'd never invited me to use his first name. "Um . . . Manny, you can tell us. We're not the press. What's *really* going on here?" I asked. "Griffon Parker was having too much fun ruining other people's lives to want to end his own."

He spread his fingers in front of him as if trying to hold me back. "I'm not hiding anything. It really does look like a suicide."

"Then what are *you* doing here? I thought you were a homicide detective."

"I am. It's standard procedure to do a full investigation whenever there's a questionable death. We never really know what we'll find. Although what you see on the surface is usually exactly what happened. And that seems to be the case here."

"Oh." I bit my lower lip. The team of medical examiners had taken away Parker's body. A uniformed police officer wearing latex gloves bent over and picked up a brown pill bottle from the step where Parker had died. He dropped it into a paper evidence bag. A female officer nearby was dusting the step for fingerprints.

"It's all standard procedure." Manny rubbed his mustache again, making it poke out at odd angles. "Procedure that we religiously follow to the letter. I don't care what Parker wrote in his column last week, the D.C. Police has some of the best professionals out there. We know how to do our jobs, and we care deeply about the public we're trained to protect."

"Parker has been attacking the police department in his column? I'm surprised. I thought he was strictly a White House correspondent."

"Oh, don't be surprised. He's done it before, usually after getting burned up over a parking ticket or something trivial like that," Manny said.

"I didn't know."

"You're telling me you haven't read the articles? If that's true, I bet you're the only person in the greater D.C. area who hasn't."

"After what he wrote about me and the unflattering editorial cartoons he'd inspired, I'd stopped reading anything by him."

"I read every word," Annie announced. She hadn't taken her eyes off Manny or his distinctive mustache. Her shyness seemed to fade away as she met his gaze. "I knew right away what he'd written about the D.C. Police was nothing but bunk." She reached across the yellow tape to touch Manny's arm. "Not a month after my husband passed away a few years ago, someone tried to break into my home. The police responded to my call practically before I'd hung up. They took up and charged the thief that same night." Her fingers trailed lightly up his arm. "I sleep soundly in my lonely bedroom knowing that you are out there protecting me."

"I . . . um . . . I . . ." Manny cleared his throat. "Thank you, Annie. That's kind of you to say."

"So the department's been taking a lot of heat because of these articles?" I asked.

"Have we ever! Several politicians are calling for the chief's resignation, which is stupid. Chief Rankin is the best chief we've had in years. Came up through the ranks and really knows how to handle the city's unique quirks and problems. Honestly, I'm not sad to see Parker gone." He hitched his thumb in the direction of the statue.

"Especially if he killed himself?" Annie added.

"Exactly. I don't see how anyone could live with himself as long as he did while knowingly going out of his way to destroy so many careers and lives." Manny shrugged unapologetically.

Coincidences happened every day. Just because Francesca and I had been talking about how to stage a murder, it didn't necessarily mean that Francesca had anything to do with Parker's death.

"So there was a note?" I asked.

"I can't talk about the details of the investigation," Manny said. "I'm sorry."

Undaunted, I pressed on. "I saw the pill bottle beside Parker. Do you think he took an overdose of pills?"

"We won't know what killed him until after the autopsy. But as I said, it looks like suicide."

"Then no poison in his tea or anything as grim as that?" I said as a wave of relief washed over me. Perhaps Parker hadn't been able to face losing his position as a White House correspondent.

It wasn't murder.

*Thank goodness.*

"We did find a travel mug. There was a bit of stinky tea left in it," Manny said, forgetting his earlier promise to keep quiet about the details. "How did you know that?"

"Good guess?" I suddenly had a difficult time catching my breath. Francesca had mentioned that she planned to put poison in his tea. Well, not *Parker's* tea specifically, but . . .

Oh, hell, if I were to be honest about it, the poison in the tea had been my idea.

I knew I needed to say something to Manny, but I didn't want to get Francesca in trouble before I had all the facts.

It still could be suicide.

I needed to step back and think.

"What was he doing drinking hot tea on a day like today?" Annie asked. "It's hot enough to blister the paint off a roof."

"Don't ask me." Manny started to watch me intently. "Casey," he said, his voice low and cautious, "is there anything you want to tell me?"

I pressed my lips tightly together and shook my head. As much as I wanted to say something to him, I couldn't. I wouldn't get Francesca into trouble. Not until I gathered more information about what had happened.

If what Manny said was true and Parker had killed himself, the rest was just coincidence.

That had to be it.

Manny began to return to the work waiting for him at the crime scene when Annie whirled toward me. "My God, Casey. How could you?" She pressed both hands to her mouth. "The tea! I should have remembered right away. Francesca told me all about it. You said you'd put something—oh, yes, an extract from the yew leaves—into his tea. And here he's been found with tea and a pill bottle. The murder is set up exactly how you said it should be done."

"I didn't—" I started to say.

Detective Hernandez had stopped to listen.

"I didn't plan to kill anyone. I didn't *kill* anyone," I protested, but the seeds of doubt had already been planted.

Detective Hernandez's gaze hardened.

Annie finally noticed him watching us. "I'm so sorry, Casey! I shouldn't have said anything. It's just that . . ." She waved her hands nervously in the air. "I shouldn't have said anything."

"What's going on?" he demanded.

"Nothing. Really. Nothing," I said firmly.

"Are you sure?"

Swallowing hard, I nodded.

A news van with *Media Today*'s distinctive logo emblazoned on its side careened around the corner and squealed to a stop in the middle of the road next to the park. Kelly Montague, dressed in a tan business suit and light blue blouse, vaulted out of the van followed by a cameraman.

Manny swore a colorful oath. "How did she find out so quickly? If she's here, I'm sure the other vultures can't be far behind. I need to get over there and deal with her questions." His authoritative gait carried him over to where the news van had parked and the cameraman was setting up. As he walked past one of the uniformed officers, I heard him say in a low voice, "Make sure the ME includes a search for yew extract in the tox screen."

"Yew, sir?" the younger officer asked.

Manny glanced back in my direction. The muscles in his jaw tensed. "You heard me. Yew. As in the plant. Now don't waste my time. I have work to do."

Alyssa rushed over to Annie and me, her keys dangling from her hands, her sundress swishing around her legs. "You wouldn't believe what it took to park. I'm four blocks away. What's going on? What did I miss?"

# Chapter Six

*What kills a skunk is the publicity it gives itself.*
—ABRAHAM LINCOLN, THE 16TH PRESIDENT OF
THE UNITED STATES

"**P**LAIN and simple. A suicide," Alyssa declared after
hearing the details of Parker's death. She pried the
tray of petunias from my hands. "It's shocking and tragic.
And by tomorrow, the news cycle will have moved on to
something else. Parker will be forgotten."

"You think so?" I asked.

"I wouldn't say it if I didn't." Alyssa introduced herself
to Annie. The two women discussed their clothes and
where they shopped while I watched Kelly Montague stand
calmly in front of the camera and from under the shade of
a towering oak tree report on her co-worker's death. Before
Kelly had finished, three additional news vans had pulled
up to the curb.

"I suppose Imogene's not around?" Alyssa asked, her
gaze scanning the dispersing crowd for the senator's wife.
Griffon's body had been taken away and the police seemed
to be winding down their investigation. With the excitement over, the onlookers had started to return home.

"She's not," I said. "Annie warned the volunteers not to

come. That reminds me." I reached into my purse, scribbled my cell phone number on a scrap of paper I found in there, and handed the paper to Annie. "Use this number if you need to contact me in the future. I hope we'll be able to reschedule the planting soon."

"I do, too." Annie folded the paper over and tucked it into her purse.

"Well, since there's nothing left for any of us to do," Alyssa said, "let's get out of here. I'm taking you to my favorite restaurant for breakfast. You rushed me out the door so quickly this morning I didn't get a chance to eat even a crumb."

"I'll see you Monday at the garden," I said to Annie, bidding her a hasty farewell as Alyssa herded me away from the park.

On the way to the restaurant, Alyssa canceled all of her afternoon plans. For the rest of the day, she stuck close by, keeping me distracted and away from the television news long into the evening. We were like a pair of college kids, ordering in pizza, eating ice cream from the carton, and watching old movies until we fell asleep on the sofa in the small hours of the night.

Griffon Parker's death made the front page in the Sunday edition of the national newspaper *Media Today*. The television reporter and the reason Parker's job had been in jeopardy, Kelly Montague, had written the front page's short article. It started out flatly stating that Parker had taken his own life, citing the pending loss of his White House correspondent position. Tucked near the end—if I'd blinked I might have missed it—was Detective Manny Hernandez's standard statement, "The investigation is ongoing."

"So that's it," Alyssa said as she read the article over my shoulder. "It's over."

"I suppose so."

Coincidences did happen.

But what was Parker doing in Burberry Park?

And why would he take his own life *before* publishing

the damaging article against Francesca and Bruce Dearing? It might have saved his job.

He didn't even hang around long enough to publish the article he'd threatened to write against the First Lady's kitchen garden.

I could understand how someone as proud as Parker would be devastated over losing his prestigious White House assignment, but he hadn't lost the assignment yet. And I couldn't believe he'd take his own life without trying to take one or two people down with him. That was the miserable kind of guy he was, the kind who enjoyed spreading his misery around.

Not my business.

Griffon Parker was dead. The world believed he'd killed himself. Who was I to say otherwise?

*STAY OUT OF THE PICTURE.* **THIS CARDINAL WHITE** House rule had been drilled into my head from day one.

Like the insects and worms silently toiling deep in the soil to keep the garden healthy, the White House staff worked behind the scenes to keep the President of the United States well fed, on time, and looking perfect as he worked to keep the country safe and the government running. Very few citizens cared to watch the ushers, maids, and gardening staff shuffling about any more than they'd wish to see those wiggly insects and worms living below ground come flopping up to the surface.

It was the colorful floribunda and tea roses blooming in the Rose Garden that the press and the public wanted to see; it was the President, First Family, VIP visitors, and the First Dog they wanted to see. There was no room on the staff for publicity seekers or showboating. It simply wasn't done.

I didn't need the reminder, thank you very much.

Seth Donahue, the First Lady's social secretary, however, apparently disagreed, if his frantic gestures were any indication. His lanky body moved like an undulating fish as he tried to push me from a great distance. Even his bleached blond hair, so light that it looked colorless, gleamed in the morning light like fish scales.

I didn't know why he was so adamant. Perhaps he thought I was planning to dive into the picture as the First Lady's photographer snapped pictures of Margaret Bradley surrounded by the volunteers who'd spent the last several months helping out in the vegetable garden.

To placate him, I took a half step to the left.

Honestly, after the harrowing morning I'd had, I was more than ready to stand back and let someone else— *anyone* else—take over.

That Monday morning I'd arrived at the White House bright and early with Fredrick's thank-you violets to find the back stairs and hallways abuzz with rumors and speculations about Griffon Parker's death. Not surprising, really. The staff—while adapt at keeping a lid on White House affairs when speaking with outsiders—loved to gossip with each other.

Parker had been a fixture in the White House press room for more than a quarter decade. Everyone was keenly aware of his absence.

*Had he really killed himself*? many of the staff were asking. Others wondered if someone from the White House, someone who benefited from his death, had killed the crusty old reporter.

It wasn't my business, I reminded myself—a sentiment with which I prayed Detective Hernandez would agree.

What I needed to do was immerse myself in the tasks of the day. Only then would my nerves settle down. *The devil never bothers with busy hands*, Grandmother Faye had told me time and again. Well, I don't know about the devil, but busy hands are adept at scaring away unproductive thoughts.

The First Lady's first harvest was in two days. Advanced publicity photos were planned for today. And with all the last-minute changes to be worked out, there'd be no shortage of tasks demanding my attention.

I'd hoped no one would notice me or want to talk with

me as I kept my head down and headed straight for grounds office underneath the North Portico.

"Casey." Steve Sallis, a Secret Service agent from the President's protective detail, dressed in a nondescript black suit, stood like an unmovable pillar blocking the door to the office.

Everyone at the White House knew Steve. Whenever he had a free moment, he'd stop and chat with the gardening staff. Steve was a handsome man with blond hair and an easygoing smile. This morning, however, his friendly smile was nowhere in sight.

He crossed his arms over his chest and frowned.

"There's nothing to see here. Move it along," I wanted to tell him. But instead I said with a hopeful lilt, "Morning, Steve. If you don't mind stepping to one side or the other, I've got a busy day." I tried to ease around him and get inside my office.

"Casey"—Steve put his hand on my shoulder—"we've got a problem."

"A problem?"

As in Parker's death?

As in Francesca's murder mystery dinner that might have turned real?

My anxiety level notched up by only, oh, one hundred and ten percent. I tried to act like I had no idea why the Secret Service might want to talk with me, but my voice squeaked when I asked, "What problem?"

"In the garden, I'm afraid."

"The garden." *Thank goodness.* My tense shoulders dropped at least two inches. He wasn't here to grill me about Parker or attempted murder.

Wait a minute. Did he say *the garden*? "Which garden?"

He rubbed the back of his neck and shifted his weight from one foot to the other. "Um . . . I'm afraid the problem is with the First Lady's kitchen garden."

"*You're* afraid? Then that would make me freaking terrified. What's happened?"

"I'm not sure. Sometime over the weekend Milo must

have gotten to the vegetables. I noticed it last night. Several of the plants have been dug up."

"I thought we'd trained him to leave the plants alone." I sighed. "No problem. We should be able to fix it." Even if I needed to remove a few plants, there should still be plenty left in the vegetable bed for today's pictures and Wednesday's harvest.

The main problem would be if the First Lady's social secretary got hold of the news and decided to use the opportunity to make me look incompetent. Or worse, he might panic and give everyone on the White House staff a blazing headache.

"Does Seth know?" I asked.

"No. I was directed to tell either you or Gordon, and no one else."

"Good." It was still early. I could fix the garden before Seth found out. "Wait a minute. You were directed to come tell me?"

"Or Gordon," Steve said.

I wondered why Jack Turner hadn't volunteered to come tell me about this. He'd sought me out on Friday to tell me something, not that he'd stuck around long enough to tell me what. I wondered what it could have been.

Perhaps Jack had been ordered to stay away from me because of what had happened this past spring. I hoped that wasn't the case. Because if it was, I'd never find out what he was going to say to me last Friday. Not that I cared.

He'd shown no faith in my ability to pass the Secret Service's training session, a training session everyone else had passed without any trouble. Sure, he'd been right. I *had* failed. Miserably.

*Forget Jack.* Yes, he'd saved my life this past spring. But he'd simply been following orders. And yes, he did make my heart race, and not in a scary I'm-having-a-heart-attack sort of way, but with a tingly, warm, fuzzy I'm-running-through-a-summer-rain kind of thumping heartbeat. But none of that mattered.

I needed to focus on what was important—the garden.

I nudged Steve aside and unlocked the grounds office door.

"We're really sorry about this, Casey," he said as I turned on the lights and dropped my backpack on my desk. "None of the agents know how this could have happened. We've been watching Milo."

"And Gordon and I have been working with him on his garden manners. Not to mention the extensive work the dog trainer's done with him. But he's still a puppy, and puppies are notorious for doing naughty things."

As if on cue, Milo trotted into the office and plopped down beside my desk. Although not yet fully grown, he already weighed more than fifty pounds. He had shaggy golden fur with one white leg and a wide white stripe running down his chest.

"Well, Milo, what do you have to say for yourself?"

At the sound of his name he started to wag his tail so vigorously his entire bottom half wiggled. His bright pink tongue lolled out the side of his mouth.

As much as I wanted to be upset with him, I couldn't. He was too darn cute.

"You're stuffed full of puppy energy, aren't you, my sweet boy?" I tousled the long curling fur on the overgrown pup's head, earning myself a sloppy kiss on the hand.

"I'd say he's mostly dog slobber." Steve chuckled as I searched for something to wipe off my dripping hand. I ended up wiping the back of my hand on my khakis.

I tossed a couple of trowels and several pairs of gloves into my large sweetgrass basket, tucked my well-oiled gardening shears into a leather holster on my belt, and grabbed my wide-brimmed garden hat. "Let's go have a look."

Wednesday was Harvest Day on the White House's South Lawn.

Seth Donahue had added the capital letters. I think he was on the verge of making them bold and golden after I'd called him at home over the weekend to tell him about how Francesca had booked us Gillis Farquhar as our guest celebrity. Not to be outdone, Seth had spent the weekend inviting several other celebrities, political power brokers, and all the major television and cable news networks to take part in what I'd initially intended to be a small affair designed for local schoolchildren.

In advance of Wednesday's big-top circus, the First Lady was scheduled to pose for pictures with the volunteers at nine this morning followed by a brief preview of the garden for the press at ten. On the way out of the office, I checked the large industrial clock hanging over the door. It was nearly seven o'clock.

Thank goodness I liked to come in early.

Despite the troubles Milo had caused and the headache it would no doubt give me, as I walked with Steve down the hill, past the President's putting green, around the flat portion of the lawn where Marine One landed, and toward the vegetable garden, my step felt lighter. Plants, I understood and could handle. They were what I loved.

Milo loped alongside us. With a happy bark he dashed off to chase a squirrel up a linden tree, but soon returned wagging his tail.

"Oh, Milo," I cried when I saw the mess he'd made of the garden.

This was much worse than the time he'd pulled most of the pea plants from their ladder trellis. Heads of lettuce the size of basketballs had been pulled out by their roots. I wandered through the rows. As I inspected the damage, I stepped over a small head of red oak-leaf lettuce, a pile of ripped-up kale large enough to have fed a family of four, and a long, uprooted cucumber vine teeming with yellow flowers.

Milo didn't follow. Instead he stopped at the edge of the garden and dropped to the ground. With a moan he lowered his head between his front paws.

Was I imagining a guilty gleam in his eyes?

Gordon had worked with Milo to teach the naughty puppy that he needed to keep out of the First Lady's vegetable garden. He'd done a great job. We'd gone all season with only the damaged pea plants.

What had happened this weekend to cause Milo to run amok?

"We're awfully sorry about this, Casey." Steve's face darkened with embarrassment. "I don't know how it happened. President Bradley was busy with the budget negotiations all weekend, and you know Mrs. Bradley is extremely protective of her vegetables. So it had to have happened when one of the agents was watching Milo. But . . ." He rubbed the back of his neck and shook his head. "I assure you the agents weren't pulling a prank on you. We wouldn't do this. Not on this scale."

The Secret Service had pulled a few pranks last spring, letting Milo run wild in the Rose Garden. The puppy had dug up a few small rosebushes, so I understood why Steve might worry I'd suspect the tampering had been intentional.

"What's done is done." I drew on my gloves and picked up a young tomato plant that had a damaged stem but was salvageable. With quick movements I dug a shallow trench and placed the tomato into the hole, leaving only the top two rows of leaves above the ground. In time roots would sprout along the full length of the buried stem, giving the plant a solid base from which to grow.

"Could you leave a message for Gordon and Lorenzo to let them know I'll need some help?" I asked as I picked up another damaged plant to inspect.

"Of course." He headed back up the hill with Milo prancing alongside him. "And we're going to find out who's responsible for letting this happen. You can count on that."

Although at first glance the garden looked like a disaster, with the help of two of the newer members of the National Park Service's grounds crew, Jerry and Bower—although they weren't really that helpful—and several volunteers who'd arrived early for the photo shoot, Gordon, Lorenzo, and I managed to save most of the plants. Pearle Stone and Mable Bowls happily dug shallow trenches for the damaged tomatoes, tucking them back into their beds while smiling like silly teens at Gordon. As they worked, the two speculated on everything from Griffon Parker's death to Francesca and Bruce Dearing's future.

"It's like a scarlet letter pinned to our poor dear's pink frock," Mable concluded. "I know of two reporters already sniffing in that direction now. The scandal will eventually come out. There's no stopping it now."

Once all of the uprooted vegetables had been replanted and the damaged lettuce leaves and stems had been trimmed, the garden looked nearly as lush and healthy as it had when we'd left on Friday.

I was on my knees, studying an unsalvageable shredded head of cabbage—there didn't seem to be any tooth marks—when I spotted three Secret Service agents heading down the hill. Several yards behind them Barton Bailey, the First Lady's official photographer, snapped shots of Margaret Bradley as she gracefully descended the South Lawn and made her way toward the kitchen garden.

The third youngest First Lady in U.S. history, edging Jacqueline Kennedy from that spot of honor by just one week, Mrs. Bradley also held the distinction of being the first wife of a President to be pregnant while her husband was in office since Jacqueline Kennedy. And according to the news reports, Mrs. Bradley was the only First Lady to be pregnant with twins while in office.

Soft-spoken Margaret Bradley was elegant in everything she did, and the press enjoyed making comparisons between her and Jacqueline Kennedy.

As her belly grew, Margaret had let her dark auburn hair grow out as well. She now sported a shoulder-length cut that softened the look of the former Wall Street professional. Six months pregnant, she seemed to celebrate and welcome each change happening to her body.

The pale yellow sleeveless dress she had picked out for the photo shoot accentuated her blossoming figure and emphasized her radiant glow. A gentle smile played on her lips as she spoke briefly with one of the Secret Service agents walking alongside her.

As she approached the garden, I hastily gathered up the plants that couldn't be saved.

"Good morning, Casey," Mrs. Bradley called with a sunny smile. "I heard there was some excitement in the garden."

"A bit," I answered and discreetly dropped the plants I'd grabbed into the small compost pile tucked into the corner of the garden. "Nothing we couldn't handle."

"Oh! How wonderful!" She crouched down and inspected a bell pepper that was about the size of her fist. "I can't wait for the chefs to start harvesting these. They're my favorite. When I was a child, my mother would stuff the peppers from our garden with rice and sausage and hard-boiled eggs. The rich flavors—" She paused when Seth bent down and whispered in her ear. The First Lady's smile faded as she listened. "Now?" she said with a sigh.

"I just received notice of it myself," Seth said, sounding genuinely contrite. "Do you want me to text back and tell Frank to hold off until after the pictures are taken?"

"No, don't do that." She forced a smile as she let Seth help her stand up again. "We could use some positive press. John could use it. I'm sure the volunteers will be thrilled." She turned to me. "Frank Lispon is bringing down some of the pool reporters to interview the volunteers while we set up for the pictures. Do you mind helping out with that, Casey?"

"I'd be glad to," I said, thankful the garden had been put back together before Frank and the press descended.

After "Watercressgate's" ridiculous charge that the White House had created a fake garden, I didn't need the press speculating that instead of fixing the garden this morning, the volunteers were in fact "creating" one.

"I'm curious," I said, "why the change in plans? And why the West Wing's interest anyhow? I thought you were directing things."

"You'll have to ask Frank," Seth said.

As soon as the White House press secretary arrived with the reporters, I did.

"Thank Griffon Parker for dying so suddenly," Frank Lispon answered. "The reporters are having a feeding frenzy with the stories he'd been working on, including your work with the First Lady's garden. The story is about to break wide open."

"What story?"

"Watercressgate."

# Chapter Seven

*Most men aren't scolded out of their opinion.*
—MARTIN VAN BUREN, THE 8TH PRESIDENT OF
THE UNITED STATES

"WE didn't plant watercress," I protested. "Does no one fact-check anymore?"

Frank leaned back as he chuckled. "Only you would latch on to that, Casey. It's not what they're calling the budding scandal that has me worried. What pulled me down here this morning is the fact that someone thinks a scandal exists, and others are listening."

"Who's listening?" I demanded. "I saw the article. It was nothing but a jumble of lies printed in a throwaway newspaper that no one reads."

"Someone read it," he said.

Frank Lispon towered about a foot over my five feet seven inches. A man well into his late fifties, he kept in shape. His runner's body was extra lean and sinewy. In his youth, he'd competed in the five-hundred-meter track and field event and gone all the way to the Olympics. That same winning drive combined with his naturally friendly manner made him an effective press secretary. Most members of the press actually liked him, a rarity lately in this town. Everyone on the staff liked him, too.

"Well, for heaven's sake, Frank, tell whoever read it that the article is wrong. And while you're at it, tell those reporters that they should be ashamed of themselves for believing such a tall pile of stinky manure."

The corners of his eyes wrinkled with worry as he dug his hands into his pockets. "We can't do that, Casey. The damned thing's gone viral. Hundreds of blogs have repeated the claim over the weekend. Watercressgate is trending on Twitter. It's also in the top ten of hot search items on Google. It'll only be a matter of hours before some crackpot is quoted on a major network claiming to have helped create the First Lady's 'fake' kitchen garden."

"But there's no proof. Why would a reputable news organization report lies?"

"In this twenty-four/seven, breaking-news-every-half-hour news cycle, not everything gets fact-checked before it hits the air. The news media can skirt around the need to check sources by reporting what the blogs are saying. They aren't reporting on whether it's true. They're just reporting what is on the Internet. It's up to the viewer and future news reports to dig up the truth. But for the White House—especially my office—that's too late. I'm scrambling to get the facts on the air while others are shouting about cover-ups. I don't want that to happen here. And in order to stop that from happening, we all have to act preemptively and with care."

"That's why you want the press to talk with the volunteers this morning?" I asked.

He nodded. "I know it interferes with the First Lady's tight schedule, but I believe this is necessary. The *President* believes it's necessary. I can't tell you how glad I am that Margaret invited so many well-known society mavens to volunteer in the garden. That'll help. The general public may not know their names, but the press sure as hell knows and respects them. They have to if they ever hope to snag an invitation to one of D.C.'s power teas. No reporter with any sense will go blabbing on the news that these women haven't been doing the work they say they've been doing out here."

"They have power teas?"

"You better believe it," he said.

"Why the heck haven't I been invited to one yet?"

He chuckled again. "I'm glad to see you understand what's going on. Just do what you can to help the reporters get their story. Here they come. Excuse me."

I was surprised to see *Media Today*'s new hotshot TV reporter, Kelly Montague, among the journalists who'd turned out to cover the garden. Stories concerning the First Lady's kitchen garden were generally considered too "fluffy" for serious journalists.

I would have thought she'd be more interested in covering the back-to-back budget meetings packing the President's schedule.

As I continued to look around, I recognized several other high-profile journalists, including Simon Matthews, a young reporter with thick glasses and a round belly, who reminded me of a computer geek. Matthews and the other reporters meandered into the First Lady's garden, stomping through—not around—the delicate garden soil.

The First Lady had noticed them as well. Together we gently guided the straying reporters back to the stone paths—freedom of the press notwithstanding, no self-respecting gardener would allow anyone to walk through extensively prepared and tended garden soil. The soil was perfect, dark and fertile and the consistency of cake batter.

We'd created it using a sheet composting method, where layers of organic matter were sandwiched between rich compost and garden soil. As the organic matter broke down, nutrients were released to the plants. It was sort of like growing a garden on the top of an active compost pile. It wasn't something you wanted people stomping through.

Once the journalists were back on the grass at the edge

of the garden, I introduced them to some of my most dedicated volunteers.

Francesca Dearing still hadn't arrived. She had both the gardening expertise and experience dealing with negative press. Not only that, she could use this opportunity to garner some positive press for herself and her husband. I was sorry that she was missing out.

Annie Campbell, bless her dear heart, was talking with Kelly Montague over near the peppers. Annie did her best, but she had no clue what she was talking about as she answered questions about the many varieties of vegetables planted in the garden.

"That doesn't look like spinach," Kelly said, her brows furrowed with disbelief after Annie had incorrectly identified a plot of lettuce.

"I think what Annie meant to say is that this lettuce is an heirloom variety from Monticello's gardens," I offered as I rushed over to stop Annie from embarrassing herself. "Thomas Jefferson praised this variety, 'tennis-ball' lettuce, as being easy to grow. It doesn't need too much care or attention. And it actually tastes like something, unlike the watery iceberg lettuce commonly sold at grocery stores."

"So it's not spinach," Kelly said. Her gaze remained fixed on Annie. Poor Annie's cheeks began to flare red. "You'd think your volunteers, if they were actually involved with the garden, would know—"

"Although we have volunteers of all experience levels," I cut in, "every single one of them has done his or her part in the garden. Even the press secretary has had his hands in the dirt a few times. But don't ask Frank about the plants. The last time he was down here, he weeded out every pea seedling while leaving clumps of henbit and chickweed untouched."

"Is that so?" Kelly asked as she wrote furiously in a small notebook. Her astute gaze latched on to me. "And what else has gone wrong? Have you had problems with any of the other volunteers? Were they picked for you by the First Lady's staff, or did you get some say over who worked in the garden?"

Why, oh, why did I always seem to put my foot in my mouth around the press? "Please stop writing this down. I didn't mean to criticize the press secretary or any of the volunteers. It was a joke. We have all had a great time working out here in the garden, haven't we, Annie?"

"Oh, yes," Annie agreed with a sigh of relief.

"But, Mrs. Campbell, didn't you say"—Kelly pressed her pen to the notebook, ready to capture whatever embarrassing bit of information might pop out of either Annie's mouth or mine—"that the garden practically appeared overnight?"

"I—I didn't actually mean—" Annie stuttered while Kelly diligently wrote down every word. "I mean, we worked . . . we had so many volunteers . . . I'd say it was as if the garden grew over a weekend . . . well, perhaps not that fast . . ."

"Kelly, have you had the pleasure of talking with Mable Bowls?" I interrupted to save Annie from herself. It was easy to get flustered. I've rambled on and on when I should have kept my mouth shut around the press far too many times. "Mable is one of the matrons of D.C. society and a past president of the garden club." I glanced around and found that the grand old lady had attracted quite a crowd of reporters already. "She's been invaluable to us in the garden. Please, let me introduce you."

After getting Kelly settled with Mable, who preened with pleasure over the well-deserved attention she was receiving, I led Annie away from the reporters and gave her the task of rolling up the hoses we'd used that morning to water the vegetables. The grounds crew had installed an inconspicuous water spigot under a nearby stand of linden trees for keeping the garden watered.

The South Lawn had several water spigots concealed in boxes buried throughout the lawn and gardens. During dry periods, we'd drag out our long hoses and use the spigots to water the parts of the lawn and gardens that couldn't be reached by the rather old irrigation system.

"Is everything ready?" Mrs. Bradley's photographer asked after the interviews started to wind down.

"We're still waiting for a few of the volunteers to arrive." Most notably Francesca. "If the First Lady agrees, I'd like to give them a couple of minutes. In the meantime, we can arrange where you want the volunteers who are here."

I peeled off my gardening gloves, dug my cell phone out of my pocket, and dialed Francesca's cell, forgetting that she'd changed her number to one that came up as "Unavailable."

If the press were looking for scandal in the garden, I supposed they were also putting pressure on Francesca and Bruce Dearing, considering how they'd been under the spotlight already with Griffon Parker's investigations. Bruce might have even warned Francesca about the impromptu press event and advised her to stay away.

I'd just about given up on Francesca when she walked past, a blur of pale pink linen.

"There you are!" I jammed the phone back into my pocket and fell in step with her. "If you have a moment after the photos are taken, we need to talk."

"I—I don't know," she said and brushed past me. A bright red flush stained her cheeks and her eyes looked puffy, as if she'd been crying.

My mouth dropped open as she rushed to stand at the back of the group. I'd expected her to snag the choice spot in the photo next to the First Lady.

Once everyone was in place, the photographer started snapping pictures.

"What's with that paper?" The photographer lowered his camera. "It's getting into the picture."

A small scrap of paper in the garden flipped around in the light breeze.

It really wasn't too noticeable. But when everyone turned to watch it, Milo, who'd been bribed into posing for the picture with pieces of hot dog the First Lady held in the palm of her hand, couldn't pass up the chance to play a game of chase.

With a puppy bounce, he broke away from Mrs. Bradley's side and bounded into the garden. He crushed lettuce and cabbage and tomato plants underneath his large puppy paws as he chased the paper's erratic movement. He looked like he was just fur and legs as he bounced after the paper.

"Milo, come!" I dashed after him before he could wreck even more damage.

Seth gestured wildly. "Get out of the picture! Get out of the picture!"

I grabbed Milo's collar just as the oversized puppy snapped up the paper in his jaws. Pleased to have his prize, he let me lead him out of the garden. With his head held high and his tail wagging like a victor waving a flag at a soccer match, I returned Milo to his position beside the First Lady, pried the half-chewed paper from his mouth, and stuffed it into my pocket.

"Sorry about that," I said and then stepped out of the picture.

From a spot well outside the frame I watched Barton Bailey, the photographer, work his magic. The volunteers who'd helped repair the garden had ended up looking wilted from the summer heat and a bit muddy. I thought it added a delightful touch of authenticity to what would have been a dry, staged photo.

Barton continued to snap away. Milo seemed happy to stay where he belonged. I leaned back on my heels and let my head fall forward.

"Careful where you close your eyes. Barton will take a picture of you asleep on the job and post it on a wall where everyone can see it," a deep male voice whispered in my ear.

I opened my eyes to find a deadly handsome member of the Secret Service's elite military arm, the Counter Assault Team, smiling at me.

His black hair was cut short. He was dressed in a short-sleeved black battle dress uniform, which had to feel like an oven in all this heat. Although, come to think about it, he didn't look at all sweaty.

"Jack!" I was surprised to see him.

His crooked smile set my heart racing.

Pounding, actually.

And my mouth went dry.

"Before Friday, I hadn't seen or heard from you in weeks." The complaint slipped out of my mouth before I could catch it. "And then on Friday you didn't stick around long enough to say two words to me."

There was no reason I should have seen him before now. CAT agents kept mainly to themselves. When they weren't actively protecting the President, they were training.

"Sounds like you missed me." Jack tilted his head toward me. "I was traveling with President Bradley and then sent on another training detail."

"Miss you?" I snorted and tried to play it cool. "Puh-leeze. Why would I miss *you*? I'm just surprised to see you pop up so unexpectedly. And for a second time, at that."

Had the Secret Service sent Jack to spy on me to find out if I was involved in Griffon Parker's death?

"I mean, it's not as if I need protecting or—"

"I get it. I wasn't missed." The corners of his mouth lifted even more. "Wednesday is your big day, Casey. I wanted to be around to see it."

"The harvest is about Mrs. Bradley, not me. It's her garden, not mine."

Still, my stomach did a huge flip-flop. He came back because of *me*?

I ducked my head to hide the burning flush that rose to my cheeks under the broad brim of my floppy straw hat.

"*Alyssa*," I hissed.

My roommate kept telling me that sparks flew every time Jack and I were together. Just this weekend, she'd slipped into the conversation that Jack and I should be doing the horizontal mambo together. I wished she'd stop saying that. She was only making me act even more self-conscious and awkward around him.

Jack and I had become friends. That much was true.

But the rest was nuts.

He obviously hadn't thought I was worth the time to call. I wasn't even worth the time for him to wait for me to get off the phone for him to tell me whatever he'd needed to tell me.

Whatever.

I didn't like guns or men with guns. End. Of. Story.

"What are you mumbling about?" Jack tipped up the brim of my hat and asked.

*Gracious sakes.* Had I said that last bit aloud? What the devil was wrong with me?

"I wasn't saying anything. Just muttering a list of things I need to get done today." A fresh wave of heat scorched my cheeks.

"Mm-hm," he said.

"The harvest has kept all of us busy."

"Not too busy. I heard you were in the park when they found Griffon Parker."

"I knew it! The Secret Service did send you to spy on me."

"You've got your letters confused there. I'm a member of the C-A-T, not the C-I-A. Besides which, spies don't wear uniforms with team logos emblazoned on them . . . unless they're uniforms for the other side." He tapped a patch on his bulletproof vest with "Secret Service" embroidered below a monochrome American flag stitched all in white. "Didn't you watch Saturday morning spy shows growing up?"

"Grandmother Faye believed kids should be playing outside, not vegging out in front of a TV."

"How horrible! You missed out on an entire generation of bad TV."

"I know. It was horrible! Growing up, I never understood any of my friends' references to popular shows because Granny wouldn't turn on the TV until after I went to bed."

He suddenly turned serious. "Um . . . Casey, you aren't planning on investigating this time, are you?"

"Me? No, of course not. What's there to investigate? Parker took his own life."

"True," he said.

"I don't have a death wish or anything like that. So you don't have to worry about me. Not that you have been. You've been too busy with other things, which is fine. I understand."

Did I understand? Then why did I sound upset?

"Okay. Okay." He started to walk away. "I suppose I'll see you around, then."

"Wait. What did you want to tell me on Friday?" I asked.

"Um . . ." He opened his mouth, but hesitated. Perhaps he wanted to ask me out for dinner after work. I'd like that.

"Yes?" My heart hammered in my chest despite my intense desire that it not do that.

Jack's smile faded. He appeared to be listening to the small receiver plugged into his ear.

Alyssa had been wrong about Jack's feelings toward me. And even if I wanted a relationship with him, which I didn't, Jack clearly wasn't interested. We were as incompatible as beans growing next to onions. We'd stunt each other's growth.

"Oh, no," Jack said. He grabbed my arm. "*What have you done*?"

"Well, I've been really busy with the vegetables—have you seen the eggplants?—coordinating with the volunteers, pulling together the events for—"

He held up his hand. "Then tell me why Detective Hernandez with the D.C. Police is here to question you about Griffon Parker's murder."

"Did you say murder?"

He nodded.

"But yesterday's newspaper said Parker killed himself."

"Ms. Calhoun is with me," Jack reported into his radio. "Affirmative. I'll escort her there now."

# Chapter Eight

*If one morning I walked on top of the Potomac
River, the headline that afternoon would read:
"President Can't Swim."*
—LYNDON B. JOHNSON, THE 36TH PRESIDENT OF
THE UNITED STATES

I bit down on the inside of my cheek as I followed Jack up the South Lawn's hill toward the White House.

I had nothing to worry about, right? Detective Hernandez was just putting together a timeline of the last hours of Griffon Parker's life and wanted to ask me about what the reporter had said to me on Friday night. That nonsense about poisoning Parker with yew leaves . . . certainly Detective Hernandez—*Manny*—didn't believe anyone would use a hedge as a murder weapon. That was just . . . just . . . *stupid*.

On the way to meet the detective, Jack detoured to a small seating area beneath the massive waxy-leafed Jackson magnolia tree.

The bright red roses in the adjacent Rose Garden rustled in a sudden breeze as Jack took my hand. He stood in front of a white wrought-iron bench, but he didn't sit. In the shade of the magnolia, we stood toe to toe.

Jack's hold on my hand tightened just a bit as our eyes met. "I don't know what's going on or what you've gotten yourself mixed up in this time," he said.

"I haven't—"

"You don't have to explain yourself to me. I just want you to be careful, Casey. Don't offer any information unasked. Don't let the police lead you to say anything that could be twisted around to implicate you. If you feel at all uncertain, stop the interview and call your lawyer."

"But I don't have a lawyer." Did I need one? "Why would I have anything to worry about? I didn't do anything wrong."

"Your guilt or innocence doesn't matter. What you tell the detective is what's important."

"Detective Hernandez knows me. He's simply gathering information. Isn't he?"

"I hope so." Jack gave my hand a squeeze and then released it. "It's just that everybody knows about that perfect murder you were planning with Francesca."

"Everybody?" I asked.

"Everybody."

My cheeks heated. Jack hadn't even been around, hadn't even bothered to call me, and *he* knew about it? Heavens. I was in trouble. "It was for a charity dinner."

"Please be careful, Casey." His voice sounded rough and husky, as if he truly did care.

I don't know why his show of emotion surprised me. We were friends. Friends cared about each other. It didn't necessarily mean he wanted to take our relationship to the next level. Nor did it necessarily mean I wanted to deepen my relationship with him, either.

I didn't, did I?

Still, I was touched to know that he cared enough to be worried. A lump formed in my throat. Swallowing hard, I nodded. "I'll be careful."

"They're waiting for us," he said and cleared his throat. He nodded toward the glass-paned door that led into the Palm Room and the two grim-faced men who were standing inside the room watching us.

The sunny Palm Room, with white latticework on the walls and colorful tropical plants in its corners, was one of

my favorite places in the White House. Located on the
ground floor, it served as a gateway to the West Wing. Double glass-paned doors led out to a covered colonnade.
Another set of glass-paned doors led to the interior of the
White House. And on the opposite end of the room was an
oversized set of solid double doors that opened out to the
North Drive.

Detective Manny Hernandez, wearing a brown suit and
a golden tie that looked older than my nearly forty years,
stood with his hands jammed into the pockets of his rumpled suit coat. A second police officer, dressed in the D.C.
Metro Police's distinctive black uniform, stood beside
Manny with a wide stance and his hands clasped behind him.

They both wore bright red visitor's badges around their
necks.

The White House's very proper chief usher, Ambrose
Jones, dressed in a crisp black suit, personally served as
their escort. Ambrose, who followed his own code of Victorian manners, prided himself on running an efficient,
elegant household. He strictly prohibited any kind of drama
from those working under him.

"Ms. Calhoun," he said stiffly, "the police say they wish
to question you. I hope there isn't a problem."

He raised his brows as he put a strong emphasis on that
singular word, "*problem.*"

"If there is, I'm sure as heck not the source of it. The
detective is merely following every lead possible to put
together the last hours of Griffon Parker's life." I looked to
Manny for confirmation.

He nodded. "We're leaving no stone unturned."

Ambrose wasn't impressed. "He's not questioning any
other members of our staff. Only you, Ms. Calhoun. I find
that . . . disturbing."

"I'm also interviewing many members of the White
House press corps," Manny said. "Is there someplace
nearby and private where I can ask Ms. Calhoun a few
questions?"

"The Map Room," Ambrose said. "Please, follow me."

Jack gave a wordless nod of encouragement as I followed Ambrose's slow, steady stride and crossed through the glass-paned double doors. A blast of air-conditioning chilled my bare arms. Ambrose led us down the White House's vaulted center hall, past the gleaming pale pink marble walls and through the heavenly scents of spicy curry and fresh vegetables emanating from the kitchen.

"President Clinton testified before a grand jury in the Map Room regarding his relationship with *that* woman," Ambrose muttered, shaking his head with each dignified step. "The presidency survived the scandal. Don't know if it'll survive Cassandra Calhoun. In all my days, I haven't had this much trouble from a gardener. Good people they are. Salt of the earth."

Ambrose stopped at the Map Room and opened the door.

"When you are finished, Barney will escort you to the gate," Ambrose told Manny and his sergeant.

A uniformed division officer emerged from the Secret Service's satellite office located directly across the hallway. "I'm Barney, sir," the officer said to Manny and took a position standing next to the Map Room door and folded his arms over his muscular chest.

The shadowy Map Room, decorated in Chippendale style, had a cozy fireplace and dark mahogany furniture that dated back to the 1700s. Several presidential portraits hung on the white-paneled walls. Named for its use as a situation room by Franklin Roosevelt during World War II, the room now functioned as a private meeting room.

Manny indicated that I should sit in a Queen Anne chair with bright red upholstery. I brushed off the seat of my pants before perching on the edge of the chair. Manny's sergeant sat wide-legged on a matching sofa and pulled out a notebook and tape recorder.

"I apologize for having to pull you away from your work, Casey, but some questions have cropped up that we need to have answered." The corners of Manny's eyes crinkled with concern as he pulled out a pen from his jacket pocket and fiddled with it in his hands. "It's important that you answer our questions as completely as possible. Do you understand?"

I nodded.

Manny's gaze latched on to my mouth. Was he looking for signs of nerves? "As you might have already heard, Parker's suicide setup was a ruse. The full results of the tox screen won't come back for another week or two, but we do now know from the preliminary medical exam and lab tests that Griffon Parker was poisoned."

I nodded again and dug my teeth into my bottom lip.

"The poison was in his tea." Manny continued to watch me intently for a reaction. I squeezed my hands in my lap, making damn sure I didn't give him one.

He sighed and started to pace the length of the Map Room's rose-colored Oriental rug. "Here's the problem we have, Casey. You were seen publicly arguing with Parker the night before he died. The last thing Parker scrawled in his notebook was your name."

"Really?" I supposed he'd jotted my name into his notebook after our confrontation.

"Yes. And there's more. At the crime scene your friend Annie all but accused you of putting poison in his tea. Francesca Dearing has also told us that you came up with a plan to murder Parker by putting poison in his tea."

"Francesca told you that?" Un-*freaking*-believable. A wave of heat scorched my cheeks.

"Is it true?" Manny asked.

I opened my mouth to deny it, but I *had* come up with the idea of the yew leaves in the tea. Was it time to call a lawyer? No, I needed to explain myself. "I was helping Francesca plan a charity murder mystery dinner to support her neighborhood's garden club. She wanted to come up with what she called 'the perfect murder.' It was going to be a game people would pay money to play while sipping on drinks and nibbling on gourmet delicacies. It was never about Griffon Parker."

"And yet, Parker was poisoned," Manny said. "Game or not, when we spoke with Annie Campbell this morning she described in great detail how you'd planned his murder."

"Am I a suspect?" My voice squeaked.

"Our lab is testing specifically for yew extract," he said instead of answering the question. "Tell me, will the results be a positive hit for the plant?"

"I don't know."

Manny stroked his mustache thoughtfully.

"Tell me about the yew bush," he said.

"What yew bush? What do you mean?" I was still reeling over the shock that I might actually be a suspect in Parker's murder. "There aren't any on the White House property."

"Just in general, what do you know about yew bushes?"

"I suppose you mean the European yew. Although it can be used as a hedge, it's actually a small conifer tree. It's an evergreen with short, needle-like leaves."

"I see. And what part of the plant is poisonous?"

"Pretty much all of it, except the red berry. Its scientific name is the Greek word for poison. The seeds have the highest level of toxin, followed by its leaves. The alkaloid taxine is a toxin specific to the yew. If you ingest enough of it, studies have shown that it can cause cardiac arrest. Actually, if that's what killed Parker, he was lucky that he died quickly. I've read case studies detailing attempted suicides where yew was ingested, but death didn't happen immediately. The patients lingered for days and in terrible pain, but the damage done to the internal organs was irreversible and fatal."

"You seem very knowledgeable," Manny pointed out.

Jack had warned me not to offer information too freely, and here I was making myself look like an expert in poisonous plants.

"I'm a trained horticulturist. I can bore you with all sorts of information about the European yew and any number of other plants. So can Gordon and Lorenzo."

"You're talking about the other two White House gar-

deners, Gordon Sims and Lorenzo Parisi?" Manny asked
while his sergeant noisily wrote down their names in his
notebook. "Are you suggesting that one of them may have
had a reason to poison Parker?"

"No. I'm not saying anything like that."

"Then you're saying that you're the only one with a
motive?"

"No! I'm not—" I closed my eyes and took a deep
breath. This wasn't going nearly the way I'd expected.

"Casey, we're trying to get all the facts. We need you to
be completely honest with us," Manny said. "The argument you had with Parker the night before his death, what
was it about?"

"Oh, it was stupid. He'd chased me down as I was leaving for the night. He demanded an impromptu interview
even though he knew I didn't have the authority to talk
with the press."

"But you were seen talking with him. Why?"

"He claimed to have a source that could prove the First
Lady's kitchen garden is a sham. I told him that his source
was wrong."

"And then what did you do?" Manny asked after a long
silence. "Did you follow him?"

"No. I did nothing. *Media Today*'s new White House
television correspondent, Kelly Montague, had chased
after him and accused him of stealing some papers from
her desk."

"Is that so?" He exchanged a look with his sergeant.
"What kind of papers?"

"I don't know. She wouldn't tell me."

"And you didn't follow Parker to a parking structure?"

"No. Kelly Montague rushed off in the same direction
that he'd taken, toward Seventeenth Street. I don't know
where either of them was heading."

Manny seemed satisfied by that. "What did you do after
you left the White House Friday night?"

"I went home, ate dinner, and went to bed."

"Are you sure you didn't go back out later that night?"

"Yes, I'm sure. I was tired so I stayed home all evening."

"Did you invite anyone over to visit you?"

"No. Why?"

"Are you sure you didn't hook up with Griffon Parker late Friday evening, perhaps after midnight? Did you have a sexual relationship with him?"

"Good God, no!" Manny actually thought the mean-spirited Parker and I had shared bedroom refreshments? "Ewww! That would have never happened." I shook my head, desperate to get rid of that awful image.

Manny shrugged. "You never know."

"Believe me, I wanted nothing to do with him." I felt like I needed a glass of water to wash the nasty taste out of my mouth. Make that a shower and some bleach.

Manny smiled at my disgusted grimace. "It's my job to ask uncomfortable questions."

"Well, now you know the answer. If we were the last two people on earth, the human race would be doomed."

He followed up with some other questions regarding my past experience with Griffon Parker. Manny had a kind voice and a fatherly way about him, which no doubt made him an effective investigator. While I remained cautious, I found myself offering suggestions and providing as much assistance as possible to help move the investigation forward. Jack had been wrong. I had no reason to clam up around Manny. I wasn't guilty. I had nothing to hide.

In response to my answers, Manny would smile and nod and plunge in with another question. And then it was over. Manny's sergeant closed his notebook and turned off the tape recording.

"One last thing," Manny said as we headed toward the door. "Just a little thing. Don't leave town without contacting someone in the police department first, preferably me."

"Don't leave? Why?" He wouldn't want to keep a close eye on my whereabouts unless . . . "You—you actually think I killed Griffon Parker?"

"It doesn't matter what I think. It's my job to follow the evidence." His fatherly smile slipped away. He turned his gaze up to the ceiling and heaved a loud sigh, as if he truly regretted what he was going to have to do next. "Right now, the evidence is pointing us toward you."

Yesterday I'd refused to believe Francesca capable of murder. Today I was starting to wonder.

"You should understand by now how this works, Casey." Manny's resigned manner sent shivers down my arms. "Motive. Means. And opportunity. You have all three."

# Chapter Nine

*That's all a man can hope for during his lifetime—to*
*set an example—and when he is dead, to be an*
*inspiration for history.*
—WILLIAM MCKINLEY, THE 25TH PRESIDENT OF
THE UNITED STATES

MY mind buzzed as I stepped out of the Map Room
and into the vaulted, pink-marble-walled center
hallway. I felt as if I were trapped in a fog-shrouded nightmare as I headed toward the grounds office. With each step
I tried to get my hands around what had just happened and
define the emotion coiling around my chest.

Anger?

Sadness?

Fear?

No. No. And no.

I think I was in shock. Was that an emotion? It felt more
like the absence of one.

How could anyone, especially a trained investigator like
Manny, think I would murder Parker?

Because he'd found my name in Parker's notebook?
Parker disliked my garden, and he hadn't forgiven me for
surviving his attempt to ruin my organic program this past
spring. I'm sure my name showed up in his reporter's note-

book many, many times as he'd plotted new ways to make my life as miserable as his own sorry one.

And how in blooming hell could Manny believe for even a microsecond I'd let Parker into my bed? I'd always considered Manny a highly skilled detective with sharp instincts. What would cause his instincts to say, "Now, there's a woman who likes her men as cranky as a rabid coon and old enough to be her father?"

And what about Francesca?

What game was she playing now?

"Casey?" Jack caught my arm as he followed me down the hall. "Are you okay?"

"Sure," I said, my voice tinny and as tight as my chest. "Why?"

"Detective Hernandez suggested I should check on you, that's why. What happened in there?"

"Nothing happened. I answered his questions. I don't know why everyone is making such a big deal out of Parker's death."

"The man was murdered," Jack reminded me, "which also means there's a killer at large."

"But that's none of my business. I learned my lesson. I'm not Miss Marple." I winced as I remembered the disastrous Secret Service training session that drove home how ill equipped I was to protect either myself or anyone around me. Compared with the other staff members, who had passed with flying colors that day, my instincts were sorely lacking. "I don't have the skills to confront a killer."

"God, I can't tell you how glad I am to hear you admit that," he said. "I don't want you to do anything that would put your life in danger."

He didn't need to worry. I hadn't done anything. Someone else had apparently done it to me. Was Francesca capable of murder? Was she trying to frame me for Parker's murder? I started down the hallway again.

"Casey, don't run off. Talk to me."

I stopped and turned to face him. "I wasn't running. I have work that needs to get done."

"You're upset," he said.

"I'm not—" I nodded to an usher and two maids who hurried past. I stepped closer to Jack and lowered my voice. "I'm okay. I'm not going to charge into the middle of a murder investigation."

"I know you're not." He sounded so damned calm. So reasonable.

"Then why are you worried?" I flapped my arms in frustration. "I'm fine."

"Are you? You walked right past me just now. Even after I called your name, you kept walking."

"Did I?" I shook my head.

His expression softened. "I think you should sit down. The physician's office is right back there. You could grab a chair in the nurse's office for a moment to give you time to catch your breath. Or you could sit in the Secret Service office. I'm sure the duty agents won't mind."

I gave a pained smile and shook my head. "I may be rattled, but you don't have to worry about me. Really, Jack. Remember I have the Calhoun family's backbone of steel. It's withstood much worse storms."

"I know."

I cringed remembering just how much he knew about me. He'd read my security background report. He knew how my father had abandoned me in a time of great danger. Jack had read the police reports detailing my mother's murder. He knew I'd also been shot and left to slowly bleed to death at my dead mother's side. But I hadn't died.

I drew a deep breath and straightened my spine.

"If you can get away for a few minutes, I could use some coffee," I said.

His furrowed brows relaxed. "Are you buying?"

"Only if you're sharing state secrets with me," I countered. We'd started back toward the Palm Room when I remembered that frustrating thing called work. I had piles of it waiting for me. "I know I invited you, but—" I reached into my pocket to pull out my cell phone to check the time. Every Monday, Gordon held a staff lunch in the grounds office to review the progress of our various projects. With everything going on, it was a meeting I couldn't miss.

Along with my cell phone, Milo's mangled piece of paper from the garden fell out of my pocket. I'd like to tell you that my first thought was to throw the paper into the nearest trash bin, but the devil made me curious. I unfolded the paper and read the handwritten note.

My chest tightened.

I read it again.

"This is impossible," I said.

"What?" Jack asked as I hurried past him.

"I have to catch Manny. He has to see this."

With Jack racing alongside me, I jogged back to the Map Room, where I found Manny and his sergeant being escorted toward the Palm Room by Barney, the uniformed division officer who had waited outside the Map Room door.

"I didn't write this," I said and thrust the paper into Manny's hand.

He gave me a curious look as he unfolded the paper and read. "What is this?"

"I think the 'what' is pretty obvious. It's the 'who' that should concern you."

Manny accepted that gem of advice about as well as my aunt's old bulldog, Beauregard, accepts his medicine. I half expected Manny to spit it back at me.

"Where did you get this letter?" he demanded after herding his sergeant, Jack, and me back into the Map Room and shutting the door behind us.

By this time adrenaline was pounding through my veins with such force I felt short of breath. "The—the paper was blowing around in the garden when the volunteers were having their picture taken this morning. I hadn't taken the time to look at it until just now. Actually, I was going to throw it out, but thought I should take a look at it first."

"You almost put this in the garbage?" Manny shook his head.

"That was before I read it."

His expression grew all the more intense as he continued to study the note. "What did you do to it? Why is it soaking wet and torn?"

"Well, I didn't find the note. Milo did. It tore when I pried it from his mouth."

"This was in a dog's mouth?" Manny clutched the mushy paper and started to pace again. "I doubt we'll get DNA or fingerprints off it, but you never know."

Jack tried to pretend he wasn't interested, but his gaze kept traveling over toward Manny's shoulder in an attempt to read the note.

"Sergeant Turk, I need an evidence bag and tag for this."

The sergeant nodded and left to fetch them, with Barney serving as his escort.

Manny grabbed his recorder and set it back on the coffee table. "Who was in the garden at the time?" he asked me.

"What's written on the paper?" Jack demanded at the same time. "Evidence or not, that piece of paper was found on White House grounds, in the President's dog's mouth at that. The Secret Service will have to review it to make sure that it's not a classified document before allowing you to take it, Detective."

I didn't know if what Jack said was true or not, but his deadpan, just-the-facts delivery and hard, no-nonsense gaze as he held out his hand convinced Manny to relinquish the crumpled paper to Jack.

Jack read aloud the short but disturbing note. " 'No law would take me up and stop me, but what I've done was wrong.' "

Jack looked up at us. "Take him up?"

"I think he means arrested," Manny said with a shrug. "Although he ruined people's lives with those damned articles of his—like he tried to do to our police chief—he didn't break any laws. Believe me, we've paid close attention to his actions. He walked up to the line but never crossed it as far as any of us could tell."

Jack continued, " 'I can no longer live with myself for the pain I've brought on others. That is why I have decided to take my own life. My only sorrow in this is the knowledge that, because of the life I've lived, no one will grieve my passing.' And there's the hastily scrawled signature of Griffon Parker."

"He didn't write that note," I said. I'd read enough of Griffon Parker's articles to recognize his writing style. This note had none of the pompous attitude he liked to pile onto his vile prose.

"I agree," Manny replied, "which raises the question— who did? We'll need to review the surveillance video of the garden from this morning." He addressed this to Jack, who nodded his agreement.

"In the meantime, Casey, I need you to tell me who you remember being in that area of the garden. And I mean everyone."

I closed my eyes and pictured the volunteers and staff who had been near the tomatoes where I'd first noticed the paper. "The reporters had tromped through there, but Kelly Montague stood near the peppers to interview Mable Bowls and Pearle Stone. And then there are the volunteers. They helped me clean up the mess Milo had made over the weekend. But it was mostly Mable and Pearle who worked in that area. Oh, and Annie Campbell. I believe she helped out over there, too."

"Anyone else?"

"I think I was in that area when I talked with Frank Lispon. Jerry and Bower, two of our newest members on the grounds crew, might have spent some time over there, too, not that they were much help. Those two are lazy. Margaret Bradley walked throughout the garden, checking on its progress, but the First Lady, she wouldn't have written a fake suicide note."

"No," Manny agreed, but I noticed him writing her name in his notebook even as he added, "I can't imagine that she would. Is there anyone else?"

"No, I think that's it."

"I saw Francesca Dearing rushing through that part of the garden to join the group for the picture," Jack said.

Manny nodded and added her name to the list.

"I can't believe she could murder anyone," I said, despite the fact that she'd obviously tried to turn the focus of Manny's murder investigation to me. Who was I kidding? Francesca had a huge motive for wanting Parker dead.

"The murder mystery dinner was her idea. She asked me to help plan it," I said. "I now wish I hadn't agreed. She also had quite a bit to gain by the reporter's death, including saving her husband's career and her lofty social position."

And, again, she seemed only too willing to blame me.

"Francesca and Bruce Dearing both have alibis for Friday night," Manny said. "They went to dinner, then a late-night jazz concert that lasted until one in the morning, and their housekeeper was adamant that then the two were in for the night until seven the next morning."

"If not Francesca or Bruce, then who killed Parker?" I asked, not because I wanted to join in on the investigation, but because I wanted out of the suspect pool.

Manny shrugged. "We're just gathering names. Don't you worry, Casey. We'll catch the perp. Turner, can you arrange for me to review the videos now?"

Instead of answering, Jack looked at me. His dark brows were drawn with concern.

"We can talk later," I said and excused myself to let Jack arrange things for Manny.

As I'd said before, despite the black cloud of suspicion hanging over my head, the investigation had nothing to do with me. Really it didn't. I could walk away from this and not look back.

And that was exactly what I did. I walked away. I felt pretty damn proud of myself that I was able to hand over the evidence and trust that the police would find Parker's killer. I felt no need to get involved. None at all.

Thank you very much.

*However . . .*

How did an obviously fake suicide note end up in the First Lady's kitchen garden? And why would the killer write something like this and then not use it?

# Chapter Ten

*If I were two-faced, would I be wearing this one?*
—ABRAHAM LINCOLN, THE 16TH PRESIDENT OF
THE UNITED STATES

"**Y**OU need to be careful, Casey," Gordon said, echoing the concern Jack had expressed earlier. "You can't open your life to that detective and hope for the best."

"But I did nothing wrong. As I've said"—many times already—"I gave Manny the fake suicide letter. The killer must have written it. Who else would have a reason to want to make Parker's death look like a suicide?"

Gordon Sims and Lorenzo Parisi both watched me as they ate their lunches at the staff meeting in the grounds office. We'd purchased sandwiches from the cafeteria in the Eisenhower Executive Office Building and were sitting around Lorenzo's drafting table. I took a bite of my eggplant parmesan sandwich.

Gordon had ordered his usual tuna salad sandwich. Lorenzo had ordered a spicy meatball sandwich, quite a change from his regular turkey and Swiss. He'd glared when I'd started to mention that.

By the time we'd finished our sandwiches, we'd made it

halfway through our projects list, checking off completed items and adding new tasks. As usual, we'd already added nearly as many items to our to-do list as we'd removed. With Wednesday's vegetable harvest looming, I felt antsy. I'd already lost half a day to talking with Detective Hernandez. I had more important things to do than worry about a murder investigation that had nothing to do with me.

We would have breezed through the staff lunch in record time if Gordon hadn't kept insisting we discuss what the police may or may not be thinking . . . about me.

Lorenzo watched me as he noisily sipped Diet Coke through a straw. I'd expected a snide comment or two from him, but he was keeping uncharacteristically quiet about the entire affair.

"You need to consult with a criminal lawyer," Gordon concluded.

Alyssa had told me the same thing when I'd called to warn her that the police might contact her to verify my alibi for Friday night. My roommate had gone a step further than just providing advice. She'd surveyed several of her colleagues on the Hill. After sorting through the stories of politicians who had escaped prison sentences, she had called me back with the contact information for the top criminal defense attorney in the D.C. area.

I'd jotted his name and phone number in the margin of my yellow notepad, but I hadn't called him. The thought of bringing in a defense attorney made my stomach churn. Hiding behind a lawyer felt too much like an admission of guilt.

"I'd much rather focus on gardening and getting ready for Wednesday," I muttered to myself.

"What's that?" Gordon asked, but then continued without waiting for me to answer. "It's not that I'm worried about your guilt or innocence. I know you could never harm anyone."

"Thank you." I appreciated his vote of confidence.

"You do realize, however, that if the press learns that the police are digging into your affairs, they might start calling you a murder suspect, which would be a disaster. The President needs to protect his own reputation. Even the illusion of wrongdoing could spell the end of your White House career."

"I hadn't thought about it that way," I said. "I'm sure several reporters are already trying to retrace Parker's steps in hopes of uncovering the scandal Parker almost published about Bruce Dearing. That's going to cause trouble enough for the President."

Considering the number of mystery novels I'd read over the years, you'd think I'd know exactly what to do if the spotlight of suspicion ever shone in my direction.

"I love the work I've been doing at the White House. I don't want to leave."

"I don't want you to leave, either," Gordon said. "No one does. Before I forget, one of us needs to have a talk with those two new guys on the grounds crew."

"Jerry and Bower?" I asked. The two new National Park Service crew members assigned to work in the gardens did seem to need a lot of supervision.

"Sal said he saw both Jerry and Bower wandering off toward the Children's Garden when the rest of the crew was working in the Rose Garden," Gordon said. Sal Martin, who acted and dressed as if he still lived in the groovy seventies, had worked on the grounds crew for more years than I'd been alive. If he thought the two new guys were doing something they shouldn't, then it was the truth.

"I'll talk with them," Lorenzo offered.

"Really?" I nearly fell out of my chair. Lorenzo almost never volunteered to interact with the grounds crew. He almost never volunteered to do *anything*. He shrugged and slurped his diet soda. His gaze glided over to the clock over the door. "Aren't you supposed to be at another meeting, Casey?"

"I don't have anything on my schedule . . ." I glanced at the day planner on my desk.

"You don't?" He pulled his straw up and down so that it

squealed against the plastic lid. "That must be why Seth phoned. You were with that detective, I think. Seth said something about a meeting with Francesca Dearing and Gillis in his office at one o'clock to discuss the harvest. He wants you to be there."

"Why are you only telling me about this now?" It was ten minutes after one. I dumped all my harvest organizational paperwork into a file folder and started for the door. "We're supposed to be a team."

His dark Mediterranean eyes widened as if he had no idea why I was upset. "What? I thought you knew about the meeting."

A frustrated growl escaped my throat as I dashed out the door.

"Lorenzo . . ." I heard Gordon's low voice echo down the hallway. "That's not what I expect from you."


**I HURRIED THROUGH THE HALLWAY TOWARD** the East Wing and Seth Donahue's corner office on the second floor. The overstuffed file folder flopped against my arm with each step.

At least I'd gotten my wish. I had no time to worry about murder investigations or mysterious notes.

Although I was late for the meeting, the bright sunny day tugged at me as I passed a line of windows overlooking the Jacqueline Kennedy Garden. I'd rather be outside in the garden watching out for signs of aphids or a wilting disease than stuck in yet another meeting. My step slowed as I took in how the afternoon light made the colorful blooms on the beds of geraniums, impatiens, ageratums, and lilies glow with life.

When I was stressed, I gardened. I'd plunge my hands into the cool earth to feel the natural world pulsing all around me. It was almost July, almost time to prune the impatiens back to about an inch above the ground to encourage a new burst of color that would last until late fall. But under the heat of the intense afternoon sun, I'd do more harm than good if I were to poke or prod or prune my green darlings in their beds right now.

One of the necessary duties at the White House included participating in life-draining organizational meetings. Okay, perhaps not life draining. But close.

Gordon called them colossal wastes of time. He always found an excuse to miss them, sending either Lorenzo or me in his place. Being the new girl in the garden, I usually pulled the short straw.

This particular meeting promised to be more interesting than the rest because it was actually necessary. Without it, the harvest festivities might succumb to chaos.

The main thing that worried me about the meeting was Seth Donahue. The First Lady's social secretary seemed particularly fond of meetings. I suspected it was because he enjoyed the sound of his own voice. He rarely let anyone else talk.

Before devoting his time to public service at the White House, Seth had owned a party planning company that catered to the rich and glamorous. High-strung and short-tempered, he often acted as if he were the only qualified employee at the White House.

Other staff members scattered whenever they spotted him storming down the hallway. He was a walking, talking headache.

Unfortunately no one could deny that he had a gift for pulling together impressive events. Most of us simply wished he would make the effort to work with the rest of us instead of fighting us every step of the way. It'd also be nice if he could let down his guard and smile.

As I reached the top of the stairs in the East Wing, laughter filled the hall. More laughter followed.

The happy sounds were coming from Seth's office.

I stopped outside his door and double-checked the nameplate.

"Casey," Seth called out from where he was sitting with his feet propped up on his desk. I don't think he'd ever looked at me without a scowl before. "Come in. Come in. We have a lot of ground to cover."

Francesca Dearing rose as I entered and she grabbed both my hands. "Casey, dear, I'm so glad to see you," she purred, with none of the cold shoulder she'd given me earlier in the morning.

"Francesca." I pried my hands from her grasp. How could she act so friendly after coldly brushing me off this morning? I wondered if her abrupt mood swings were a sign that she'd suffered a mental collapse. Or was that how she covered her guilt? "Do you have time to talk after the meeting?"

"Of course, my dear," she said, smoothing out a nonexistent wrinkle on her jacket's linen sleeve. "I'd hoped you'd have time for me."

"Och, it's my favorite bonny fan." Gillis, dressed in a sedate black kilt and dark purple button-up shirt, rose from his chair in the corner to brush his lips against my cheeks. "Seth moved mountains to fetch the necessary security credentials so I could come inside the White House instead of being tucked away in that old musty building next door."

"Actually, I filled out the paperwork Friday night," I said, but I realized immediately how petty that made me sound. "Francesca helped," I added.

"Och," he said, his brown eyes twinkling. "My warmest thanks to the both of ye, then. I look forward to helping out with your kailyard."

"Kailyard?" I asked.

"Your wee vegetable patch."

"Ah."

I apologized for arriving late and then suggested we get started with the meeting.

"I should scold you, Casey," Seth said once we all were settled. His smile was still there. I hadn't imagined it. If I didn't know better, I would have thought the man had been drinking. "You should have told me that you'd attracted the finest gems of D.C. society to volunteer in the kitchen garden."

I glanced at Francesca and then said quietly, "It was Mrs. Bradley's idea."

From the moment she'd moved in to the White House, Margaret Bradley had surrounded herself with her trusted friends and family from New York City. As a result, she'd neglected the social elite of Washington.

The unintentional snub had driven a wedge between the White House and D.C. power brokers. Angry wives of congressmen, diplomats, and high-paid lobbyists had convinced their better halves to return the favor and snub John Bradley. Individuals the President had counted on to provide enthusiastic support for his programs and policies in the past had started disappearing.

Margaret Bradley, a keen power broker in her own right, had recently started to take aggressive steps to remedy her mistake. One of those steps had included personally inviting the Washington society ladies to help fill all East Wing volunteer positions—including working in the vegetable garden.

"I should have known. The plan has Margaret's sharp style written all over it," Seth said. "I would have taken a more active role if I'd known about the illustrious names you forced to work in the dirt." He tsked. "I never would have allowed that to happen."

"Almost all of them are accomplished gardeners. They are happy to get their hands in the soil. And their help has been invaluable," I pointed out.

Francesca nodded. "We are glad to do the work."

"Will there be many volunteers on hand Wednesday?" Gillis asked, leaning back in his chair. "I'll have to bring signed copies of my book to hand out. On that subject, I was thinking I should give a speech detailing my organic gardening methods and how they should be utilized in the kitchen garden."

"The First Lady is planning to give a short talk to the schoolchildren. This is her project. The focus should be on her," I pointed out.

"Gillis, your speech could follow Mrs. Bradley's," Seth said. "I think that's a splendid idea. The press will love it."

"I hope my speech will inspire the First Lady as well. I'd love to see her garden converted into an organic garden."

"We're already following organic practices," I said. "If you have the time, I'd be happy to go over them with you."

Gillis waved off the offer. "I've read accounts about your little projects here and there. But, lass, one or two little changes won't turn a *midden* into an organic garden."

"We're following *all* recommended organic practices," I repeated. "I assure you the changes have been quite extensive."

"Is the garden certified organic?"

"No, and because of past fertilizer practices, we'd have to dig up and replace all existing soil in order to gain certification, but—"

"If the garden's not organic," Seth broke in, "perhaps you should listen to Gillis. He's an expert in these things. His book on the topic moved up to the number three spot on the *New York Times* bestseller list last week."

I narrowed my gaze as Gillis raised his brows with smug satisfaction. Was Gillis the unnamed source who told Parker that the First Lady's kitchen garden wasn't actually organic? "You didn't happen to contact a certain reporter, Griffon Parker, about your thoughts on the White House's gardening practices, did you?"

"That crusty old goat?" Gillis asked. "Gave him a copy of my book to review. Suppose that won't happen now."

"Did he even do book reviews?" I asked.

"You're talking about the dead reporter?" Seth sat up. He leaned toward me, propping his elbows on his desk. "Considering the police's interest in your involvement in the man's murder, Casey, I don't think you should be talking about him. Don't look so surprised. Everyone's heard about how you were interrogated this morning."

I glanced at Francesca. Her self-satisfied smile remained eerily fixed. She had to realize the difficult position she'd created for me by telling Detective Hernandez I'd planned Parker's murder.

"Perhaps we should move on." I flipped open my file folder and began going over the events.

I hate to sound bitter or ungrateful. Francesca did us a great favor by getting a popular celebrity like Gillis to the White House, but the more time I spent with him—someone I thoroughly enjoyed watching on TV—the more I started to dislike the famous gardener.

He dominated the meeting even worse than Seth.

Whenever I would explain what we already had planned or suggest an idea from my fat file folder, a folder I'd spent weeks developing, Gillis would roll his eyes and interrupt. "Och, we can do better than that, lass," he said more than once. Often he added, "On my television show we'd . . ."

Both Francesca and Seth lapped up his ideas as if they were kittens at a saucer of milk.

"This is wonderful, Gillis," Francesca cooed after the schedule of harvest festivities had been completely reworked. She reached over and squeezed his arm. "You're wonderful."

"I don't know what we would have done without your input," Seth said.

The three of them then turned to me. I supposed they expected me to add my praise to the chorus. I couldn't. By that time my jaw was clenched so tightly I could barely speak.

"You may want to check with the chef. Several of these changes will affect her programs," I managed.

"Good point," Seth said. "Actually, I have a meeting scheduled with her in an hour. She seemed most accommodating when we spoke earlier." He paused. Three pairs of eyes turned toward me again.

I didn't doubt the chef was accommodating. She had a reputation for being a superwoman. She could think on her feet, whip up a masterpiece even with the meanest of ingredients, and with a soft-spoken word keep Seth happy. I quite admired her.

"Well, then, if that's all . . ." I rose and, hugging my file folder of hard work to my chest, headed toward the door.

"Wait a minute, Casey," Seth called. "You'll want to hear this. Gillis is interested in lending his expertise to the gardens, like a regular member of the White House staff."

"He is?" The news hit me like a two-by-four to the gut.

Gillis struck the pose he used at the end of his television shows. His hands on his hips, his chin up, his eyes staring straight forward. "That I am, lass."

"I wish you luck," I mumbled.

"I hope this will be the start of a long relationship between you and our gardens." Seth vigorously shook Gillis's hand. "We can use some celebrity talent around here."

"And I can bring it, mate," Gillis agreed. He looked over at me and smiled. "Talk with Mrs. Bradley, Seth. Tell her how invaluable I'd be to her."

"We have plenty of gardeners on staff right now," I cautioned.

"Och, dinna mean to stomp on your toes, lass. It's just that . . . well . . . you never know when circumstances might change. Opportunities might open up. Have you read my book?" He picked up a copy from a stack he'd left on Seth's desk and handed it to me. "My brand of organic gardening, which is the only way, promises to grow into a nationwide movement. The White House should lead the way, not follow."

I tucked the book in with the file folder, even though what I really wanted to do was toss it right back at his smug face. "Francesca? You said you had a moment to talk?"

"Hmm?" She tore her adoring gaze away from Gillis just long enough to answer me. "Oh. Of course, Casey. Gillis, you are a wonder," she added and kissed his cheek. "I'll see you this evening for dinner?"

The meeting had taken too long, and I still had several things I needed to accomplish before Wednesday. This workday and the next promised to stretch long into the night.

Francesca walked with me as I headed down the East Wing stairs.

"He *is* a wonder, isn't he?" she repeated, still beaming.

"I suppose."

"The First Lady is going to love him. He has that effect on people, you know. Everyone loves Gillis."

"So I've noticed. He also seems very interested in taking over my job."

I wondered if he and Francesca were working together and spreading stories.

# Chapter Eleven

*I have tried so hard to do right.*
—GROVER CLEVELAND, THE 22ND PRESIDENT OF
THE UNITED STATES

"**D**ON'T you think you're being overly sensitive?" Francesca laughed. Her twittering echoed down the stairwell. "Why would Gillis want your job?"

"I don't know. He has his television and radio shows, book deals, and hordes of fans." It did sound rather silly. "I suppose he wants to act as a consultant. Is he campaigning for a spot on the Grounds Committee?"

"Honey, what else would he have time for?"

The White House Grounds Committee was made up of horticultural professionals from the American Association of Nurserymen. The committee oversaw design and implementation decisions. When I'd proposed the White House grounds go all organic, the Grounds Committee had balked at the plan until I modified it to take place over several years in a slow, phased process. "Gillis, with his passion for organic gardening, might actually be an asset on the committee," I had to admit. "But to hear him speak about his working with the gardens, it does sound like he's trying to push me out of a job."

*That peacock sure knows how to strut.* My aunt Willow's colorful way of describing some of our Charleston neighbors seemed to fit Gillis. *He's been strutting around so much he hasn't noticed that he's all feather and no brain.*

Okay, that last part might have been an unfair characterization of Gillis. I hadn't yet read his book. He might have some new ideas. Good ideas.

At the moment, however, I was more interested in asking Francesca about Griffon Parker and her murder mystery dinner that someone had served up weeks before the charity event than in learning a new approach to organic gardening.

Oh, good gracious, if Francesca had killed the crusty reporter, would that also mean she'd slept with him?

Ew! Eww! Ewww!

I shook that nasty image out of my head and out of my body.

"Is something wrong?" Francesca asked. "Are you having a fit?"

"I think I must be. I feel as if I've lost my mind."

"It's the stress, dear. It's getting to you."

"Not this time, although I'll probably have to be peeled off the ceiling if anything else happens today. This was a delayed reaction to something Detective Hernandez asked me. He wanted to know if I'd slept with Griffon Parker on Friday night. Apparently the cranky fellow got lucky before his luck ran out."

"Heavens," Francesca whispered, her hands flying to her lips with genuine surprise. "You must have been mortified. I'm mortified for you."

"Manny . . . er . . . Hernandez didn't ask you the same thing?"

She shook her head. "I would have given him quite a set-down if he'd even suggested I could be unfaithful to my Bruce with a *journalist*!"

I grabbed Francesca's wrist. "How can you be so devil-may-care about Parker's death? Friday afternoon you told me that you wished you could get away with murder. Then that evening you ran off after insisting we confront Kelly Montague, who is now—conveniently—Parker's replacement. Where did you go? And why is Detective Hernandez telling me that all the evidence points straight at me? Why are you blaming *me* for your murder mystery game?"

"I—I never meant—" Francesca stammered. She waved her elegant hands in front of her as if she were trying to wipe away my accusations. "What is happening to this town?" She didn't sound at all like a woman capable of murder, but that didn't mean I was going to let her get away without giving me some answers.

"What is going on with you?" I asked, but the words had barely made it out of my mouth when Assistant Usher Wilson Fisher, the king of government forms—in triplicate— hurried toward us.

"Ms. Calhoun!" His sharp voice filled the East Wing's wood-paneled lobby. "I've been looking everywhere for you." His hooked nose twitched with every agitated step.

"I just got out of a meeting and am piled under with the harvest plans right now, Fisher," I warned.

"Perhaps I should go." Francesca tried to pull away from me, even though her security clearance required she stay with an escort when in the White House.

My grip on her wrist tightened. "No."

"Ms. Calhoun, I need those forms," Fisher said, thumping his finger into the palm of his hand for emphasis. "The digitization process can't start without them."

"What forms?" I had no idea what he was talking about, but then again, I rarely understood any of his formspeak.

"Didn't you read my memo? I sent it with form 53-421-A."

"I'm sure it's somewhere on my desk."

"I put it in your in-box," Francesca murmured.

"Oh, thanks. Apparently it's in my in-box. I'll look for it there this afternoon," I said, hoping he'd leave it at that.

"Ms. Calhoun"—my name shot out of his mouth like a couple of bullets—"I can't wait any longer. The memo, if you'd read it, clearly stated my timeline. In an effort to streamline our procurement process, we're going digital. But in order to do that I need to digitize all of our old purchase orders, which means every office needs to send me their archives. I have everyone's files except for the grounds office's."

"Can't this wait until after the harvest?" Fisher always wanted this form or that from me. I honestly couldn't keep up. He loved his forms with the same passion a mother feels toward her babies. I found it all a bit unnatural.

"I've already waited long enough, Ms. Calhoun. Those forms are vital to the operation of the White House. Are you willing to jeopardize the President's comfort and safety because you are too busy to do this one thing? Certainly you don't think you're more important than the President."

"Of course not, but it's archived paperwork. I can't see how gathering decades-old procurement forms a week or so late would bring the wheels of democracy grinding to a halt." I hoped he'd agree with the reasoning in that.

But no, he started huffing as if I'd suggested we rip out the North Lawn's historic boxwoods and replace them with invasive privets.

"If it's that important, I'll do it now." The grounds office kept boxes of old paperwork in a storage closet. Retrieving the boxes wouldn't take that long and it would give me the opportunity to talk with Francesca in private.

Francesca and I left Fisher still huffing. We hurried down the center hall, past the curator's office, and toward the stairs that led down. There were two basement levels beneath the ground floor of the White House.

The basement mezzanine housed the dishwashers, flatware, and dishes. There were some other miscellaneous storage rooms on that level, but the one assigned to the grounds crew was one level below that, in the subbasement. Both of these levels were added when the White House was completely gutted and rebuilt during the Truman administration.

Once we were alone in the narrow utilitarian stairwell that descended deep into the bowels of the White House residence, I confronted Francesca again. This time I was determined to get an answer out of her. "You never answered me before. Why did you tell Hernandez that I was responsible for planning Parker's murder when you know that it's not true?"

Francesca stopped near the bottom of the stairs and, after looking to see if anyone was around, whirled toward me. The cold look she leveled in my direction gave me cause to wonder if it was a good idea to go anywhere with her alone. "I didn't kill Parker," she said, biting off each word as if it tasted bitter in her mouth.

"Then why would you want to make it look as if I did?" The occasional metal bangs and constant drone of the mechanical systems filled the stairwell.

"I didn't kill Parker," she repeated.

"I never said you did."

"Didn't you? Well, missy, I wasn't the only one who benefited from his demise. He seemed to be ramping up his campaign against your work as well. And then you publicly accused me of the crime."

"I never accused you of anything. I wondered, yes. Accused, no."

"Didn't you?" Her breathing grew quick, agitated. "Annie told me how you hissed my name to the detective at the crime scene. And that was before the detective even suspected a crime had been committed."

"I didn't mean to—"

"You didn't mean to frame me? He died exactly as *you* had planned for him to be murdered. I couldn't hide that information from the police, especially after finding out how you were already working to pin the crime on me. After all I've done for you—I saved your precious harvest celebration from ruin—I can't believe you'd turn on me like this . . . unless you committed the crime."

"Oh, my." I held up my hands to calm her down. "Annie misunderstood. I don't even remember saying anything to

Detective Hernandez about you. If I did, I'm sure he didn't take it to mean that I was accusing you, because I wasn't. No way. No how. And I had nothing to do with Parker's death. He could have attacked my gardening practices as much as he wanted. I'm doing the right thing. Unless he was ready to out-and-out lie"—which I wouldn't have put past the weasel—"I don't see how he could have hurt the work we've all been doing in the kitchen garden."

"Is this true? You aren't trying to frame me for murder?"

"Are you trying to frame me?"

She closed her eyes. The stress of the past week had taken its toll on her. Her light brown hair hung limp about her face. Her pink linen suit hung as if it were a size too big for her slender frame. And she looked pale underneath her perfectly applied makeup.

For the first time since I'd known her, Francesca looked wretchedly . . . human.

I touched her arm. "Francesca? Are you okay?"

She jerked away from me. "Why wouldn't I be? Parker is dead. What could be wrong with that? All of my problems are solved." Despite her assurances, she sounded absolutely miserable.

I nodded to an usher who appeared, startled to find us blocking the stairwell.

"We'd better get going," I said. We continued down the steps to the White House's lowest level, the subbasement. This floor housed the laundry facilities, more storage for the kitchens, men's and women's locker room facilities for the ushers and maids, mechanical and electrical equipment rooms, and, tucked behind the incinerator, a storage closet designated for grounds crew use.

In the short time that I'd worked here, I'd witnessed some ugly battles waged over these storage spaces. The grounds office most assuredly had more than its fair share, considering we also had a greenhouse on the roof, a storage shed on the grounds, and a greenhouse facility across town, in addition to this storage closet.

I pulled a key from my pocket and unlocked the gun-metal gray steel door. The hinges whined as I pushed the heavy door open. With a flip of a switch, the fluorescent lights flickered on. The bulb in the back started to buzz.

"It kind of makes my messy desk look organized," I admitted.

Francesca just shook her head.

Three seven-foot-tall metal shelves had been crammed inside the storage closet. The packed shelves reminded me of the Island of Misfit Toys, but for gardeners. There were gardening shears in need of repair, ancient bags of potting soil, beautiful ceramic pots that were chipped or stained, bottles of chemicals that I wouldn't want to touch without rubber gloves and tongs, and the ever-present boxes of old paperwork.

"When I get some free time, I'm going to organize this closet and toss out over half this junk. Most of it is past its expiration date."

The room had the bitter smell of a gardening center's pesticides aisle. I wiggled my itchy nose and pushed aside a few boxes that hadn't made it to the shelves as I searched for the file boxes Fisher needed.

"Look here," Francesca said.

She'd squeezed to the back of the closet and was frowning at the bottom shelf, where a dozen or more ten-pound plastic bags with faded labels sat.

"I can't believe the Secret Service would allow anyone to bring these bags into the White House," she said.

I dusted off the label of one of the bags to read it. "Ammonium nitrate."

"Both Annie and I grew up around this stuff. My dad worked as safety inspector in a coal mine back in West Virginia. The miners use ammonium nitrate not for fertilizer, but as a powerful explosive."

"So I've heard."

The bags weren't mixed with other fertilizers, but were pure ammonium nitrate.

"This stuff wouldn't explode if we dropped a bag. We'd need to add some kind of fuel and a detonator in order to make it into a bomb," I said. "Still, it's a risk storing it down here. I should get rid of it."

"I agree. Annie's dad was killed in a mine explosion. That's not something you want to fool around with."

My disastrous session out at the Secret Service's training facility replayed in my mind. What should I have done when they'd suspected that a bomb had been planted in the West Wing?

In the end, I could only come up with one solution: Don't let a bomb get into the White House in the first place.

I grabbed a bag and hauled it out of the closet. "It's not like we're going to use it on the lawn. These bags look like they're at least a decade old."

The fertilizer, high in nitrogen, had probably been used by the grounds crew in the past to give the lawn a quick burst of green color. While satisfying in the short run, the excess nitrogen often makes grasses grow too quickly, opening the door to disease. Not to mention the need to trim the lawn more often. Don't even get me started about the problem with runoff and the trouble nitrogen causes in our waterways.

The constant application of chemicals like these over time could make the grass dependent on the higher level of nutrients, weakening its ability to handle stress and, again, opening the door to disease.

This past spring, I'd started to implement an organic lawn care plan for America's first lawn, weaning the tall fescue grass off chemical fertilizers and pesticides. We'd raised the mower height from two and a half inches to three. The taller the leaf blade, the stronger the roots, which meant it'd need less water and be less susceptible to weeds, insects, and disease. We'd also started to water deeply and less frequently, and always on mornings when there was no wind, to give the grass roots the best chance to absorb the water.

Ammonium nitrate didn't fit into this plan. No, sir. It had to go.

After locating all of the boxes for Fisher, I found a handcart next to the freight elevator.

"Francesca, I need to ask you about something else."

"Um . . . sure, Casey. I guess."

"Why did you disappear on me Friday night?" I asked as I rolled the cart to the closet. "I felt stupid when you pushed me into Kelly Montague like that."

Francesca shrugged as if it were nothing, but I could tell she felt uncomfortable. Her arms suddenly grew tense and her movements resembled a marching wooden soldier as she followed along beside me. "I had remembered something that I needed to do before I met up with Bruce for dinner."

"Do you know Kelly?" I asked, recalling how strongly Kelly Montague had reacted at the mention of Francesca's and Bruce's names.

"I've never met the woman."

"Really?" I asked.

She shrugged.

"She's taking over for Parker," I said as I dropped a box onto the handcart.

"So I've heard. She's beautiful and smart. A real asset to *Media Today*'s team."

"Aren't you worried she might report what he found out about you and Bruce?"

"No."

"You sound pretty sure of that."

Francesca clicked her painted pink nails together. "I'm not sure of anything anymore. Unfortunately I don't think the rumors will die with Parker. It'll only be a matter of time before another reporter digs up the story, probably that young know-it-all Simon Matthews, but not Kelly."

"How can you say that?" I asked. "How can you predict the actions of a reporter you've never met?"

"You're right. I can't. Perhaps Kelly will be my downfall." She smiled that brittle smile of hers, the one that looked as if she might break. "I think she's investigating Parker's death."

"I wish her luck. Who better than a reporter to poke around? Perhaps she can find what Manny has obviously overlooked." Mainly, my innocence.

Francesca's expression tightened as she ran her hand along a seam in the cinder-block wall of the storage closet. "I suppose one could look at it that way."

"But you don't." I bit my lip. "You need to tell the police about this mysterious scandal everyone has been talking about. If Parker knew about it, it might be the reason he was killed."

Francesca grabbed my shoulder and turned me toward her. "Casey"—her voice dropped to a whisper—"this isn't a pretend murder mystery dinner that we're talking about anymore. A man's been killed. You need to tread carefully, very carefully. I've been in this town for nearly a lifetime. I know how these things play out. You can get away with only a certain level of eccentricity before you find yourself packing your bags and heading home . . . or worse."

"Worse?" Was she warning me? Or threatening?

"Don't get involved."

"Why? What's going on?"

"Don't get involved." She refused to say anything else on the matter. Her movements turned quick, mechanical again as she grabbed a box of paperwork and dropped it onto the handcart.

"So you'll just whistle into the wind waiting for the scandal to break?" I asked as I picked up another ten-pound bag of fertilizer.

"No." She dropped the last box of paperwork onto the handcart. It landed with a loud clang.

"Then what are you going to do?"

"Drop it, Casey. I can't talk about it, okay?" She paused as if reconsidering. "I won't talk any more about it. Let's just get this done. I have wasted enough time down here already. I should never have agreed to help you."

I tossed several of the ammonium nitrate fertilizer bags on top of Fisher's boxes of paperwork. "I'll come back for the rest later," I said. "I don't want to waste any more of your time or risk tipping the cart over." I'd already learned that lesson. A few months earlier, when Lorenzo and I were delivering potted plants to the offices in the West

Wing, I'd turned the cart too sharply around a corner. Pots, plants, and soil had gone flying.

Francesca and I took the freight elevator to the ground level. I tugged the heavy handcart through the hallway in search of Wilson Fisher.

Before we got very far, a piercing alarm sounded.

"What's going on?" Francesca shouted and pressed her hands over her ears.

"I don't know."

Two Secret Service agents dressed in identical black suits darted out of their nearby satellite office. Come to think of it, that was where that godawful sound was coming from. Jack Turner, along with several other CAT agents, jogged down the hallway toward us.

"Jack?" I was so glad to see him. "What's going on?"

"There's a bomb on this floor," he answered as he continued down the hall.

*A bomb?* I staggered backward, falling over the handcart of paperwork and fertilizer.

# Chapter Twelve

*Take time to deliberate; but when the time for action arrives, stop thinking and go in.*
—ANDREW JACKSON, THE 7TH PRESIDENT OF
THE UNITED STATES

**G**LORY be, this was the disastrous training session all over again! But this time it was for real!

Francesca and I had walked into the eye of the storm.

"The bomb must be somewhere over here," a burly, neckless Secret Service agent barked. He frowned as he scanned the area directly around Francesca and me.

"We should take cover," Francesca said, pulling on my arm.

According to my training, we should move as quickly as possible to the nearest exit, but I didn't move. I watched wide-eyed as the agents systematically searched every crevice. Someone had mercifully turned off the piercing alarm, but that didn't stop the ruckus. Ushers, maids, chefs, curators all came pouring into the hallway to see what was happening.

"Get back! Get back!" an agent shouted at them. "I need you to stay away from this area."

"This is the sensor that was triggered," Jack said, pointing to a doorway leading out to the Jacqueline Kennedy Garden.

"Sensor?" I asked.

Jack and the rest of his team were too busy searching for the bomb to answer.

"Help me get Jack's attention," I said to Francesca. "I need to ask him about the sensors."

She didn't answer. I glanced behind me. She wasn't there.

She'd pulled that slippery gardener act on me again. "Francesca?" I called.

Wilson Fisher, however, came running up, his hard-soled shoes slapping loudly against the stone floor, his long nose twitching with excitement. His voice was labored and breathy. "The sensors are sensitive . . . electronic . . . sniffers have been set up at all entrances designed to detect . . . explosives."

Jack turned on his heel. Our eyes met for a moment. His gaze then shifted to the large bags of fertilizer on my handcart. A sick feeling gurgled in my stomach.

"No one came in this door," Agent Steve Sallis reported as he jogged up to join the search. "The dogs are being dispatched. Thatch is bringing the handheld bomb detection unit."

Another agent held his hands wide and guided the crowd away from the area like a border collie herding sheep. He kind of looked like a border collie, with his alert gaze and long, sleek facial features.

"Um, Jack," I said. He kept frowning at the fertilizer bags I'd hauled up from the storage room while a half dozen Emergency Response Team members charged in from outside and fanned out around the doorway, their P90 semiautomatics held at the ready. Panic gurgled in my chest at the sight of all those guns. I started my deep breathing exercises. I was inhaling another deep breath when a uniformed agent arrived with a bomb-sniffing dog.

I swallowed hard and held my ground at the cart of fertilizer. Wilson Fisher, his nose still twitching, remained at my side. "Casey, we need to get this paperwork to safety. If the bomb blows up, there will be no replicating my forms."

"It's okay," I said. "There's no bomb."

"Not unless you've got some gasoline and an electrical source on that handcart," Jack agreed, looking up at me again. "No bomb."

"The paperwork." Fisher tried to pry the handcart's handle out of my grasp. "It has to come with me."

"Aren't you listening? There's no bomb," I said, my voice louder than necessary. "It's the fertilizer. It set off the sensors."

"The paperwork needs to be saved!" Fisher latched on to the handcart just below its handle and gave a vicious tug.

"Fisher, stop that." I tugged the handcart back toward me, struggling to keep the assistant usher from running off with the evidence.

"I found the problem," Jack called to the rest of the team. "Just some bags of fertilizer."

The hallway fell silent.

"It's the ammonium nitrate. They set off the sensors, didn't they?" I asked even though I already knew the answer.

"It's happened before." Jack then spoke into his radio. "Looks like a false alarm. Just the gardeners and their fertilizers."

A large black and tan Belgian Malinois came over to the cart, sniffed, and barked his agreement.

"You put explosives on the handcart with my files?" Fisher demanded. He jumped as if a nettle had stung him. "*My files*? There are explosives on top of my files?"

"It's okay," I said.

"You need to be more careful, Ms. Calhoun. Those files cannot be replaced."

"Really, the fertilizer's not volatile. It's just one component in making a fertilizer bomb."

"Well, then." He straightened his suit coat and regained his nose-in-the-air composure. "I'll take those boxes." He called over several of the ushers.

"Casey Calhoun. I should have known you'd be at the center of this." Mike Hatch, the special agent in charge of the Secret Service's Counter Assault Team, arrived, followed by a handful of scowling CAT agents. "Do you know how much trouble your fertilizer has caused the President?"

"I didn't—"

"If you don't mind, I'd like to take my files now," Fisher said.

Thatch held up his hand. "Nothing on this cart is leaving. The Secret Service will need to confiscate it."

"But—but—" I started to protest. My notes and to-do list for Wednesday's harvest were on the handcart. I needed them.

"We had to pull the President out of an important budget meeting to evacuate him to a safe location." Thatch stood too close. I could feel his hot breath on my face. I tried to back up, but he followed.

"Do you know how much of a disruption you've caused? Those are delicate negotiations. I'd hate to think the government shuts down because you carried fertilizer into the White House."

"Out. I was carrying it out."

"Did you or did you not cause the alarms to go off? You did. So don't try to wiggle out of the blame."

I thought he was done. He'd backed away, but he swooped back in like a bird of prey after a mouse and stuck his finger under my nose.

"Need I remind you—and everyone here—how miserably you failed your safety training? Next time an alarm sounds, I expect you to get the hell out of the way. That's all you need to do. Get the hell out of everyone's way."

Jack gave me a pained look before he started to push the handcart down the hall.

Wait a blasted minute! "My notes," I called. "My notes for the harvest are on the cart. I need them."

I also needed to warn them about the rest of the fertilizer bags in the storage room. "And the fertilizer, there's more in—" I started to explain. "Jack, wait!"

"Don't you think you've already said enough?" Thatch

said. "Turner, what are you waiting for? Get that stuff out of here!"

"I just—" I needed to explain about the other fertilizer bags, and I needed my notes.

"You just cause trouble," Thatch shot back. "You've been a thorn—"

"Thank you, Agent Thatch." Margaret Bradley's appearance stunned everyone. The First Lady, dressed in a dark blue maternity dress, moved with remarkable grace through the throng of Secret Service agents. Milo bounded, all puppy legs and golden fur, alongside her, followed by three harried-looking staff members. "I appreciate the care you take in protecting both me and my husband." She touched a hand to her swelling stomach. "I sleep soundly at night thanks to your efforts."

"Thank you, Mrs. Bradley." Thatch stood a little taller as he faced her.

"Now if you'll excuse us, I need to have a word with Miss Calhoun about Wednesday's harvest."

"Of course." He bowed his head and stepped back, finally giving me room to breathe and to escape.

"I'm not done with you," he threatened as I passed.

"What an inventive way to liven up a Monday afternoon," Margaret Bradley said after she'd led me out the door and into the Jacqueline Kennedy Garden. With a raised palm, she stopped her staffers from following.

"I didn't know the fertilizer would set off the sensors. I didn't even know the sensors were there. I'm so embarrassed."

Milo darted between us and out into the garden. He took a wide circuit around the path, barking at the squirrels, before flopping down on a thick patch of grass. He rolled around on his back, expressing his pleasure with a series of contented grunts and growls.

Margaret smiled at his puppy antics. She then took my hand as we strolled toward a pergola lush with budding Concord grape vines. "Mistakes happen. I should know. I've been making the lion's share of them around here lately," she said as she sat on a white cast-iron bench and invited me to join her. "By the way, the vegetable garden is looking so healthy. I can't believe how tall the pepper plants have already grown."

"Lordy, please, don't let the press hear you say that. As you know, some joker is telling anyone who'll listen that we're sneaking in healthy plants in the middle of the night."

"Whether you're trucking the plants in at night or growing them in the ground, I don't care as long as I get a chance to eat some of those bell peppers. My mouth was watering this morning. It's amazing."

"It's not just me. The volunteers have done tremendous work. And all this heat—the peppers love the hot, humid weather. The lettuce, not so much, but they'll get pulled and eaten on Wednesday."

"The volunteers." She sighed. "Do they seem happy?"

"I believe so." Milo, I noticed, had started to nibble on a planting of rosemary. I clapped my hands and clicked my tongue. He looked up at me and stopped.

"I should have invited the lionesses of D.C. to tea the day after the inauguration. I'm afraid my efforts now are too little, too late." Margaret shook her head. "It's just part of the game, though. John's been playing it his entire adult life. I'm new to it. And right now I'm having a difficult time even caring about D.C.'s endless political and social wrangling." She rested her hand on her swelling belly. "I simply want to be a good mother."

While I could grow a garden, I knew nothing about "birthin' babies." So I smiled and nodded and wondered if this was her way of scolding me about causing so much trouble at the White House today, starting with Manny questioning me in connection with Parker's murder. If I were an expectant mother, my first order of business would be to kick all suspected murderers out of the White House.

"Griffon Parker," she said, confirming my worst fears.

My stomach twisted into a knot.

I nudged the gravel between the seating area's pavers with my toe while waiting for the ax to fall. Grandmother

Faye and my aunts, Willow and Alba, would welcome me back to Rosebrook with open arms. So I wouldn't be homeless. It'd take time and hard work to reestablish my landscaping business, but I wasn't afraid of either of those things.

"I understand," I said to save her from having to actually fire me.

"You do?" She shifted in her seat and looked at me askew. "Then you must be a better investigator than the Secret Service gives you credit for."

I struggled not to let my confusion show as I met her gaze and nodded.

"His investigation was bad enough, but now he's dead. Poisoned." Margaret glanced around to make sure none of the Secret Service agents were close enough to hear. "I heard that you found the fake suicide note in the garden. The implication of how it might have ended up among my pepper plants terrifies me. If you happen to find anything else or hear anything about anyone—"

"You want me to play sleuth?"

"No. God, no, Casey. Nothing so drastic. You need to guard your reputation and your personal safety. Don't cause any trouble for John." Milo's ears perked up in response to her vehement answer.

"No, I wouldn't want to do that."

She patted my hand. "I want you to be my eyes and ears in the garden and report back anything you learn or *find*. The sooner the police catch whoever killed Griffon Parker, the better I'm going to sleep at night."

"I—I—" My heart pounded with excitement. She did want my help.

"If you hear any new whispering about the Dearings in the garden, I hope you'll let me know about that as well. John stubbornly refuses to distance himself from Bruce, so I need to make sure I'm in a position to protect him. I need to know what's going on with them. You helped me this past spring. I trust your instincts and your ability to keep confidential matters confidential. Can I trust you to do this for me?"

How could I refuse her, a worried mom-to-be and First Lady of the United States?

"Of course you can count on me," I said. She simply wanted me to ask a few innocent questions, questions I needed to know the answers to as well.

# Chapter Thirteen

*We cannot do everything at once, but we can
do something at once.*

—CALVIN COOLIDGE, THE 30TH PRESIDENT OF
THE UNITED STATES

I T wasn't as if I planned to do anything that would put
my life in danger. I would ask a few questions. As the
First Lady had aptly pointed out, Griffon Parker's murderer had access to at least the White House garden. This
also meant the murderer had to be either one of the gardening volunteers, a pool reporter, or a staff member. What
else could explain the appearance of that suicide note?

Although I felt confident the Secret Service would be
checking and rechecking the background of everyone present at the photography session, I was equally convinced the
murderer, whoever he or she may be, would have a clean
background . . . save for a secret Griffon Parker had been
on the verge of exposing.

Which brought me back to Francesca.

I closed my eyes and sighed.

Francesca was too smart to be so obvious. Why would
she kill Parker in the same manner that we'd planned for
the murder mystery dinner when too many of her friends
already knew the details? Apparently we weren't nearly as

discreet as I'd hoped. Everyone—Jack included—seemed to know all about how we'd been planning the perfect murder.

Dig a hole and push me in, because I was about to die from embarrassment.

But I had to wonder, did everyone who had been working in the garden before the fake letter showed up actually know the specifics of our planned "perfect murder" for the dinner party or was that information known to just a select few? That was the first thing I needed to find out. Luckily for me I had the unique advantage of daily contact with nearly everyone who had been on hand during the photo session.

Asking a few carefully worded questions about a charity dinner party Francesca and I had been planning shouldn't make the killer nervous.

I kept following that line of thinking as a means to console my troubled conscience as I left the Jacqueline Kennedy Garden and returned to the scene of "Casey's great fertilizer bomb debacle." That was what the Secret Service agents were now calling the false alarm if the two agents I'd overheard laughing outside were any indication. The center hallway had been cleared, leaving no trace of the earlier excitement.

Francesca had also vanished, a rather irritating talent of hers. I hoped she wasn't wandering the halls unescorted. I had been her escort and was responsible for her. I didn't think the Secret Service would appreciate hearing from me with another problem so soon.

After asking around, I discovered Francesca and Wilson Fisher had started talking and had hit it off. Fisher confirmed he'd escorted Francesca to her husband's office.

With that under control, I headed back to the grounds office. Gordon and Lorenzo stood at the door waiting for me.

"Gordon." I held my hands up in front of me like a shield. "Don't say anything. I honestly didn't know the fertilizer would set off alarms and trigger a bomb scare."

"The grounds office is getting quite a reputation," Lorenzo

said. "Before you started work here, we happily flew under the radar."

"Which wasn't necessarily a good thing," Gordon added, bless his tender heart. He tested out a grin. "On the upside, we're gaining a reputation for being a bit dangerous. Maybe the kitchen staff will think twice the next time they want to try and take over our storage room."

In the silence that followed, Gordon turned a meaningful glance in Lorenzo's direction.

Lorenzo cleared his throat a couple of times. "Casey, I apologize for not telling you about the meeting. I should have given you Seth's message before our lunch meeting started." His voice was unusually subdued. "Is there anything I can do to help you prepare for Wednesday's harvest?"

"The harvest," I sighed. "The Secret Service confiscated all of my notes and lists of things that need to be done."

"You mean this list?" Lorenzo picked up the overstuffed file folder from my desk.

"Where did you get that?" I snatched it from him and flipped the folder open. Everything was there, including my five-page to-do list.

"Jack Turner dropped it off a few minutes ago," Gordon said. "He thought you might need it, so he made sure to get it back to you ASAP."

"Thank you." I hugged the folder to my chest. "I'll have to think of a way to thank Jack as well." It was nearly five o'clock, and it would take several more hours to get through the list of things that needed to get done today. "I hate to ask you to stay late, but I could use help with—"

"Don't worry about the time. Let me have a look at what needs to be done." Lorenzo held out his hand as he stood stiffly beside my desk. I handed over my notepad and pointed out some of the more challenging tasks. With a nod, he ripped off the top two pages from the notepad. "I'll get these done before I leave tonight. First chance I get tomorrow, I'll take care of getting the rest of that fertilizer out of storage."

"And properly disposed of?" I asked.

"I'm not a novice," he shot back. "I'll take care of it."

"Hand me a page from your to-do list as well," Gordon said, grinning as he watched Lorenzo shuffle back to his desk and pick up the phone. "Seth being Seth, I'm sure there are a million last-minute additions."

"Not quite a million," I said, ripping off another page from the to-do list, feeling thankful that I'd taken thorough notes about what needed to be done. "Just let me know if you have any questions."

I took a seat at my desk, picked up a pen, and read the first item on my now mercifully shortened to-do list: Deliver a copy of the kitchen garden specs to the First Lady's social secretary as well as a copy to Frank Lispon, the White House press secretary.

I also noticed that someone had left a sticky note on my desk with a barely legible "Lispon's office" scrawled on it.

"Did you put this here?" I asked Lorenzo. "Do you know what it could mean?"

Lorenzo shook his head and grunted. Gordon didn't know about the sticky note, either. "Francesca and Fisher did pop in looking for you. Ambrose passed by as well. Perhaps one of them left the note," Gordon offered.

After e-mailing a copy of the press packet I'd put together for Frank, I started to wonder if the note meant that Frank needed to see me. He might have had questions.

*I* had questions for him.

Had he known the details of Francesca's perfect murder? He'd been in the garden shortly before the fake suicide note appeared. It could have dropped out of his pocket. Griffon Parker must have been a constant thorn in Frank's side with Parker's string of damaging "investigative" reports. Had Frank snapped and silenced Parker permanently?

Also, with all the work we'd been doing lately with the harvest plans, I couldn't remember when anyone had checked on the plants in the West Wing. The poor leafy darlings were probably in desperate need of water or a trim or something.

"I'll be back in a half hour," I announced. I gathered up the hard copy version of the press packet and a small watering can and headed off toward the West Wing.

**FRANK LISPON'S OFFICE DOOR WAS CLOSED,** which surprised me. The press secretary preached and practiced an open-door policy.

His office served as a clearinghouse of information for the press who covered White House affairs. This time of day, late afternoon, was his busiest time, when reporters would put their finishing touches on stories for the six o'clock news or the late edition of Internet sites and newspapers. Both his cell phone and office phone would be buzzing with calls and text messages as requests poured in for last-minute details or clarification on statements made earlier in the day.

This evening, with the end of the daily budget meetings, I'd expected his office to be packed with staffers helping to disseminate information.

Occasionally Frank would pop into the Press Briefing Room unannounced for an impromptu Q&A session if some important news was unfolding. Hoping to find him in there, I headed back down the West Wing's carpeted hallway.

Bruce Dearing lumbered toward me.

"Just the lady I need to speak to." His voice rumbled. "If you want to have any kind of career in Washington, you're going to have to start schooling what you say to people around here, especially before you spout wild accusations about me and my wife. Do you understand me? Stay out of matters that don't concern you."

"I haven't spouted anything that wasn't true, and I assure you that I have not gone out of my way looking for trouble. It keeps finding me."

"Come now, Ms. Calhoun. You have a reputation for sticking your nose where it doesn't belong." He wagged his meaty finger in front of my face. "Understand this, missy, that pointy thing has no business anywhere near my affairs."

My nose wasn't pointy. I'd been told more than once it was button shaped. And he had no right telling me where I should or shouldn't be sticking that particular cute-as-a-button appendage.

"You're wrong," I said. Two words I was certain he rarely heard. "When you and your wife suggested to the police that I was responsible for Griffon Parker's death, all of this"—I gestured with the watering can—"became my business. I'm not going to let anyone destroy my reputation. Not even you. And I'm certainly not going to let a killer escape justice."

We glared at each other like a pair of feral cats squaring off to fight. Although Bruce Dearing, with his decades of connections in this town and a reputation for acting as both a kingmaker and an executioner, scared me, I knew I needed to stand my ground or I'd find myself plowed under by his political wrangling.

He puffed out his already rounded chest. "This isn't a war you want to fight."

"I agree with you there," I said with a grin, which seemed to surprise him. "I don't want to fight anyone."

"I don't understand you, Casey Calhoun." He shook his head, making his thick jowls dance. "Tread with care around my family."

"Again, I agree with you. I'm only trying to protect what's mine. I wasn't at all pleased to be grilled by the police this morning, especially when they'd been fed half-truths. So I suggest you turn what you've just said back around and apply it to yourself. If you stomp through my flowerbed, I can't say I won't do the same."

He barked a gruff laugh. "I see why my wife likes you. You've got a spine. It's amazing how many don't around here," he said as he ambled down the hallway. "The spineless . . . God bless them. They're damned easy to climb over."

* * *

**DESPITE BRUCE'S WARNING, I WAS STILL DETER-**
mined to find and talk with Frank. After all, someone had
left his name on a sticky note on my desk. When I stepped
into the dark blue Press Briefing Room, with my watering
can in one hand and press packet in the other, the dozen or
so journalists spread out in the theater seats and hunched
over laptops all looked up at me like they'd spotted a tasty
morsel on a sparsely stocked buffet table.

"Oh. You're one of the gardeners," said Simon Matthews, a twenty-something young man with thick glasses
and a laptop that looked as if it had come from a spaceship.
He sounded disappointed.

"I am." I held up the watering can. "Have you seen
Frank Lispon?"

"Check in the zoo," Matthews answered and went back
to typing furiously on his laptop's keyboard.

The zoo, or cube zoo, was what journalists called the
cramped cubicles and tiny offices in the adjacent press
corps offices. I'd seen it only once: on the efficient, but
overwhelming, tour the chief usher had given me on my
first day at the White House.

At the back of the Press Briefing Room, past the bank of
electronic equipment the television and radio crews used to
broadcast press conferences, I found a door tucked into a
corner that opened up into the bustling press corps offices.

With so many people talking, on phones and to each
other, I couldn't imagine how anyone managed to concentrate in here. After a quick look around, I spotted *Media
Today*'s new solo reporter, Kelly Montague, in a small
office near the door. She was talking so loudly on her
BlackBerry cell phone I had no choice but to listen in on
her half of the conversation while I searched for the press
secretary.

"I will not be bullied into anything," she rasped. "How
did you get this number? I don't even know who you are."

There was a pause as she listened, her entire face darkening.

"*My father?*" Desperation, a feeling I knew too well, tightened her voice, raising it an octave as she squeezed out, "Do you know where I can find him?"

She frowned as she listened.

"No!" she shouted and disconnected the call.

"I couldn't help but overhear your end of the conversation," I said to Kelly; then I quickly added, "If someone is harassing you, I have friends in the Secret Service who might be able to help."

"What?" She gave a startled jerk and quickly covered a stack of papers on her desk with her arm. "The Secret Service? Oh, no. Thank you. No. I'm fine. It's just a stupid misunderstanding. I can handle it."

I watched her, my concern growing as she moved to more fully cover up the papers on the desk in front of her. Her hands were shaking. The media types—like the Secret Service—didn't rattle easily. Most thrived on conflict. The greater the conflict, the better the story and all that. So I had to wonder what was going on with Kelly that would make her this nervous and yet was not something she felt she could turn into a front-page story.

"Have you seen Frank Lispon?" I asked her. "I have some information for Wednesday's harvest to give him."

"Frank?" She leaned out her office and looked around, her gaze flitting nervously around the busy room. "I haven't seen him. No one has." She huffed loudly. "I need to get a list of figures for tonight's broadcast, and he's ignoring my texts. I was told that Lispon was one of the best press secretaries ever to have worked these halls. But so far, I've not seen that."

"A man was murdered over the weekend, your co-worker," I pointed out. "This isn't your typical Monday."

"Of course." Her cheeks darkened again. "You'll have to forgive me. This is my first full week at the White House, Parker's no longer around to help me out, and I don't want

to mess up this opportunity. The jackals"—she gestured to
the other reporters in the room—"want to see me fail;
either that or they want to steal my story. That Simon Matthews seems eager to take over Parker's role as hard-nosed
reporter around here. I can't let him sabotage me as he tries
to climb the rungs. I really do need to get these figures
checked."

"Try texting Penny in the press office. She should be able
to help you." I gave her the number. Now that I was thinking
about her, I realized Penny might be able to help me as well.

Kelly thanked me for the number. I started to leave but
then thought of another question.

"Did you manage to retrieve the papers Parker took
from you?" I asked with a meaningful look at the papers
she was clearly trying to hide from me.

"I don't know what you're talking about."

"Friday night. You were arguing with Parker in Lafayette Square because he'd taken some papers from you," I
said.

"Right. I'd forgotten that you'd overheard that. I'd rather
you didn't tell anyone about the theft. They weren't for
work." She glanced down at the papers and pushed them
under a stack of newsprint. "They were personal."

"White House employees are models of discretion," I
assured her, but then I remembered my conversation earlier
in the day with Detective Manny Hernandez. "Shoot. I'm
afraid, however, I did tell the police about your missing
papers and your confrontation with Parker when they questioned me about what happened on Friday night."

"I hope they don't . . ." She shrugged and then forced a
smile. "It was nothing. Really, nothing. You had to tell the
police about what happened on Friday. I wouldn't want you
to lie. I'm sure nothing will come of it."

"And did you find them?"

"Find what?"

Was she being deliberately dense?

"The stolen papers. After Parker's death, were you able
to find them?"

"No. I haven't had a chance to look. They really weren't that important anyhow. Now, if you'd excuse me, I really do have a deadline to meet."

"Not important?" Then why was she upset to hear that I'd talked to the police about them? And why wasn't she still looking for them? The reason was as obvious as powdery mildew on a crepe myrtle—Kelly was lying.

Did she get her papers back from Parker before his murder or after? And who was threatening her on the phone just now?

"How well do you know Francesca and Bruce Dearing?" I asked her, wondering if she knew about the details of the murder mystery dinner Francesca had cajoled me into helping her plan.

"I've never met them. Sorry," she answered without lifting her head from her phone.

While Kelly texted Penny, I did a quick search in the rest of the press corps offices for Frank Lispon. No one had seen him. Most were anxiously waiting for him to return their calls and texts. When I passed Kelly's office on my way out, she—along with the interesting stack of papers on her desk—was gone.

I FOUND PENNY IN THE PRESS OFFICE. SHE WAS talking on the office phone while texting on her iPhone.

"You have the kitchen garden press packet?" she asked me. "No," she said into the phone, "I was talking to someone in the office."

"I do," I whispered and set the press packet on the corner of her desk. "I've also e-mailed a copy."

"Thanks," she mouthed and then added aloud, "Frank's been looking for this. No, sorry, I was talking to someone in the office again. Yes, I am listening to you," she said into the phone.

"Have you seen him?"

She shook her head. "When I find him—" She pantomimed choking him.

"Good luck with that," I said with a laugh. "I found a note on my desk that said 'Lispon's office.' Do you know what that could be about?"

She shook her head.

After watering the peace lily on her filing cabinet, I left her office. On my way out, I passed Frank Lispon's office again. The door, which had been closed, was now slightly ajar.

Good, I thought, I needed to check on the young Ming aralia, an indoor Asian houseplant with an exotic bonsai look, in his office. It was a thirsty critter, and Frank never bothered to water it. I was certain it needed some tending.

I'd raised my fist to knock on the door when I heard Frank's voice say, "What are we going to do about Casey Calhoun?"

I froze.

"We?" Bruce Dearing countered. I'd recognize his gravelly voice anywhere. "She's your problem. I expect you to handle her like you handled Griffon Parker. Only try to be more discreet this time."

"I *was* discreet with Parker." Frank's cool voice chilled the blood in my veins.

"I saw you in the parking garage inches away from slugging the bastard Friday night. Thank God there weren't any other witnesses. What was that about?"

"He'd—"

"He what?" Bruce demanded.

"Nothing. It's not important. I'll take care of Casey. Don't worry. It'll be handled before the end of Wednesday."

"See that it is. And this time, for God's sake, don't let the press get hold of it," Bruce said.

Was this the reason Francesca had warned me to stay away from anything involving Parker's death? Did she know that Frank and her husband might turn their murderous sights on me?

The door started to swing open.

I needed to move *and fast*! I didn't need to give either man more reason to . . . to . . . want to kill me.

With my heart thudding in my throat, I darted down the hall. I'd rounded the corner when I heard, "Casey?"

I didn't care who had called my name. All I cared about was getting as far away from Frank and Bruce as possible. As I blasted through the glass doors leading out of the West Wing and onto the West Colonnade, I ripped my cell phone out of my pocket and dialed Jack Turner's number.

"Please, answer. Please, answer," I prayed, but his phone flipped over to voice mail.

"Casey?" Frank called as I pushed open the door to the Palm Room. I didn't look back. I didn't slow down.

If two of the top members of the President's own staff had a hand in Griffon Parker's murder, I shuddered to think who else might be involved.

*The Secret Service?*

*Jack?*

I needed to get away from the White House while I still could.

# Chapter Fourteen

*A regret for the mistakes of yesterday must not,
however, blind us to the tasks of today.*
—WARREN HARDING, THE 29TH
PRESIDENT OF THE UNITED STATES

**M**Y heart was firmly lodged in my throat by the time
I reached the White House's northeast gate. My
hand shook as I reached for the gate's latch. It clanked as
it opened. I'd kept my head down. So far no one had noticed me.

"Casey?" Fredrick popped his head out of the whitewashed guard hut beside the gate.

I stopped. So did my heart.

"Y-yes?" I hoped I looked calmer than I felt.

"Is everything okay? You don't look so good."

"Probably something I ate at lunch. Can't talk now. I'm
in a hurry," I said and swung the iron gate open with more
force than was necessary.

"Oh, okay, then," Fredrick said as the gate clanged
behind me. "Um . . . thanks again for bringing the violets
for my Lily. She's going to love them. Have a good evening
and good luck on Wednesday."

I kept moving away from the White House at a fast clip,

but glanced back over my shoulder. Fredrick stood at the gate with his hands on his hips, watching me and frowning.

How deep did Frank and Bruce's conspiracy go? Who else was involved?

Not Fredrick.

Not Jack.

What if Jack was involved?

Panic surged through me.

I started to jog when I turned the corner at Seventeenth Street and hurried down the hill toward the Tidal Basin. This path took me farther away from my apartment, a deliberate choice. With Frank and Bruce—two of the President's most powerful men—targeting me, the brownstone was the last place I'd feel safe.

Despite the oppressive heat that still hung heavy in the early evening air, the crowds were as thick as I'd ever seen them. A large family, clearly tourists, stepped in my path. The father stopped abruptly in front of me. Bending down on one knee, he pointed out the Washington Monument to his young blond daughter in pigtails. The child squealed with delight.

My chest tightened.

Nearby a group of local teenagers practiced in a field in the Ellipse. They kicked a soccer ball from one to the other as they ran down the field while their proud parents watched from the sidelines. A father cheered when a smaller boy sent the soccer ball sailing.

I hugged my arms to my chest and hurried farther down the hill, weaving my way through a large tour group. With all these people and all this action surging around me, I felt more alone now than ever.

At least I was safe. I'd gotten away from the White House, and no one had tried to stop me.

But why would either Bruce or Frank try to hold me against my will? They knew how much of a scene I'd make if they tried to drag me back to the White House. And wasn't that exactly what Bruce had told Frank to avoid?

They were smart men. They knew they had me backed into a corner.

What could I do? Run to the police and say, "Hi, Manny, you're not going to believe this. Two of the President's most trusted advisers are murderers. And by the way, they're also trying to kill me."

Manny would probably send me straight to St. Elizabeth's for a psychiatric evaluation. I didn't have any proof. I didn't even understand why the men thought they needed to "handle" me.

Damn it, this wasn't fair. Just two days before the First Lady's first harvest and this? I wanted to scream in frustration, but that would attract too much attention.

I passed the World War II Memorial and then turned back around. With the Lincoln Memorial in view just beyond the reflecting pool, I descended the long, grassy steps into the memorial, where the sound of whooshing water from the fountains in the central pool soothed.

The people wandering through the memorial spoke in hushed tones. The memorial, laid out like an amphitheater, had a series of pillars adorned with bronze wreaths representing every state and U.S. protectorate during World War II that stood like silent sentries at the periphery of the memorial.

A white-haired gentleman wearing a camouflage hat and leaning heavily on a cane ambled past.

He stopped and asked without turning back around, "Are you okay?" After a pause he half turned toward me. He had a kind and vaguely familiar face that made the tension in my shoulders ease.

I smiled and nodded. "Everything is going to be fine," I said around a lump in my throat even though I felt anything but okay. I had no idea what I needed to do or where I needed to go.

The man leaned on his cane and tilted his head. I recognized him now. He was one of the regular protesters who sat outside the White House's North Lawn, the unfriendly guy who didn't talk to anyone. "This is a good place to come and think. I come here often. The water"—he gestured with his cane to the center fountain—"can clear your mind of all the unnecessary noise. It can help you focus. To see what's real and what's not."

"I hope so." I sat on the edge of the center pool and watched the light from the sunset dance on its glassy surface. "My father once told me that the sparkling spots of light on the water were diamonds only the faeries could touch," I said.

I'd forgotten about that.

"Faerie diamonds?" The old man chuckled. "Your father must have had some imagination."

"I don't know. I don't really remember him," I answered, still mesmerized by the sparkling water.

"Are you sure you're okay?" the man asked. "If you need something, anything—" He looked up suddenly. A smile pulled up the corners of his lips, smoothing out his wrinkles. He nodded to someone beyond me. "I have a feeling you're in good hands now."

I jumped to my feet and whirled around to find Jack Turner standing about a yard away from me. No longer dressed in his black battle dress fatigues, Jack looked no less deadly in worn jeans and light gray T-shirt. There was an intensity about him. I don't know of any other way to describe it.

He was a trained killer. He made me nervous, and I was beginning to realize that a perverted part of me liked that about him.

He closed the distance between us. "Casey?" he asked, while his eyes flicked a questioning glance toward the older gentleman.

"Jack!" I was so glad to see a familiar face, I threw myself into his arms, which he wrapped protectively around me. I pressed my cheek to his chest and breathed in his scent.

"What's going on?" he asked.

Where did I start? The bomb that wasn't a bomb and what the First Lady had asked of me afterward? What I'd learned from Kelly Montague? Or didn't learn? The over-heard conversation between Frank and Bruce?

Or . . .

Jack, a member of the White House's Secret Service detail, might be part of the plot. Maybe I shouldn't trust him at all.

I pulled out of his comforting embrace. The older gen-tleman, I noticed, had left.

"Um . . . Jack, maybe I should be alone." As alone as I already felt.

He didn't move so I did. I followed the edge of the cen-ter pool toward one of the two towers. One side said "Pa-cific." I moved toward the opposite tower, the side called "Atlantic."

"Casey." Jack's voice was low. "You called me."

"You didn't answer."

"I was in a meeting about the suicide note you found." He looked away. Was he trying to hide his guilt? When he looked back, all I could see was concern. "I'm here now."

"How did you find me?" Was I being followed? I searched the crowd of tourists for plainclothes Secret Ser-vice agents, not that I had any hope of spotting one.

Whenever the President or First Lady made a public ap-pearance, the Secret Service placed several agents within the gathered crowd to ferret out trouble.

I'd heard that the Secret Service also used plain-clothes agents on other assignments. Did one of those assignments include following White House employees—employees that needed to be "handled" and who were wearing targets on their backs?

"How did you find me?" I asked again, moving even farther away from him.

He remained by the reflecting pool. "Fredrick watched you leave. He told me which direction you went. If you didn't want to be followed, you should have turned off your cell phone. It has a GPS in it. And if you think you're in danger, you should change roads and directions several times. I could give you lessons on—"

"I'm not—" I blurted out. Several people stopped to stare at me. "I'm okay," I said, lowering my voice. "I'm okay." I hoped that if I said it enough times, I'd start to believe it.

Jack crossed his arms over his chest. "Talk to me, Casey. You ran out of the White House as if terrorists were chasing you. What's going on?"

He'd followed me to the memorial either to help me or to help Frank and Bruce destroy me.

I wanted to trust Jack, truly I did, but sticky tendrils of fear wrapped around me, whispering into my ear that I couldn't trust him. I couldn't trust anyone.

My father had taught me that lesson.

I drew a deep breath and held it.

No, I wasn't going to let my father's mistakes color my world. Jack was a good guy. One of the best.

Even if the Secret Service was a part of the conspiracy to silence Griffon Parker and now me, Jack wouldn't go along with that. He wouldn't.

"I know who killed Griffon Parker," I said.

Jack grabbed my arm and ushered me away from the crowds. He didn't stop until we had left the World War II Memorial and found a relatively secluded spot beyond the "Pacific" tower and underneath one of the National Mall's American elms.

This tree in particular had stood against the powerful Dutch elm disease and survived. While the fungal disease had killed a majority of the elms in municipalities across the country, this tree had given arborists new hope for the elms' future survival.

Using this disease-resistant tree and others like it that had been planted as part of the National Mall's original planting of elms in the 1930s, scientists had developed the "Jefferson" American elm, a cultivar that promised to survive against a foe much stronger than itself. In time, clones of this tree might help bring back the iconic American elm to the National Mall and to communities across the country.

I prayed I could be so strong.

"I know who killed Parker," I said again.

"Is that so? Despite your promises to stay out of the investigation, apparently you've turned into a regular Nancy Drew," he said.

"*Miss Marple*," I corrected. "Nancy Drew is too perky."

"And you're not perky?"

I sneered.

He released my arm. "In case you've forgotten, you promised me and your saintly grandmother that you wouldn't get involved with another murder investigation, that you wouldn't put your life in danger."

"It wasn't as if I went looking for trouble." Griffon Parker's death was none of my business. I understood that. "I wasn't playing sleuth. I wasn't."

I didn't tell him about the side project the First Lady had asked of me. It wasn't as if I'd started asking questions in that direction anyhow. Not really. Kelly Montague hadn't been any help at all. "This isn't my fault. I didn't do anything other than talk with Detective Hernandez. And I didn't go to Manny. He came to me, remember?"

Jack nodded, which I knew didn't mean that he agreed with me. It only meant that he'd heard what I was saying. Sometimes, like right now, I wished he'd talk more. Trying to puzzle out the workings of Jack's mind was like trying to win one of those giant stuffed toys at the fair, the kind with all the dust on them.

"Tell me what happened," he said as he casually leaned his arm against the trunk of the sturdy American elm. "What has made you so frightened?"

Anyone who saw him would mistake his easygoing manner as just that. I'd worked around the Secret Service long enough to know that Jack—like all the other agents—maintained razor-sharp reflexes and senses beneath his facade of calm.

"I overheard Frank Lispon and Bruce Dearing in Frank's office talking. They were discussing me."

Jack raised his brows with interest.

"I wasn't eavesdropping."

His brows hitched up a bit higher.

"I wasn't. Not intentionally. Not at first. I was delivering the press packet for Wednesday, and I heard angry voices as I passed Frank's office. Bruce told Frank that he'd have to 'handle me' the same way he'd handled Griffon Parker."

Jack rubbed his chin. "The press secretary and the Chief of Staff said this?"

I nodded.

"You're sure?"

I nodded again.

His hand moved to the back of his neck.

My heart dropped into the pit of my stomach.

"I don't know what to do, Jack. No one is going to believe me. *You* don't even believe me."

"I don't?" Jack asked.

"D-don't you?" I was afraid to hope, afraid to trust.

"Why else would I be standing here? Why else would I have followed you here?"

"Because Bruce or Frank ordered you to find me, to keep an eye on me until they could figure out how to get rid of me like they did with Griffon Parker."

He didn't say a word to that.

"It's not that I don't want to believe—" I started to say, but he raised his hand and walked away.

I closed my eyes and sighed. What in the world was wrong with me?

Why did I say that? Why did I push him away?

*Honey child*, my aunt Alba used to tell me when I complained about being socially inept in high school, *you're not supposed to know all the answers. If you did, God wouldn't have put you down here to learn 'em.*

She was right, of course, then and now. I would have hoped, however, I'd have learned a thing or two about trust in my nearly forty years on this confounding planet.

Despite the panic welling in my chest as I watched Jack

walk away, something deep inside me kept me from calling out to him. God knew I couldn't do this alone. I needed help.

I needed Jack.

Forget that my story sounded crazy, even to me. Jack believed me.

Why couldn't I believe in *him*?

# Chapter Fifteen

I pressed my palm against the American elm until its bumpy bark bit into my skin. I closed my eyes and prayed the long-lived tree would lend me some of its strength.

"Stop," I whispered as my heart clenched. "Jack, please stop. I need—"

"Damn it, Casey. Do you push everyone away or am I the only one who gets the special treatment?" He stalked back toward me. "When I refused to help you this past spring, you did everything you knew how to win me over, including bribing me with gourmet coffee every morning. Now that I'm willing to lend a hand, to be your friend, you're the one pulling away. Tell me. What has changed? Where's my damned cappuccino?"

I blinked. "You want coffee?"

"No, I want answers."

"I—I—"

"Whether you trust me or not, you need me."

"I do need you," I whispered.

In a rare show of raw emotion, Jack ripped off his sun-glasses and glared. Anger burned steadily in his green eyes. "Have I ever lied to you? Have I ever hurt you? Tell me, Casey, what have I done to deserve your keeping me at arm's length?"

I hadn't meant to question his honor.

"Well?" He crossed his arms over his chest.

"I . . ." My voice trailed off.

He waited.

"Because . . ." He didn't really want me to say this, did he?

He waited.

"Because if I let you get too close—" I said with a rush and then stopped myself. Fire scorched my cheeks.

I couldn't finish that thought.

If I said any more, I'd have said too much.

"Oh, Jack, you're a good friend to put up with me." I playfully punched his arm. "I'm sorry I doubted you. Must have watched too many *X-Files* reruns lately. They've made me obsessed with conspiracies."

He stared at the spot on his arm where I'd punched him. His silence unnerved me, so I kept talking.

"I did overhear Frank and Bruce talking. And I'm scared. That's not me being crazy. Who else in the admin-istration is involved? I don't know. Even if it's just the two of them acting alone, they're powerful men. I need help. I don't know what to do."

He finally dragged his gaze away from his arm. "You could call the police."

"Detective Hernandez thinks I'm a suspect," I reminded him. "He'll probably think I'm trying to confuse the inves-tigation. Besides, it's my word against Frank's and Bruce's. I don't have proof."

"That is a problem." He slipped his sunglasses back on and stepped back.

"If you stick around and help me with it, I'll—I'll not only buy you that cappuccino you seem to like so much, I'll also take you out for dinner," I said, ignoring my grandmother's number one rule for dating—*nice girls don't ask men out.*

Well, it wasn't really a date. It was dinner. Between friends. Friends ate dinner together all the time. Didn't they?

"If you don't want to go out for dinner," I continued, blathering on like an idiot while wishing he (or anyone) would stop me, "we could just have that cappuccino. Friends have coffee together. And we could talk. Or whatever you want. Just name it and I'll do it. I need you, Jack. I need help."

Alyssa had already warned me not to wait up for her tonight. The most recent amendments to the budget still needed three more votes, votes that she needed to help find, so she wouldn't be available to help me out of this.

If Jack abandoned me, I didn't know what I would do.

"You still don't get it," he grumbled. He walked away, shaking his head. "Come on," he said when I didn't follow. "I'm hungry, and you'll probably want to stop by your office and pick up your backpack and check the garden for slugs or something before heading to dinner."

He was right. I did have work to finish up.

Back at the White House, while Jack conferred with another CAT agent, I headed to the grounds office. Lorenzo and Gordon had finished most of the to-do list in my absence and were heading home. I thanked the two of them and promised to treat them to lots of gourmet coffee and pastries from the Freedom of Espresso Café over the next week. Once Lorenzo and Gordon had left for the night, I finished up the tasks that couldn't wait until morning and met back up with Jack. He followed me out to the vegetable garden. In the gray twilight, we stood side by side at the garden's periphery. I breathed in the scent of the vegetable blooms.

Some of the lettuce had bolted in all this heat. Dry seed pods hanging from the tall stalks rattled in the evening breeze. On Wednesday local schoolchildren would harvest those seeds and take them back with them to plant at their schools in the fall.

Like my grandmother's garden had done for me, the First Lady's garden would give several dozen children the gift of gardening that, if nurtured, could last them a lifetime.

I crouched down to stroke a downy eggplant leaf.

"Are you ready?" Jack asked.

Afraid my voice might crack like a nervous teenager's on her first big date, I nodded and grabbed my backpack.

As we walked through the downtown, neither of us talked. I was close to bursting at the seams with everything that had happened, but Jack discouraged it. "Let's go to your house, where it's private," he told me. "Then we can hash out what we know."

He was right. The last thing my career needed was for me to talk about these things in a restaurant. The way my luck had been going lately, I'd probably be seated next to an investigative reporter anxious to find his next big story, like that young Simon Matthews. I'd heard rumors about such things happening from other members of the White House staff. Whether those stories existed merely to scare us into practicing discretion or if they were actually true, it didn't matter. I had enough trouble on my hands. Lord knew I didn't need to go and do something indiscreet.

"Are there any yew bushes?" Jack asked as we entered the brownstone's small front yard.

"The European yew is actually a tree. And no, there aren't any in my yard."

He nodded, his gaze taking in the flowers crowding the twin beds that lined the walkway up to the front steps.

In exchange for a reduced rent, I'd agreed to upgrade and maintain the landscaping. I'd designed the small front yard to resemble the Victorian garden that might have flanked the front stairs when the brownstone was new.

I'd used a modernized version of the Victorian "Persian rug" planting that was popular on estates in the area during the late nineteenth century. Low-growing mondo grass formed the borders for a double interlocking diamond pattern. Within the diamonds, blooms created the fields of colors for the "rug," including pink and white dianthus and cosmos bursting yellow and orange.

"Are any of these poisonous?" Jack asked.

"Not particularly."

"What's in the back?"

"There's a small fenced area. I've not had an opportunity to do anything with it yet. It's mostly exposed dirt. I think the renters before us had a dog that liked to dig."

After he'd taken a look around the front, I let Jack into the apartment. He immediately conducted a thorough search of the rooms on the first floor.

"Do you think Frank or Bruce might be hiding behind the curtains?" I joked.

"Not really," he said with a smile, although he did peek behind the curtains in the living room once I'd mentioned it. "I'm looking for surveillance equipment . . . just in case. Better safe than sorry, you know? I'd like to see the backyard, too, if you don't mind."

The small backyard was accessed through a door in the small laundry room/pantry off the kitchen. We were losing what was left of the waning twilight as we descended the old wooden steps that led into the backyard. A streetlamp in the alleyway behind the brownstone flickered on. Soon, moths and other flying insects started to buzz around it.

The tiny backyard with bits of weeds popping up through the compacted soil looked as desolate as the last time I'd ventured out there. The small space didn't get enough sun during the day to grow vegetables. When I had a free moment, I planned to create a raised-bed border along the fence where I would plant shade-loving grasses. A small wall fountain would go nicely on the brownstone wall. The trickling sound of water and the rustle of the breeze in the grasses would help transform the dreary space into a garden oasis. I planned to cover the rest of the bare ground with stone pavers where Alyssa and I could keep a couple of lounge chairs and there'd also be room for an outside dining area.

"What's that?" Jack pointed to an untidy pile of branches near the wooden gate that led out to the alleyway.

"I don't know. That wasn't there when I took out the garbage yesterday."

I followed Jack to the pile of branches. They couldn't have come from the yard. Other than the few spots of weeds, the landscape was bare.

I picked a branch up and turned it over in my hand. The cut looked fresh—the interior of the branch still had a green tinge and felt soft when I pressed my nail against it.

"I don't know where these could have come from," I said.

"Can you tell what they are?"

I shook my head. "Someone peeled all the leaves off." I smelled it. "It's got a piney scent."

"Like an English yew?"

I dropped the branch as if it had stung me. "You don't think the leaves from these branches were used to make the poison that killed Parker, do you?"

"What I'm wondering is why these branches are here."

"Jack, I didn't kill Parker!"

He nudged one of the branches with his toe. "I never thought you did. You're not a killer, Casey."

I wouldn't go that far. Jack would change his opinion about me if he knew about the violent dreams that had haunted my sleep lately. For months now, I'd been dreaming I found the man who murdered my mother and his companions. Sometimes I'd gouge their faces with my fingernails until there was nothing left of their ungodly smirks. Other times I'd blast them so full of holes with a gun their bones would turn to jelly. And other times . . .

I shut the door on those thoughts and fisted my hands to stop the trembling. The memories of my mother and that horrible night were ancient history. They had nothing to do with my life now.

Jack flicked a glance at my fists, but didn't say anything.

I needed to focus. "These can't be the branches used to poison Parker's tea." I picked up the branch I had dropped. "Look here. The cut is too fresh. Whoever pruned these branches did it today."

"Then someone is trying to make you look guilty."

"Perhaps. You know, Frank was in the First Lady's kitchen garden this morning. He could have dropped that fake suicide letter. This could be his attempt to 'handle' me by making me look guilty of murder."

"How? Why would the police find these? Will he call in a tip? That seems risky."

"I don't know. I don't understand what's going on."

"I don't, either." Jack pulled his cell phone from his pocket. "We need to tell Detective Hernandez."

"Why? Didn't you just say someone would need to report the branches in order to make me look guilty?" Jack, Gordon, and Alyssa had all warnèd that I needed to tread carefully around the police. Their advice had finally taken root. "Besides, what are we going to tell him? 'Hey, Manny, someone left a pile of branches in my backyard'? I say we toss them in the Dumpster at the end of the alleyway."

"That's not a good idea. We need to report it."

I grabbed the phone from Jack.

He sighed. "Someone is deliberately trying to make you look guilty. Is it Frank or Bruce? I don't know. But I do know that we need to make sure Hernandez understands what's going on here before the killer, whoever that may be, completely ruins your career."

"Okay. Okay, I get that. Let me make the call. It's my yard, my word, my future."

MANNY HERNANDEZ ARRIVED ABOUT A HALF hour later looking rumpled. Both his shoulders and his mustache were drooping.

"Casey said that these weren't here yesterday," Jack told him as we stood around the branches. Manny kept a flashlight beam shining on them.

"The cuts are fresh. I think someone must have put them here this afternoon," I added.

"I wonder if it happened before or after you gave me that fake suicide note." Manny stroked his salt-and-pepper mustache thoughtfully.

"Have you been able to find out who dropped that note?" Jack asked.

Manny shook his head. "The angle on the video is all wrong. We can see who walked through the garden, but we don't see the note until you wrestle it out of the dog's mouth."

"So what do we do now?" I asked.

"I'll test these branches for prints, but . . ." He sighed. "It's still early in the investigation."

"I touched one of the branches," I warned.

"That shouldn't be a problem."

"There's something else you need to know." Ready the net, boys, I was about to prove to him that I'd lost my mind.

Manny clasped his hands behind his back, waiting for me to continue. Jack gave me an encouraging nod.

I drew a deep breath. "I know this will sound far-fetched." Not the best way to build confidence. I don't know why, but I cared about what Manny and Jack thought about me.

"Go on," Manny said. "Out with it."

"Frank Lispon and Bruce Dearing. I think they killed Griffon Parker."

"Go on," Manny said.

I repeated the conversation I'd overheard earlier that day. Manny listened. He nodded in all the right places. He even jotted several things down in that little notebook of his.

"Is there anything else you'd like to tell me?" he asked when I finished.

I thought for a moment before saying, "I don't think Francesca Dearing is involved, but she might know something. I think she tried to warn me this afternoon. And someone left a note that said 'Lispon's office' on my desk. Perhaps it was a warning."

He flipped the notebook closed and pushed it back into his jacket pocket. "Okay," he said. "I'll have another talk with Francesca. If that's all, I'll make sure these branches get tested."

"You don't believe me."

"I believe you overheard something," Manny said.

"But you don't believe Frank and Bruce poisoned Parker and are now planning to kill me," I said.

"No, Casey, I don't."

# Chapter Sixteen

*Man cannot live by bread alone; he must
have peanut butter.*
—JAMES A. GARFIELD, THE 20TH PRESIDENT OF
THE UNITED STATES

"**T**HOSE two men hold important positions in the government. They don't have time to play games like this." Manny pointed to the branches.

"But because I'm a gardener I have time for petty games and murder, so I'm a suspect?"

"You're deliberately twisting my words around, Casey."

"And you didn't do the same thing to me earlier today? Frank was in the First Lady's garden right before the photo shoot. The fake suicide note could have fallen out of his pocket," I reminded him. "Frank has just as much motive as I do. Parker has been a thorn in the administration's side from day one. You should have heard how the staff would curse Parker and his slanted articles. That's motive. He had tons of it. More motive to get rid of Parker than you think I have."

Manny shook his head. "It's not the same thing."

"You're right it's not the same thing. I didn't do anything wrong!"

"Calm down. I didn't mean to imply—"

"You didn't?" Jack quickly jumped to my defense.

"Questioning Casey at the White House made damned sure everyone on the staff wondered whether she put the poison in Parker's tea."

Manny pulled on a pair of latex gloves and stooped down to shovel the branches into a plastic bag. "I was only doing my job."

"You could have quietly asked her to come to the station to answer a few questions, and you know it. You made a point of singling her out."

"So?" Manny grunted.

"So, your interest in Casey regarding the murder and then the bomb scare this afternoon made the top brass at the Secret Service sit up and take notice. They're wondering if Casey is a security risk. If I hadn't fought for her, she might have lost her security clearance this afternoon."

"What? I almost lost my security clearance because of this?" If that happened, I'd miss the harvest. I'd be useless to Gordon and the First Lady. My White House career would be over.

"Yes. And if Hernandez keeps the investigation centered on you, your days at the White House will be numbered."

"But—" I started to say.

"Someone wants you to look guilty of murder," Jack said, "and is willing to use the police as a tool to ruin you."

"But I'm not guilty of anything!" I flapped my hands in frustration.

"Look, Casey," Manny said, "it's not that I really believe you are involved in Griffon Parker's death, but Jack's right. Someone wants us to think you are guilty by using the details of the murder mystery dinner you and Francesca had planned as the method for murder, and then there are these branches. I put some pressure on you; these branches popped up. Makes me wonder what else the killer might do to keep the spotlight of suspicion on you."

"I don't like it. You're playing with Casey's future and her safety," Jack argued.

"Manny, there has to be some other way I can help the

investigation. Whoever killed Parker has access to the White House gardens, which is my territory. If nothing else, I can serve as the eyes and ears for you there."

The detective seemed to consider this before nodding slowly. "Maybe there is something you can do."

**"DON'T BE A FOOL WITH YOUR LIFE, CASEY,"** Jack warned as he watched the detective put the branches in the trunk of his black sedan and drive off.

"I'm not being foolish. I only promised Manny that I'd ask a few questions around the garden." Why not? I'd already promised the First Lady as much.

"That's taking too much of a risk"

"No, it's not. I think I've finally started to see things clearly. If Frank and Bruce want me to take the blame for the murder they committed, if that's how they plan to 'handle' me, they won't hurt me no matter what I do. That would ruin their plan."

"Wrong. The killer, whoever that is, will hurt you if you are a threat."

"So I'll be careful."

Jack punched the wrought-iron railing in frustration, but followed me up the stairs.

His stomach grumbled.

"You're hungry. Shoot. I asked you out for dinner and then didn't feed you." Some date this had turned out to be. By the time Manny had left it was close to ten o'clock. "We could order pizza."

Jack shook his head. "With all this traveling I've been doing with the President lately, I'm burned out on fast food and pizza. I should probably just go home."

I didn't want him to leave when he was still upset. I didn't want him to leave at all. "Wait. You promised to help me come up with a plan. I don't have a plan yet. If you come inside, I'll fix you something."

*I'd fix him something?*

The offer had tumbled out of my mouth before I realized what I was doing. I knew how to bake a damn good chewy, gooey pan of brownies. But that one recipe summed up my entire culinary repertoire. If Jack wasn't in the mood for pizza, I doubted he'd welcome a dish of brownies.

"I image your grandmother taught you how to make all sorts of Southern dishes, like collard greens and hoppin' John." He smiled as he said it, probably imagining I'd whip him up some Southern fried chicken with all the fixin's.

"Um . . . yes . . . my *grandmother* is a fabulous cook."

Jack followed me through the apartment and to the kitchen in the back. "Would you like a beer?" I offered as I leaned against the open fridge door and peered into its frosty depths.

Milk. Soy milk. Beer. Soda. Jar of salsa. Lettuce.

Discouraged, I pushed the door closed, poured Jack's bottle of beer into a glass, and handed it to him. I then peeked in the freezer. Behind several half-eaten pints of Ben and Jerry's ice cream I found a package of chicken.

"Chicken!"

I grabbed the package and held it above my head as if I'd just won a gold medal at the Olympics.

"That'll work for me," Jack said with a chuckle.

But what the heck should I do with the chicken? I turned the pink foam package over in search of cooking instructions. There weren't any.

"Excuse me for a minute." I sidled toward the living room. "I . . . um . . . promised my grandmother I'd call her tonight. She'll be in bed soon, so . . . um . . . I'd better call her right now."

I stood in the front foyer as I dialed the phone number for Rosebrook, the stately mansion in Charleston's South of Broad neighborhood that had served as home-sweet-home to generations of Calhouns.

"Hello? Casey? Why are you whispering? Speak up. I can barely hear you," Grandmother Faye said after answering the phone.

"Is that Casey?" I heard Aunt Willow's voice in the background.

"Casey? Hand me the phone," Aunt Alba shouted. "I need to tell her about an article I read on the outbreak of violence in the D.C. area. She needs to—"

"Shush, girls. I can barely hear the child as it is. How are you doing, dear?" my grandmother asked.

"I'm good."

"Speak up, Casey."

"I'm good, Grandmother," I said loudly as I jogged up the stairs and sat on the top step so I could speak without worrying about Jack listening in. I mean, what self-respecting Southern girl didn't know how to—at the very least—fry up some chicken? "You remember Jack Turner, that Secret Service agent I told you about?"

"The nice young man who helped you this past spring? Of course I remember him."

"I've invited him for dinner, but I don't know what to make."

"He's sitting in your kitchen waiting to eat, I suppose?" Grandmother Faye knew me too well.

"Casey has a man in the house?" Aunt Alba squealed in the background.

"Good for her! A man will want to eat meat," Aunt Willow called out. "A bloody steak."

"I had thought we could go to a restaurant," I explained, "but it got late so quickly. I have chicken." I listed what else I'd found in the fridge.

"Honey child," Grandmother Faye scolded, "you need to stock up for occasions such as these. A proper lady doesn't let her guests go hungry."

"She shouldn't have a man in the house at this hour," Aunt Alba shouted. I heard the click of a second line being picked up. "You shouldn't have a man in the house at this hour," Aunt Alba said. "Not only is it unseemly, it's dangerous. Who knows what he'll expect you to do? And what if you don't do it? What then? Will he force—?"

"Shush, Alba. You'll scare the child," Grandmother Faye said. In my loving grandmother's eyes I'd forever be a child. Not that I minded.

"Should I try and fry the chicken?" I asked, hoping to get back to the reason I'd called.

"*No!*" both Grandmother Faye and Aunt Alba shouted.

"Lordy, you're liable to burn the entire house down," Aunt Alba said.

"Listen to me, Casey, don't try and fry anything," Grandmother Faye warned. "Do exactly what I tell you to do. Put the chicken in a baking dish. Cover it with the salsa."

She explained how to bake the chicken and suggested I toss up a light salad to accompany it. I tried to keep the directions straight in my head. Did I put the oven on broil or not? It wasn't easy to follow Grandmother Faye's instructions with my aunts constantly interrupting with warnings and advice.

"Don't use salsa, use mustard and lemon," Aunt Willow said. She must have wrested control of the second line from Alba. "And cook it in a skillet. If you have a potato, cook that as well. Men love potatoes. They also love steak. Are you sure you don't have time to go buy some steak?"

"Give me that." Aunt Alba wrested control of the phone again. "Broil the chicken. It'll taste better that way. And if he tries anything, hit him exactly like I showed you. That'll stop him dead in his tracks."

"Don't tell her that!" Aunt Willow shouted. There was a scuffling as the two sisters fought over the phone again. "She's going to end up a withered-up old maid like the two of us thanks to your meddling. You've made her terrified of men."

"I'm not terrified. Grandmother, tell them I'm not terrified of men. And tell them that Jack is a *friend*. Just a friend."

"I will, honey child. Enjoy your evening."

*I can do this*, I told myself after assuring my doting family that I loved them and would visit as soon as I found the time. I disconnected the call and headed back down the stairs toward the kitchen.

Years ago my aunts, who rarely agree on anything, had both tried to teach me to cook.

At the same time.

In the same kitchen.

As a result, while I could grow a cornucopia of vegetables, I didn't know how to prepare even a simple chicken dish for dinner.

*I can do this,* I repeated. All the dishes my aunts and I ever made during those cooking lessons ended up fit for only one place . . . the garbage can.

So what did Grandmother Faye tell me? Should I bake the chicken at four hundred degrees? For how long?

"How is your grandmother?" Jack asked when I returned.

Did she say I should put the oven on broil or not? "What? Oh, she's good." I turned the oven on and set it to broil. Broiled chicken sounded fancier than baked.

"Did you tell her about Parker's murder?"

"Um . . ." I placed the frozen chicken fillets in a baking pan and sprinkled some salt and pepper on them (like they do on cooking shows). "No. I didn't want to worry her about any of that. She worries about me too much already."

I slid the pan onto the oven's top shelf.

"Do you need a hand there?" Jack asked, rising from the kitchen chair.

"No, I've got it." I flashed him a forced smile and prepared an oil and vinegar dressing for the salad. "Thank you."

"Ohh-kaay," he said, eyeing the oven as if he thought it might explode or something.

"Don't worry. It's electric," I assured him. Grandmother Faye had told me to add the salsa when I turned the chicken over. Which reminded me, I needed to set a timer.

Once that was done, I pulled two more bottles of beer from the fridge, refilled Jack's glass, and poured one for myself.

I dropped into the kitchen chair across from Jack and sighed. "Been one hell of a day," I said after taking a sip of the beer.

"Uh-huh."

"You're still upset with me. You wouldn't be frowning so hard otherwise."

"I risked my life to protect you this spring. I didn't do it so you could get yourself killed three months later."

I sank down a little in the chair. "I'm not going to get hurt."

"You told Hernandez that you were willing to play games with a killer. I'd say the express train to disaster has already left the station. If you're lucky, you'll end up in the hospital. If not, you'll take that train all the way to the morgue." He lowered his voice. "I don't want to go to your funeral, Casey. I won't."

"What can I do? If Frank and Bruce poisoned Parker, it looks as if they want me to take the blame. It's not as if I invited them to use the details of the murder mystery dinner to carry out the deed. I certainly didn't want the police breathing down my neck at the White House. Nor did I ask anyone to dump a bunch of yew branches in my backyard. What do you want me to do, sit on my hands and hope enough evidence builds up against them so Manny has no choice but to believe me? What if that doesn't happen? What if it goes the other way and I'm arrested for Parker's murder?"

"We need to be smart about this." I liked the way he said "we." I really did want his help. "What we need to do is make it impossible for the killer to keep throwing the blame your way."

"I agree. Even if Manny doesn't think I killed anyone, a trial by the press would end my White House career."

"We can't let that happen." Again he used the "we" word. I bit my lower lip in a failed attempt to hold back a smile.

"What do you suggest *we* do?"

Always cautious, Jack took a moment to think about the question before answering. "First, let's cut through the conjecture and nail down what we do and don't know."

I fetched a pen and a pad of paper to take notes. "I know Frank and Bruce killed Griffon Parker."

"That's conjecture."

I frowned even though I knew he was right. "Okay, I overheard them talking. Frank was seen arguing with Griffon Parker the night of his death."

"What were they arguing about?" Jack asked. "That's something we need to find out."

"Right." I sat back in the chair. "We also know that the killer, who might be Frank, dropped the fake suicide note in the garden this morning."

"There's a good chance that the killer dropped the note, although that's not a known."

"You're too logical, you know that, don't you?"

"Perhaps you jump to too many conclusions," he tossed back at me with a smile. "But getting back to the fake note. Someone connected with the murder or the cover-up wrote that note and was in the garden this morning. Who in the garden also had a connection with Parker?"

"A motive, you mean?"

"Let's start with a connection. Motives can be tricky."

"You're right. Miss Marple mysteries often follow the thinnest threads to get to the murderer." I tapped my finger on my chin. "Francesca Dearing—along with her husband—was the subject of Parker's investigative report. Both she and Annie told Manny about the murder mystery dinner, but made it look as if I'd come up with the entire scenario."

"Were all three of them in the garden?"

"Bruce wasn't."

"Well, for now, let's put all three of them down."

I wrote their names on the list even though Bruce was the only one of the three I believed capable of murder.

"Let's see, Kelly Montague, the new *Media Today* star reporter, was in the garden. Parker had stolen papers that belonged to her. She was pretty upset about it."

I told Jack about my conversation with her and how she had tried to hide the papers sitting on her desk from me. I also told him about the threatening phone call she'd received.

"That makes her sound more like a victim of the plot than the villain," I concluded.

"I'm not ready to strike her off our list yet. Didn't Parker's death mean she's now *Media Today*'s top White House reporter?" He tapped the notepad. Reluctantly, I wrote her name on it.

We went through the list of everyone who had been at the photography session that morning. The only other person who had a connection to Parker was the First Lady. Griffon Parker was always writing damaging articles about her, the administration, and her husband. Despite that, neither Jack nor I felt it necessary to add Margaret Bradley's name to our short list of suspects.

"So these are our suspects?"

"Unless there's someone else we don't know about or haven't thought of yet," Jack warned. "What else do we know?"

"The killer put the yew branches in my backyard. That's a clue we can follow. Can you find out whether Frank or Bruce left the West Wing this afternoon?"

"I can," Jack agreed. "But Casey, let's not jump to conclusions. We don't know who put the branches in your yard or why. It might not be related to the murder."

"You can't be serious. It has to be—"

"I'm being cautious. Jumping to conclusions too quickly might prove dangerous. For you. I'm not willing to take that risk."

Touched, I quickly looked away and cleared my throat.

"So what am I going to do tomorrow and Wednesday at the harvest?"

"Nothing. Act normal. Keep your ears and eyes open."

"And ask those questions I told Manny I'd ask?"

"Are you trying to kill me?" Jack asked.

"What? You've tasted my cooking before?"

We both laughed.

"I just wish Francesca would tell me what's going on with her. She's upset. I'm afraid it's because of the story

Parker was going to write and that her husband and Frank 'took care of matters' before the story could get written."

"Besides the Dearings and Kelly Montague, who else was Parker investigating?"

"Me," I hated to admit.

We talked more about the evidence that Manny had against me. Griffon Parker had written my name in his notebook. It had been his last entry.

"I think Gillis Farquhar might have talked to Parker about me. He had nothing but complaints about my—I mean, the First Lady's—organic program for the gardens. And he admitted to knowing Parker," I said. "I'm sure my name was in Parker's notebook because of the article he was planning to write about the First Lady's garden."

"Let's not jump to conclusions about that," Jack said. "We don't know what line of research Parker was following when he jotted your name down."

I didn't agree, but to keep the discussion moving along I let him have the last word on that. After a while, I managed to steer us back to my main focus: Frank Lispon and Bruce Dearing.

"Those two have a long history together," Jack told me as he sat back in the chair. "They roomed together in college and have worked together in politics for decades. I haven't seen it myself but I've heard other agents talk about Frank. When we're traveling, he'll sometimes go off radar for a while. The speculation in the ranks is that he's meeting someone."

"Well, he's a good-looking man for his age and not married."

"Bruce sometimes disappears as well," Jack added.

"You think they might be out trolling for women when they travel?"

Jack shrugged. "It could be the scandal Parker was planning to spring."

"I don't know. The way the society lionesses were talking about it, they made it sound as if it had to be something bigger. What's so shocking about an affair? Those seem to erupt on a monthly basis. There has to be a nasty twist. Wait a minute, Lorenzo was telling me about some rumor about Frank and Bruce that was going around the White House last year. Do you know anything about that?"

Jack closed his eyes as he thought about it. "There was something . . ." He opened his eyes. "Oh, it was pretty far-fetched. Some of the other guys were saying that Frank and Bruce were close. More than friends."

"You mean . . . ?"

Jack nodded. "Romantically involved. I never believed it. I've seen those two together. They aren't involved in that way. Or if they are, they're experts at hiding their feelings for each other."

"That reminds me," I said. "Manny told me that Parker had sex the night he died. Don't ask me how he knew."

Jack started to explain forensics. I stopped him.

"I don't want to know," I said. "If the killer slept with Parker, which Manny seems to believe happened, and the killer is either Frank or Bruce, perhaps the rumors are true. That would be an embarrassing scandal for Francesca, and it would likely ruin Bruce's political career."

"So we need to find out if Parker preferred men or women?" Jack asked.

"I'll let you handle that one. Thinking of Parker getting down and jiggly with anyone makes my skin crawl."

"It's not something I want to picture, either, but I'll do it," Jack said.

"I'm not sure who he slept with even matters. Frank killed Parker."

"That's conjecture," Jack reminded me.

"You're probably right about that. Francesca seems to know what Parker had been threatening to expose. If the scandal did involve an affair between Frank and Bruce, I can't imagine Francesca would stay with Bruce knowing that that was going on behind her back. I simply can't imagine she'd put up with something like that. Besides, Annie insisted that Bruce and Francesca were above reproach, that they were the perfect power couple."

"Perhaps Annie doesn't know her longtime friends as well as she thought. Or perhaps she does and doesn't want to say anything."

"I'll ask Annie about this," I said. "She's known Francesca since childhood and Bruce for nearly that long. She should know what's going on."

"In the meantime, I think you should be careful around Bruce Dearing. He's got a nasty way of destroying his enemies both politically and professionally."

"And perhaps also literally," I added. "As in murder."

Jack made a face. "I think the chicken's done."

"It can't be. The timer hasn't gone off yet."

Narrow ribbons of gray smoke danced in a spiral pattern as they escaped around the door's seal.

I jumped up and threw open the door. The room filled with a cloud of smoke just as the fire detector started to scream.

"Open a window," I shouted over the deafening sound. I pulled on a thick oven mitt and rescued the chicken from the billowing smoke.

I quickly set the table and served the salad—a mix of romaine lettuce, hydroponic cherry tomatoes, and the oil and vinegar dressing. By that time most of the smoke had cleared and the fire detector had, blessedly, stopped screaming.

"Alyssa and I usually opt for takeout or delivery," I admitted, eyeing the chicken's thick black crust. I had to use a metal spatula to scrape the fillets from the pan onto a glass platter. I poked at them with the side of the spatula. Perhaps if I scraped off the blackened crust . . .

"It's fine." Jack took the platter and pushed one of the unrecognizable lumps of meat onto his plate with his fork. He chiseled off a blackened corner. "I've had . . ." He took a bite and chewed.

And chewed.

And chewed.

Finally, he washed it down with half his beer.

I put the other unappetizing piece of chicken on my

plate. Even though I rarely ate meat, I cut into it to find that although the outside had burned to a crisp the center was not only raw . . . it was still frozen!

"Don't eat that." I grabbed his plate before he could bravely carve off another piece, and I dumped the chicken into the trash. I then piled his plate with more salad.

"You would have been better off with the pizza," I said and set the plate back in front of him. My insides clenched. What Jack must think of me! I'm worthless in the kitchen. Worse than worthless. What with the looks of the charred chicken and the bitter stench of smoke lingering in the air, I thanked providence I didn't burn down the apartment. "I could make you a peanut butter sandwich."

"No, Casey. Don't worry about it. I appreciate the effort you made." He shoveled the salad into his mouth. "This tastes . . . different. What did you put in the dressing?"

"Just vinegar, oil, and a dash of Italian spices."

He swigged his beer. "I can really taste the vinegar."

I took a bite of the salad and was nearly knocked out of my chair from the vinegar's sharp tang. "Gracious, I must have added too much." I really did know better. My aunts had given up on my cooking lessons before we reached the salad section in the famous Junior League cookbook *Charleston Receipts*.

"It's different," he said just as his cell phone beeped. Frowning, he read the screen and punched in a quick reply.

"Is there a problem?" I asked.

"No. Not really." But he kept frowning. He shot a glance to the clock on the wall. "I'm sorry, Casey, I've got to run. Dinner was . . ."

*Awful*?

*Stomach pump worthy*?

I put my hands on my hips as I waited for him to finish that sentence he'd left dangling. I'd never known him to lie to me.

He cleared his throat. "Next time, I'll cook."

"Good idea."

He leaned toward me, his lips nearly brushing mine.

Suddenly I couldn't breathe.

Closing my eyes, I drew my tongue over my lips and waited for him to close the distance between us.

"Don't do anything rash, or even slightly daring," he whispered. "I won't be able to watch your back like last time. I've not been assigned to protect you. This time, Casey, you're on your own."

A featherlight kiss brushed my cheek. When I opened my eyes he was gone.

# Chapter Seventeen

*We can draw lessons from the past, but we cannot live in it.*
—LYNDON B. JOHNSON, THE 36TH PRESIDENT OF
THE UNITED STATES

**N**OT long after, Alyssa stood in the middle of the kitchen with her hands on her hips and her nose crinkled with concern. I'd just finished telling her about my day, every embarrassing and frustrating detail. Not that I needed to spell it all out. Evidence of my mortifying meal could be found in the blackened baking dish that sat soaking in the sink filled with warm soapy water and in the bitter stench of charred meat lingering in the air.

"It was a disaster," I told her, wringing my hands. "Not one thing went right today. Not one blasted thing. If I'd read my horoscope, I bet it would have warned me to hide under my bed."

Alyssa looked at the soaking pan with its blackened bottom, then at me, and broke out laughing.

"It's not funny," I protested, which only made her laugh harder. "First the garden—"

"Yeah, yeah. A disaster," she said, grabbing her knees as she continued to laugh.

"Detective Hernandez—"

"I know, I know." Tears filled her eyes.

"And Gillis—"

"Terrible." Her shoulders shook so hard that her black hair slipped free from its tortoiseshell barrette.

"And the fertilizer—"

"Yes. Yes. I'm mortified for you." She snorted, which made her laugh that much harder.

"And then this." I swung my arms wide.

She started laughing so hard she couldn't speak.

"What do you find so blooming funny about this?" I demanded.

"Because"—she had to gulp for air—"honey, you—you served a trained killer f-f-frozen chicken and he choked it d-d-down for you! You know what that means, don't you?"

I crossed my arms over my chest. "No. What? That Jack's got terrible taste in food *and* women?"

"No, silly goose." She straightened and pulled me into her arms as she twirled in a circle. "It means I've been right all along. Jack lo-o-oves you."

"Did you even listen to me?" I pried myself loose from her well-meaning but overbearing grip. "He—"

My cell phone chirped that overly cheery Katy Perry song. I was going to have to change the ringtone. I was not feeling at all cheery or perky.

With a violent yank, I flipped open the cell phone. The readout said "Unavailable."

Francesca's calls had been coming from a blocked number so I didn't hesitate to answer.

"Stay out of the garden," a gruff voice warned. I couldn't tell if the strange voice was that of a man or a woman.

"What? What garden? Who is this? Francesca?"

"Stay out of the garden or else you might turn up at the bottom of the compost pile."

"Who is this?" I demanded.

The line went dead.

I lowered the phone from my ear and stared at it.

"Who was that?" Alyssa asked.

I shook my head.

Alyssa grabbed my shoulders and guided me to the nearest kitchen chair and sat me down.

"Who was that?" she asked again.

"I don't know. I didn't recognize the voice and the call information had been blocked."

"Well? What did this mystery person say that has you looking so pale?"

I drew a slow, deep breath. And another. "Just someone trying to scare me."

"What exactly did the caller say?"

"That I needed to stay out of the garden." I started to dial a number on my cell phone. "Manny needs to know about this. It could be the killer trying to discourage me from asking questions tomorrow."

"You need to call Jack."

"No. Not Jack. He'll worry."

"Of course he'll worry. He's in love with you. I think it's romantic. Call him."

"No! I can't. It's not romantic. It's sad. I can't count on Jack—or any man, for that matter. He'll find a flaw or a prettier, younger woman or simply get bored. And then"—I snapped my fingers—"he'll abandon me."

And there it was, no matter how hard I fought it, at the root of everything that was wrong in my life.

*My father.*


**THE NEXT MORNING I WOKE UP AN HOUR EAR-**lier than necessary. My nerves felt raw and prickly as if a flock of starlings had been pecking at them all night.

Manny was still working on tracking down who had threatened me the night before. I'd told him to check Frank Lispon's phones, but Manny informed me that it wouldn't matter. The cell phone the caller had used was a prepaid throwaway phone.

He could tell me the general area where the call had been made—somewhere worryingly close to my brownstone apartment—but not who had made the call. Not something I wanted to hear.

I snapped at Alyssa when she asked if there was any coffee left in the French press, and then after getting dressed for the day I stomped out of the house itching for a fight. I wanted the killer to jump out at me so I could unleash the full force of my ornery self. No one, not some cowardly killer and certainly not a crank caller, had the power to keep me from my garden, not while I still breathed.

I was no longer the frightened little girl my father had practically handed over to a gang of assassins back in Phoenix, Arizona, so many years ago, and I refused to let the echoes of those little-girl fears drive my life.

With my homemade pepper spray—from potent habanero peppers cultivated on my kitchen windowsill—readily accessible in my front pocket, and an arsenal of gardening supplies along with my tattered copy of Agatha Christie's *Murder at the Vicarage* tucked inside my backpack, I marched through the early morning D.C. streets with such a determined stride that even the panhandlers avoided eye contact.

It was one thing to put yew branches in my yard. It was quite another to try to scare me out of my garden. The slug responsible for Griffon Parker's death had better watch out.

Halfway to the White House, I turned down a street that ran past Burberry Park. A young mother sat bouncing a toddler on her lap on the same statue's marble stone base where Parker's body had been found. Although the police had removed all signs that anything sinister had happened there, I shivered.

Parker, even from beyond the grave, wouldn't welcome my attempts to help him.

"I don't care what you think, buster. Whether you want me to or not, I'm going to help you find your peace," I said with an edge to my voice.

Across the street, I spotted Annie Campbell emerging from one of the more modest brownstone town houses. She locked the door behind her and hurried down the steps. I hadn't realized she lived so close to the scene of the crime. Had she seen something that morning? Was she covering up to protect her best friend's husband? I needed to talk with her about so many things.

I called out to her, but she didn't hear me. She scurried down the street with just as much determination in her step as I had in mine. Naturally, I followed.

Annie, wherever she was heading, seemed to be in quite a hurry. She pushed aside an old homeless woman who'd stepped in her way.

The poor woman stumbled. Her green and white carpet bag—which probably held all her worldly possessions—went flying. I caught the older woman before her knees hit the concrete sidewalk. After making sure she was steady on her feet again, I gathered up the few belongings that had spilled from her bag and handed it back to her.

"For you," the woman said with a hacking cough. She reached into her pocket and pulled out a shiny copper penny.

I tried to refuse, but she pushed it into my palm and closed my fingers around it. "For luck," she said as she continued on her way down the street. "For luck."

By that time, Annie had gotten far ahead of me and had turned a corner. I jogged to the corner, hoping to catch up, but she had disappeared again. Thankfully, she hadn't gone too far. At the next cross street I caught sight of her as she ascended a set of brick stairs that led up to an elegant clapboard-sided town house. We were still only a few blocks from Burberry Park.

Annie banged on the door until it flew open.

Frank Lispon, looking as angry as a rabid hound, emerged from the town house. I gasped at the sight of him.

Did Annie realize the danger she'd put herself in?

Instead of grabbing her and dragging her into his home, the press secretary stepped onto the front stoop and closed the door behind him.

He was dressed in gray suit pants and a white "John

Bradley for President" T-shirt that looked as if he'd hastily pulled it on over his well-developed chest. His feet were bare.

I moved in closer. Annie turned her head, searching up and down the street. I stepped behind an oak growing in the planting strip along the sidewalk before she could see me.

Frank, his mouth set in a grim line, crossed his arms over his chest and leaned forward. He towered over Annie's petite frame.

She did all the talking and poked him in the chest several times until he caught her hand and pushed it away.

She then reached into her pocket and pulled out something. I squinted. It looked like a sheet of paper.

Whatever it was, Frank hadn't expected to see it. He tried to snatch it out of her hands, but she danced down the steps and took off running.

Frank followed down to the bottom of the steps. With his running ability, I was sure he could have caught her if he'd really wanted to. I had my hand on my cell phone, ready to call for help if he tried to hurt her. But he spotted me and pushed his hands into his pockets and watched her run away.

Once she was out of sight, he shrugged and turned to head back up to his town house.

"Frank!" I called out.

He stopped midway and turned back around. "What do you want?" he asked, narrowing his gaze as I approached. "What are you doing here?"

"Walking to work," I said, amazed at how well I hid my jangling nerves.

"Oh. Have a good morning." He started back up to the house again.

"I didn't know you lived so close by. I should call for a ride when it's raining." Presumptuous, I know. But I couldn't think of anything else to say until I blurted out what I really wanted to find out: "I didn't know you and Annie Campbell were acquainted."

"We're not."

"But I just saw her leaving here."

He glanced down the road as if he expected her to return. "Yeah, I was surprised she knew where I lived. We've met here and there, usually at parties at the Dearings' house. The last time I saw her was shortly after the inauguration."

"Huh, that's odd. She's one of my volunteers. I expect to see her tomorrow afternoon at the harvest. Would you like me to talk to her to find out what she wants? She's a widower. Perhaps she's lonely."

"Annie definitely isn't looking for *that* kind of companionship from *me*."

"Then what did she want?" I pressed.

"She seemed to be upset that the rumors surrounding the Dearings are persisting and wanted me to do something about it."

"I've heard they've been friends since childhood."

"Well, I guess that explains it." He shrugged again. "I'd better get inside before the neighbors start to talk. I'll see you around, Casey." He took the steps up to his brownstone two at a time. I waited until he disappeared inside and the door closed behind him.

Frank had lied to me about why Annie had popped up at his door. She had something—*evidence*?—that Frank desperately wanted to get away from her.

Would he now feel compelled to "handle" her like he'd promised to "handle" me and had already "handled" Griffon Parker? If that was his plan, he'd have to go through me first.

Unlike my father, I'd never abandon someone in need.

# Chapter Eighteen

*Labor disgraces no man; unfortunately, you occasionally find men who disgrace labor.*
—ULYSSES S. GRANT, THE 18TH PRESIDENT OF
THE UNITED STATES

I hurried to the White House feeling hopeful that I could quickly knock my to-do list down to a reasonable size so I could take some time off to find Annie and figure out how I could help her. But at the grounds office door I found Janie Partners, one of the female members of the Secret Service's Presidential Protection Detail, waiting for me.

Even though she always dressed in a conservative black suit with a white blouse as seemingly required by Secret Service, Janie let her personality shine through in little ways. She dyed her hair a stark white blond and wore it in a short pixie cut. Tiny embroidered yellow squashes dotted the dark green scarf she wore around her neck.

"We have a problem," she said before I even had the chance to greet her.

"Not the First Lady's garden again." I groaned.

She nodded.

"But Steve promised that Milo would be watched."

"Milo's been locked up all night. I noticed when the

First Lady took him on his morning romp around the grounds this morning that something had ripped apart several of the plants in her vegetable garden."

"Again?"

Janie nodded.

"How did the First Lady take it?"

"She wasn't pleased but handled herself with her signature grace. She appeared confident that you'd be able to fix it."

"Well, in that case," I said as I slid my gardening shears into the leather holster I wore on my hip and scooped up my basket and wide-brim straw hat, "I'd better get to work."

The garden looked as chaotic as it had the day before. The only difference was that this time when I made it down to the garden, I found several staffers from the West Wing and the White House kitchen, including the top toque herself, with their sleeves rolled up and starting to repair the damage.

"We're here to support you," Penny from the press office said with a smile. "And look, none of the First Lady's favorite peppers were damaged."

"It's not much, but I'll take that as good news." I pulled on a pair of gloves and joined the others in repairing the garden.

Perhaps a raccoon was sneaking into the garden in the middle of the night. But, oddly, although the plants had been pulled from the ground and trampled—some beyond repair—none of the vegetables had been eaten. Wouldn't a raccoon or squirrel or rat have feasted on the bounty it found?

Just to be safe, with the assistance of Jerry and Bower, the two troublesome members of the grounds crew, I installed netting designed to keep garden pests away from the plants we intended to harvest the next day.

I also took the opportunity to talk with Jerry and Bower about their past work habits and what was expected of employees at the White House.

"No one told us that they weren't happy with our work," Jerry argued.

"Didn't Lorenzo talk with you?" He'd volunteered to do it.

Both men shook their heads. "We joked around with Lorenzo for a bit," Bower said. "He's got a twisted sense of humor." Both men laughed. "Didn't say nothing about our work."

Well, I did. I told them they needed to worry about doing their work and not go wandering around the grounds. Jerry shrugged and walked away. Bower gathered up the rest of the tools. "Lorenzo was right," I heard him mutter as he headed to the storage shed. "*Bitch*."

"What did you say?" I asked sharply. My temper was already sparking, and those two layabouts with molasses in their britches weren't helping.

"I said 'peach.' It's just peachy. Everything is peachy," he called over his shoulder without breaking his stride. "Got work to do."

"Yes, you do." And so did I.

Lazy. Lazy. Lazy. My aunt Alba would say of men like them—and she said it often—that even dead fleas wouldn't fall off those boys. And she'd be right.

Once my work in the garden was done, I tried to call Annie's number. Her voice mail picked up so I left her a message to call me back.

I then called Jack's number to tell him about Annie's confrontation with Frank. His phone also went to voice mail. I left him a short message and asked him to call me back.

I had a bad feeling about Annie. Perhaps I needed to go check on her. I was heading that way when Lorenzo grabbed my arm.

"You have to help me, Casey," he said. "Jerry and Bower were going to help with the Fourth of July plantings, but I can't find them."

"I just spoke with them. They were heading toward the storage shed." I gestured in that direction. "I thought you were going to talk to them about their work habits. They said—"

"I tried to talk with them." Lorenzo huffed. "They're

worthless. Those two need to be fired, but we don't have time for that right now. Can you help me? The plantings can't be put off any longer. Please, Casey. I shouldn't have let it go this long. I need your help."

What could I do? If the planters didn't get done on time, it would put yet another negative spotlight on the grounds office. I couldn't let that happen to Gordon.

Lorenzo and I drove the grounds office's nondescript white van over to the White House greenhouses, located on the outskirts of D.C., to make holiday planters.

We grew many of our plants for the gardens and various special projects within the greenhouse facility's long, domed structures. Today, using the same thirty-gallon concrete Grecian urn–shaped containers used for the Easter Egg Roll, Lorenzo and I designed two dozen Fourth of July displays to be placed around the exterior of the White House.

Because of the summer heat, all the vents in the greenhouse were open and the large fans on the far wall ran constantly. Even so, it was hot and humid and ear-splittingly loud inside the building.

I wiped sweat from my brow before checking my cell phone. Annie still hadn't called. Neither had Jack.

Even though my ability to concentrate was nonexistent, I pulled on my gardening gloves and tried to work. Each planter would get a red, white, and blue display. The tallest plant—sweetgrass that I'd brought from my grandmother's backyard in Charleston—went in the back of the container. The tall grass with its light purple flower stalks mimicked a spray of fireworks blasting into the air. In front of the sweetgrass we planted dwarf blueberries that were heavy with the bright blue fruit. Then came bachelor's buttons (or cornflowers) thick with white blooms, and at the front of the container we planted calibrachoa (or million bells). These looked like tiny petunias, blooming like crazy with a profusion of deep red flowers that cascaded down the front of the container. The end result produced festive red, white, and blue layers.

Lorenzo hummed tunelessly as his hands moved with a smooth motion. He finished one planter and started another

before I could finish one. He added a few ornamental
onions from the species *Allium schubertii* to his pots. A
brilliant choice. The pale pink flowers looked like minia-
ture exploding fireworks blasting out of the pots.

That tiny detail transformed the plantings into something extraordinary.

Lorenzo shrugged when I told him that.

"Did you do anything fun over the weekend with your
new girlfriend?" I asked, trying to strike up a friendly conversation with him.

"Not really," he mumbled, and he started to hum again.
Although he wasn't the most personable gardener I'd ever
worked with, I respected his skill and his eye for design.
He placed the plants in the potting soil with the same care
a father would take tucking his son into bed.

He gently patted the soil around a blueberry plant. "I
heard that *Organic World Magazine* will have an article
about your kitchen garden in its next issue.""

"It's not my garden. It belongs to the First Lady." I
picked up a pot with a sweetgrass plant. "I'm glad to hear
that the garden will finally get some good press."

"I didn't say that," Lorenzo said. "They faxed a copy of
the article to the East Wing this morning, and the office
made a copy for Gordon."

"And?" My heart started pounding. Hard. I respected
*Organic World Magazine*, read every issue from cover to
cover.

"According to them, the garden is contaminated with
lead, and you—yes, they named you specifically—were
putting the First Family's lives in jeopardy. It also mentioned that you were doing a shoddy job going organic and
gave some suggestions on how you could improve."

The trowel in my hand clattered as it dropped to the
wooden potting table. "They said there were dangerous
levels of lead in the soil? That's . . . that's crazy."

Lorenzo gave one of his trademark shrugs. "Crazy or
not, the magazine hits newsstands tomorrow."

I was shocked, shocked down to my toes that my work

would be attacked by my fellow gardeners—organic gardeners at that!

"The article didn't happen to suggest that the White House let Gillis Farquhar take over, did it?"

Lorenzo clucked his tongue. "Jealousy looks ugly on you, Casey. Gillis is a good guy. He's spending his own dime and taking time out of his busy schedule to help the White House. And you're blaming him for an article that has nothing to do with him. I bet if you could, you'd pin your garden troubles and Parker's murder on him as well."

"I wouldn't do that," I protested. "Wait a minute. You know Gillis?"

"Yeah, I've known him for years. I worked on his show when he was just starting out. Talk about a neurotic professional. He expected everyone around him to be as hard-working, nose-to-the-grindstone focused as he was. That was before he went off the deep end and became an econut and all, but you have to respect the guy. He knows his plants, and he's generous with his knowledge."

"If it's not Gillis, then who is feeding lies to the press? Who is trying to hurt the First Lady's reputation?"

And mine?

"How should I know? Let's get these planters done. It's hot as hell in here."

It took some effort, but I picked my trowel back up and carefully eased the sweetgrass from its plastic pot.

Lorenzo had already turned his focus back on the plants in front of him. Humming that same tuneless note, he tucked another plant into its soil bed.

I carefully pressed the plant into the rich potting soil and then checked my phone. Was this thing working? Annie should have gotten my message and called by now.

My mind kept circling back to what Annie knew about Frank's involvement in Parker's death. Why hadn't she gone to the police? Was she scared for her life? Or trying to protect Francesca?

By lunchtime, Annie still hadn't returned my call. I tried her again. No answer.

I tried Francesca's old number. Still out of service.

I tried Jack's number. No answer.

Lorenzo and I packed the patriotic planters into the van and headed back to the White House. All the way back, I worried for Annie's safety.

As soon as the van had passed through security, I jumped down from the passenger seat.

"There's Jerry and Bower. They can help you unload the planters. You don't mind, do you? I have an urgent errand to run," I told Lorenzo, who grunted.

No one answered the door at Annie's house. I knocked again, louder this time, while calling both her cell phone and her home phone.

"She's not home," a woman called to me.

"Do you know when—?" I turned around to ask when Annie might return. My mouth stopped working when I saw the woman heading across the road from Burberry Park. "Kelly? What are you doing here?"

"I—I'm not sure." Kelly Montague stopped at the bottom of Annie's steps. Although her dark purple suit looked perfect, her dark hair was a mess, as if she'd pulled her hands through it multiple times. "Annie Campbell's neighbor"—she pointed to the adjacent town house—"said she left this morning and hasn't returned. I was hoping to ask Mrs. Campbell some questions."

That last part made my neck muscles tighten. "Is this about an investigative report you inherited?" I had hoped she would prove to be a serious reporter. Not one that just looked for flash.

But why shouldn't she go for the flash? Going after the sensational stories would bring in the ratings, which in turn would boost her career.

"I know that you lied to me the other day. I saw the papers on your desk you were trying to hide. Not that I'm surprised about it. I heard how all the news organizations are digging around, trying to figure out what Parker was working on when he died. I would understand why you'd want to break the news story before anyone else. After all, the story belongs to *Media Today*."

She paled. "I wouldn't do that. Even if I wasn't receiving those threats, I would never pursue the story Griffon had . . ." She glanced down the street. "He stole that story from me. If I had never come to D.C., he'd still be alive. I'm sure of it."

"You are? Have you told the police this?"

Tears sprang to her eyes as she violently shook her head. "I can't."

I led her back toward the park. "Talk to me, Kelly. Tell me what's going on here."

She twisted away from me. "I can't. I can't talk about it."

"Why? What's going on?"

"He's in danger. That's why. Because of me, he's in danger."

"Who is in danger?" I forced myself to ask calmly when I wanted to shake her and scream at her. If someone's life was in danger, she needed to go to the police. And if the police refused to listen, she needed to keep talking, write articles, and do news reports until she got the help she needed. "Talk to me, Kelly. If not me, you need to talk to someone. If a life is in danger, you have to act."

Her entire body trembled as she stared at me. Was she trying to decide whether she could believe in me, trust me? I didn't know what I could say to convince her that I wanted to help her. In this town, it sometimes felt as if everyone was out for themselves, that it was an eat-before-you-get-eaten kind of world.

But while some people in the nation's capital lived that way, not everyone did, not by a long shot. Being the new girl in town, Kelly had no way of knowing that yet. Nor did she know which of her colleagues and which of her friends she could trust. I understood that.

Heavens, I was struggling with enough trust issues to give a seminar on the subject.

I grabbed Kelly's hand. "I don't want to exploit you for

a news story. I don't care what kind of trouble you are in or why. I'm not here to judge you. I know what it feels like to be alone in the world." More than she could ever guess. "That's why I want to help you."

She swallowed deeply.

"Whose life is in danger?" I asked again.

"I don't know!" she cried.

# Chapter Nineteen

*I may be president of the United States, but my private
life is nobody's damned business.*

—CHESTER ALAN ARTHUR, THE 21ST PRESIDENT OF
THE UNITED STATES

"YOU don't know?" I demanded. How could that be
possible?

"I can't talk here," Kelly said and yanked her hand from
my grasp. "I'm being watched."

At that moment her cell phone chimed. She blanched as
she glanced down at it.

"Who is it?" I asked.

She showed me the caller ID readout. "Unavailable."

"It's the killer." Kelly glanced around. "And I'm sure
we're being watched."

I grabbed the phone as it continued to chime. All of the
calls I'd received from Francesca had said "Unavailable"
on the caller ID. "Let me answer that."

"No!" Kelly and I played tug-of-war with the phone.
I won.

It didn't matter, though. The call had already been sent
to voice mail. I handed her back her phone.

"So what do you want to do? Do you really think you
can keep on ignoring this? Do you think doing nothing will

stop the killer? It won't. And can you really let Parker's murderer go unpunished?"

She shook her head as I asked that last question.

"I can't do this alone," she admitted. "You said you had connections with the Secret Service. Do you think some-one there could help me? *Quietly* help me? I don't want to be the reason anyone else gets killed."

"I'm sure we can find the right person. Now will you tell me what's going on?"

"Not here." She hurried out of Burberry Park.

When I didn't immediately follow, she whirled back around. "We're being watched. The phone call is evidence of that. We need to leave. Now."

I dialed Jack's number as I followed Kelly. I'd read enough mystery novels to know I needed to tell someone else my location and what was going on. Kelly had been in the First Lady's garden shortly before the fake suicide let-ter had been found. Had she dropped it? Also, I hadn't for-gotten how she'd landed Parker's choice position in the White House press corps after his death.

The threatening phone calls could easily be staged. Why else wouldn't she want me to answer the phone?

I had to be careful.

Jack's cell phone went directly to voice mail. Again. I hung up and texted him that I was with Kelly Montague and was leaving Burberry Park.

"What are you doing?" Kelly demanded when she noticed I had my phone out.

"Texting my location to a friend."

"That friend doesn't happen to be with the D.C. Police, does he?" Her voice rose. "I told you that I can't go to the police. If I do I'll be responsible for someone's death. You said I could trust you!"

Actually, I hadn't told her that. Not explicitly. I was hav-ing a hard enough time finding trust in my own heart that I wouldn't ask it of others.

"I'm not contacting the police. I'm doing exactly as I

said, texting my location to a friend. There's a murderer on the loose. I don't know who the killer is." Even though I had strong suspicions that Frank Lispon was guilty. "Or what that person is planning."

"You think that I'm—"

"I think I have to be careful." I lifted my hand as I clarified. "You should be careful, too. Neither of us should go off without letting someone else know where we are. It's simple common sense."

She glared at me as I finished up the text and hit the "send" button.

"Tell your friend that you're going with me in my car." She gestured to a shiny black Range Rover parked at the curb. "I need to get away from here. If we drive to the zoo, it's public, but there are private spots where we can talk."

"I have a better idea," I said. "Let's go to the U.S. Botanic Garden. It's at the base of the Capitol Building and there are plenty of private niches. Even if we are followed, no one will bother us there." And I knew the garden like the back of my hand, unlike the zoo.

"I don't know . . . Maybe I shouldn't be seen with you. It might be dangerous."

"Kelly . . ." I didn't want her to run away now. If she knew something about Parker's murder, she needed to start talking about it. "Put together another short piece about the White House, about its kitchen garden."

"But a report about the garden and nothing else is so . . ."

"Fluffy? Yes, yes. That's what Parker thought, too. He'd only bother with the garden if he could dig up a scandal, which was why I assume you were in the kitchen garden interviewing my volunteers yesterday. You were out there hoping for dirt. Well, here's a story for you. Someone has been feeding lies and half-truths about the garden to the press. Case in point, there's an article coming out in tomorrow's *Organic World Magazine* that claims the First Lady's kitchen garden is contaminated with deadly levels of lead.

I don't know where the author of the article got that information, but it's wrong."

"Is it?" Kelly's brows shot up. "That's a serious charge."

"Yes! It is wrong. We did the soil tests. They're available for public review. Yes, there are traces of lead in the
soil. This is an urban area. It would be odd if there weren't
some sign of lead in the soil. That's why we tested for it in
the first place. But there's not enough lead to be dangerous,
not by a long shot." I wondered if the article's author even
bothered to look at the test results. "This isn't the first negative article. I think someone is acting behind the scenes to
discredit the First Lady." Or me.

"Can I quote you on that?"

"No! Gracious, no." Now I started to get nervous. I was
no longer working with dear old Southern ladies. While
what I said in the backyards of Charleston could and did
sometimes get repeated and turned around to my detri-
ment, my thoughts and opinions never ended up making
the six o'clock news or the morning edition of a national
newspaper.

"But there is a story here," I said. "An explosive story."

She thought about it for a moment. Her lips relaxed into
a smile. "Yes, there is a story. I'll get my editor to run a
teaser on the TV scroll. That should explain to anyone who
might be watching me why I've been seen with you.
Get in."

The United States Botanic Garden, practically in the
shadow of the Capitol dome, sits at the far end of the
National Mall. In the middle of the day and at the height of
the tourist season, it took forever to find a parking spot.
The Metro would have taken less time.

George Washington, Thomas Jefferson, and James
Madison all had a hand in the development of the Botanic
Garden. It had opened on the National Mall in 1820. The
facility, with its gardens and glassed conservatory, moved
to its present location in 1933.

Several of the horticulturists who worked or volunteered at the Botanic Garden greeted me with excitement

and hugs. With everything that had been going on in the First Lady's kitchen garden, it had been a while since I'd gotten a chance to visit with my friends and colleagues here. I chatted with each of them briefly about their projects—they tend more than sixty thousands plants at the gardens, a staggering amount that never failed to amaze me—and introduced Kelly, telling them that she was researching a story on the First Lady's garden.

Once the niceties had been taken care of, I found a relatively secluded bench underneath a large cocoa tree in the main glass conservatory. It was a spot where we could watch people passing by. The tree backed up against the greenhouse wall. It would be difficult for anyone to sneak up from behind and listen in on our conversation.

Kelly paced in front of the bench.

"This is difficult," she said several times.

I watched her in silence. She'd either tell me what she needed to tell me or she wouldn't.

I hoped she would.

"I know this may sound silly coming from a journalist and all. I mean my job is to publicize the truth, to get people talking about events that are happening. And here I am, anxious to hide what is possibly the most important event of my life. I don't want people talking about this. It's private."

"White House employees are the models of discretion. We don't go blabbing what we know to anyone. And the Secret Service has 'Secret' in their title for a reason. Believe me, they know how to keep what they know to themselves. To a fault. Drives me insane how secretive they can be."

Kelly nodded.

She swallowed deeply.

And then mumbled something.

"Pardon me?" I leaned forward. "I couldn't hear what you said."

She sat down next to me and squeezed her hands between her knees. "I said I'm searching for my father."

"What would you do that for?" popped out of my mouth

before I realized it. I cleared my throat. "Your father, you say?"

She nodded. "That's why I pushed to get this assignment. I could have had the weekend anchor spot for *Media Today*'s national morning news. That's a big position, a step away from the weekday anchor. I turned it down in favor of the White House assignment because I wanted to find my father. I wanted to know if he even realizes I exist."

"I see." It was my turn to swallow deeply.

"A few days ago I was convinced I'd found both my father and my mother. Not that I really care to find my mother. She left me on a doorstep in rural Virginia in the middle of the night. I was only hours old. It was winter and snowing. And she leaves me outside? How can I forgive her for that?"

"But you were found? Saved?"

"The neighbors saw a car pull away and investigated. The family who owned the house where I was left were away." She smiled as she looked into the distance as if peering into a memory. "My adoptive parents were the neighbors who found me. They took me in. They cared for me and loved me as if I belonged, as if I were their natural child."

"You were lucky."

So was I. My father may have abandoned me, but I had a grandmother and two aunts who loved me like they loved no other.

Kelly nodded. "But no matter how loved I was—how loved I *am*—at home, the questions about my birth parents never go away. I have long fantasized of the day I would meet my father. Would he recognize me? Would he be surprised to learn I existed? When I started this search I had little to go on, only an investigative reporter's instincts and a longing to learn the truth."

"And have you found him?"

"I thought I had. But I was wrong. I thought Bruce Dearing was my father. I even thought his wife, Francesca, could be my mother. I do look a little like her. But look at me."

"What about you?"

"I'm African American, or at least partially. They're not. We couldn't be related. And my blood type and Bruce Dearing's . . . it's not a match." Her shoulders dropped. "I was so certain. And now . . ."

"Parker stole the research you were using in your search for your birth parents?"

She nodded. "Parker seemed to know more about all of this than I did. About twenty-five years ago, the presidential election cycle would have been heating up. Ronald Reagan, a two-term president, couldn't run again, which left the slate of candidates wide open for both parties.

"Parker told me that there'd been a rumor of an indiscretion surrounding one of the popular politicians at that time. He hinted that he was talking about the presidential candidates."

"Do you know which politicians were vying for the presidency?"

Kelly nodded. "Besides George H. W. Bush and Michael Dukakis, Bruce Dearing had entered the race as a dark horse. Some thought that if he didn't get the nomination, he'd be a shoo-in for the vice presidency. A young, unattached John Bradley was also running for Congress for the first time. I mention that because when Parker found out about my research, President Bradley was the first person he mentioned."

"Do you know why?"

"When I asked, Parker got all twitchy and secretive. Said there'd been a scandal that had been hushed up at the time. 'It's an explosive story I wanted to tell, but I didn't have all the details, and my editor pulled the plug on me,' he said. He then stole my papers. And then was found dead in that park the next morning."

"That makes you a suspect," I pointed out.

"I know. The police keep asking me questions about what I was doing Friday night. But I had no reason to want Parker dead. I never wanted his job. I simply want to find my father. And yet I'm sure my searching for him caused Parker's death. So doesn't that make me guilty of something?"

"I don't know. Everyone in D.C. wanted to see Parker gone."

"You're right about that. Every day I meet someone new who loathed Parker. Actually, I wasn't convinced about the connection between my research and his death until I started to get the threatening phone calls."

"Can you tell if the caller is a man or a woman?"

She shook her head. "The voice is gruff. Muffled."

"You need to tell the police about the phone calls. It could be the big break Detective Hernandez needs to catch the killer."

"No! I can't! You don't understand. The caller is telling me that if I talk to the police my father will be murdered! Murdered before I can find out who he is!"

Several people turned to stare.

"Oh, God." Kelly jumped up. "What if the killer followed us here? What if he heard me?"

I glanced around. Frank Lispon and Bruce Dearing weren't anywhere in sight. "I'm sure it's fine. Sit down."

"No! I shouldn't have come. I've put my father's life in danger by talking to you." She ran out of the conservatory. I chased after her.

I made it through the heavy double doors and had caught her arm when a black town car—a common sight in D.C.—screeched around the corner at a most uncommon speed.

"Look out!" I screamed as the car jumped the curb.

I dove out of the way, dragging Kelly with me.

Too late. Too late.

Kelly's arm tore from my grasping fingers as the sedan slammed into her. Her head cracked against the sedan's windshield before she was thrown onto the sidewalk.

The car sped away. Kelly lay in a crumpled heap like a broken doll. A pool of blood formed a halo around her head.

\* \* \*

"TWO REPORTERS DEAD." SPECIAL AGENT IN
Charge Mike Thatch grimaced. His gaze dropped to the
hospital's linoleum floor.

Manny Hernandez nodded gravely.

"Kelly's not dead," I said.

She was in the ICU unit at the end of the hall on life
support. The car's impact had fractured her skull along
with several ribs and her right arm, and it had punctured a
lung, but she wasn't dead.

Thatch ignored me. "Both reporters were White House
correspondents for *Media Today*. This is clearly an attack
on a specific media outlet. Naturally we'll increase security for the press at the White House. Bryce has already
sent out an investigative team to coordinate with your men
on what happened." William Bryce was the Secret Service's assistant director in charge of protective operations.

As soon as Jack had received my many text and voice
messages, he'd rushed over to the hospital still dressed in
his black CAT fatigues. Unfortunately, in order to leave his
post he'd had to request time off from his supervisor, Mike
Thatch. When Thatch heard I was involved with the accident, he'd insisted on accompanying Jack to the hospital.

"The attack on Ms. Montague changes the focus of our
investigation into Parker's murder. Any assistance you can
provide with names of known threats would be appreciated," Manny said.

"You're welcome to our data. The FBI will have information as well."

"I've already contacted them," Manny said.

"Then it's handled. It's a shame, really." Thatch glanced
down the hall. "She was so young."

"Kelly's not dead," I repeated.

He turned toward me. His expression hardened.

"Don't you have plants to tend?"

I did.

The sky outside the window was showing the first signs of morning gray. I'd gone to the hospital with Kelly and even though I wasn't allowed to see her, I didn't have the heart to leave, not until her adoptive parents arrived.

I glanced at my watch. Five o'clock. The First Lady's harvest was to begin in a few hours. Whether I had the heart to leave or not, I'd run out of time. I had to get ready for work. Manny had already headed for the bank of elevators. I jogged to catch up to him and caught his sleeve.

"Are you going to follow up on what Kelly told me about her search for her father?" Despite my vow to keep silent about what she'd told me, I couldn't keep this information from Manny. Too many lives were at stake. Manny needed to know.

"I will pull her caller history," he said. "I'll do what I can, but honestly, Casey, I can't see how Kelly's searching for her birth father could have acted as a trigger for someone to murder Parker."

"You'll believe it once you talk with her. She was terrified, not for her own life, but for her father's life."

"I hope I do get a chance to talk with Kelly." He glanced down the hall and at the double doors that led into the ICU ward. "I sincerely hope she wakes up."

I'd heard the doctor's assessment. Her chances for survival were grim.

That didn't mean any of us needed to give up hope.

"You will get to talk to her," I insisted. "She's strong. She's going to survive this."

Manny patted my shoulder and smiled indulgently. "I hope so. If we find the folder you described with her research in it, I'll assign an officer to follow up on that information as well."

"You haven't found it? Are you saying it's gone?"

"It's still early in the investigation," was all he'd tell me.

"And Annie? Have you found her yet? I still haven't been able to get in touch with her."

Manny shook his head. "We don't even know that Annie is missing, Casey. All we know is that we have two attacks on two reporters who work for the same news organization. One is dead. One may not survive the day. As I told you before, I have to go where the evidence leads me. And the evidence is not taking me to missing fathers or murderous press secretaries."

"But—"

Manny's cell phone buzzed. He held up a hand and answered with a curt, "Tell the chief I'd be able to get some damn work done if he'd stop having dispatchers call for progress reports."

His face grew scarlet as he listened.

"*What?*" I breathed.

The string of curses that followed made me blush. He jogged toward the elevators and slammed his fist against the "down" button. The violence of his actions startled me.

"What? What's happened?" I demanded as the elevator doors slid open.

Manny stepped into the elevator and slammed his fist against the "door closed" button several times. When I tried to follow, he blocked me. "I don't need a damned gardener nipping at my heels. Get Jack and go home."

"What's going on?" I called out as the doors started to close.

"Another White House reporter has been found dead. Looks like—" The thick elevator doors clanged into place.

# Chapter Twenty

*Don't hit at all if it is honorably possible to
avoid hitting; but never hit soft!*
—THEODORE ROOSEVELT, THE 26TH PRESIDENT OF
THE UNITED STATES

"JACK? Wake up."

He was slumped down in the plastic chair in the waiting room. His arms were crossed over his chest. His head, tilted at an awkward angle, rested on his shoulder. How he'd managed to fall asleep with the commotion erupting all around him, I couldn't imagine.

"Jack?" I lightly touched his arm.

He stretched. The chair creaked as his weight shifted.

He took one look at me and shot, fully awake, to his feet. "What's wrong? What's going on? Kelly's not—"

"Kelly's condition is unchanged. Manny won't listen to me." Tears sprang to my eyes.

I should have pushed harder, asked more questions. My voice broke as I told Jack, "Another reporter has been murdered."

"My God. What happened? Which reporter?"

I couldn't answer. I had to get out of there. I started to run back toward the bank of elevators.

Jack followed. "Talk to me, Casey. I mean it."

I flapped my hands as tears rolled down my cheeks. I felt as helpless now as I did when I was six years old. I couldn't stop the murders.

And damn it, I didn't want to cry.

Jack grabbed my shoulders, pulled me into his arms, and held me against his chest. I wrapped my arms around him and held on as if my life depended on his embrace.

I'd spent so much energy not trusting him, not letting him get close. And for what purpose? To protect me from getting hurt? I felt more alone and hurt now than ever before. I needed Jack. Desperately.

I don't know if I lifted my head or if Jack lowered his. Perhaps we met somewhere in the middle. His lips pressed against mine with a fierce need.

I responded with a neediness of my own.

The antiseptic hospital corridor, D.C., and the world, for that matter, melted away. Everything I was, every hope, dream, fear, and insecurity, poured into that kiss.

The moment lasted a lifetime and was over too soon. Pain stabbed me in the chest as our lips parted.

"What was that about?" I whispered.

"Us," he answered.

As much as I liked how that sounded, this wasn't the time for there to be an "us." Another reporter had been killed because I'd not asked enough questions. I pushed at Jack's shoulder to get him to back up.

A mistake.

My knees had gone all watery on me. My legs buckled, and I started to fall.

Jack caught my shoulders.

"I . . . um . . ."

"Come on," Jack said. "Let's get out of here."

From dangerous stud to just dangerous, Jack transformed into a warrior on high alert as we exited the hospital. The lights in the adjacent parking structure glowed an eerie yellow as we crossed several rows of cars and followed a ramp up one level.

Wheels squealing, a car rounded a corner.

Jack grabbed me and pushed me between two parked SUVs. The car whipped past us. And kept going.

"Just a careless driver," Jack said. "My car's over there."

He pointed to a battered Jeep. Its faded red paint had been completely worn off in several spots. The fenders were dented. The soft top had a rip that had been meticulously mended.

"A Prius would be more economical," I said.

He smiled and shook his head.

"Where are we going?" I asked after climbing into the Jeep's passenger seat. "I have to be at the White House in about an hour."

"I know. I do, too. I'm taking you home."

"Good. I need to shower and change."

On the ride through the quiet D.C. streets, Jack got on his phone to one of his Secret Service buddies.

As he talked, I sat on the edge of the passenger seat. My nerves were perched at the edge as well.

"What? What did he say?" I demanded as soon as he hit the phone's "end" button. "What did you find out?"

Jack tossed his phone to the Jeep's dashboard and turned a corner before answering.

"Simon Matthews was found dead in his apartment a few hours ago."

"Matthews?" I pressed my fingers to my lips as I pictured the young reporter with those thick glasses peering at me from over his laptop. "Everyone has been saying that he was vying to become the next Griffon Parker."

"It won't happen now. The police still need to do an autopsy. At the moment, though, it looks as if he was poisoned. His computer was smashed."

"He didn't work for *Media Today*. Manny will have to listen to me now."

"I learned something else," he said as he pulled to a stop in front of my brownstone apartment. "They found the car that hit Kelly. The bastard drove it to a secluded boat landing on the Potomac and set it on fire. The license plate, which was registered to a blue Nissan, matched the plate you saw on the black town car."

"I can't believe someone would do that. Kelly had said that someone was following her, but I didn't see anyone on the drive over to the Botanic Garden," I said as I opened the passenger door and slid out of the Jeep.

Jack followed. "The police still don't have a description of the driver. But they're pushing hard to find an eyewitness, a security camera along the route, anything."

"Have they questioned Frank Lispon regarding his whereabouts yesterday?" I asked.

"Sorry, Casey, he's not even on the police's or the Secret Service's radar. It may make good reading for a thriller— press secretary cracks and goes on a killing spree, knocking off the White House press corps—but it's not real."

"He's not targeting everyone in the press corps, just the ones who were on the verge of finding Kelly's birth father."

I pulled out my keys to the front door. Jack stood beside me, a pillar of strength when I felt ready to collapse. His kiss still tasted fresh on my mouth. I wanted to forget the harvest, the murders, all of it, and wrap my arms around him and kiss him forever. Just thinking about it left me more than a little dizzy.

"So what do we do now?" I asked.

"You let me in."

ALYSSA WAS STILL ASLEEP AND WOULD BE FOR another half hour. Jack waited on the sofa in the living room while I went upstairs, took a quick shower, changed into my best work clothes, and pulled my hair into a ponytail.

When I came back down the stairs, Jack followed me into the kitchen. "I'm making oatmeal and toast," I said. "Would you like some?"

"No. Thank you, but no. I'll pick up something at the White House." He hightailed it out of the kitchen as if pursued by wolves.

Once I'd finished heating the oatmeal and had the toast safely buttered on my plate, Jack leaned into the kitchen to survey the danger. Finding none, he crossed the room and poured himself a cup of coffee I'd brewed, smelling it before taking a tentative sip.

"Not bad," he said as he sat down at the small maple kitchen table with me.

"I'm not a complete disaster in the kitchen," I said as he smiled into his coffee mug. "Nothing was destroyed the other night. The fire department didn't have to be called."

"Good for you. Set that bar high." He set down his coffee mug. "Something's been bothering me about what happened yesterday. How do we know the town car that hit Kelly wasn't aiming for you?"

"Because . . ."

I didn't have an answer for that.

Jack did. "You're the one who's been asking questions."

"Not that many!"

"Did Kelly find yew branches in her backyard?" he was quick to ask.

"No, but she was getting threatening phone calls. I overheard one of the calls."

"So you both were at risk. She gets the calls. You get the branches in your yard. I don't like it, Casey."

"Actually, after you left the other night I received a threatening phone call, too."

"You did? Casey! Why didn't you call me?"

"I called Manny. He traced the number. So far he's hit a dead end. The call came from a throwaway cell phone."

Jack took several deep breaths before asking, "What did the caller say?"

"He—I think it was a he—told me to stay out of the garden or else I'd end up at the bottom of the compost pile. Well, that's not happening. I'm not going to stay out of the garden."

Jack held his coffee mug so tightly his knuckles turned white. "You and Kelly are both at risk. But while she'll be well protected in the ICU, you are a walking target."

"What do you suggest I do?"

"First we're going to the White House. That's the safest place for you right now. And then—" He hesitated. "Damn it, whoever's doing this is getting desperate. The police will move swiftly, but I'm afraid they're going to end up pushing our killer to strike again. And soon. When that happens, I'm afraid the killer will come straight for you."

"And Kelly's father."

"Yes, his life is in danger, too."

"He may have already gotten Annie," I said. "I can't let anyone else get hurt or killed. I have to do something, Jack."

"I hate to say this, but I think you're right. Stay at the White House. It's the safest place for you. No, let me finish. While there, use your contacts with the gardening volunteers and find out everything you can about Francesca's scandal and Kelly's birth father."

Jack was encouraging me to ask questions? "Do you think Francesca and Kelly are somehow connected?"

"I don't know. We don't even know if that's the reason Parker and Matthews were killed, but we need to find out. The police and the Secret Service are focusing on searching for a mental or a terrorist who has a grudge against the White House press coverage. For all we know, that's the motive. But if it's not, if someone is killing in order to keep a scandal from becoming public, then anyone connected to that scandal is in danger. The fastest way to stop what's happening is to expose the secret that the killer is desperate to hide. Kill the motive, we stop the murders."

"I like that plan." I quickly swallowed the last of my orange juice and grabbed my backpack. "Let's go."

IT DIDN'T MATTER THAT I HAD NO SLEEP. I FELT alert and ready for anything.

"I know that the White House's security is second to none," I told Jack after he accompanied me through the White House's iron gates, "but I have a bad feeling something's going to happen at the harvest."

Jack stopped abruptly in the middle of the small parking lot near the East Wing. "The Secret Service will be on the South Lawn in full force to protect the First Lady and everyone else. What could happen?"

"I don't know. Just the other day the killer dropped that fake suicide note in my garden."

"You mean the First Lady's garden," Jack corrected.

"Smart aleck. Of course that's what I mean. Everyone who was in the garden the day I found the note is going to be back today. Except perhaps for Annie. I pray she's okay."

"I do, too. Look, I trust your instincts. I'll talk with Thatch and Bryce about having some extra guys down there. If anyone lifts a finger the wrong way, the Secret Service will see it."

"Really? You trust my instincts? After my disastrous training session, I thought you'd do the opposite of whatever I said."

"That training session? Didn't I tell you already? There was no possible way you could have passed."

"No, you didn't tell me that."

"Oh, I meant to. I remember—you were on the phone that day, and I only had a few minutes before I needed to herd another group of staffers out to the training center. Well, I'm telling you now. Thatch threw everything at you, including the kitchen sink."

"He did? Why?"

"I don't know. To embarrass you? To discourage you from getting involved in our work? We occasionally do no-win training sessions like that. They encourage us to think outside the box, to keep us alert. We know that any given training session could be an impossible one. You didn't."

"Then why were you upset with me that day?" I asked.

"I wasn't upset with you. I was upset with Thatch for pulling such a dirty trick. I tried to catch up with you afterward, but you left so quickly."

"Wouldn't you have done the same thing? I was embarrassed."

We had to move when a car pulled into the parking lot.

"Why didn't you call me after that?" I asked. "I thought we were friends. Friends call each other."

"You could have called me," he countered. And then he smiled. "Listen to us bicker. Between the training sessions and traveling with President Bradley, I barely had time to change my shirt before we were off to another location. Believe me, I'd much rather have dinner at your house than shovel down a cold take-out meal in a plastic container."

"That's not a smart choice. My cooking doesn't get much better than it did the other day."

"It's what I want."

I was speechless.

"You can do this," he whispered and brushed a brief kiss against my lips before heading off toward the West Wing, where the Secret Service offices were housed.

What did Jack want?

*Me*?

Really?

I couldn't believe it. No man in his right mind would willingly want to eat my cooking, especially after having tasted it.

He had to be lying.

Only, Jack never lied. *Honey child, the only man a woman can truly trust is her daddy*, Aunt Alba had once told me.

"No, Aunt Alba, you're wrong," I said as I headed toward the North Portico and the grounds office below it.

Trust wasn't an award presented to only a select few, but a gift I needed to learn to give to myself.

It had become too dangerous not to.

# Chapter Twenty-one

*Farming looks mighty easy when your plow is a pencil and you're a thousand miles from the corn field.*
—DWIGHT D. EISENHOWER, THE 34TH PRESIDENT OF
THE UNITED STATES

I stopped by the grounds office just long enough to check my messages, grab my gardening shears, basket, and wide-brimmed straw hat before making my way to the kitchen garden.

Although the White House hadn't seen the likes of a kitchen garden since FDR's victory garden, a time when forty percent of the country's produce came from home gardens and backyards, the practice of raising vegetables for the household on White House grounds actually dated back to its very beginning.

John Adams, the first president to reside in the White House, demanded only one thing before he'd agree to take residence. He wanted a vegetable garden large enough to supply food for the coming winter. Throughout the White House's history, everything from ponies to sheep to turkeys have munched on the lush South Lawn. It was once as American as apple pie and fireworks on the Fourth.

So why did so many journalists and pundits feel the

need to publish scathing criticisms of the current First Family for reviving one of the most basic home and hearth traditions?

Some said the garden was a fake. Others said it wasn't organic enough. Still others complained that it was too organic and that the President was forcing his weirdo organic preferences into hardworking Americans' backyards.

Just that morning Lorenzo had forwarded me an e-mail that had gone viral. The e-mail claimed to have insider knowledge of President Bradley's sinister plans to force every American family to grow a kitchen garden of their own. Too tired to do anything about it, not that there was anything I could have done, I deleted the e-mail.

If only I could concentrate on gardening and ignore everything else.

I needed to make today about the First Lady and her garden, but I also needed to dig up all the information I could about who knew that Kelly had been searching for her birth father.

Annie Campbell was still not answering her phone. Kelly Montague was still in the ICU, her condition unchanged. And Simon Matthews, the young go-getter geek, was dead.

"No more," I said. This was going to end today.

From the top of the hill, I spotted several West Wing staffers and the White House pastry chef standing at the edge of the garden. I frowned at that.

Those volunteers had spent enough time in the garden to be able to weed and pluck insects without waiting around for supervision. Actually, many of them had made it a habit to start their day in the garden as a way to grab a piece of solitude before diving into the problems of the world demanding their attention. None of them had gotten to where they were in the world today by standing around and waiting for someone to tell them what to do.

Something had to be wrong. I picked up my pace.

Jerry and Bower from the grounds crew joined me on the walk down the hill.

"Remember, we're not making any major changes," I told them.

"God, look at that," Jerry said and nudged his buddy in the ribs with his elbow. "A giant Pepto-Bismol bottle is heading this way."

I followed Jerry's gaze and spotted Francesca Dearing swathed from head to toe in a vibrant pink pantsuit with a white straw hat. She hurried across the lawn from the southeast gate. The tail ends of a pink paisley scarf tied around her neck fluttered in her wake.

Bower chuckled. "Looking at her makes my stomach ache."

Jerry laughed even harder.

"Stop that," I snapped.

The two men's gazes shifted toward me. They glared for several seconds before Jerry shrugged and moved away. Bower followed. I suspected from their smirks and nudges that they were still talking about Francesca's brightly colored outfit.

Enough was enough. I pulled them aside and gave them a quick but stern lesson in White House decorum.

Before I'd finished, a White House workman dressed in a dark blue uniform and wearing black gloves tapped me on my shoulder. His team was busily erecting a white canopy tent at the bottom of the hill and had several questions for me. He knew the White House chefs planned to use the tent as a workstation for preparing and serving the harvest lunch, but wasn't sure about the configuration.

I explained what had been decided. "We'll also need extra tables for the schoolchildren so they can help prepare lunch." I then showed him where they should put the four extra tables.

"Busy day, today," Francesca said. "What do you need me to do?"

"I'm planning to make a quick sweep down the rows and check for problems and then pull out the hoses to water the plants. I could use your help." We walked over to the edge of the garden together. I raised my voice to address the volunteers who were waiting. "Pull any weeds that might have popped up overnight. Clip off any dead leaves or branches. If you have a question about whether something should be removed, ask me or Gordon, who'll be along soon, before—"

*Get a feather and knock me over.*

"Is this a prank?" My voice squeaked as I stared in horror at a vegetable garden I didn't recognize.

Over two dozen bloodred chili peppers, long and skinny, bounced in the stifling, humid breeze. The spicy devils reminded me of dead men swaying from the gallows, their legs curling in agony.

Or perhaps the feeling of agony came from the growing tightness in my throat.

*Three months of work.*

"We didn't plant red chili peppers."

*Frank Lispon had already provided the press with a detailed list of the garden's vegetables and had let the press loose in the garden to interview the volunteers.* It had been his idea to do those things. He'd stepped in and changed the East Wing's plan for press coverage.

Was this his doing?

The First Lady preferred large, sweet bell peppers to their spicier brothers. Where were the red, green, yellow, and chocolate-colored bell peppers?

I'd spent at least an hour every day, sometimes seven days a week, keeping watch over the vegetable crop contained within the fifteen-hundred-square-foot plot. Nearly all of the plants had been started at the White House greenhouse facilities from heirloom seeds provided by Thomas Jefferson's historical gardens.

In less than three hours, two busloads of inner-city schoolchildren, along with Washington's major power players, were scheduled to descend on the First Lady's garden for its first public harvest. Not to mention the press hungry for a scandal. A feast, prepared using the freshly picked fruits and vegetables, was to follow.

The press was going to feast on this all right. They'd gather like aphids on lettuce.

The First Lady had entrusted me with her garden.

The bamboo teepee trellises were still there, but the tomato plants—already bursting with flowers and immature heirloom tomatoes—that had covered the trellises had vanished sometime in the night.

And over there. How did *that* happen? Round globes of cabbages squatted in the section of the garden where Thomas Jefferson's favorite variety of tennis-ball lettuce had thrived just a day before.

"This . . . this is a disaster."

"Back up! Casey's going to faint," Francesca declared with such passion that the oversized brim of her white gardening hat flopped down and swatted her in the face.

Francesca, however, was sorely mistaken. I had no intention of fainting, thank you very much.

Before I could tell her just that, she brushed her hat's wide brim back into place and grabbed my wrists. "You need to take deep breaths, my dear." With a powerful jerk, she raised my arms above my head.

The brightly dressed Francesca didn't seem to notice the other volunteers watching us with their mouths gaping in various stunned expressions. "Don't let some silly chili peppers bother you, Casey."

"But—but we didn't plant chili peppers, and the tomatoes—"

"Never cared for tomatoes. If you ask me, they're grossly overrated."

"The heirlooms we planted were dripping with flavor," I argued. "Did your husband do this?"

"Bruce? Why would he care about—"

"Or was it Frank? Is this how they plan to get me out of the way? To destroy me? Is this why you invited Gillis? So even more members of the press would be here to witness this?"

"Now, dear, don't be fanciful. No one wants to destroy you. You're working yourself into a dither. Breathe with me," she commanded while yanking my arms up and down in a broad motion and taking exaggerated breaths. Her arms held surprising strength under her bright pink linen suit.

I closed my eyes and drew in a deep breath in concert with Francesca before shaking my wrists free.

Tears sprang to my eyes when I looked at the garden again. I quickly blinked them away. As my grandmother Faye said to me time and again, the Calhoun women weren't born; we were forged from steel.

My ancestors stood against marauding Union soldiers, crippling economic depressions, and the insidious boll weevil. I could handle a few misplaced plants. I just wished I wasn't so darn tired.

"Thank God." Gordon Sims grabbed me and threw his arms around me in a tight hug.

"Mhat grff fuffn?" I tried to ask, but it came out all muffled. I wiggled out of Gordon's surprise embrace. "What's going on?"

"You're safe. When I heard about the attempt on your life yesterday I aged at least ten years," he said.

"This has aged *me* twenty." I pointed to the garden.

"Oh, my." Gordon stood silently beside me. His hands, timeworn and leathery from years of working the land, clasped and unclasped several times before he said anything. "None of the White House staff, not even the staffers from the West Wing, would behave in such an unprofessional manner and pull a prank like this."

"No, they wouldn't," I agreed. Everyone at the White House, especially the household staff, took great pride in serving the family in residence with the utmost efficiency and grace.

This may be the People's House, but to us, we served a family who considered the White House their home.

"If not someone on the staff, then who? Who could have done this?" I turned toward Gordon. "How could this happen? The White House is under constant surveillance. No one could have sabotaged the garden without being seen. Do you have any ideas?"

"It's rather like one of those lockbox mysteries, isn't it?" he said.

"I believe it's called a locked-room mystery."

"Whatever you call it, I'm sure once you put your Miss Marple skills to work, you'll track down the plant thieves."

I had to clasp my hands behind my back to keep from wringing my skin clear off. "This has to be related to Parker's murder," I muttered. "The killer is trying to scare me off. Or get me fired."

Gordon's silver eyebrows shot up. "Casey, you need to stay clear of that. You could have been killed yesterday."

"But I wasn't."

He kept his eyebrows raised.

I had to bite my tongue to keep from telling him that I felt pretty damn certain Frank Lispon and Bruce Dearing were behind not only Parker's and Matthews's murders but also the attempt on Kelly's life and this . . . this . . . garden catastrophe. "If I happen to stumble upon the identity of a murderer, that's good, right?"

Gordon paled. "Just how deep have you gotten yourself involved with the investigation? Was that car aiming for you yesterday?"

"I don't know. I've not asked enough questions to have anything figured out. That's something I plan to remedy today. Don't look at me like that. I need to protect myself. If I didn't know better, I'd say Parker was trying to ruin me from beyond the grave."

"Casey, I hope you remember what happened the last time you started asking questions."

"We don't have time for a waltz down memory lane," I said. "Right now we have to fix the plants, and we have to do it before the schoolchildren, the VIPs, and, *heavens*, the press arrive."

Gordon watched me for a few moments and then sighed. "You work on the garden. I'll talk with Mrs. Bradley"—he gulped before adding—"and Seth Donahue."

"Bless you, Gordon." I kissed his cheek.

"Don't bless me too quickly." He stopped me with a

hand to my shoulder. "We also need to apprise the Secret Service of what happened. *You* need to do it."

"Unless . . ." My thoughts swirled as if caught in a hurricane. "What if we can get the garden cleaned up before the harvest celebration? Certainly we don't need to alert the—"

"If we don't . . ." He shook his head. "Trust me on this, Casey. Get the Secret Service in on what's happening now."

I didn't like it, but I nodded. Gordon had thirty-plus years as White House gardener. He knew better than anyone what needed to be done first.

As Gordon hurried back up the hill, I called the volunteers out of the garden and had them wait under the shade of a stand of linden trees. Francesca helped by answering questions and keeping the volunteers entertained and occupied.

Jerry and Bower, I noticed, had disappeared. Again.

"What am I going to do?" I muttered to myself as I paced the length of the garden.

How did one solve a locked-room mystery . . . in the middle of a garden? Was such a thing even possible?

The fences. The twenty-four-hour surveillance. If Frank or Bruce wanted to frame me for murder, why muddy the waters by sabotaging a defenseless garden? The *First Lady's* garden, at that.

Perhaps they were trying to keep me busy so I wouldn't have time to best them at their game. Was that the reason? Or was this about something else?

Why embarrass the First Lady?

I rubbed my temples to ward off the start of what promised to bloom into one wicked headache. I didn't have time for aches or pains. In a couple of hours several members of the White House press corps were going to descend that hill to prowl over every inch of this garden in search of controversy.

A small weather station stood watch over the small slice of Eden we'd created like a silent sentry, dutifully recording the temperature and moisture. Honeybees buzzed about the blueberry bushes and raspberry vines, while slender green lacewings patrolled the raised beds of deep green rhubarbs in search of insurgent pests.

Gone were the eight varieties of heirloom tomatoes that the volunteers had tended, dutifully tying the tomatoes' reaching vines to a system of bamboo latticework. Only the latticework remained.

At least the Three Sisters were still intact. The corn, beans, and squash had been planted together in mounds where the three plants could benefit and support each other, an ancient Iroquois practice that naturally renewed the soil for future crops.

Had I laid the foundation for ruin, both mine and the garden's, by taking an interest in Parker's murder? No, I refused to believe that.

However, Frank Lispon knew what kind of damage a garden fiasco would cause for me. He knew that a major part of the harvest's press kit included a list of the plants along with a colorful schematic of the garden's layout.

By sabotaging the garden, he would give credibility to the reports on fringe blogs calling the kitchen garden a fake, a conspiracy to fool the American public. A disaster like this would pull those fringe reports over to the main-stream media.

Frank had occasionally joined his colleagues and volun-teered in the garden, not that he knew his plants. I hadn't forgotten how, early in the season, he'd pulled out an entire row of young pea seedlings he'd mistaken for weeds.

Had that been an early effort to discredit me?

Poor Milo had taken the blame when Steve Sallis dis-covered the garden had been damaged over the weekend. Raccoons had been blamed the second time. But what if it had been Frank all along?

Perhaps Annie had seen Frank sabotaging the garden and confronted him with the evidence of his misdeeds the morning before.

I knew of one sure way to find out. I whipped out my cell phone and dialed Jack's number. Not his personal number, but the number to the Secret Service office in the basement of the West Wing. "We've got a problem," I said to the agent who answered. "I need a team to meet me in the First Lady's garden ASAP."

"We don't have time for problems," a deep voice rumbled directly behind me. The owner of that voice must have stepped through the bushes surrounding the nearby Children's Garden.

I whirled around and found myself standing toe-to-toe with the devil himself.

Frank Lispon.

# Chapter Twenty-two

*We do not need to burn down the house to kill the rats.*
—HERBERT HOOVER, THE 31ST PRESIDENT OF
THE UNITED STATES

STARTLED by Frank's sudden appearance, the word that popped out of my mouth was colorful enough to have painted a bright flush on Grandmother Faye's cheeks.

"Things that bad, eh?" Frank asked. He pushed his hands into his pants pockets.

He was dressed in a dark blue tie and light gray suit pants. He must have left his jacket in the office, smart man. The temperature had already climbed close to ninety degrees. The sleeves of his white shirt were rolled up to his elbows. His dark skin glistened with a light sheen of sweat thanks to this heat wave that refused to break.

"I should have worn something cooler. We're all going to be dripping wet before this damn harvest is over. I hope I'll have time to change before I have to tackle this afternoon's press briefing regarding the budget fight," he said as I stared, my mouth gaping.

I pressed my lips together and wiped a layer of sweat from my forehead with the back of my hand. I had to swallow a couple of times before I managed to get my voice to work enough to hurriedly finish my call with the Secret Service agent.

"I know what's going on," I said to Frank. My voice sounded low, menacing, like a warning growl. I knew I'd told Jack that I'd only ask questions, but after finding the garden in ruins how could I not confront Frank? "I know why Annie came to your house yesterday morning."

"I see." He straightened his shoulders, making himself appear even taller. "What do you plan to do about it?"

"What—what do I plan to do? I'm going to tell everyone. What else would you expect?"

"I don't know what I expected from you. You're from the sheltered South. I suppose the choices I've made must sound shocking to you. In D.C., I assure you my lifestyle is more common than you might think."

"Lifestyle? Common?" I shouted. "Are you insane? I can't believe . . ." No, wait, I could believe it. Washington, D.C., wasn't like my genteel, old-world Charleston. Some of the people here, especially those with political aspirations, seemed to live in a different world. They played by different rules, rules where winner takes all, and the mentality was always to win at any cost.

Facts had to be carefully checked, because everyone in this town lied.

*Not Jack.*

Everyone *else* lied.

"I'm surprised you don't deny it," I said, my anger at Frank and the political environment that had spawned him growing stronger with each beat of my heart. "Lie. Cheat. Steal. Kill. All in a day's work, isn't it?"

My words seemed to bounce off him.

"Did you run down Kelly Montague yourself? Or did you pay someone to do it? All she wants is to find her birth father, you know. She wasn't writing a story."

"Kelly was doing what?"

"And Matthews? He seemed like a good guy. Now he's dead, too."

"If you think his death didn't affect me, you should—"

"Do you even care that your latest stunt hurts the First Lady? If you're trying to protect the President, wouldn't you want to protect her as well?"

"The First Lady?" His head jerked back. "What do you mean I'd hurt the First Lady? I'd never—"

"This!" I swung my arm to point at the garden so hard that I actually stumbled to my knees.

"Have you lost your mind? What are you talking about?"

"This disaster! I expect you to fess up and fix it!"

"Fix what?" Frank reached out a hand to help me up and then withdrew it. His gaze shifted toward the White House. "What the hell is going on? What the hell did you do? The press is going to be all over this."

A CAT dressed in their battle dress uniforms charged down the hill toward us, rifles held at the ready. Behind them, an Emergency Response Team followed with their menacing P90 assault weapons. With all that firepower coming in our direction, a raw memory of another time, another place, slammed into me with the force of a speeding bullet.

I'd locked that memory away so tightly, I'd forgotten all about it . . . until today.

I was four or five years old at the time that it had happened. My father had charged into our tiny cottage in France. His face was flushed, his breathing quick. A gun was in his hand.

"Get our things," James Calhoun barked at my mom. "Now."

"Did you get it?" she asked.

"Yes." He handed her a package wrapped in a linen handkerchief that she slipped into her dress's pocket.

"Did they see you?" She pulled out the box she kept under the kitchen table.

"I don't know."

"What's going on?" I asked. "Why are you scared?"

Daddy had no answers for me. He pulled back the drapes. Standing off to one side, he peered out the window.

"I've been followed. Go out the back way. I'll slow them down."

"Are you sure?" Mom asked.

"Daddy!" I wailed.

He grabbed my shoulders, gripping me so tightly it hurt. "I need you to do exactly what Mom says. Don't talk. Don't make a sound. Your life, my life, your mom's life depends on you obeying us. Understand?"

I nodded, even though I didn't understand at all.

"Go!" he shouted.

Mom grabbed the box and my hand. I had to run as fast as my tiny legs could carry me to keep up with her.

We were at the back door when I heard a splintering crash.

"Daddy!" I twisted out of my mom's grasp and ran back to the front of the cottage.

A man had kicked down the door. He was dressed in a uniform. Like a policeman?

Dad stood his ground. His arm was outstretched, the gun gripped tightly in his hand.

Without hesitation, he fired.

He fired again.

And again.

"Daddy!" I screamed and threw myself to the hardwood floor. I wrapped my hands over my head. To block out the sound. To block out the sight of the dead man lying at Daddy's feet.

"Casey? Casey! What's going on? Are you okay?"

I peeked out from under the arm I'd wrapped protectively over my head to find Jack crouched down beside me.

"Jack, what's with all the firepower?" I asked while uncurling from my embarrassing impression of a turtle. "I asked for assistance, not an invasion."

"The last time you needed assistance on the South Lawn someone was trying to strangle you," Jack reminded me as he helped get my feet under me again.

"That was months ago." Still, instinct had me reaching for my neck.

Jack brushed a clump of grass from my hat. "I'm sorry

we scared you. It must be hard seeing men running at you with guns. That's how it happened with your mother, isn't it? And those men shot you as well. You were what? Six? Seven years old?"

"Six," I answered. My body shook. There was nothing I could do to stop it, so I hugged my arms to my chest. "That was a lifetime ago. I don't want to talk about it."

My father had killed a man. Was that why we were always on the run? Was that why he'd moved us to Phoenix, Arizona, shortly after the shooting in France? Was that why he'd abandoned me and my mom?

Those men who'd killed my mother had escaped justice. Had my father escaped justice, too? A lump formed in my throat that refused to go away.

Justice demanded payment. Then and now.

It didn't matter that Griffon Parker had made life difficult for everyone at the White House. Frank Lispon may have thought he was doing everyone a favor. He was wrong. He needed to pay for taking Parker's life. And now Matthews's life.

While I couldn't change the past or fix what my father had done, I could make sure justice was served now.

I closed my eyes and rubbed my hand over my face.

"What's going on?" Jack asked.

"I tripped," I said. Embarrassment bloomed anew at how gravelly my voice sounded. I lowered my hand, wiping my damp eyes as I cleared my throat a couple of times. I hoped Jack wouldn't notice my misty eyes, but what should I expect? He was a trained observer.

"Are you sure you're okay?" he asked, his voice gentling. "Talk to me."

"Where's Frank?" I asked.

Jack tensed. The grip on his rifle tightened. "What did he do?"

I spotted Frank standing next to Francesca and the group of volunteers. He said something to Francesca and then gestured toward me. Francesca shook her head.

What was the press secretary up to now?

"Talk to me, Casey," Jack demanded. His tone turned eerily calm as he kept his gaze on Frank. "Don't lock me out. What did Lispon do? Why the hell are we down here? I was told you required Secret Service assistance ASAP."

"Frank did this." My father may have escaped justice. I wasn't about to let Frank get away with murder. I grabbed Jack's arm. "Look." I pointed to the garden again. This time I didn't topple over.

Jack looked at the mishmash of wrong and missing vegetables and shook his head. "What?"

"The garden. The plants. They're not what we planted. Frank did this, and he also killed Parker and Matthews. He must have."

I explained what had happened. Jack nodded as he patiently listened. He then called the big guns to come take a look.

No, not the snipers. They're nice guys, by the way. I would have preferred that he called them to come and help out in the garden instead of William Bryce, the assistant director in charge of protective operations, and Mike Thatch, Jack's supervisor.

The look on Thatch's face said everything as his cool gaze scanned the garden. His jaw clenched and unclenched.

This wasn't the first time the Secret Service had to be called in for advice concerning the kitchen garden.

Growing food for the President of the United States, or POTUS, was considered a matter of national security from the get-go. The clashes . . . er . . . discussions began at the planning stage with the site selection for the garden. The best location for any vegetable garden is right outside the kitchen door. When tucked away at the bottom of the yard, a garden is often forgotten, neglected.

Not that the First Lady's garden would ever have been in danger of neglect. But still, the White House kitchen garden was to serve as an example for others to follow, especially during an economic downturn when a little effort in the backyard could have a big impact.

I'd explained quite clearly three months before to Wil-

liam Bryce that a garden's success often relied on how
close it is located to the house. He'd nodded and smiled and
told me he understood.

Understanding something and agreeing with it were two
very different things for him. While he understood the reasons I'd given him, he disagreed that the garden should go
where I'd initially proposed. The plants would intrude into
the safety zone the Secret Service had established around
the White House perimeter, a zone that had to remain clear
of any impediments. I got the feeling that if it were up to
Bryce he'd tear down every bush and tree within a five-
hundred-foot radius.

At the same time, the garden couldn't be too close to the
fence, where someone could potentially tamper with the
food the President might consume. After a lengthy back-
and-forth, we had finally come to an agreement. The garden would be placed at the bottom of the South Lawn in a
niche that protected it from the damaging winds that
Marine One stirred up during landings and takeoffs.

It was a location that gave tourists the opportunity to
stand outside the iron fence at the edge of the Ellipse and
see—but not tamper with—the garden for themselves. So
even though the garden's location wasn't my first choice, I
admit that it was the best choice.

I hoped the outcome of this clash . . . er . . . discussion
would be just as advantageous and that Frank would be
sent to jail.

"I don't want to alarm anyone," I said, trying to remain
calm myself. "The tomatoes and—"

Thatch held up his hand. "Jack," he said, his tone sharp,
impatient. He wouldn't even look at me. "The situation?"

Jack's version took much less time than mine to tell.

William Bryce, who'd listened with much more interest
than his CAT counterpart, nodded gravely. "This is a problem. Surveillance should have picked up and alerted our
men on the ground to any suspicious activity."

"But you can go back and check the tapes and review

what happened, right?" I asked. They'd catch Frank red-handed. "You can see who did this, can't you?"

"We haven't used *tapes* in decades. But, yes, we can review what happened in the garden. You say the trouble occurred sometime between yesterday evening and early this morning?"

I nodded and gave him the exact time frame along with the time frames for the other two times the garden had been damaged, which Bryce jotted down in a small note-book he'd produced from his jacket pocket.

"You did the right thing calling us, Ms. Calhoun. It's imperative we act before anyone gets hurt," Bryce said. "God only knows the dangers those things might present."

"They're pepper plants, not a group of marauding pro-testers," I said.

The bright red chili peppers bounced as a warm sum-mer breeze pushed through the garden, rattling the leaves around us. The plants were leggy. Their narrow stems looked too weak to hold the peppers' weight. And the leaves were a pale green. That tended to happen to plants grown inside without enough natural light. Not only would they easily break in a storm, they'd be susceptible to pests and disease.

"I'm going to pull out the peppers and the cabbage," I told them. "Do you need them for evidence, or would it be okay to dump them in the compost bin? I also need to replace the missing tomatoes. I think I have enough seed-lings back at the greenhouse. There's nothing I can do about the spinach. I don't know what we're going to do about this afternoon. The chefs were planning on including it in the salads the kids were going to make for lunch. This is a disaster."

"Yes. Yes," Thatch said irritably. "We understand the situation, Miss Calhoun. Plants are missing."

"Please save the specimens you remove. We'll want to analyze them," Bryce said. His gaze narrowed as he sur-veyed what was left of the First Lady's kitchen garden. "All of the remaining plants will have to be ripped out as well."

"What! All of them? The First Lady is counting on me. I can't let her down."

"We don't know what else was done to the garden," Bryce pointed out. "Is this a prank or something more sinister? If we let you go ahead with the harvest, you'll be putting the schoolchildren, the First Lady, and anyone else who might eat the food harvested from here in danger."

I didn't want that, but to pull out all the plants on the off chance that there might be something wrong with them? No, I couldn't do it. I *wouldn't* do it. I paced the length of the garden, desperate for a solution.

Jack frowned as he watched me. "With all due respect—" he started to say, but stopped when Frank Lispon hurried over.

"Will, I couldn't help but overhear. What's this nonsense about canceling the harvest?" Frank flashed me a don't-worry-about-it smile.

For a killer, Frank was damn good at hiding his guilt.

He thumped Bryce's shoulder. "It's good to see you, by the way." They looked like two old college buddies meeting up after years apart. They clearly had a history together, but also wariness, as if Bryce didn't quite trust the press secretary.

Of course there'd be wariness. Bryce and the members of the Secret Service like him had made a career working at the White House, while Frank Lispon served the President and would leave at the end of this administration's term.

Yet, those same members of the Secret Service who had weathered many changes in administrations could find themselves demoted and assigned to a turkey farm—a type of career-killing move where the work assignments completely dried up—or worse, fired, if the current President was unhappy with their service.

"I'm sure if we all put our minds together, we can come up with a solution that won't embarrass either the First Lady or the President. No one here wants that," Frank said.

"Of course not," Bryce agreed, "but—"

"I understand there's a problem with the plants. Some joker changed a few things around," Frank pressed on as I watched in amazement. If he'd damaged the garden in an attempt to destroy my reputation and career, why was he helping out now?

Could I have misunderstood what I'd overheard two days before about how he was going to "handle" me like he'd "handled" Parker? But what about the following morning and what I saw transpire between him and Annie? And why would he readily admit to wrongdoing if he was innocent?

Frank flashed a smile that showed off his white teeth. Both Bryce and Thatch seemed to shrink back a bit.

"Why don't you review the security feed and let us know exactly which plants we need to avoid?" Frank said. "We'll steer clear of those during this afternoon's harvest. Everyone will be safe, and the First Lady won't be embarrassed by the Secret Service's obvious breakdown in security."

"Now, see here—" Thatch protested.

"I'm not placing blame," Frank continued smoothly. "Mistakes happen. Even breaches in security, I suppose. The Secret Service can't be expected to be everywhere at all times. There's bound to be occasional mistakes. It's our job to make sure those mistakes don't interfere with the activities of the First Family."

Thatch opened his mouth and then closed it again.

"Hell," Bryce said.

"Well?" Frank asked, his brows raised. "What would you like me to tell the President about this breach in security?"

"Tell him that I'll see what we can do," Bryce said.

"We don't have to cancel?" I asked, not ready to believe it.

"No, damn it, you won't have to cancel." Bryce bent down and ripped a pepper plant out by its roots. "I'll rush a random testing of the harvest through our lab. We'll call in off-duty agents to help with the investigation. This'll be cleared up before the kids arrive. No one gets poisoned on my watch."

He looked straight at me. "Give us an hour to do what we need to do in the garden and we'll start checking the surveillance feed from last night. After that, you can do whatever you want in here. In the meantime, stay out of trouble."

# Chapter Twenty-three

*Character is like a tree and reputation like a
shadow. The shadow is what we think
of it; the tree is the real thing.*
—ABRAHAM LINCOLN, THE 16TH PRESIDENT OF
THE UNITED STATES

"**D**ON'T worry." Isn't it odd that those two words when
put together always seem to have the opposite effect?
I crossed my arms over my chest. Not only did I not
trust those two words, I also didn't trust the mouth that had
formed them. "I'm serious, Casey," Frank continued, his
smile as easygoing as ever. "You can handle this. There's
no reason for you to worry."

I had just returned from the White House greenhouse
facility and had climbed out of the grounds crew's nondescript white van filled with replacement vegetable plants
when Frank had grabbed my arm and pulled me aside.
Gordon and Lorenzo had nodded in my direction and
started directing unloading the van.

"Let me help there, lads." Gillis, who must have just
arrived and was dressed in his flowered kilt as if he were
ready to tape his show, rolled up his sleeves and grabbed a
tray of plants. I didn't have a chance to say two words to the
celebrity gardener. Frank had already dragged me several
yards away.

"If you don't get your hands off me, I'll scream," I warned Frank.

Although there was little he could do on White House property, I wasn't about to take chances with my life. Despite what Jack thought, I liked my life and intended to keep on living it. "I mean it. I'll scream loud enough to scare the snipers on the roof."

Frank released my arm so quickly his movements looked like a blur. "I know you and I don't see things eye to eye right now, Casey. I know you don't approve of . . . what I've done, but I need your cooperation. Margaret needs you."

"Margaret, the First Lady?" I asked with great care. Was she involved in this?

Perhaps if I played along with him, I could catch him making a mistake. One slipup. That was all it would take for me to prove Frank had a hand in Parker's and Matthews's murders.

"This afternoon, after the schoolchildren have harvested the vegetables and are working with the chefs to prepare the lunch, I've scheduled a small Q&A session with the press. I want you to be the one to answer the questions."

Okay, I thought, here it comes. The hammer was about to fall.

"Me? I shouldn't be the one talking to the press. I'm an assistant. The First Lady has always been the spokeswoman for the garden. It's her garden. And if she isn't available, Gordon should take the lead. He's the head gardener."

"True." Even though no one was close enough to us to overhear our conversation, Frank lowered his voice. "This has to do with Griffon Parker's death."

I knew it! I simply didn't realize Frank would admit to it so readily.

I leaned forward slightly and whispered, "Go on."

"As you know, Parker left *your* name in his notebook, not the First Lady's, not Gordon Sims's. Your name. I'm sure you're well aware of the rumors making their way across the Internet, the ones insisting the garden is a fake—an elaborately staged fake. Those rumors are now connected to you and your organic gardening program. Add to that, this morning the latest issue of *Organic World* came out, and it claims there's lead contamination in the soil, and it also names you."

"But none of that is true. The East Wing already issued a statement correcting the *Organic World* article. I wrote that statement last night when I was sitting in the hospital waiting room. And it's true the garden might not be exactly like a home gardener's. The White House has a horticultural staff along with an endless supply of off-site experts and volunteers available to answer questions and lend a helping hand. But the organic practices we've implemented are simple and can be used in any backyard."

"Great. That's what I want you to explain at the Q&A."

"But why me?" I asked. "Why do I have to be the one to talk to the reporters?"

"It's your blood the journalists want to taste."

"And you're only too glad to hand me over to them? Is that it? Is that the reason you destroyed the First Lady's garden? To chum the water?"

"What? You think that I—" Frank shook his head. "Why would I want to hurt Margaret or John? That garden is Margaret's sanctuary, her quiet spot away from the rumors, partisan wars, and budding scandals. I would never take it away from her."

He sounded so convincing. He'd also sounded convincing two days ago in his office. "I heard you tell Bruce Dearing that you'd handle me like you handled Griffon Parker and that you'd do it by today. And what do I find this morning? The garden in shambles."

"You thought I was talking about hurting you? I was talking about the negative news reports popping up all over the Internet. I'm all about the message, the image this administration presents, and the positive message that we convey." With a violent swing of his arm, he thrust his pointed finger toward the garden. "That's not the message I would ever

want to send out. Ever. Parker's death caused more trouble
for me than it could have ever solved. I could handle one
pain-in-the-ass reporter. His death has caused every damn
reporter in the press room to act like him and go all 'investigative' on me. The wild garden rumors are just one fire in
a forest of fires that I'm battling. If I lose control over this
one, the reporters will only be more rabid when it comes to
the next big problem to hit. So I ask you, Casey, are you a
team player? Are you willing to help get Margaret's harvest
back on message?"

What could I say to that? "Of course I'll do what I can
to help the First Lady."

"I'll be right next to you. If you stumble on a question
I'll jump right in. This is how the game is played. This is
how we win back control of the message." He patted my
arm. "Trust me."

Trust him?

That was too big a leap for me to take. "I'll answer the
reporters' questions." But I sure as hell wasn't going to
trust Frank to have my back. I started to walk away, but
Frank called me back.

"What did you mean when you said earlier that Kelly
Montague has been searching for her birth father?" he
asked.

"I meant just that, and you darn well know it. She
believes someone in this administration is her father. Perhaps Bruce Dearing. Perhaps even President Bradley.
Someone didn't want the scandal to come out twenty-five
years ago and that same person is now willing to kill to
keep the story from coming out today.

"You're the ever-loyal friend to both Bruce and John
Bradley. You've long been the go-to guy they could count
on to keep the public image and message on target. I suspect you've gone to extreme measures more than once to
do just that."

"Kelly believes either Bruce or the President is her
father?" He shook his head. "Bruce can't have children.
Neither can John."

"But Margaret's pregnant."

"Casey?" Francesca called from the garden. "Where did you want to plant the okra?"

"Excuse me," I said to Frank. "I have a garden to repair."

Why should I believe Frank? It was his job to promote the story he wanted others to hear.

**"OH, DEAR, WE SHOULDN'T SPEAK ILL OF OTH**ers," Mable Bowls protested. She waggled a replacement tomato seedling at me. "It's wrong to gossip."

The entire grounds crew and all the volunteers I could find were making quick work of tearing out the leggy, unhealthy vegetables that had appeared overnight and planting the crop I'd been growing in the greenhouses across town. Revised schematics would be handed out to the press within the hour.

Like a well-oiled machine, everyone was pulling together, even Gillis, and we were certain to accomplish what should have taken all day in just under a few hours. Standard fare for the White House staff, who regularly made major changes at the last minute for events of world-wide importance.

"Very wrong," Pearle Stone agreed. Her hands moved with seasoned grace as she tucked a replacement pepper plant into the soft ground.

"Two men are dead," I reminded them.

"Is this about that silly murder mystery dinner you and Francesca were planning? I heard Parker's murder followed the details you devised to the letter."

"You knew the details of the mystery dinner murder?" I asked.

"Darling, we discussed it at our weekly tea. Not very clever to leave a bottle of pills," Mable said.

"It would have been better to keep the police guessing instead of giving them something to test for," Pearle added.

"The two of you frighten me."

They both smiled angelically.

"I do need your help," I told them. "Kelly Montague is in the hospital. I was talking with her right before the hit-and-run attack. She was worried that she'd uncovered a long-forgotten scandal, a scandal someone has been willing to kill to keep secret. She thought the scandal dated back about twenty-five years ago. There was a baby—does that sound familiar?"

Both women shook their heads. "That was so long ago."

"How about today?" I tried. "Do you have any idea what Griffon Parker found out about Francesca and Bruce Dearing?" I asked. "Was Bruce having an affair?"

"It couldn't have been about Bruce's philandering ways. Everybody knows about that," Mable said.

"Really? Bruce? Does Francesca know?"

"Honey," Pearle said, "that girl was never one to sit at home like a good wife. She has always lived an active side life as well."

"If it works for them, who are we to criticize?" Mable said.

"News of an affair wouldn't be news at all with either Bruce or Francesca. The way Parker was talking, he must have learned something truly explosive about those two," Pearle said.

"Like a secret baby?" I asked.

"Bruce can't have children." Pearle moved down the row to plant another healthy bell pepper. "Poor Francesca. She wanted to adopt. Her friend Annie offered to help out."

"Poor Annie, her husband mismanaged their money," Mable added. "When he died, all he left her with was a pile of bills."

"Francesca is overly generous with Annie," Pearle said. "She pays for everything."

"But what about Francesca? Why didn't she adopt?" I asked, trying to keep the two on the subject.

"Bruce wasn't interested in doing that."

"He can't have children? Are you sure?" I followed her. I have to admit, I'd stopped working.

"It was quite the talk back when it looked as if he might

get the presidential nomination. When was that?" Pearle asked.

"Nineteen eighty-eight," I said.

"Ooh . . ." she replied and then moved on to the next plant.

Again, I followed.

"What happened back then? What was everyone talking about?"

"I suppose it really wasn't a secret at the time, so it's not gossip now. At Francesca's urging, Bruce had gone to one of those fertility clinics. He was none too happy when everyone found out. He never went back. Never would talk to Francesca about children again, either," she said.

"Did that hurt his political aspirations?"

"What's that, dear?"

"His political aspirations?" I moved closer to her and repeated. "Did that damage them?"

"Oh, my, no. A little middling like that? Just made him red faced at some of the parties around town for a month or so."

That seemed to be all she'd say about that, so I had no choice but to change course.

"Someone recently told me that President Bradley can't have children, but the First Lady is pregnant with twins. Have you heard anything about that?" I asked, expecting to catch Frank in his lie.

"Poor Margaret." Mable tsked. "No wonder she didn't have time to attend any socials or teas. Someone did tell me that she'd been going to a fertility clinic for the past year and a half. I heard her biological clock was ticking and she wasn't willing to wait a moment longer."

"I heard that the babies are the President's," Pearle added, "but they had to work hard to make that happen."

"I see." So Frank had been telling the truth about that. "What about Frank Lispon? Has he ever been the focus of a scandal?"

"Now, Frank. What a dynamic guy. He started out all hot and heavy with the younger ladies, a real heartbreaking

Casanova, and then—" Pearle interrupted herself. "Don't look now, that handsome Gordon Sims is coming our way." She swept off her sunhat and fluffed her hair.

Once Gordon arrived, I couldn't get either Mable or Pearle to leave the man alone long enough to tell me what they knew about Frank Lispon.

**SO FAR ALL OF MY QUESTIONS ONLY LED TO** more questions. What dangerous game was Frank playing? Why would he sabotage the vegetable garden if his actions hurt the President and First Lady more than they hurt me? Most Americans didn't know, or care, that I existed.

I doubted most reporters knew my name. By parading me in front of the press, did Frank really think he could turn the tide on the negative news reports? Was that even his goal? Or was he planning something else?

I couldn't do this on my own.

"Jack, do you have a moment?"

Jack excused himself from the other uniformed Secret Service agents who'd stationed themselves around the garden's perimeter in advance of the First Lady's arrival for the harvest activities.

"The garden looks . . . healthy," he said as the other agents watched us. It was unnerving having so many prying eyes on me when what I wanted to say to Jack felt so damned private.

"Um . . ." I tried to ignore their curious gazes. And failed. Miserably. "Must they stare?"

He looked over at his fellow agents as if only now noticing them. "It's their job to keep a watchful eye. That's how assassins and mentals are stopped before the gun comes out of the coat. We have a duty to notice things before bullets can fly and lives are lost."

"Who wears a coat on a hot summer day like today?"

"Mostly mentals with guns in their pockets."

"Ah."

"Come on. Walk with me," he said. He led us past the

First Lady's vegetable garden, which had been patched back together quite nicely. We passed the South Fountain and walked toward a shady area beneath the South Lawn's large white oaks. The leaves rustled above our heads as a couple of squirrels chased each other through the canopy.

"Sure, they're cute now. Soon, though, they'll be munching on the strawberries and raspberries," I muttered to myself. "Netting. We'll need to install netting next week."

"What's up?" Jack asked.

"Nothing. Jack, I want to apologize for how I've been acting toward you." I grimaced. "I know the other day you told me not to count on you to be around to save me . . . or not save me, but . . ."

Jack kept silent as he watched me struggle for words.

I needed him to understand that I wanted him in my life. That I—this was difficult to admit even to myself—I wanted to trust him. I needed to trust him. But I couldn't just snap my fingers and become the perfect, unbroken girlfriend Jack deserved.

"My father—" I started to pace. I didn't want to think about that man. I didn't want to think about how he could coldly take another's life. "As you already know, he left my mother. He left me. I thought it didn't matter. I thought I didn't need him. He left. So what? He's a jerk. He's most likely a dangerous criminal who I wouldn't want in my life. But . . ." But what if he'd stayed? Would he have been able to fight those men and save my mother?

It hurt too much to put voice to those thoughts.

"I had a wonderful childhood without him. It shouldn't matter that he wasn't there."

"It does matter," Jack said for me.

"Stupid, but yeah, it matters. It didn't before. But this spring all those memories of my parents came flooding back. It changed everything. Those memories killed the carefree gardener you met this spring."

I wondered how this most recent memory was going to affect me. Was it going to destroy me to know that my father was no better than the men who had killed my mother? That he, too, had wrecked lives before slipping past the bonds of justice?

"Did those memories change you?" Jack took my hand. "Or did they force you to see the reason why you are afraid?"

"I'm not afraid of anything." I pulled away. "I'm . . ."

Confused? Oh, so terribly confused.

"Have you ever had a long-term relationship with a man?" Jack asked.

"That's an abrupt subject change."

"No, it's not. Have you ever had a long-term relationship with a man?" he repeated.

"Yeah, in college." But after a couple of semesters the engineering student turned cold toward me. He pushed me away. Hadn't he?

I couldn't remember.

"A few years later another boyfriend ended the relationship after about a year and a half. He complained I was emotionally unavailable. But he doesn't count. He'd been seeing a therapist who, I'm sure, totally turned him against me."

"Okay. Have you ever broken off a relationship first?"

I thought back.

"I've never had the chance."

"Interesting," Jack said.

"What's interesting about that? That I'm totally dumpable? Is that even a word? It's the guys who are too picky. Always looking for something wrong. They can't be trusted to stick around for long. But that's okay. I don't want a long-term relationship. I just want to have fun."

"I'm sure that's it. I'm sure your past relationships with men weren't influenced at all by your father leaving you and your mother at such a dangerous time in your lives."

He let me stew about that for a while.

"Okay, perhaps I have always been afraid."

Jack took my hand again. "I'm sure your father didn't intentionally—"

"I don't want to talk about him." The memory of him

killing a man was too fresh in my mind. The pain too raw. "Jack, I just wanted to tell you that I'm sorry I've been having trouble trusting you. You're not the problem. I am. Trust me, I'm working on that."

"Trust you?" He smiled.

It was infectious. I smiled back.

The moment stretched out for miles, but then I remembered the reason I needed to talk with Jack in the first place.

"Remember the threatening phone call I received two nights ago?"

His smile faded. "The one you didn't tell me about until this morning?"

"I told Manny about it."

"What about the phone call?" Just like that, his bad feelings faded away and he was ready to help.

"He—I think it was a he—told me to stay out of the garden or else I'd end up at the bottom of the compost pile. If Frank had made that call, why would he want me to stay out of the garden? He needs me here if he ripped out the First Lady's plants to discredit me."

"We don't know that Frank's the killer."

"*I* know," I said.

"He stood up for you and the harvest. If not for his fast thinking, Bryce would have canceled everything and ripped out the plants."

"That confused me at first, but I think I've figured out why he did that. I want to know what you think."

"Go on."

"Frank has arranged for me to be grilled by the press this afternoon. He said it was so I could discredit the rumors that the garden is a fake."

"So you think Frank sabotaged the First Lady's garden to make it look as if you've been fooling everyone, volunteers included, into thinking the garden was actually producing vegetables?"

"Exactly. See, I knew you'd agree with me. Frank is up to no good."

"No, I don't agree. Taking you apart professionally

would hurt the President and the First Lady. Why would Frank want to do that? If he killed Parker, wouldn't you think he did it to protect the President? Isn't that what you're thinking?"

"Yes, President Bradley or Bruce Dearing, but—"

"Then why would he turn around and dig up the kitchen garden? Why not simply focus on framing you for murder?"

"So you don't believe me." I started to walk away. "I have work to do."

"Why do you have to be so pigheaded? All I'm saying is that I'm not going to form any opinions until I know more about what happened in the garden last night. Bryce is putting all his available men on this. We'll know who sabotaged the garden before the schoolchildren arrive. But remember, we don't know if the garden joker is connected to Griffon Parker's murder."

"Isn't the Secret Service worried that the murderer could be a member of the President's staff?"

"Of course we are. Trust me, if there's a killer walking the White House halls, the Secret Service will find him. We're not sitting on our hands waiting for the D.C. Police to follow the clues. We're taking an active role in the investigation."

"You are? Why didn't you tell me?"

"Do you really want me to answer that?"

"No, what I want is for you to spill the details. What do you know that you've not told me? There's a gourmet iced coffee in it for you."

He chuckled. "I wish we did know more. I could use an iced coffee right now. Look. No one liked Griffon Parker. Several staffers and reporters had good reasons to dance on his grave. But where's the evidence? Who had the motive? The means? And the knowledge?"

"Francesca Dearing. But she has an ironclad alibi."

"And what about you?" Jack asked. "You had just as much motive as Francesca and you don't have an alibi."

# Chapter Twenty-four

*When you get to the end of your rope,*
*tie a knot and hang on.*

—FRANKLIN D. ROOSEVELT, THE 32ND PRESIDENT OF
THE UNITED STATES

"**YOUR** murder mystery dinner that turned into a real murder makes you look guilty," Jack warned as he walked beside me back to the kitchen garden.

"It wasn't *my* charity dinner."

"That's what people think, though." Jack held up his hand to keep me from interrupting him. "All I'm saying is that it's easy to jump to the wrong conclusion."

Jack was right. Everyone I talked to seemed to know about that damned murder mystery dinner. And blamed me for instigating it.

"Don't forget that I heard Frank Lispon and Bruce Dearing plotting against me. I didn't make that up."

"I believe you, Casey. Because of you, Manny has asked those two some difficult questions. But at the same time William Bryce and Mike Thatch are both wondering if you made the story up to protect yourself from further scrutiny."

"But—"

"I believe you," Jack repeated. "But remember, it's dan-

gerous to jump to conclusions. Damn, I'm being called.
I've got to go. Be careful, Casey. Frank and Bruce are powerful men with powerful connections. It's only a matter of
time before they discover you've been telling people that
you think they murdered a reporter. They won't think twice
about pointing the finger back at you with a great deal of
force."

HAD I MADE A BIG MISTAKE BY CONFRONTING
Frank?

I hoped not.

The schoolchildren were going to arrive at any moment,
and we were still waiting to hear from the Secret Service
about whether the children would be allowed into the garden and whether anyone would be allowed to eat the vegetables.

I hoped the Secret Service cleared us soon. I didn't want
Frank to win this one.

"It'll work out," Gordon said as he rolled up a hose. I
couldn't figure out how he could remain so calm when I felt
as if someone had stuck needles into my neck. "Look at
Gillis entertaining the volunteers. Isn't he a wonder?"

"Yes," I said through clenched teeth. As much as I hated
to admit it, I appreciated Gillis's help repairing the garden
this morning. "He knows his stuff and isn't afraid to work."

My volunteers were just as valuable. They had to endure
the heat and humidity while we waited for the buses to
arrive. I owed Francesca, Mable, Pearle, and Annie—

"Annie! Gordon, when did Annie get here? I've been
trying to get in touch with her since yesterday."

"She must have just arrived. I haven't seen her all morning. Is there a problem?"

"There might be. Annie!" I jogged over to the white tent
where the volunteers had gathered. "Annie!"

She turned toward me with a look of surprise.

"Where have you been?" I asked. "Why haven't you
answered your phone? Why haven't you been home?"

She took several steps back. "I don't understand why you're so upset. And why are my whereabouts any of your business?"

"I've been worried about you. I saw you arguing with Frank Lispon the other day at his house. I was worried that he might—"

"Annie, you went to see Frank?" Francesca paled. "Why? What did you tell him?"

"I didn't tell him anything." Annie's bright red hair bounced with agitation. "I didn't! I went to him to demand he rein in those nasty reporters."

"Is that all?" Francesca asked warily.

Annie nodded, sending her hair bouncing again.

"Where have you been?" I demanded. "Why haven't you returned any of my calls?" I'd left an embarrassing amount of messages.

"I've been with Francesca." She looked surprised that I'd even question her about this.

"Yes, she's been staying with me," Francesca said. "With Bruce so busy right now, poor Francesca has had to fend off the press alone. She's even had to buy a new cell phone with an unlisted number. Until this all blows over, I decided to keep her company."

"Are you okay?" I asked Francesca.

She looked at Annie and then nodded. Annie patted her shoulder.

"Do you think I shouldn't have gone to Frank?" Annie asked and swallowed deeply. "Gracious, you don't think he had anything to do with the reporter's death, do you?"

"I don't know. Just be careful. Kelly Montague, another reporter for *Media Today*, was hit by a car yesterday. She's in the hospital. And Simon Matthews—"

"Kelly?" Francesca gasped. "No! That's—that's—"

Annie looked ready to faint. "D-do you think I need police protection?"

"It couldn't hurt. What did you show Frank? Was it evidence?"

"It was just a newspaper article that Parker had written.

I wanted him to stop the reporters from attacking Francesca."

"Then why did he try to snatch it away from you?"

She shrugged. "Did he? I don't really remember. He was just so angry with me. I think he wanted me and the press just to go away."

"What happened to Kelly?" Francesca asked.

"Do you think Frank will try to hurt me?" Annie said at the same time.

"I honestly don't know. As I was saying, the police found Simon Matthews dead this morning. He'd been poisoned, too."

"Simon Matthews? I believe he came to my house trying to get an interview yesterday. Will Kelly be—" Francesca started to ask, but Annie cut her off.

"Perhaps I will call Manny. He was so kind to us the other day. I—I can't believe I did something so foolish. I was just trying to protect Francesca. Oh, my. Look, the schoolchildren are here."

Two yellow school buses loaded with schoolchildren from the inner city entered through the outer gate.

Several members of the President's cabinet who had also volunteered to help arrived. Bruce Dearing rocked on his heels. He looked impatient as hordes of laughing children poured out of the buses.

I checked my watch. We still hadn't heard from the Secret Service. They were cutting things pretty close. I looked up at the sky. Not a cloud. If we had to cancel, we couldn't use the weather as an excuse. We'd have to make do with the unvarnished, ugly truth. I was certain some members of the press would grab on to the cancelation as proof that the garden was a fake.

"Jack, where are you guys?" I muttered as I started to pace.

The chefs waiting under the white tents stood next to tables draped with white tablecloths that hid coolers of spinach and miscellaneous vegetables for the kids to eat if the Secret Service didn't clear the garden produce for this afternoon. The chefs wouldn't let any guest leave the White House hungry.

I called the switchboard and was put through to Bryce's office. The call went to voice mail.

I called Jack's personal number. It also went to voice mail.

"I'm going to have a nervous breakdown before this day is over."

"Everything will work out, Casey," Gordon said. He matched my stride as I paced. "It always does."

I swiftly turned, changing directions. "But we haven't heard from the Secret Service."

"I have." He nodded to the hill. The doors to the Palm Room opened and several agents started in our direction. "The vegetables are fine. We're cleared to go."

"We are?" I hugged Gordon. "That's wonderful news!"

Most of the kids looked anxious to dash into the garden right away. The schoolteachers and chaperons herded them to stand near a podium that had been set up for the First Lady.

Many of the kids had owl eyes as they gazed at the White House.

Near the back, a skinny little girl with black curls clung to her mother's hand. The child looked terrified. I started toward her with the intention of reassuring her. Today was about having fun. Gillis crossed in front of me and made it over to the girl and her mother before I could.

"You look just like my wee lass," he said loudly. "She's just about your age and has curls, too. Thank you for coming out to my harvest."

The girl's eyes widened to the point that they looked like they might pop. She huddled behind her mother's legs.

Gillis was having none of that. He reached down and lifted the child into his arms, swinging her wide into the air.

I gasped. He was going to terrify that poor child, scar her for life.

"There you go, my darling dear!" he sang and set her

back on the ground. With a grand sweep of his arm, he kissed the top of the startled girl's head and whispered something in her ear. Her face instantly brightened. She nodded as she released her mother's hand and bounded off toward a group of children that looked about her same age.

I was stunned.

Gillis smiled widely and snapped his fingers in the air. Jerry and Bower rushed over. Both of them had stacks of Gillis's book in their arms. Gillis grabbed a book from Bower and handed it to the blushing mother.

"For you, lass," he said to the mother and sauntered away, his colorful kilt swishing. "A signed copy."

Jerry and Bower, moving faster than I'd ever seen either move, followed Gillis like a pair of happy puppies as they helped hand out his books while Gillis worked through the throng of children, patting heads, handing out books to the adults, and winning everyone over as if he were the Pied Piper of the garden.

"That Gillis is a wonder," I found myself saying. Even if he did seem to be after my job, I had to admit he made a great spokesman for organic gardening methods. He'd even managed to inspire Jerry and Bower to look as if they wanted to be at work for once.

"Could the two of you please come with us?" Special Agent Janie Partners requested of Gordon and me. She and Special Agent Steve Sallis were both dressed in dark suits and wearing the standard earpieces. They moved through the crowd of students and parents with the lazy grace of panthers.

"What's going on?" I asked Gordon as we followed the Secret Service agents.

He shrugged and looked as surprised as I did.

Janie went over to Jerry and Bower and spoke quietly to the two men.

"Would you mind taking care of these?" Steve handed us the books the two lazy gardeners had been lugging around for Gillis.

"I told you we'd find out who damaged your garden, and

we have," he said before helping Janie discreetly lead Jerry and Bower up to the White House. Gordon and I watched with our mouths gaping. We were stunned.

"Jack," I called out when I spotted him stationed at the garden's periphery, "what's happening?"

"They're your garden saboteurs," Jack said quietly after he approached.

"What? Why?" Gordon asked.

We moved away from the students and set Gillis's gardening books on a table.

"That's what we plan to find out. Have you seen anything suspicious that we need to be on the lookout for?" he asked.

"Annie's here," I said.

"Really?" He spotted her in the crowd and nodded. "Good. This is the safest place for her and Francesca right now. If you see anything the least bit odd, don't hesitate. Call me. I have permission from Bryce to keep my personal cell phone with me and on for the rest of the day."

"Thanks, Jack, but your concern is unnecessary," Gordon said. "Now that those two jokers are gone, everything will go back to normal."

"I hope you're right," Jack said and headed back to join his team fanned out on the periphery of the South Lawn. Soon the First Lady arrived.

She stepped out of a black town car that had driven her to the bottom of the hill. Her flowered dress was tailored for her growing belly. The skirt swished around her legs like waves at the beach. She carried with her a large straw hat to shield her from the worst of the sun.

Although her trademark serene smile grew wide enough to crinkle the corners of her eyes, her steps were slower than usual. Her complexion had lost much of its rosy glow.

The stress from the budget talks and the budding scandals was clearly taking its toll. I worried about her health and the health of her babies. She needed to get away from the political beehive and rest. However, as soon as she saw the gathered schoolchildren, she seemed to come alive like an actor turning on for her audience. She stepped up to the podium and welcomed everyone to her garden.

Her enthusiasm proved contagious. The kids were bouncing up and down, chanting that they were ready to eat their vegetables.

As we'd discussed, Gillis stepped up to the podium after the First Lady to talk about organic gardening. He kept it brief and on a level that held the third and fourth graders' interest.

"Chemical free! Fresh produce, yum!" he led the kids in chanting as we all headed into the garden.

"There you are, lass," Gillis said as he dumped a pile of his books into my arms. "Stick with me. You might learn a thing or two."

Grinding my teeth to keep from saying something I knew I would regret, I had no choice but to follow Gillis. People gathered around him like flies to honey. He was loud and flamboyant and, okay, he could talk knowledgeably about plants. He was also preventing me from keeping a keen eye out for trouble. Frank, I noticed, had vanished. I needed to find out where he'd gone, and I couldn't do it with these books in my hands.

"Annie," I said as I dropped the books into her arms, "I hope you don't mind."

"Mind?" she said, shifting the books in her arms. "I love his show! I love him!"

"Great." I wished I could share her enthusiasm, but I had a harvest to oversee and a killer to follow.

Apparently, though, Gillis's sparkle wore off quickly for Annie as well. The next time I noticed him, Francesca was lugging his books around. Annie was nowhere in sight.

The harvest couldn't have gone better. Within twenty minutes, the schoolchildren had filled their baskets with several varieties of lettuce, kale, leafy collard greens nearly as tall as the youngest children, snap peas, beans, rhubarb, and one tiny cucumber.

Thanks to the Secret Service's quick actions, not only was sampling permitted as they harvested the vegetables, it was encouraged. My chest tightened as I watched the kids scamper through the garden. I'd once been exactly like them, learning about the joys of harvesting a garden from my grandmother and aunts.

The constant click, click, click of the press photographers' cameras reminded me of my Charleston childhood and the hum of cicadas in the summer heat.

I missed my family. I missed Rosebrook.

Maybe I should take some time off, go back to Rosebrook, and let my grandmother and aunts pamper and spoil me.

I smiled at the thought.

The kids carried their bounty over to the tents and the chefs took over. The volunteers started to carry the gardening supplies back to a nearby small storage shed screened by bushes.

I drew in a deep breath. It was time for the press Q&A.

Frank was still missing.

Seth Donahue, looking unusually happy, patted Gillis on the shoulder and waved me over to the podium. The gathered reporters moved to where schoolchildren had stood not more than an hour earlier.

"It's time," Seth said.

"Good luck, lass," Gillis added.

I glanced around. Frank had promised to stand by me, to jump in if I got in over my head.

He had the charm and the necessary skills for dealing with the national press. I, on the other hand, was a simple girl from the South. If you looked hard enough, you'd find the turnip truck that took me into town.

So where the hell was Frank? Had this been his plan all along? Had he wanted to so humiliate me that I'd have no choice but to run back to Charleston?

I knew it. I knew he was up to no good.

# Chapter Twenty-five

*A man who reads nothing at all is better educated than a
man who reads nothing but newspapers.*
—THOMAS JEFFERSON, THE 3RD PRESIDENT OF
THE UNITED STATES

**T**HE First Lady, bless her, stepped away from the
cooking tent and joined me at the podium. The nearly
dozen reporters gathered fell silent.

"Where's Frank? He promised he'd be here," I whispered.

"He must have been called away. Don't worry." She
squeezed my hand. "You'll do fine."

She looked out from behind the podium and smiled.

"I know there have been several biting reports out there
that claim I have delegated all the work of my vegetable
garden to the grounds crew. Well, I'm here to tell you that
it's true." She rested her hand on her growing belly. "Bending over has become quite difficult lately."

Several reporters chuckled.

"I'm grateful to Cassandra Calhoun and to the rest of
the staff and our volunteers for keeping our gardens green
and the vegetables fresh and healthy. As requested by many
of you, Casey has agreed to answer some questions about
the garden and how it was developed. Now, if you'll excuse
me, it's been a long day and my ankles are swollen."

Seth moved quickly to assist the First Lady. She leaned heavily on his arm as they walked over to a waiting black town car to drive her back to the White House.

Steeled for the worst, I cleared my throat and stepped up to the podium.

"As the First Lady said, many hands made this garden possible. The chefs played a major role in selecting the plants, many of which are heirloom varieties from Thomas Jefferson's Monticello. These are seeds that are available to any home gardener.

"We prepared the soil using a method of sheet composting, also known as lasagna gardening. No, we weren't growing pasta."

A couple of reporters chuckled.

"Sheet composting is a method of planting on top of a modified compost pile that feeds the plants as they grow. We started with a layer of paper—"

"This month's issue of *Organic World* reports that dangerous levels of lead have contaminated the soil," a reporter from the *New York Times* tossed at me.

"Yes, I have read the article." I'd expected that question and had come prepared. I retrieved a copy of the soil report from my pocket. I explained how the White House regularly tested the soil for nutrients and contaminates and pointed out that testing the soil is a practice any home gardener should follow. "Many local cooperative extension offices offer soil testing. What we found was that the lead levels in the soil here was ninety-three parts per million. That may sound surprising, alarming even, but you have to understand lead commonly occurs in urban soils. According to the EPA, anything below four hundred parts per million is safe."

"But other countries require much lower levels than even ninety-three parts per million," the reporter shot back.

I smiled. "I'm glad to see that you've done your research. That level of lead was our starting point. We amended not only the existing soil, we planted above the soil using the sheet composting method that I was explaining. To avoid further contamination, all of the amendments and compost material came from organic sources. At the end of the season, we will run another soil test and, like before, make the results publicly available. With those changes I expect to find that the lead levels have dropped to under twenty parts per million."

The reporter nodded, seemingly satisfied with the answer.

"Do you wish to respond to the Watercressgate reports that the garden is an elaborate fake?" another journalist asked.

"I'd be glad to." I took a deep breath. "You can ask any volunteer who spent hours under the blazing sun that most of the plants we harvested today were in the ground the day we broke ground and planted the garden."

"Most? But not all?" someone else asked.

"That is correct. We are practicing succession planting in the garden. This means that we plant some varieties over a period of time to ensure the chefs have a steady stream of vegetables. You wouldn't want all the tomatoes to ripen over one weekend, for example."

I started to relax as the questions continued along that vein. It was easy to talk about something I felt so passionate about.

I explained the placement of the garden, along with the back-and-forth that the gardeners had had with the Secret Service. I talked about the varieties of vegetables. How we used integrated pest management methods. I even explained the difference between being certified organic, which the White House garden was not, and following organic practices, which we did.

The press conference kept going along smoothly until a young male reporter shouted, "Cassandra Calhoun, isn't it true that you've been questioned in Griffon Parker's death?" The cameras snapping pictures and filming the press conference seemed to close in on me. "Isn't it true that Griffon Parker had been planning to write a scathing exposé detailing the shenanigans taking place in this garden?" He did air quotes as he said "garden."

"He had mentioned—" I started to say.

"Isn't it true that you brazenly planned his murder out in the open, calling it a game, and that you drew on your horticultural education, an education that included several classes on poisonous plants?"

"I didn't—"

"Come now, everyone knows about how you were planning the perfect murder for a 'charity dinner.' And isn't it true that shortly after Parker's replacement, Kelly Montague, interviewed you about this garden"—again with the air quotes—"for an article she was planning to write, she was run down and nearly killed?"

"She was, but—" He didn't give me a chance to answer any of the questions he rapid-fired at me.

"And isn't it also true that the garden we see today was planted only hours ago?"

Expecting him to continue, I didn't even try to answer that last one. Unfortunately, he had no more questions. My silence seemed to last forever.

"I—I don't know what to say to that," I stammered. "Yes, some plants had to be replaced because of damage that occurred last night. The replacements came from our greenhouses. They—"

"Did you kill Griffon Parker to cover up the ruse that is happening in this garden?" he demanded.

Where the hell was Frank?

I looked around, searching desperately for the curiously absent press secretary. Or his assistant. Or anyone with experience dealing with the press. My hesitation sounded like guilt.

"Stop this havering. It would take more work to fake a kailyard like this than to simply grow one in place," Gillis jumped in to say. "Although the First Lady's kitchen garden doesn't follow all the methods outlined in my book *Gardening the Farquhar Way: Organic!*—celebrating its fifth week on the *New York Times* bestseller list and currently number three—it is as organic and pure as Highland snow. The rest of your questions are bollocks and don't merit answering by Casey or anyone else."

"I think Casey has answered enough questions." Penny, Frank's assistant, had finally shown up. "If you need any follow-up information, I'll be happy to arrange that for you."

"Thank you," I said to Gillis, stunned that he'd jumped in and helped me. "That last reporter—I didn't know how to begin to answer his charges."

"Don't thank me, just look happy. Didn't an American coin the phrase 'Never let them see you sweat'?"

"In this heat, all I seem to be doing is sweating."

Gillis flashed his trademark grin and, after tossing his arm over my shoulder, struck a pose for the cameras.

As the cameras flashed, Special Agents Steve Sallis and Janie Partners came to stand a few feet out of range of the pictures. They both looked grim. I tried to keep from staring in their direction—it wasn't good for the picture—but my gaze kept traveling back to them.

"Stop frowning," Gillis managed to say without altering his flashy smile. "The papers always print the worst pictures out of the lot. It's up to you to always look your best."

I forced a grin to my lips. But my brows remained furrowed.

"There, we're done. That should get my face on the front page of several papers." Gillis lifted his arm and sauntered over to the press. "Do you have a copy of my book?" he asked the reporter from the *New York Times*.

At the same time Steve and Janie moved in.

"What's happening now?" I asked them.

They continued past me without answering.

"Mr. Farquhar," Steve said, his voice calm and polite, "will you please accompany us to the White House?"

"Och!" Gillis boomed. "Looks as if the President needs my advice on how to solve the budget crisis. If you have any questions about my work or my media empire, my publicist's name is on the book's front flap."

He waved as he followed Steve and Janie to the West Wing.

I hurried over to where Jack was still stationed. "What did Steve and Janie want with Gillis? Please don't tell me he actually scored a meeting with the President."

Jack held up his hand. His mobile gaze brushed over me as if I didn't exist.

"Jack?" I was starting to get nervous.

He nodded. "Sorry about that," he said to me. His entire body remained tense as if on high alert. "Jerry and Bower are talking. The garden sabotage wasn't their idea. According to Bower, someone paid them handsomely to make you look bad."

"Who? Who paid them?"

"Apparently, your charming Gillis Farquhar."

# Chapter Twenty-six

*You do not lead by hitting people over the head.*
*That's assault, not leadership.*
—DWIGHT D. EISENHOWER, THE 34TH PRESIDENT OF
THE UNITED STATES

"**G**ILLIS?" I couldn't believe it.

Wait. I *could* believe it. "That scheming, no-good showman! He tried to ruin me just because he wanted to sell more books?"

"I suppose your instincts about him were on the nose. Detective Hernandez is on his way to interview him. I haven't heard why, but I'd have to assume the homicide detective wants to question Gillis in regard to Parker's murder."

"Gillis?"

"He might be our murderer," Jack said.

"No." Frank was the killer. I stopped myself to rethink everything for a moment. "No. Unless Gillis fathered a child twenty-five years ago, when he was—what—ten years old or so, he wasn't involved."

I spotted Thatch heading our way. "We can talk about this later," I said. I didn't want to get Jack into trouble.

Penny was busy directing the press now that the Q&A was over. The chefs were winding down their activities as well. The kids soon boarded the buses and headed back home.

Frank was still absent.

Francesca was talking with her husband near the South Fountain. She waved me over.

After exchanging polite greetings with Bruce and Francesca, Francesca asked, "Have you seen Annie lately?"

"She was helping Gillis," I said, but come to think about it, I hadn't seen Annie since I'd handed her Gillis's books. A band of worry tightened around my stomach.

"I'm sure she's okay," I quickly added. With all the stress Francesca had been under, I didn't want to alarm her needlessly.

Francesca frowned. "Bruce, have you seen her?"

He shook his head.

"Perhaps she left with the children," I offered. "That's when Pearle and Mable went home."

"Perhaps," she said.

"I'm sure she's okay," I said to assure both Francesca and myself. "This is the safest place on earth."

"She's right, honey," Bruce grumbled. "You worry too much. I'm sure it's nothing."

Francesca didn't look convinced. She rose up onto her tiptoes as she watched the White House workmen dressed in dark blue uniforms and wearing black gloves take apart the tents and stack the tables.

"Let me thank you, again, for all your work with the harvest, especially you, Francesca," I said, hoping to distract her. "I know the First Lady was thrilled with its success."

At the mention of the First Lady, Francesca seemed to pull herself together.

"I'm sorry Mrs. Bradley wasn't able to stay longer," she said. "I didn't have a chance to say two words to her."

"You'll have more time to speak with her at the volunteer appreciation tea."

"Do you really think so?" She sounded uncertain and not at all like herself. This was Francesca Dearing, after all, one of the most influential and powerful society ladies in D.C.

"Are you sure you're okay?" I asked her. "Why are you so worried about Annie? Do you know something?"

"No," she answered too quickly. "I'm fine. Everything's fine. It's just been a long day." She turned to Bruce, who'd tightened his grip on his wife's arm.

"If you need anything," I told her, "anything—call or text me anytime."

I didn't like the way Bruce was keeping a tight hold on her. Bruce and Frank were up to something. And Francesca looked truly worried about Annie's whereabouts.

Had Frank returned to the West Wing or had he gone somewhere else? And where was Annie? I tried both of their cell phone numbers.

No answer.

I left them both text messages to call me.

The back of my neck prickled. Jack had worried that the killer was growing more and more desperate and needed to silence anyone who threatened him . . . and the secret he'd already gone to such lengths to protect.

"You shouldn't frown so," Gordon said. Using a long compost fork, he'd been turning the vegetable garden's three-bin compost system and incorporating the harvest's fresh plant waste into the first bin. When I approached he leaned against the compost fork's bright blue handle. "You should be pleased. Despite a series of disasters, today was a success. Everyone left smiling. That's how things happen around here. It's chaos behind the scenes and perfection to everyone else."

"I could do with less behind-the-scenes chaos."

Gordon agreed, but insisted, "Stop worrying. It's over. You can't change what did or didn't happen today. You need to slow down and enjoy these moments."

"I will as soon as I find Annie Campbell. Francesca has been looking for her. Have you seen her?"

Gordon shook his head as he thought about it. "I think I

saw her with the group helping clean up. Lorenzo is directing some volunteers as they put equipment away in the
storage shed."

"Thanks, I'll look for her there."

"Is there a problem?" he asked. "No, wait. Don't tell me
if something is going on. After this morning, I think we've
all had our monthly allotment of disasters. Make that two
months' worth. I'm going up to the office. I have some
phone calls to make regarding the lead in the soil article."

"Ugh! I wish I could rip up every copy of that magazine.
You know it used to be my favorite publication. I hate to do
it, but I'm canceling my subscription."

"Don't cancel. This isn't the first time misinformation
has been printed about the gardens. It won't be the last. I
have plenty of contacts who can help us get the correct
information into the right hands."

"You do?" I grabbed the compost fork from him. "Then
what are you doing here just standing around?"

He pulled the brim of my hat down over my eyes and,
laughing, walked away.

I carried the compost fork to the far end of the garden
and ducked under the nearby stand of linden trees. It was a
shortcut that led to a walkway near the southwest security
gate. The tree-lined path took me to a metal storage shed
located across from the White House's small basketball
court. On the way, I tried to call Annie again.

I then tried Frank.

I finally dialed Jack's number. With the First Lady and
visitors gone, he and the rest of the CAT agents had left the
garden.

No one picked up.

I slammed the phone against my hand. In response, the
phone vibrated and beeped. A new text message from Jack
that had been sent more than an hour earlier appeared on
the screen. "Kelly condition guarded but stable," it read.

That piece of good news would have put a smile on my
face if not for my confusion over why it had taken so long

for the message to get from Jack's phone to mine. Was this Frank's doing? Was he trying to cut me off from anyone who could help me?

If this were a game show I'd pick door number three, the one with the raving lunatic behind it. I think the heat and stress were finally getting to me. How could Frank block my phone? Because of the amount of security and jamming equipment around the White House, this wasn't the first time my cell phone had acted wonky.

The shed door was closed, which was odd for this time of day. I slid it open. "Annie?" I called. My voice echoed as it bounced off the metal walls.

It felt cool in the shed's darkness. Despite being on one of the most famous properties in the United States, the shed carried the same smell of damp, grass clippings, and fertilizer found in any backyard. This was where the push lawn mowers—no ride-on mowers here—meticulously clean hand tools, hoses, pots, and various chemicals were stored. The fish emulsion and compost thermometer were examples of recent additions to the storage shed since the implementation of my organic gardening program.

Unlike the grounds office's messy storage closet, everything in the shed had its place. The mowers were parked right inside the sliding door. Most of the hand tools were hanging from hooks on Peg-Boards lining one wall. The other equipment sat on three seven-foot-high metal shelving units identical to the ones in the basement closet.

Using only the light from the door, I found a rag, wiped off the compost fork, and hung it on its spot on the wall. The hook next to it, which usually held a red-handled shovel, I noticed, was empty.

It probably was still in the garden. I was about to go searching for it when I heard a scraping sound near the back of the shed. And then a clatter.

Sounded like a rat. I closed my eyes. I hated rats.

I'd started to hightail it out of there when a gonging thunk, followed by a soft groan, stopped me.

The shovel.

"Annie?" I rushed past the shelves to the back of the shed and skidded to a stop.

"Frank!"

The tall press secretary was sprawled facedown across the concrete floor. My first thought was that it was a trap, a clever ruse to get me to let down my guard around him. Backing up, I told him not to move.

He didn't.

He wasn't moving. Not at all.

Expecting him to jump up at me at any moment, I moved closer and nudged his arm with my toe. Still no movement. Biting my lower lip, I knelt down beside him to take his pulse.

His skin felt hot to the touch. He must have come in the shed hours earlier to hide out, planning to ambush me or Annie, and, while waiting, collapsed from the intense heat.

"You're in for it now, Frank. Once they get you back to health, you're going to have to explain how you planned to handle me."

I ripped my phone from my pocket and punched the first two numbers for the White House switchboard.

A metallic crash stopped my fingers cold. The phone slipped from my hands as I watched as if in slow motion one shelving unit tipping over onto another. Like giant dominoes the metal shelves tilted toward me, spilling their bags of soil and chemicals, heavy clay pots, and assortment of sharp tools.

# Chapter Twenty-seven

*It would be judicious to act with magnanimity
towards a prostrate foe.*
—ZACHARY TAYLOR, THE 12TH PRESIDENT OF
THE UNITED STATES

I grabbed the nearest tipping shelf with both hands in the hope that I'd be able to stop it from crushing me and Frank.

With the other two shelving units pressing down on top of it, the shelving was too heavy. My feet started to slip. Pots smashed against the concrete floor as they slid from their neatly stacked locations on the shelves. A ten-pound bag of fertilizer slid off the top shelf and between my arms to slam into my chest. I lost my grip on the shelving and fell backward, landing with a thud sideways across Frank's back. The darn fertilizer bag then dropped on top of me. It seemed to explode in a puff of white powder as the shelf smacked down on top of the bag not a second later.

Wait a minute. I recognized that bag of fertilizer. It was one of the bags of ammonium nitrate Lorenzo had promised to toss out. He must have stored it in here instead of properly disposing it.

Ohhh! Lorenzo could make me so angry sometimes!

Ohhh! It hurt my chest to be angry.

Breathing as shallowly as I could manage, I stared up at the seams in the metal roof above me. If not for the fertilizer bag, I might have been seriously injured.

True, the shelves pressing against my chest hurt. I couldn't move. I felt like a turtle unable to right herself. It was quite an embarrassing predicament. With my arms pinned at my sides, I couldn't get the leverage to lift the shelving. But it could have been worse.

I could be dead.

I could be lying on a dead body.

Neither had happened. With each breath Frank took, he pressed my chest against the fertilizer bag. It didn't feel good, but as I said before, things could have been much, much worse.

My head hung off Frank's side at an awkward angle. I tried to lift it. Ow. Ow. Bad idea.

A pillow or even a block of wood would have been a godsend right now.

I turned my head left and then right. I spotted my cell phone on the floor not too far away. One call, and all kinds of help would pour my way. In some ways the White House complex was like a small city within a city. In addition to the President's personal medical staff on the White House's ground floor, a full medical team was housed in the Eisenhower Executive Office Building. They were like a mini ER. If I asked nicely, perhaps one of the nurses would even bring me a pillow.

With those blessedly soft thoughts floating in my head, I wiggled my arm. It took some work, but I managed to move my arm out from under the shelf and reached for the cell phone.

"Ohhh!" A sharp pain jabbed my chest as I stretched.

*Keep reaching.*

The tips of my fingers brushed the phone. Panting through the pain, I reached some more. I touched the phone's plastic casing.

*Just a little more.*

Each effort to bring the phone closer with just my fingertips nudged it farther and farther away until it lay just out of reach.

I stared at the shed's ceiling again.

Someone would come looking for me. Eventually.

In the meantime, I'd be fine . . . as long as I didn't have to breathe.

Sharp pain bloomed like a razor-edged flower each time I inhaled. I tried holding my breath. A huge mistake. I could only hold it for so long before having to gulp in air spiked with stinging barbs.

Taking small, shallow breaths seemed to spare me from the worst of the pain . . . and panic. Who knew how long I'd be stuck in this sweltering storage shed tucked away from anything else on the White House grounds? Those tiny little breaths also had the added benefit of making my head feel light, as if it might float all the way up to the ceiling.

I closed my eyes and decided not to count the seconds. Someone would come looking for me and for Frank, if for no other reason than the fact that unaccounted staff members posed a serious security risk.

"Casey?" Francesca's voice never sounded so good. I heard her moving around outside the shed. The metal door scraped as Francesca slid it open. "Casey? I thought you said you saw her come this way."

"I did," Bruce growled. "She must have left already."

"But she told me she'd look for Annie."

"Well, apparently she didn't."

"*Help*!" I wheezed. Ohhh! That hurt!

Not only that, the plea came out about as loud as one of Pearle's or Mable's whispers. Considering my shallow breaths, I considered that quite an accomplishment. Both the half-deaf but wholly dear matrons had quite loud whispers. As I breathed through the pain shooting up and down my chest from the effort, I prayed it had been loud enough for Francesca or Bruce to have heard.

"Come with me back to the West Wing. I have work to do. I'll call for a car to take you home," Bruce said. The shed's metal door scraped closed.

"I suppose," Francesca agreed, her voice fading as they passed the storage room.

"*Help!*" I called again. "*Ple-ease.*"

I groaned as pain bloomed in my chest. If I could wiggle a little to my left, perhaps I could take some of the weight off that one rib that really seemed to hurt.

I wiggled. Groaned. Wiggled.

And didn't move an inch.

"Stop kicking about," Frank grumbled from beneath me. "Oh, my head. What the hell happened? Why are you on top of me?"

I was still reeling from my attempt to move. My chest muscles weren't too happy with me at the moment.

"Casey?" Frank groaned. "What happened?"

"I found you"—shallow breath—"lying on the ground. You"—shallow breath—"were unconscious. Passed out from"—shallow breath—"the heat."

"It wasn't the heat." He sounded irritated about it. "Someone hit me. With a shovel."

"Why? Were you trying to hurt Annie?" I managed to shift to where, if I whispered, it didn't hurt too much to talk. "Did she fend you off?" If that was the case, help would be on its way.

"Annie? What? I don't know anything about what's going on with Annie. I have nothing to do with her. I don't know why anyone would hit me. I turned and saw the shovel coming at the back of my head just before—" He groaned. "My head's splitting. Is help coming soon?"

"No one knows we're in here," I said.

"Oh." I didn't like how that sounded. I was pinned to the ground with a man who had already killed twice that I knew of and had nearly killed Kelly. And I'd just told him that he had all the time in the world to knock me off the mortal coil.

*He's going to snap my neck and blame it on the shelving collapse.*

"Don't even think about it," I told him.

"What don't you want me to think about?" he grumbled.

"Getting out of here? Because all I'm thinking about right now is how to get off this dirty floor. Don't you gardeners ever sweep in here?" He smacked his lips. "What's that foul taste in my mouth?"

"Fertilizer. It's in my mouth, too."

"It's not going to kill me, is it?"

"Depends on how much you swallow," I said.

That reminded me . . . "If I die in here, Jack will know you killed me."

"What? Who?"

"Special Agent Jack Turner," I said too vehemently. Needles of pain stabbed me in my chest. I closed my eyes and took several shallow breaths. When I could talk again, I whispered, "I told Jack all about your cover-up. So if you kill me, he'll know."

"You're crazy. Not just a little crazy, but certifiable. You think I want to kill you? I suppose you think I killed Parker, don't you?"

"I know you did. I heard you admit it to Bruce Dearing. You were going to handle me like you'd handled Parker."

"With the media, doll cakes. I already told you that it's my job. Spin the story. Why else would I be parading you in front of the media like that?"

"To ruin my reputation. To discredit me. You promised to stand by me at the Q&A, and yet when it started you were nowhere to be found. You left me to be trampled by the press."

"I did no such thing. The garden isn't the only political fire burning around here. I was called back to the West Wing to deal with the budget crisis, but I sent Penny."

"She didn't show up until it was all over," I said. "I think you planned it that way to ruin me."

"I didn't plan anything."

"And then you rushed down here to silence Annie."

Frank groaned. "You're crazy. None of that would help this administration one whit. If I wanted you gone, there's much quieter ways to get rid of you."

"Like murder?" I knew it! I knew he was guilty.

"No! Not murder. To be honest with you, I came back to the garden hoping to get a moment alone with Annie. I wanted to make sure she understood that I was doing all I could to help Francesca and Bruce and that she didn't need to . . ."

"Need to what?" I asked.

"Nothing," Frank grumbled. "I don't know why I bother explaining anything. You're like a broken record. Talking to you makes my head hurt. So let's stop."

"Fine."

His back, which was pressed against mine, felt like an oven. Sweat stung my eyes and dripped down my neck. When would this heat wave break?

After several minutes of baking in the shed's heat, I said, "At least you have the cool concrete under you."

"I'd be happy to trade places."

A long silence followed.

"Move your elbow," he said. "It's jamming into my back."

"Maybe your back is jamming into my elbow. Is that better?"

"Not really."

Jack would come looking for me soon. I had to trust that he'd wonder why I hadn't called to badger him about what Manny found out when he questioned Jerry, Bower, and Gillis. I had to trust that he'd worry.

I simply had to trust.

To pass the time, I started to count the seconds after all. I was getting close to two thousand when the shed's metal door scraped open.

I screwed my eyes shut tightly and sucked in a lungful of needle-sharp air.

"We're in here!" I shouted. "Ohhh!"

"Casey?" Gordon called. "What happened in here? How did these shelves fall over?"

"*Here*," I whispered, panting desperately as my chest paid a steep price for that deep breath I'd taken.

"Back here," Frank shouted.

"Don't move," Jack said, as if that was a choice.

Jack! He came!

I knew he would.

Jack and Gordon lifted one shelving unit. Then another. Finally the last one was lifted from my chest.

Gordon grabbed the fertilizer bag.

"I thought Lorenzo was going to get rid of these," I wheezed.

Jack gingerly lifted me into his arms just long enough to get me off Frank's back. With great care, he placed me beside Frank on the cool concrete floor. Finally, my head could rest at a natural angle.

"Are you okay?" Jack asked.

I lightly touched my chest. "I think I bruised a rib or two."

Jack nodded. "Don't move," he said again.

I turned my head and watched as he and Gordon helped Frank roll onto his back. Frank managed to sit up, but ended up cradling his head in his hands. Gordon had found a clean cloth and wiped the spilled fertilizer from Frank's nose and mouth. He then came over and did the same for me.

"How could this happen?" he demanded. "Those shelves are heavy. I've never known them to tip over. Never mind. We're getting you to the hospital."

I nodded and closed my eyes. It was over. I was safe.

I listened as Jack spoke quietly with Frank. Slowly, blissfully, my mind started churning again. The shelves wouldn't have tipped over by themselves. Someone had to have pushed them over. Besides, I'd left the door to the shed open, but Francesca had opened the shed door when she'd come looking for me.

Frank couldn't have done it. He was unconscious on the floor at the time.

Gillis had been in police custody.

Bruce?

Francesca?

Who else had been around? Who else needed to keep

Parker's investigative report from ever seeing the light of day?

"Jack?" I opened my eyes. "Jack?"

He was immediately at my side.

"I need to talk to Manny."

When I tried to sit up, Jack gently put his hand on my shoulder and pinned me to the concrete floor with very little effort.

"You need to be still," he said.

"I can't. Someone just tried to kill me," I said. "And it wasn't Frank."

"You think?" Frank quipped. "At least no one conked you in the head with the flat end of a shovel. Why would someone do that?"

I stared at Frank. His dark skin. His winsome good looks. His height.

The sticky note left on my desk with Frank's name on it hadn't been a warning. It had been a clue of where I needed to look.

"My God," I said as I turned toward Frank. "You're Kelly's father."

# Chapter Twenty-eight

*A brave man is a man who dares to look the Devil
in the face and tell him he is a Devil.*
—JAMES A. GARFIELD, THE 20TH PRESIDENT OF
THE UNITED STATES

"**D**ON'T waste your time with me. Go on." Frank waved his large hand, shooing away the three-team medical staff who'd rushed to the shed. "Casey is in desperate need. Check her for head injuries. She's saying crazy things. I'm not anyone's father."

My heart twisted when I heard him say that.

"Kelly nearly lost her life searching for you." A surge of adrenaline propelled me into a sitting position. "You just don't get it. I can't believe I didn't see it before. Parker is dead because he got his hands on the research Kelly had gathered in her search for her birth father . . . *you*. Kelly had been getting threatening phone calls, telling her to back off or the killer would come after you. And now he has."

"Proof positive that she hit her head. What a fiction she's dreamed up. First I was a killer. Now this. I'm not anyone's father," Frank repeated.

"When Kelly wakes up, talk with her." I fended off the nurse who tried to get me to lie down. She asked me a question, perhaps many questions. I was too focused on getting Frank to listen. "Find out if her information and your history match. Can you do that much?"

"No, I can't. It'd be a waste of time. I'm not anyone's father."

"Why are you being so stubborn?" I demanded.

Would *my* father reject me as soundly if I were to go looking for him? No need to wonder. I had no plans to find the murderous coward.

"What harm could come from talking to Kelly, from comparing notes?" I asked.

"You're delusional. It'd be a waste of time."

A doctor wearing a white coat and a kind smile knelt down beside me. He introduced himself and asked what had happened. I pointed to the shelving and quickly explained how it had fallen on me. He nodded.

"This might hurt a bit." He lightly touched my ribs. I dropped to the floor as if he'd punched me.

"Watch it," I wheezed.

As I lay on the concrete floor, I struggled to breathe. Not from the pain, which was quite intense now that I felt it again, but from Frank's disinterest in the woman who could be his child. What kind of man ran from fatherhood? It wasn't as if I were handing him a baby to raise. She was an adult, an accomplished one at that. "Can't you keep an open mind about this? Kelly is in the hospital because of you."

"First she thinks I killed Parker and Matthews. Now she's saying I fathered one of the White House reporters. There has to be some kind of neurological damage causing those wild thoughts. Or mental illness. Either way, get her some help!"

Gordon paced as he wrung his hands. "These shelves should have been bolted to the floor. I can't imagine what could have made them tip over like that."

Jack had stepped out of the way. His gaze hardened as he scanned the shed's interior.

Everything that followed passed in a blur. The doctor

and the nurse tossed around scary diagnoses like broken ribs, internal bleeding, and collapsed lungs. Nothing was certain. It could just be a bruise. (I'd added that last diagnosis.)

I was told not to move while they examined Frank. He objected vehemently at first, but in the end he let them lead him to the ambulance.

Poor Kelly. Her father would be at the same hospital as she, and he wouldn't even visit her. She could die never knowing that he existed.

Perhaps it was for the best. Frank didn't deserve Kelly. She was too good for him. She deserved to be loved, cherished—things Frank obviously didn't know how to give.

"Please, don't cry, Casey." Jack squeezed my hand before two EMTs lifted me onto a stretcher. "I can't come to the hospital with you. I'm still on duty. But I promise I'll come by as soon as I'm able. You're going to be okay."

I nodded.

I knew I'd be okay. I didn't need a father.

My tears were for Kelly, damn it. She was the one who'd wanted to find her dad.

Not me.

Never me.

**"THIS HAD BETTER BE GOOD, COLOSSAL GOOD,** not that run-of-the-mill bull," Manny growled. His salt-and-pepper mustache stuck out at all angles as if he'd been scrubbing his fingers through it nonstop. "I'm busy. Whatever you wanted to tell me, you could have told the uniformed officer I sent to take your statement." He'd added several more words to make his speech more colorful and, I'm sure, to entertain me, but my grandmother would die if I repeated any of it.

"What? No flowers?" I said with a goofy grin. I'd been given a sizable pain reliever. "I was nearly crushed by a bag of stinky fertilizer today. I think I deserve some flowers. Nothing fancy or anything. Shasta daisies. Or gerberas. Just something to bring the garden into this antiseptic space."

"You're in an ER examination room. If all checks out you'll be going home soon. You don't need flowers."

"The hospital ran a CT scan right away. The doctor noted something that he wants to check out. Casey's waiting to get an MRI to check for internal damage," Alyssa said quietly.

"I'm not damaged," I said.

Even though Jack couldn't come with me to the hospital, he'd contacted my roommate to make sure I had a friendly face with me. Gordon had crawled into the ambulance after me. He'd fretted the entire time. Alyssa, tired of his mother henning, had sent him in search of coffee. Not just any coffee but a particular kind that could only be purchased across town.

"I feel great," I said.

"That's the meds," Alyssa was quick to point out.

"They could send me home right now, but they're being pushy. How's Kelly?"

"She's starting to wake up." Manny scrubbed his grizzled mustache. "I hope to be able to talk with her tomorrow."

I started to cry. "I couldn't be happier. Wait a minute. I'm hurt, too. You'll talk to Kelly personally, but send one of your officers to interview me?"

"We've talked enough. You've already told me every harebrained theory that's popped into your head, remember?"

"Yes, but I was wrong." I waggled my finger, indicating he should lean in closer. "Frank's not a killer," I whispered.

"No kidding," he said dryly.

"There's something else you should know."

He sighed dramatically. "I suppose since I'm here already, you might as well tell me."

"My dad," I said. "He killed a man."

"Go on," Manny said, more interested now.

"I had forgotten. I was so young, so trusting. I didn't

want to believe he was an evil man. He was my daddy, you know? How can a little girl's daddy be evil?"

Manny didn't have an answer, only a sad look that said he'd seen—and had probably arrested—too many evil daddies who had broken too many little girls' hearts.

"I couldn't believe my daddy could be the villain of my fairy tale, so I chose not to remember. But today, I remembered."

"I see."

"We were living in northern France, but I'm sure you can help. I'm sure you can—"

"Wrong jurisdiction," he interrupted. "Didn't you want to talk to me about the murders of Griffon Parker and Simon Matthews? My officer told me that you had information about them, information that only I could understand. So, what is it?"

*What was it*? That was a good question. I yawned as I tried to remember.

"I wish I was back in the garden," I said groggily. "The First Lady's kitchen garden. That's where all the suspects were gathered. We could have one of those grand Agatha Christie endings. After I revealed the killer, you could spring to action and drag the culprit away."

"Let's pretend we are there now," Manny said with unnecessary sarcasm.

I didn't let his bad mood get me down. With all the pain medication flowing through my veins I didn't think I could even if I'd wanted to. I closed my eyes and pictured the rows of leafy greens, the large leafed cucumbers that were just starting to take off, and the tiny little tomato seedlings that we'd just planted that morning.

If anything, the press should accuse the kitchen garden of shrinking.

Gillis waltzed through the garden with Annie struggling to keep up, her arms laden with his books. Gillis had wanted Parker to review his book for *Media Today*. Why Parker?

Parker wasn't a book reviewer. He was a complainer

who had a taste for criticizing gardeners, well, one gardener in particular. Me.

Gillis wasn't just interested in selling his book—or should I say his revolution in the organic gardening world?—he also wanted a position at the White House . . . at least that was what I'd thought. I opened my eyes. "What's going on with Gillis? I can't believe he'd hire those two slackers, Jerry and Bower, to do anything. Lorenzo used to work with Gillis and said that Gillis expected a high level of professional behavior from those around him. Jerry and Bower are anything but professional."

"We're still talking with Gillis and checking phone records. The number that contacted Jerry and Bower apparently came from the same throwaway phone that placed the threatening call to you and the threatening calls to Kelly. Like you, he knows his plants, including the poisonous ones. And as you've pointed out, he'd been in contact with Parker."

"Don't tell me you think Gillis slept with Parker that night."

Manny lifted a brow. "He might have."

"Gillis? Really? But he has children of his own. I heard him tell a little girl that she looked just like his daughter."

"Adopted. He's been in a long-term relationship with his show's producer."

"I still don't get it. What's the motive?"

"Give us time," Manny said. "It's still early in the investigation."

"And how did Gillis manage to knock over the shelves after the Secret Service had escorted him away?"

"Accidents happen all the time. You were startled to find Frank Lispon. You panicked and set off a series of events that ended up with you crushed beneath the shelves."

"No. It wasn't an accident."

"How can you be sure? Did you see someone? Did you hear someone?"

"It wasn't an accident. I'd left the door to the shed open.

When Francesca came looking for me, she had to open the shed door to peek her head inside."

"Are you sure? He could have hit Lispon with the shovel and returned in plenty of time for your mini press conference."

"But—" I rubbed my temples, hoping to clear my foggy head. "But when I came into the shed I noticed that the shovel was missing from its hook. Then I heard a sound. I didn't know what it was at the time. Thinking back, though, it must have been the killer hitting Frank with the shovel. This all happened after you took Gillis into custody."

Manny's jaw tightened. He scrubbed his hand over his mustache, making it look even more untidy. "You're making me rue the day you moved to D.C. Were you this much trouble for the Charleston PD?"

"I never made any trouble in Charleston. It's not me. It's this city."

"That's what they all say," Alyssa said, wiggling her hips like a modern-day Mae West.

"I have the coffee." Gordon burst into the room with two tall cups. "What did I miss?"

Alyssa took one look at me, one look at the insulated cup Gordon offered to her, and said, "I wanted iced coffee."

His shoulders dropped. "Oh." Gordon turned around and left again.

"Quickly now, Casey, tell Manny what you remember. The pieces are in that complicated head of yours. You know all the players. Who killed Parker and Matthews?"

She was right. The pieces were all there.

But something was missing. Something felt . . . off.

"The sticky note I found on my desk with Frank Lispon's name. It wasn't a warning to stay away from him like I first thought. It was a clue. I think Francesca left me that note. She told me to stop asking questions or else I would get hurt. Shortly afterwards, the note showed up on my desk. I'm sure she left it for me. Somehow she knew Frank was Kelly's father. She's afraid of someone hurting me for finding out. She's afraid of Bruce perhaps? That's why she's keeping quiet. I think she knows who is killing the reporters and why."

"Do you still have the note? Do you have any proof that Francesca is involved?"

I shook my head. "The pain medication is making me feel . . . drowsy. I'm sorry I wasted your time, Manny."

"That's all I seem to be doing lately." He rested his hand on my shoulder. The lines in his face looked more deeply drawn tonight. His tone was ashen. He needed to take better care of himself.

"Have you eaten dinner?" I asked him.

"Not yet. I've got a few more things to do tonight. I hope you're okay and you get to go home soon."

As Manny left, a nurse came in all smiles, promising us that I was next in line for the MRI. She took my vital signs and checked my chest for any changes in color or swelling. She then asked about my level of pain and if I needed more medication.

My pain level?

So many lives ruined in such a short span of time. Kelly had given up a better job so she could go in search of her birth father. Parker and Matthews had chased an explosive story. And Frank Lispon—the man who, like my father, refused to act like one—had done nothing.

And me, I wished I had never had a father, wished I could erase the shocking memories of him that had dribbled back into my life.

Even if Manny managed to find the man responsible for the deaths and unhappiness, nothing was ever going to be the same for any of us.

And the nurse wanted me to quantify on a scale of one to ten what the pain felt like? I couldn't. All I knew was that it would take much more than a pill to chase away that kind of pain.

# Chapter Twenty-nine

*Well, there doesn't seem to be anything else for an ex-president to do but go into the country and raise big pumpkins.*

—CHESTER ALAN ARTHUR, THE 21ST PRESIDENT OF THE UNITED STATES

A week later I was back at work and glad to be in the garden again. It hurt when I bent over to pinch off the tops of the chrysanthemums in the Jacqueline Kennedy Garden—that was what cracked ribs did for you—but that pain paled in comparison to the sting I felt when I thought about Parker and Matthews's murderer still walking around.

At least the heat wave had finally broken. It was nearly fifteen degrees cooler that morning than it had been the previous week.

"You don't have to be here, Casey," Gordon said as he accompanied me on my routine morning trek to the First Lady's kitchen garden.

"I want to be here." After a day of sitting around on the sofa with nothing to do, I'd been more than ready to get back to work.

"Don't push yourself." He took the bucket of soapy water from my hand. "You need to give your body time to heal."

"With my cracked ribs I'm supposed to take deep

breaths and stay active, do jumping jacks and whatnot. Otherwise I might catch pneumonia."

"I don't remember the doctor saying it quite that way. I hope you're not doing jumping jacks." Gordon had eventually returned to the ER and stayed, entertaining me and driving Alyssa crazy, which was also entertaining. When the pushy hospital staff finally agreed with me that nothing had been seriously broken or punctured and let me sign the release papers, Gordon had accompanied Alyssa and me home. At the brownstone, he'd left Alyssa to help me get into my pajamas but had soon returned with takeout for dinner and an easy-to-heat precooked breakfast that he slipped into the fridge.

We ate. Talked. Gordon then sat up with me as we watched TV long after Alyssa had called it a night. He'd stayed, keeping me company, watching over me as I dozed, and texting Jack periodic updates on my well-being. I couldn't have asked for a more devoted friend. Or a better nervous mother hen.

"You've seen the size of my apartment, Gordon. I'd go mad if I had to sit on the sofa day after day with nothing to do but watch gardening shows." I took back the bucket of soapy water. "I need to keep these hands busy or else the devil might get after them."

"You do know what today is, though?"

"I know." The First Lady's volunteer appreciation tea was scheduled for this afternoon, the same event that both Gordon and Lorenzo had found reasons to miss. "I have a dress all ready to go back in the office."

"I suppose if you're feeling up to it . . ." Gordon said, watching me carefully.

He'd been such a help all that past week. No, that wasn't quite right. Gordon had been my champion from the first moment I'd stepped foot in the grounds office nearly six months before.

"It shouldn't be that bad," he said, but at the same time he breathed a sigh of relief that he wouldn't have to fall on that particular sword.

We'd reached the kitchen garden.

Although we'd harvested the spring plants, my morning garden routine hadn't changed. The summer crop still needed water, food, and weeding. As I did almost every morning, I surveyed the garden. No signs of major damage from critters of the four-legged or two-legged variety. I squatted, groaned, and started to look for the smaller pests, the kind that generally had six legs and wiggly antennas.

Gordon pulled out the hoses and began to water. He stopped when a couple of the chefs arrived to pick baby eggplants for a lunch dish they were preparing. It sounded delicious.

As the chefs gleaned, I plucked a hornworm from a tomato plant and dropped it into the bucket of soapy water. My hand passed over a second hornworm that was dotted with white beneficial wasp eggs. That worm would soon die from the parasitic wasps. The wasps would then hatch, reproduce, and infest other hornworms.

Gruesome, I know. But that was nature keeping itself in balance. If we were to spray insecticides on the plants, we could inadvertently kill off the wasps that did a darn good job of keeping the hornworm population in check, not to mention the damage we might inflict on our pollinators.

The garden was a tiny ecosystem that, when in balance, took pretty good care of itself with each plant and creature playing its specific part.

Speaking of each of us playing our parts, I felt as if the murderer had designed a part for me to play, which I'd played brilliantly. And a part had also been designed for Gillis Farquhar.

"Any word on Gillis?" I asked Gordon.

"Nothing in this morning's paper. I still can't believe it."

"I can't, either. I don't think he's guilty of anything besides a bloated ego."

Gillis had been charged with damaging the White House gardens. Whispers in the White House hallways were that he would soon face both attempted murder and murder charges.

In my opinion Manny was making a huge mistake in taking his investigation in that direction, but after I'd left him several messages saying just that, he was no longer taking my calls. I don't suppose I blamed him. It wasn't as if I had any alternative theories.

According to newspaper reports, the more Manny dug into the case, the more evidence piled up against Gillis. Bank records showed several withdrawals from Gillis's account that exactly matched the amount of money that Jerry and Bower received. But who had tipped over the shelving units in the shed? Gillis had already been taken into custody.

Did Gillis have an accomplice besides Jerry and Bower?

Did someone simply not like me?

Or had the murderer done an impenetrable job of framing an innocent man?

I simply didn't know.

Later that morning when I was deadheading the roses that surrounded the South Fountain, someone standing behind me cleared his throat. Expecting Jack, I started to jump up to greet him and was sharply reminded about my cracked ribs. Cupping my hand over my eyes, I turned and smiled in his direction.

"Hello, Casey." Not Jack.

I tried not to let my disappointment show.

"Good morning, Frank. How's your head?"

He touched his forehead as if remembering. "It's good."

He continued to tower over me with apparently no real purpose, all suit and long legs.

"Yes?" I said.

"You said the other day you knew my secret."

"I—I—" I'd thought he'd figured out by now that I was wrong about him . . . apparently about everything. "I'm sorry about that," I was quick to say.

"Sorry?" His expression darkened.

Where was the genial press secretary that everyone loved? And trusted?

"I have spent nearly all of my adult life covering for others, putting a good spin even on the worst story." He heaved a sigh. "I never thought I'd have to face my own mistakes. I thought I'd done a good job of making certain I'd never have to do this. But thanks to Parker's death, every skeleton out there is about to tumble out of the White House's closets, including mine."

"I am sorry to hear that," I said.

"Sorry?" he repeated. "You can't imagine."

"No, I don't suppose I can."

Frank watched me. His jaw twitched. "I'm going to release a statement to the press today. It's better that I come out with it before some reporter pens an article or films a segment designed to shock."

"Today?" My brows shot up in surprise. "Isn't that large press conference with President Bradley and leaders of Congress scheduled to take place in the Rose Garden this afternoon to announce the big budget agreement?" Just as the oppressive heat wave that had gripped the city finally broke, both sides of the aisle had finally found a tiny strip of common ground to stand on. "You don't mean to—"

"I do. It's the best strategy. The big news of the day will be the budget agreement. My story will get buried." He paused. "I hope."

"I hope it works out for you." I mentally patted myself on the back for not asking him for the details of his scandal. Okay, truth be told, I didn't ask because I assumed he'd finally decided to admit to the press (and himself) that he was Kelly Montague's birth father.

I pulled off my gloves and slid my gardening shears into my belt's leather holster. "Why are you telling me this?"

"You said you knew what I'd been up to and you knew why Annie had come to my house that morning."

"I did say that."

"I'd appreciate it if you didn't go to the press with your own version of my story. It's bad enough that my mother's still alive. You don't understand how difficult this will be on her and me. Although attitudes about homosexuality have grown more accepting over the years, many in the black community, like my mother, still view it as a grave sin."

"Homosexuality?" Jack had mentioned the rumors of a long-term illicit relationship between Frank and Bruce. Was this the scandal Parker had been so keen on uncovering? But what did that have to do with Kelly's search for her parents?

"It's not a lifestyle choice, at least not for me. I tried for over half my life to deny who I am, to pretend I was someone else. It was hell."

I nodded. Truly, that was all I could do.

My silence only further darkened his mood. "I hope I can count on you not to go to the press about this."

"Of course—of course you can." I stumbled over my words as I struggled to catch up. "I'm sorry you had to hide for this long."

"I wasn't exactly hiding. I was living my life on my terms, just not publicly. I would have been happy to continue that way for the rest of my life . . . or at least the rest of my mother's life. My private life is no one's damn business. I hate to think what Annie Campbell is going to say to the press about me."

"What does she have to do with this?"

"I thought you said you knew. Annie came to my house that morning—she had pictures of me on a date." He turned away. "I was kissing the man. She threatened to take the picture to the press unless I protected Francesca and Bruce."

"She's blackmailing you? Is that why you feel pressured to go public?"

"It's part of the reason. I've been doing all I can to protect those two. I don't know why that crazy friend of Francesca's doesn't understand that. The way she was acting, you would have thought the scandal Parker was investigating was about her. Like that's possible. No one even knows who she is."

"Wow." Annie was acting like a mamma grizzly protecting her babies. She may have gone too far with Frank, but I respected how fiercely she fought for her friend.

I wished Frank would show some similar parental interest in Kelly Montague. "Kelly's still in the hospital. Have you visited her yet?"

"Not that again. She's not my daughter."

"But what if she is?"

"Don't you have a volunteer tea you need to get to?"

"Shoot! I do." I started to rush away, but stopped and turned back to Frank. "I hope you're doing the right thing. You're an asset around here."

"Thank you, Casey."

His shoulders weighed heavy. He looked like a man heading for the gallows.

Perhaps he was. His press announcement, even buried within the larger news of the day, still could spell the death of his lifelong career.

# Chapter Thirty

*Leadership: the art of getting someone else to do something you want done because he wants to do it.*
—DWIGHT D. EISENHOWER, THE 34TH PRESIDENT OF THE UNITED STATES

"**C**ASEY! Casey! You have to help me. It's a disaster," Annie cried as she fluttered her hands in front of her. She did look rather like she was falling apart.

Her dark purple sundress was stained with mud. One tan sandal had broken a strap and flopped as she walked. Her bright red hair, usually styled to pageboy perfection, had completely lost its bounce.

She'd intercepted me in the Rose Garden, just outside the Palm Room, as I was returning to the White House. A harried staffer trailed alongside her, wringing his hands.

"What are you doing here?" I asked. "The First Lady's tea is being held in the Jacqueline Kennedy Garden. You should have come in the East Wing entrance."

"I—I wanted to see the Rose Garden before the press conference to see how they set things up for the President. I didn't mean to do anything wrong. Francesca was supposed to be here with me, but she's running late. She had Bruce arrange for me to be escorted to the Rose Garden before the tea." Annie gestured to the skinny, pale-faced intern standing behind her. The young man looked as if he might cry.

"I was just walking along. I didn't see it. I swear. I don't know why I didn't notice where I was going. Then I tripped. It broke. It's a terrible mess, and so am I."

She was talking so quickly, I couldn't keep up. I raised my hands. "Slow down," I said. "Why are you covered in dirt?"

"Clumsy, I know. I tripped over a planter." She pointed to one of the large urns that Lorenzo and I had planted for the upcoming Fourth of July holiday. "And it broke!" she wailed.

The urn closest to the podium where the President would stand was cracked down the middle. The plants and dirt had spilled out everywhere.

"It's nothing to worry about," I assured Annie. "We'll get it cleaned up."

"Please"—she grabbed my arm; her fingers felt cold—"let me help."

"All I need to do is get someone to sweep up the mess. There's really nothing to do. While I do that, you go home and get changed. Really, it's not a problem."

Annie's grip on my arm tightened. "But there'll be an odd number of planters. There will be a hole."

"It's not a problem. We can rearrange to make it work."

"I feel awful about this. This is such an important day with the President's press conference to announce the budget agreement. Please, let me help fix it. I saw an extra urn in the gardening shed. If we gathered up the plants, with your help, we could make it look as if nothing happened."

"I assure you, Annie, that's not necessary."

"Please." She refused to let go of my arm.

It wouldn't take very long to transfer the plants to a new urn, and it seemed to mean the world to Annie.

"Very well," I said.

"Wonderful! I can prepare the urn in the shed while you bring the plants down. I saw the potting soil on the shelf. It'll be done in no time."

I asked the West Wing intern if he'd be willing to escort Annie down to the gardening shed. While they headed down to the shed to get the pot ready, I found a handcart. I gathered up the plants from the broken urn and carefully placed them on the cart.

A couple of ushers volunteered to clean up the rest of the mess. I would have hugged them, but Ambrose didn't approve of displays of gratitude beyond a modest nod of the head.

By the time I had rolled the handcart down the path to the gardening shed, Annie had the urn filled with potting soil and ready for the plants. I was impressed. This was the first time I'd seen her take the initiative.

"Did someone spill gasoline?" I asked. The scent was strong. The West Wing intern glanced up from his iPhone just long enough to shrug.

Annie blushed to the tips of her red hair. "I don't know what's wrong with me. I've been so clumsy lately." She pointed to a red plastic fuel container sitting on a shelf and the small black spot on the concrete below it.

The shed had been put back into order with one improvement. One of the carpenters had bolted the shelves to the floor. Not even an earthquake would tip those puppies over.

"Accidents happen."

"I'm so upset today. Did you hear? Frank is going to give the press a statement after the President is done, to air his dirty laundry. I wish someone, like that handsome homicide detective, would take Frank up and stop him."

"You shouldn't let Frank's decision to tell the truth upset you," I warned. "Secrets need to come out."

Her eyes grew wide. "Not all of them."


**ANNIE GOT HER HANDS DIRTY AS I DIRECTED** where each plant was to go in the urn. The West Wing intern assigned to escort her on the short tour that had turned into a long sojourn shifted impatiently from foot to foot.

Finally we were done. We loaded the urn onto the hand-

cart. Together Annie and I pulled it up the hill to the Rose
Garden. I'd made it halfway there when a sharp pain
stabbed me. I hugged an arm to my bruised chest and kept
going. I should have never let Annie talk me into doing this.

If she hadn't looked so forlorn, I wouldn't have given in.
According to everyone I'd spoken with, she'd lived a rough
life. Growing up poor in a West Virginia mining town had
to have been difficult. And then just a few years ago, she
lost her husband of thirty years and discovered that he'd
left her with a pile of debts.

Pearle had said that Annie now lived off the generosity
of Francesca and others. No wonder the poor woman
always reminded me of an overwatered houseplant, all yellowed and drooping. The least I could do for her was to
forget about my cracked ribs and pull this damn planter up
the hill.

"I'm sorry, you can't go this way." The uniformed division Secret Service guard manning the hut at the Rose Garden's entrance stopped us. "The press conference is getting
ready to start."

Annie gave me a panicked look.

I wasn't worried. "This urn needs to go next to the
podium to replace the one that broke earlier. We'll be in
and out."

Only the press secretary and his assistant were in the
garden, making last-minute adjustments to the seating. The
press hadn't even been allowed out yet, which I pointed out
to the guard.

"Just a minute," he said and stepped into the white
guard hut to consult with someone on his radio. "Go on.
Hurry up," he said when he returned.

"Thank you," Annie gushed.

I nodded as we passed.

The Rose Garden, located adjacent to the West Wing
and steps from the Oval Office, often played host to cere-
monies and important press announcements. With the
Oval Office as the backdrop and flanked on both sides by
flowerbeds of roses in full bloom along with colorful fox-

glove, fragrant hedges of thyme, boxwood borders, crab apples, little-leaf lindens, and saucer magnolias for height, it made for a stunning setting.

The steps leading up to the West Wing doubled as a podium and raised platform large enough for the President, House majority and minority leaders, and Senate majority and minority leaders to announce their success in the budget negotiations.

Soon, the neat rows of chairs in the garden's broad center lawn would be filled with reporters searching for kinks in the plan and dramatic angles to take when writing the story.

With Annie's assistance, I maneuvered the handcart across the garden's lawn to the now gleaming spot where the other urn had once sat.

"Aren't you supposed to be at the First Lady's tea?" Jack hurried across the lawn. Even after everything he'd done for me, the sight of him in his full dress uniform made me nervous and excited and . . . happy.

"I'm heading that way. Just doing a little fix-up in the garden here."

Without prompting he slung his rifle over his shoulder and lifted the urn from the handcart. "You shouldn't be lifting anything heavier than a pencil. Where do you want this?"

I showed him.

After setting the urn down, he brushed off his hands and smiled at me.

"Just fixing up the garden? Not snooping?" he asked.

"Me? Snoop? I won't dignify that with an answer." I found his smile infectious.

For the last four days, Jack had been traveling with the President as he drummed up support for the budget deal across the country. Even though Jack had called every chance he got, I'd missed him.

After the great shelf topple, Jack had stuck close to me night and day for two days, going as far as to take personal leave from work so he could manage it. He'd been worried

that whoever had pushed the shelves over would come after
me again. That single-minded concern for my safety had
ended after he and Manny had talked at length.

The security cameras didn't focus on the gardening
shed's door, so while they couldn't reveal directly who
came and left from the shed, they could show who went up
the path that led to it. From the videos, the men determined
that no one had traversed the path until Francesca and
Bruce came looking for me.

Both Manny and Jack had started to suspect I'd done
something to knock the shelving over. By accident, of course.

Gillis, for reasons still unknown, was the villain in this
mystery. Or so everyone was telling me even though the
DA still hadn't pressed murder charges.

I wanted to stay irritated at Jack for following Manny's
line of thinking instead of mine, but his steady smile
melted my resolve.

"I suppose y'all are setting up for the press conference,"
I said.

"We are." He leaned forward and whispered, "And
you're not supposed to be here."

"I'm leaving. I'm leaving."

The West Wing intern could take care of Annie. She
was wandering around, surveying the garden and the other
urns. I hoped she'd watch where she was walking this time.

I had to get cleaned up, change into my dress, and hurry
to the tea. Aunt Willow would be proud. I was going to be
fashionably late to a White House event.

On leaving the garden, I stopped at the podium to wish
Frank luck.

"It's all planned," he said. His entire body seemed to
sag. "I'll be handing out my statement right after the press
conference."

I patted his shoulder. "You have my support."

"Frank Lispon!" Francesca burst from the West Wing
with a red-faced Bruce following closely behind.

"Fran, I'm warning you. Don't do this," Bruce's gruff
voice caused everyone in the garden to turn their heads.

Francesca made a beeline for Frank. She gripped her hands in front of her bosom. "You have no right," she whispered.

"No right?" Frank pulled back. "What are you talking about?"

"Bruce told me that you're planning on handing out a statement after the President's press conference, a statement that makes public the scandal Parker was threatening to uncover."

As she said the last part the color drained from her pink cheeks.

Frank didn't say anything. He simply stared at her.

"Francesca." Annie grabbed her friend's arm. "Let's go." Francesca batted Annie away.

"We were friends once," she said to Frank. "More than friends. I'd like to think that would mean something more than a sordid tabloid tale. How much are you getting paid to do this?"

"Paid? I'm not—"

"Francesca!" Annie's voice grew more urgent. "We need to go. Now." A couple of Secret Service agents closed in to help move Francesca and Annie along. They wanted the area cleared.

"You may think you're doing the right thing, but what about Bruce? What will your airing of dirty laundry do to him?" Francesca, teetering on the hysterical, resisted their attempts to herd her back toward Bruce. She raced after Frank, who had moved over to check on the cords to the teleprompter. I followed, hoping to help calm her down.

"Francesca," I said, "I don't think you have the entire story." I knew I sure didn't. "Frank is going to the press about his . . . er . . . lifestyle."

My cheeks burned. A proper Southern lady didn't talk about such things. Not that I was a proper Southern lady. My grandmother had tried her best, but I don't think I'd ever fit the mold.

Still, old lessons remained.

When Francesca didn't immediately react, I clarified.

"He's going to tell the press that *he's gay*. You have nothing to worry about."

Unless . . .

*What if Annie's blackmail picture was of Frank kissing Bruce?*

According to Mable and Pearle, Francesca already knew of Bruce's infidelities. She'd even had a few indiscretions of her own. But would she be as understanding if she learned that Bruce enjoyed the company of men? How would she feel about the world learning that secret?

Francesca took several deep breaths as she processed the idea of Frank coming out of the closet in front of the White House press corps.

"Is that true?" she asked Frank.

"What in hell did you think I would tell them?"

"I—" She shook her head. "I have no idea."

She knew darn well what she thought Frank would tell them. And damn it, why hadn't I put the pieces together sooner? I was so concerned about who might be Kelly's father and who might want to keep his identity secret that I'd completely ignored the other half of the equation. The mother.

It was Francesca.

She was Kelly's mother.

"You put that sticky note on my desk with Frank's name on it because you were dying to tell someone," I said. She'd abandoned her newborn baby because Kelly was half black. Francesca would never have been able to pass Kelly off as Bruce's child. And everyone already knew that Bruce didn't want to adopt. "That's why you were acting so oddly. You wanted to tell someone. Not only that, *you* wanted to meet Kelly. How did you find out that she was your daughter?"

"Parker called asking questions," Francesca whispered. "I denied that I knew anything about Kelly, but the time frame fit. She's mine." Francesca shook her head as fat tears fell off her cheek. "*She's my baby.*"

"Fran-ces-ca," Annie said, enunciating every syllable in her friend's name, "if you know what's good for you, you'll come with me now. I'm not going to ask again."

Her red hair fell even more out of place as she stamped her foot against the slate pavement underneath the West Colonnade. She didn't look or sound like a concerned grizzly bear friend. She sounded like a demanding bully.

And back at the gardening shed, Annie had said that she wished someone would "take Frank up and stop him." The fake suicide note had used a very similar odd phrasing.

A phrase from the hills of West Virginia?

Why hadn't I seen it earlier?

Her unnatural attachment to Francesca. Francesca's generosity that held no bounds. Hell, even Frank had said Annie had threatened to blackmail him. The scandal Parker had dug up hadn't been about Bruce Dearing at all. It had been about Frank and Francesca and Kelly.

And Annie . . .

I grabbed Francesca's arm and spun her toward me. "She's blackmailing you."

# Chapter Thirty-one

*The truth will set you free, but first it
will make you miserable.*
—JAMES A. GARFIELD, THE 20TH PRESIDENT OF
THE UNITED STATES

I didn't want to believe it. Annie Campbell seemed so
meek. So fragile.

"What did you say about Annie?" Francesca pulled
away from me as if I'd suddenly caught fire.

I felt as if I had.

"Poor underprivileged Annie. Your best friend from
forever. She's blackmailing you. That's how she's kept her
high-priced lifestyle when all she had inherited was debts.
She was the one who would rather die than return to West
Virginia, to her painful roots, am I not correct?"

Francesca swallowed hard and nodded.

"How far is she willing to go?"

My mind went to that urn Annie had broken. Was that
an accident . . . or another one of her plots? "How far has
she already gone? Did she kill Parker? And Matthews?
Was she driving the car that hit Kelly?"

"Lord, I hope not," Francesca breathed. "Not Annie. I
have had suspicions, but I'm afraid to ask too many questions. I'm afraid of *her*. For as long as I've known her, she's

always had a mean streak. When I told her about Parker asking questions about Kelly, Annie exploded. She told me that if I tried to contact Kelly, if I talked with anyone about Kelly, she would ruin not only me but also Bruce."

Time seemed to slow as the pieces of the puzzle started to click into place. I watched in horror as President John Bradley walked in front of the glass door of the Oval Office and stopped. We'd replaced the planted urn just a few feet away from where he was standing.

Annie had said she'd spilled gasoline in the shed.

She'd also grown up around a father who was a miner with experience making ammonium nitrate explosives. A father who had died in a mining explosion. The essential ingredients of such an explosion included fertilizer, a fuel source—like gasoline—and a trigger device.

Had the bags of ammonium nitrate been finally disposed of or simply put back onto the shelf? I hadn't taken the time to look.

Annie had been convinced Frank was going to tell the press about Francesca's secret. She'd even tried to blackmail Frank to keep Francesca's secret.

"Was it Annie's idea to invite Gillis to the White House?" I asked Francesca.

Manny was wrong. Gillis Farquhar had no connection to the murders.

"It was my idea to invite him." Francesca bristled at the question.

"This is important. I need to know the truth."

She closed her eyes. "It was Annie's doing. I don't know how she knows him."

Was Annie blackmailing Gillis? Was that how she'd paid Jerry and Bower to do her dirty deeds?

"How far will she go to keep your secret?" I asked.

Francesca refused to answer. Perhaps she didn't know. Or was unwilling to fully face the truth.

We were all players in Annie's play. Like puppets on a string, we'd twitch every time she pulled a thread.

Annie had come to the Rose Garden not to see the press

conference setup. She'd come to knock over that urn and break it. She'd come to plant a bomb.

My head started to pound.

Every bomb scenario the Secret Service had thrown at me had ended in disaster. Jack had said they had been no-win situations.

Was this a no-win situation?

After checking the teleprompter, Frank returned to the podium to set the President's notes on it. I noticed I wasn't the only one watching his progress. Annie had given up on Francesca and was watching Frank with an intensity that frightened me.

What should I do?

President Bradley and the top members of Congress were just on the other side of that glass door. A large enough blast might injure or even kill them . . . and everyone in the Rose Garden.

Bomb or not, I needed to do something.

Annie and I locked eyes. She must have seen something in my expression to tip her off that I knew what she'd done. She took off running, not in the hope of escape, but to buy herself time. She was pulling out her cell phone. That was the trigger.

"Jack!" I shouted. "There's a bomb in the urn by the Oval Office. Frank, move!"

The Secret Service agents in the Rose Garden converged toward the urn. Six members from the Secret Service's elite military Counter Assault Team, dressed in ominous black battle dress uniforms and armed with large rifles, ran past the window inside the Oval Office. I'd only seen them move in a similar fashion once before. They were moving President Bradley and the members of Congress to safety.

They were doing their jobs, but they didn't know what I knew.

I had to act as well. And if I didn't act fast, we might still all end up dead.

My breath was coming too fast. I felt dizzy as I sprinted after Annie.

"There's a bomb," she shouted as she ran. "Francesca, run!"

What a clever actress she was. She had her cell phone out and was pushing buttons as she charged out of the Rose Garden and down the South Lawn.

Annie may have been fast, but I had several inches in height on her as well as a lifetime of hard work in the garden.

I also had cracked ribs that felt like they wanted to shatter with every pounding stride. Even so, she didn't get far. I grabbed her around the waist and, spinning, pulled the both of us to the ground.

Her grip on her phone held fast. She punched more numbers.

She had to be stopped.

I had to stop her. I grabbed the gardening shears from their leather holster on my belt. "Let go of the phone," I warned.

Annie screamed. But she kept punching numbers into the phone's keypad.

When I looked at her I didn't see sweet, muddleheaded Annie. I saw the grizzled face of my mother's killer. I pulled back and slammed the sharp point of the shears into her hand until the phone dropped to the grass.

Jack grabbed me around the shoulders and pulled me off her. He lifted me and wrapped his arms around my chest as two other CAT agents pulled Annie from the ground. Annie's hand was bleeding. The cell phone was shattered.

"I should have run you down when I had the chance," she spat at me as they dragged her away. "You had no right to butt into my affairs. No right."

"It's over," Jack said as he pried the bloodied gardening shears from my clenched fingers. "It's over. We've got her."

I pressed my face against Jack's chest and fought to control the angry tears and rage pulsing through every muscle in my body.

\* \* \*

**THE ENTIRE WHITE HOUSE COMPLEX HAD TO**
be evacuated while highly trained members of the Secret
Service neutralized the bomb. The press conference, the
First Lady's volunteer appreciation tea, everything, had to
be canceled.

Because we were all witnesses, Francesca, Bruce,
Frank, and I were taken together to a Secret Service bunker
deep beneath the North Lawn. The entrance . . . well, I'm
not allowed to tell you where we entered the secret passage
that led to the secret bunker with a large conference table
and plush chairs, only that the door could be found two
floors below the grounds office. At the far end of a hallway.

For the first time since Parker's murder, Francesca
seemed to be in control again. She took deep breaths
between each carefully thought-out sentence as she
explained why Annie was blackmailing her. "You were
campaigning, Bruce. I got lonely. And Frank"—she
sighed—"was trying to prove how much he loved the
ladies."

"I have a daughter?" Frank asked.

I held my breath, waiting for him to deny Kelly or tell
Francesca that he didn't care, that even if Kelly bore his
DNA, he didn't want anything to do with her.

He didn't say a word. He gripped the arms of his chair
and bent forward slightly.

Francesca nodded. "Bruce had ended the campaign
before I started showing. Remember, Bruce? The money
ran out after you were handily defeated in that first pri-
mary election. As soon as you called an end to your campaign, I told you I needed to take care of my mother back
in West Virginia. That was a lie. I went up to our cabin.
Annie came with me."

"You'd vowed to always be discreet, as I had vowed to
you," Bruce said, his voice a low growl.

"I was discreet." Francesca spread her hands on the
table in front of her. "No one knew."

Bruce grunted and turned his head away.

Francesca grabbed Frank's hand. "You understand why I couldn't keep her and why I couldn't tell you."

Frank pulled away. "No, I don't understand."

"What made you abandon your own child outside in the cold in the middle of the night? She was a helpless newborn baby," I asked. "Kelly said that if the neighbors hadn't found her, she would have frozen to death."

"What? Annie told me that she used an adoption service. She—"

"Lied," I said.

"You should have told me about the baby," Bruce slammed his fist against the table. "We would have raised her."

"You should have told me," Frank said, still taking it all in. "I would have made it work. I have a daughter? What a miracle. I never thought I'd have a child, not after I stopped pretending to be something I could never be."

"I—I didn't know Annie had abandoned her. She'd promised me that she would make sure my baby found a good home. She'd promised—" Francesca froze. Her eyes filled with tears as she seemed to realize the magnitude of the mistake she'd made all those years ago. "My God," she sobbed. "What have I done?"

"How long did it take before Annie started demanding payment for her generosity?" I asked.

"Almost—almost immediately," Francesca answered as she lowered her head to the table and started to sob uncontrollably.

"Bruce," Frank said. "You do know you're going to have to resign? When this all comes out about the murders, you'll be a liability to the President. You already are."

Bruce's shoulders raised and lowered in a slow shrug. "I know my duty."

"So let me get this straight," Bryce said from the head of the table. "Annie poisoned both Griffon Parker and Simon Matthews to keep them from writing about Kelly's birth parents because if the story got out, she would no longer have a hold over Francesca?"

"I think that's what happened," I said since Francesca was still crying too hard to answer.

"But how did she get close enough to them to get them to drink poison?" he asked.

"My guess is she seduced them, telling them that she could be an important source to their story, that she could tell them all they needed to know," Jack said.

"She always has been Francesca's friend, the tagalong," I said. Francesca refused to look up from the table. Her shoulders shook harder. "I have a feeling that people forgot Annie was even in the room. She'd listen to conversations that she shouldn't, perhaps even see things that she shouldn't. And then she used that knowledge to her benefit."

"Like taking pictures of me," Frank said.

"What about Gillis? What's his role in this?" Bryce asked.

"She must have something on Gillis as well and used that to her benefit when she framed him for murder," Jack said. "She was blackmailing him like she apparently did with everyone else in her circle of friends."

"But why didn't Gillis tell us that?" Bryce asked.

"Maybe he didn't know who was blackmailing him. Who knows how many other people Annie has been extracting payments from?" I said. "But Francesca seemed to be Annie's main paycheck."

"Please don't hate me." Francesca lifted her head and grabbed Frank's hands.

"How can I hate you? You gave me a child." He jumped out of his chair. "She's in the hospital. She's hurt. I have to go there. I have to be with her."

He pushed aside the Secret Service agents standing in his way. "You don't understand. You can get my statement later. I have to get to the hospital. I have to go meet"—his voice cracked—"my baby girl."

# Epilogue

*Let us have peace.*
—ULYSSES S. GRANT, THE 18TH PRESIDENT OF
THE UNITED STATES

**T**HE White House came alive for the Fourth of July holiday that year. With Annie safely locked away—denying every charge—everyone seemed eager to celebrate. The last I'd heard from Manny, they'd linked Annie's phone to the threatening phone calls and the calls directing Jerry and Bower to damage the garden. Also, transactions in her bank account matched the dates and amounts she'd paid the two lazy gardeners. And, the most damaging evidence of all, the police had found three severely pruned yew trees in her backyard.

President Bradley had invited injured troops and their families to a backyard picnic. The First Lady invited all of her volunteers to the picnic to make up for the volunteer appreciation tea that had ended so abruptly. She had made a brief appearance before hurrying back inside.

I prayed that with the worst of the controversies behind us, Margaret could rest and regain her strength for both herself and those darling babies she was carrying.

Dressed in my brightest, happiest sundress, I mingled

with the First Lady's volunteers while sipping punch. After being stalked by Mable and Pearle for most of the afternoon, Gordon decided to stick close to my side.

"Now, that's a sight that makes me smile," Gordon said and nodded toward the South Portico.

I turned to follow the direction of Gordon's gaze.

Frank, beaming like a proud father, pushed Kelly in a wheelchair toward a buffet table.

"Excuse me," I said and hurried toward the happy duo.

The doctors promised that Kelly was well on her way to making a complete recovery. I was happy for her. Truly happy.

Why shouldn't she get her father and her happy ending?

I hated the part of me that felt jealous. I made certain that none of that foolishness showed as I hugged Kelly and then Frank, congratulating them on finding each other.

"If you don't mind, Frank, I'd like to have a word in private with Casey," Kelly said once the polite conversation had run its course.

"I don't know." Frank hesitated.

"Go on. It's girl stuff," Kelly said. "I won't be a moment." She reached back and squeezed her father's hand.

"Don't let the wheelchair roll down the hill," he warned me, even though there really was no danger that that could happen.

"I am truly happy for you, Kelly. You found your father," I said as I crouched down beside the wheelchair once Frank had wandered off to speak with Gillis Farquhar, who'd been cleared of all charges against him. The press coverage had pushed his book to the number one spot on the *New York Times* bestseller list, a fact he'd mentioned to me more than once that afternoon.

"He's quite a character," Kelly said as she watched Gillis hand Frank a copy of his book. "He's promised me an interview as soon as I'm healthy again."

"How are you doing? And how have you managed to keep the story about your father away from your colleagues?"

"There are plenty of other stories to tell right now," she said. "I'm sure most of it will come out at the trial. But for now, I'm glad to have Frank to myself without worrying about becoming the six o'clock news."

"That sounds funny coming from you."

"Ironic, isn't it? But that's not what I wanted to talk to you about." She reached into a pouch hanging from the wheelchair and handed me a small white envelope. "This is one of the stories Parker was working on before he died. I found it in his desk."

She put the envelope in my hand, but held on to it as she added, "I would never pursue a story like this. You can trust me when I tell you that I won't repeat what I read in there."

"Thank you." I really didn't think much about what was in the envelope. Ever since I had bested him that spring, Parker had made a habit of digging for dirt in the First Lady's gardens. Irritating, but not earth-shattering.


AS DAYLIGHT STARTED TO DIM, MY PHONE BUZ-zed in my purse.

*Finally*, I thought.

"Are you ready?" the text on the phone's readout said.

Did he really think he needed to ask?

I typed my reply as I bid Gordon good night and made my way to the nearest gate.

On the far side of the Ellipse, the large park sandwiched between the White House and the Washington Monument, crowds had been gathering throughout the day to find the best spot for watching the evening's fireworks show. I stopped and searched the faces.

"Looking for me?" Jack bumped my shoulder with his arm as he came up from behind.

I almost didn't recognize him in his casual khaki shorts and white button-up shirt, a woven picnic basket slung over his arm. He looked so *domestic*. "I hope you're not stuffed from the White House picnic. I made one for just the two of us."

I held the basket as Jack spread out a classic red-and-brown plaid picnic blanket underneath a nearby streetlamp. Once we were settled, he reached into the basket and pulled out a spread of wine, bread, and various cheeses. He sliced a piece of the bread and handed it to me.

"The bread's still warm." I moaned my delight at the rich flavor and hearty texture of the artisan bread as I ate it.

"I'm glad you're pleased. I baked it this afternoon."

"You did? This is delicious." I reached for another piece.

"My mother worked two jobs. If we wanted to eat something other than takeout, we had to learn how to cook."

I feasted on the bread and that rare personal morsel from his past that he'd shared with me.

When we finished sipping the wine and nibbling on the bread and cheese, it was nearly dark. The fireworks would soon begin. I dug the envelope out of my purse, explaining to Jack how Kelly had given it to me.

"I'm sure it's nothing," I said as I broke the seal.

An old newspaper clipping fell out and fluttered to the picnic blanket. I caught it. The paper had yellowed over the years, but was otherwise in good shape. Someone had written "April 1978" and "Phoenix Daily Record" next to the headline.

I frowned. Phoenix was the last place I'd seen my father. And April 1978 was the month and year my mother had died.

The headline screamed, "Murderer Escapes Police."

I shifted so the streetlight above us shone directly on the paper. "James Calhoun, wanted for the murders of at least six people, including his wife, was nearly apprehended yesterday afternoon. During a struggle, Calhoun killed the arresting officer, Blake Douglas, father of two young boys. Calhoun is still on the loose and is considered armed and extremely dangerous."

A weight pressed down on my chest so hard I couldn't breathe. Had I blocked out a memory of seeing my father one last time? Had he been there when I watched those men shoot my mother? Had I blocked out the memory that my own dad had pulled the trigger?

And what about that other memory (or had it been a dream?) of that time when we had lived in France? The sight of my father shooting the man who had charged through our cottage's front door replayed in my head in slow motion like a scene from a horror movie.

"What is it?" Jack asked with a note of concern.

"Nothing." I crumpled the newspaper clipping and stuffed it back into my purse. I didn't need to read the rest. "Nothing at all."

The sky exploded with a blaze of red, white, and blue as the William Tell Overture began to play over a distant loudspeaker. I grabbed Jack's hand and leaned back on the blanket.

Behind me the lights shining on the White House gleamed like a beacon of hope. In front of me a sea of revelers had gathered on the National Mall to celebrate being part of something bigger than themselves. And above me the sky danced in vibrant colors.

This was my life. This was my future. Jack was my future.

"It's time," I said. "It's time I let go of the past and live in the now."

Jack turned toward me. "That sounds like a good plan."

Not one to drag my feet before acting, I rolled over and met Jack halfway. I wrapped my arms around his neck and pulled him closer.

He took the hint and kissed me breathless as the world exploded into brilliant colors.

# A Page from Casey's
# Summer Gardener's Notebook

## June

### Week 3

**PLANTING:** Replanted mysteriously uprooted heirloom tomatoes using trench method—burying most of the stem in a long, shallow hole to promote a healthy root system.

**SOWING:** None this week.

**CULTIVATING:** The chefs are gleaning the vegetables as needed for their recipes. We'll be harvesting the spring crops and planting more summer crops next week.

**FERTILIZING:** Fertilized the vegetable and flower gardens with a complete organic fertilizer that contains seaweed, fish emulsion, and compost tea. The vegetable garden is fertilized every two weeks. With this heat, the fescue grass is turning dormant. Won't need to fertilize until sometime in the fall. In two weeks, we'll give the roses their final feeding of the summer.

**PRUNING:** July Fourth is the last call for pruning spring-flowering trees and bushes, which will soon be setting buds for next year's spring flowers. Conducted a pass through the North and South lawns and gardens. Shaped up the azaleas, rhododendrons, and especially the President Lincoln and Dwight D. Eisenhower lilacs so they will produce a showy blue flower display again next spring.

Over the next couple of weeks will prune chrysanthemums back to about half their height and cut back the impatiens to about an inch high. Doing this now, leading up to the Fourth of July holiday, will encourage new growth and blooms well into the fall.

Constantly deadheading the annuals to keep them blooming.

**WEATHER:** Hot! Heat wave has hit D.C. The First Lady's favorite bell pepper plants love it and are thriving. The lettuce is starting to bolt. I've covered part of the lettuce plot with a tarp to keep it shaded from the worst of the heat. This has kept the plants from bolting and turning bitter before next week's harvest. Pop-up afternoon rainstorms are keeping the flowers and vegetables lush and green.

**NOTES:** A new mystery for me to puzzle out. If not Milo, I need to figure out what's digging up the vegetable garden. Whatever it is, it's not eating the vegetables. Will install netting to protect the plants from four-legged pests, especially the fruits that will be starting to set and the tomatoes.

Keeping on top of weeding, as always.

# Recipe for Quick and Easy
# Sheet Composting

Sheet composting, also known as lasagna gardening, is a quick method for creating a rich planting medium for your vegetable or flower garden. Don't have a yard? You can sheet compost in planters and pots. As the plant grows, it breaks down the compost ingredients, which in turn feed the plant. Great for the lazy (or busy) gardener who is unwilling or unable to commit to the time and effort needed to tend a compost system.

No matter the condition of the soil in your yard, you'll end up with a planting bed filled with nutrient-rich, fluffy soil.

*Water from a hose*
*Newspapers or cardboard*
*Greens (fruit and vegetable scraps from your kitchen, grass clippings, tea leaves/bags, coffee grounds— ask at your local coffee shop for their used grounds)*
*Topsoil*
*Browns (leaf litter, hay)*

Determine the size and location of your planting site.

Spread a layer of newspaper or cardboard over the planting site, overlapping the sheets. There's no need to pull grass or weeds or till the soil, just layer the newspapers over the existing ground.

Using a hose, soak the newspapers or cardboard.

Add a layer of greens (see list above). Wet with a hose.

Add a layer of topsoil. Wet with a hose.

Add a layer of browns (see list above). Wet with a hose.

Continue adding layers of greens, topsoil, and browns until you have a mound/planting bed that is at least two feet high. Wet each layer with a hose.

Finally, top the mound/planting bed with three to four inches of topsoil. Wet with a hose.

Plant your garden. (There's no need to wait. The roots will help break down the compost material as your plants grow, in turn providing your plants with nutrients.)

Add a thick layer of mulch.

Enjoy!